CASCADIA FALLEN

ORDER DIVESTED

AUSTIN CHAMBERS

CREDITS

EDITOR – Emily Rollen

FINAL PROOFER – WMH Cheryl

COVER BY – Fusion Creative Works, Poulsbo, WA

ISBN Paperback: 978-1-7339593-6-0

ISBN Hardcover: 978-1-966164-91-3

Published by Crossed Cannons Publishing, LLC
P.O. Box 334
Seabeck, WA 98380-0334
pkodell.com

Cascadia Fallen
Order Divested

PROLOGUE

"There is no crueler tyranny than that which is perpetuated under
the shield of law and in the name of justice."
—Montesquieu

A Few Years Before Tahoma's Hammer

THE COURTROOM ERUPTED INTO CHAOS. The Pierce County District
Court—in this case Room 936, Judge Ronald Wixley's courtroom—
had been packed tightly by two groups of people for two full days.
At debate was what to do with…*him*. The side that supported him—
most of them used to sitting next to their own defense attorneys
when they were in a courtroom—had been unusually respectful and
quiet until that moment. The other side, almost entirely comprised
of victims and their families, had been trying the judge's patience
every time the perp's counsel had made a point.

Perp—that's what he was, not a defendant. He had already

gone to trial, years earlier. His time served, his case on this day was one of those rare cases in which the outcome was bound to upset all parties. The perp had served his entire eight-year sentence, and at stake was whether or not the people of Washington would allow him to have the freedom and new start he'd earned.

Christopher Wood, known reverently as "Sticky" by the members of his Outlaw Motorcycle Club, was a suspected murderer and a convicted Level 3 Sexual Violent Predator, the highest level in the Evergreen State. Before prison, Sticky had been the "Enforcer" in his Motorcycle Club, trusted to exact discipline on bikers that screwed up and vengeance on rival gangs. He had a beast inside him that hunted and preyed on young, blonde women. He had only been convicted of raping two, though several more had identified him after they learned he was on trial.

This hearing had largely been a formality, one created to maintain the illusion that Liberty was still controlled by the citizens. Fewer than half of all states had a civil commitment process, and fewer still had a commitment center solely dedicated to sexual predators. Washington State had both.

It was the kind of technicality that made even the most ardent conservative think twice about what he or she truly believed—that sometimes the government just may need to violate some people's rights. Should this animal be allowed out to prey again? What about the rights of those most-certain future victims?

Sticky Wood had just been sentenced to indefinite confinement as a "resident" at the McNeil Island Special Commitment Center. They were the only residents on the six-square-mile island, other than the chickens and rabbits they raised, and a few of the staff. The residents had the same type of staff they were accustomed to while in prison—counselors, guards, a warden. Like in prison, they cooked and washed for themselves. There was a large garden, a softball field, a horseshoe pit, and a pair of barbed-wire fences—everything but a ticket off the island nestled neatly west of Tacoma. That only came with a lengthy rehabilitation process and the blessings of not one but three psychiatrists.

The eruption on that day was inevitable. The Risen Dead Motorcycle Club—decked out in ties, clean jeans, and blazers—was understandably pissed that a free man who had served his time was being shipped off to indefinite exile. The victims and their families were upset about not receiving an *impossible* outcome. Most of them were in denial about what the judge's true powers were, thinking he could just tack more time onto the sentence served. Though one of Sticky's victims had committed suicide in the years since, he could not be charged with murder under the plea bargain he had struck.

Bikers and family members were starting to toe-up and get hands on each other as the usual bailiffs—and the additional correctional officers brought in just for this case—tried to insert themselves and use physical holds to maintain control. The biggest bikers, though, were in the front row, trying to grab Sticky and pull him to safety, yelling at the judge and anyone in the way of the verbal barrage. The State President of Washington's largest Outlaw Motorcycle Club wasn't just defending a metaphorical brother, but a biological one. Campbell Wood, known to bikers and law enforcement alike as "Legion", was the most respected biker in the state and the only person in the world that meant anything to Sticky. They were brothers and had grown up together in the worst and most despicable of stories, learning that the other was the only one they would ever fully trust.

Deep in the back corner of the victim's side of the courtroom was a silent and stoic man, focused not on the melee surrounding him, but on the door that the bailiffs had rushed Sticky through moments earlier. He never even got out of his seat—his life had prepared him to be calm in complete and utter chaos. He relished in it. It was this moment that he knew it was time to retire from the US Army. He was at a point where that was a reality for him anyhow. He was wrapping up a full career that had lasted the entire War on Terror.

He was still active duty, though he chose to wear civilian clothes for the hearing. He wanted to give nothing away. *Information is power,* he thought to himself. *The less the monsters have, the better.* Multiple tours to Iraq, Afghanistan, and various parts of Asia and Africa had taught him to find peace in the storm. Twenty-one years—most of them as a light-infantry sniper—was enough. He would return to Schofield Barracks in Hawaii and file retirement papers as soon as possible.

Nick Williams had been busy fighting terror when this human garbage had raped his sister and left her for dead 12 years earlier. Though she survived the monster, she could not escape the demons he'd burned into her, choosing to end it with a rope four years before the monster finished his sentence.

He stood up, realizing he had no point in remaining. His father had already passed away, and his mother couldn't bear to go to court that day. He could only hope that announcing his retirement to her would bring a small level of comfort. As he pushed his way to the nearest exit, he took one last look at the door which now represented Sticky to him. *I will kill you if it is the last thing I do,* he thought. *Your head will dissolve in red mist, and you will never know what happened.*

1

Second Wind.

Tahoma's Hammer + 18 Days.

Payton looked at a restless but finally sleeping Phil through puffy eyes. She'd run out of tears the night before, wondering if it were some sort of sign. *Am I dehydrated? Is there something wrong with me?! How come I can't cry anymore?* Time would teach her that it wasn't a matter of *can't* but more a matter of *shouldn't.* It was her turn to hold it together. Her father had been *the rock* through all the pain in the years prior—Caroline's death being the most trying time in either of their lives...until then. *I still can't believe my baby brother is...gone...*

She didn't want to wake him, but she had to. Someone at the gate needed him. *Why can't they just leave us alone for a few days?* But she knew that was as much Phil's fault as anything. Ever since Savannah's abduction, he insisted that all threat assessments be made by him personally.

"Gordon, got an ETA?" she heard the radio squawk.

It was Jerry calling from the Command Post, checking to see if she'd wakened him yet. On the open air, individuals only went by code names. Payton's was *Gordon*—named after a famous, cussing TV chef—due to her growing reputation as Lord of the Kitchen. Another newly enacted security procedure was to use separate frequencies for security and routine business, hence why Jerry was acting as the intermediary in the communications between Payton and the gate guards.

"Three minutes," she said, as she started to caress Phil's hair. "Dad...Dad..."

He started to grunt.

"Dad, wake up," she practically whispered.

Phil shook his head with a start, picking it up off the pillow and looking straight at her, but not seeing her. After a few seconds, his eyes finally constricted and he put his head back down. "What?" he said irritably, still groggy and thinking about the nightmare that had just been interrupted. Payton could see his eyes were puffy and red.

"Southwest corner called in something," Payton replied. "One person, wandering up the highway all alone, slowly, staring at our property like he's assessing it." People wandered past the property fairly regularly, but most kept their eyes straight down the road, trying to appear harmless. She knew automatically Phil would want to know what was different about this one. "He should be getting to the main gate about now." She studied his non-motion for a few more seconds. "You getting up?"

Phil let out a big sigh. "Yes. I'm up, drill sergeant." His tone was a bit more rude than usual. He pushed himself off the cot, swinging one-and-a-half legs toward the tent floor.

She stood up and left the tent, feeling sorry for her father once again. She didn't know what to make of it because she was so used to the head-butting dynamic. *Maybe the changing world will bring us back together…*All she knew was Phil and Savannah would both need her.

Her daughter had been through so much—the world as she knew it had disappeared, and the nine-year-old had no real life-experience to frame it against. In less than three weeks, she had lived through the worst natural disaster in modern history, never to see many of her friends again. She'd been abducted, rescued, and survived an attack by armed marauders. And just two days earlier, she'd learned that her only uncle was killed in a military operation to save an aircraft carrier. *My poor baby.* She worried for her daughter.

Once Phil opened the tent flap and stepped out, she trailed behind him up the path towards the main lot, heading towards the kitchen as he peeled off for the gate. Savannah was in the trailer that used to serve as a classroom and was now the kitchen and food prep area. She stepped in and saw her daughter coloring in the corner.

"Everything okay?" Teddy Wilson asked. He and Donna Gladstone were helping prep potatoes, onions, and carrots for the big stew they were preparing to hang over the range's firepit.

"Yeah…" Payton mumbled, still thinking about how her father was holding up. "I'm just starting to really worry about this whole food thing. Dad is planning some sort of big meeting tonight. People coming in from Mason and West Slaughter Counties. I think a couple of them are the leaders of groups he invited to stay here."

"And he expects us to feed them all?" Donna asked incredulously.

"Uh, no. I mean…I don't think so." She paused for a moment, looking out the door at Josh Bryant as he walked from the office to the northwest corner fighting position. Josh's brother and nephew were headed toward her at the kitchen, hauling fresh game in meat packs on their backs. "I'm just thinking in general. The 'community stew-pot' thing helps stretch the food, but I'm pretty sure that some people are starting to run low on what they brought." She could see the bulbs coming on over their heads. "This is a simple math problem—how many calories per day will everyone get to eat over winter?"

"Way to dampen a mood, girl," Teddy said half playfully. Though they'd just met eight days earlier, Payton had started developing a spirited, platonic relationship with the high-energy Teddy, something she desperately needed since learning of Crane's death. When she'd failed to respond to that, he finally broke the silence. "Hellooooo. Earth to Payton." She looked at him. "What are we doing about it?" he continued in a semi-concerned tone.

"Josh said he has an idea," she mentioned, turning back to the doorway to stare at his butt as he disappeared around a tree. *It'd better be a good one,* she thought.

THE LITTLE OLD lady known as The Godfather by her subordinates, Sandy McCallister, was only half-listening as the National Guard Soldier gave her and the rest of the Slaughter County Unified Command a vehicle tour of Bartlett. That group was comprised of a variety of civic leaders operating as one, big council. They were closing in on three weeks into this crisis. It had not escaped Major Adam Matsumoto's attention that most of the FEMA and political leaders were doing their best to stay out of the common person's line-of-sight.

It had been his turn to run the morning meeting for the UC, and so without asking permission, he scheduled a convoy of HumVees to provide an armed escort around the central and north parts of the county. He'd been hearing entirely too much politically slanted speculation in the recent meetings, and he was tired of it. The former active-duty officer and Home Depot manager was a people person. He needed these politicians to get out and see the people—and their real problems.

The fifteen-vehicle procession carried all the mayors, county commissioners, police chiefs, fire chiefs, and FEMA leaders on a tour. He wanted them to understand what it meant to be in a rig having rocks thrown at it. Anyone could say they understood, but it took seeing the rock hit the window combined with the unexpected thud to truly drive home the message he needed them to receive—people were hungry, angry, and desperate. He'd taken them through the zigzag of roads that were still operable—barely—only via a slalom course of broken bridges and fallen cell towers. They'd been sheltered. He wanted them to experience the spine-jarring driving of these roads over the worsening cracks and crevices that had formed nineteen days earlier.

They were in the final quarter of the tour, which had taken three hours. Sandy was not happy with the major. It wasn't that she didn't care about people's plight—she'd gotten into emergency management because she did care about serving her community. She just didn't like the surprise. The course of her career had evolved from one of service to one of control and influence. She was upset that she'd made it so close to retirement before all of this happened. Major Matsumoto was showing ingenuity and back-bone, and she hadn't given him permission to have those. *It's always the ones who were active duty before joining the Guard that I seem to have problems with*, she thought.

"What are those obstacles halfway up the hill on each of these crossroads?" she yelled over the roar of the giant tires, bumpy road, and diesel engine. She was asking the staff sergeant driving her vehicle. He'd been yammering about this and that for most of the trip. *Probably parroting some theme the major made him memorize*, Sandy thought before tuning him out a half-hour earlier.

"Those are the barricades, Ma'am," he replied, somewhat shocked. "Those are the check-points that each area is establishing to control who enters and exits their neighborhood." He couldn't believe she had to ask that question after all he'd been explaining.

"Why haven't you dismantled those yet?" she countered.

The staff sergeant was no fool. He had seriously contemplated pretending he had no idea as his response. It was probably the frustration of being one of the idiots that hadn't abandoned his post yet that made him provide a shot of honesty. "We're down to 230 members, Ma'am. There are 41,000 people and thirty-two square miles in Bartlett, let alone the entire county. Where do you suppose we start?" The other passengers in the vehicle sucked all the air out of it as they tried to pretend they hadn't just heard him say that. "Ma'am," he added when he realized the gravity of the error.

Sandy had the experience to let that slide and file it for later, but she knew this man would soon disappear anyway. "Sergeant," she said in her fake Southern accent. "I'm going to let that tone slide this time."

He could feel her staring. "Yes, Ma'am," was all he mustered.

"How often are you pelted with rocks and such on a patrol?" He was much too junior to let her feelings be bothered by a snide comment.

"Several, Ma'am. And once it starts on any given street, it always continues in that spot from then on. The original locations are using Molotov cocktails, now."

"So I've heard," she replied, mulling over the recent daily reports. The major's tour was having an impact, but not the one he had intended. She knew the truth already—people couldn't provide for themselves anymore. Most of them couldn't, anyway. *We need to start containing zones and let the rest fend for themselves.* Her thoughts were firing faster than her logic could track them. *Manpower will continue to be an issue. The stupid Feds can't seem to get any food up here. We are going to be hosed in an exponential way very soon. Need to get that fool of a sheriff and the major on board with resource and weapons confiscation. PR—that's our biggest issue. How to get these people to realize it's for the greater good?*

"JOE, THIS IS DOCTOR…" Phil said, dragging the last sound out while looking to Stu to fill in his name.

"Stu. Just call me Stu," he said, chuckling softly and shaking Jose Santillan's hand. "Or Doc."

"Yeah—Stu," Phil mumbled. In normal times he might offer an apology and quip about his absent-mindedness. This was a moment in his life that zero craps were given about such things. "Uh, listen… Could you maybe put Doc up in your pop-up camper with you for a bit? We've struck a deal for him to shelter here while he plans his way north. We'll try to get some info on the radio while he takes a look at our overall health profile."

"No problem," Joe, the club's fiery secretary said. "As long as you don't mind snoring."

"I'm sure it'll be fine," Stu said. "I've been in a lot worse environments the last few weeks."

"On second thought, why don't we give him a cot right in the storeroom?" Joe suggested. He was referring to the locking room at the end of the rifle line that had become their infirmary.

"Great. Whatever. Make it happen," Phil agreed. *Why do I have to decide everything?!* "Can you also give Doc a tour? Thanks." He wasn't really asking.

"Well, actually, I was—"

Phil cut him off. "Don't really care, Joe. We all got our problems." *Did your son just die, Joe? Just get on it!* He was already leaving the office and slammed the door behind him.

He made the hard right off the office deck and headed down the road between the rifle line and Bays 1 thru 4. He stopped off at his tent, dropping off his battle rifle and prosthetic leg, opting to switch to crutches for a bit. He'd been on the false leg a lot the last several days and was trying to give his stump and skin some rest periods. He crutched his way down to the conex boxes that doubled as a school and safety zone for the children and found the John Deere Gator parked there. He hopped in and made the two-minute drive up the northern road that eventually wound up in the upper area they called *The Field*. Once up there, he made a hard right towards the south end and found Jerry on an extension ladder leaning against a fir tree.

After shutting down the small utility vehicle, he heard Jerry proclaim, "You showed up in the nick of time. See that roll of tape?" He was pointing at the base of the tree.

Phil picked up the hint and retrieved the item, throwing it the twelve or so feet up to his primary HAM operator.

"Whatcha up to Jerr?" Phil asked.

"'Bout twelve feet!" Phil didn't laugh. Jerry immediately realized it was way too soon for jokes with Phil. "Sorry. Just got done setting up a new antenna, but I've had too much SWR so I'm breaking and re-wrapping the connections to check for moisture or oxidation."

Phil had no idea what that meant and regretted asking. "Sounds good," he lied. "Did you get confirmation?"

"Yep. They figure to be here around 5, 5:30." Jerry stared at Phil, then decided to come down off the ladder. "If you have time, I have some comms stuff that is very relevant to the meeting."

"Yeah, I agree. What exactly are you thinking?" Phil asked, hoping it wouldn't be a technical diatribe.

"They call it an 'SOI', which means a Signals Operating Instruction. The short version is that it is a plan and protocol for linked groups for both routine and unplanned emergency communications. I feel so strongly that all the like-minded groups need to align on this that I've been hand-writing several copies."

"You got it, Jerry. One of your trainees can cover the CP?" Phil was keenly aware that a lack of knowledgeable people running their command post was a major issue.

"Yeah. No sweat." One of Don Kwiatkowsky's grandkids was Jerry's primary trainee, and he was only thirteen years old. "James is really picking it up, and I'll have Tanya there, too."

"Good." Phil was already getting into the gator and putting his crutches in the bed behind him.

"Hey, Phil," Jerry went on before the boss could escape. "Any more thought to the latrine situation up here?"

"I think Craig said something about how they made septic systems in the old days. Once they turn one of the cedars into boards, they'll bury a big, floorless cedar box, fill it with rocks or gravel, somethin', somethin'. Not really sure, but it's gonna happen. Gotta go, Jerry," Phil said shortly.

He hit the gas and headed back down the hill to the lower part of the club. He stopped off at some of the back conex boxes near the pond where he planned on having the meeting that evening. He stared at the spot near the picnic table that was back there and recalled the day Crane had taken his training wheels off his bike. His eyes filled with tears in the solace that came with being alone for a few minutes. Soon a sob escaped as the water began to flow. *Son, I love you so much*, he thought.

"IT'S CALLED 'TANGLE-FOOT'," Josh explained. He was instructing club member John Horn and John's kids—Zach, sixteen, and Levi, twelve—in the art of building a perimeter.

"But I don't get why we have to clear all this brush," Levi complained.

"Shut it, Levi," his older brother scolded. He didn't like the manual labor any better than his sibling, but he hated the whining noise even worse.

"Guys..." John started in.

"No, it's okay," Josh said. *Maybe a little class-time will help*, he thought. "You boys want to know what being in the Army was all about? This is it." Josh decided a little break while painting the big picture would sooth them a bit. The end of the world was a lot more laborious than people were ready for. "Everyone, drop your tools and follow me."

They were on the far side of *the field*, and he started walking the small contingent to the north-east corner of the club's property. After four hundred feet, they arrived at the spot where Craig

Wageman and Tyler Wilson were using the Kubota to dig a large hole and line it with some decent sized timber. There was an abundance of trees that had fallen in the hammer, and they weren't going to let them go to waste. There was a team of people choking the fallen logs with chains and using the horses that Pam Jorgenson had brought to drag them into the field. They were using handsaws and chainsaws to take the branches off, leaving a large bare log exposed.

"This position here will be turned into a post for keeping an eye on the woods in this direction," Josh started. "This entire eastern side is a big security concern. We may have plenty of room for everyone here at the range, but there's a point where it becomes too difficult to guard the whole perimeter. With me so far?"

All three members of the Horn clan nodded, saving questions for the end.

"This position will be fortified with logs to provide cover and a roof. We'll wind up building three or four of these on the 500-ish meter length of this side of the property. There's two major issues, though." He paused because Levi was starting to throw rocks at a stump.

"Levi!" John commanded. The pre-teen huffed and turned to face Josh. "Sorry," he said to their instructor.

Josh gave John a quick look to say it's fine and turned directly to address the young man. "I know this is boring, pal, but let me ask you something." Josh knew the family had just walked to the range from their home in the north end of the county. They had probably endured their fair share of hardship by this point. "What's the scariest thing you've encountered since the earthquakes?"

Levi shot a look at his dad, who nodded for him to answer. "I guess it's the burnt-up bodies in the cars on the highway," the young man answered after pondering a few seconds.

"Yeah," Josh said. "I get that. I saw those quite a bit in Iraq, and it freaked me out every time. Now you should hear what everyone here has been scared by." He stopped to make sure he had the tween's full attention. "Several days ago, a girl was kidnapped off this property."

Levi looked like he couldn't figure out if his leg was getting pulled. Josh ignored the skepticism and kept talking. "Several of us went and rescued her, and three days ago some people came back to retaliate. See that grave over there?" He pointed to the lumber-cross planted at Fred's grave. The scumbags buried nearby had only a large stone as a marker. "That is one of our friends, killed here that night." He scanned the kid's face, which had seemed to grow a level of concern. "So, if you can't hack it out here with the grown-ups, I can make sure you go spend time in the school with the little kids."

Josh looked at John to make sure he hadn't drawn the father's ire, but John was studying his son's reaction, fully supporting the scare tactic. After several seconds, Levi looked at the ground. "Sorry," he mumbled. His older brother rubbed his head in the way that big brothers do.

"Water under the bridge, pal," Josh said. He continued the lesson. "In between these foxholes we need to install some wire. We have barbed wire rolls for some areas, but we also have regular fencing wire. We'll zigzag it back and forth between trees about waist high, but we need to do it where the bushes and grass can grow back up through it. It will be there for several years, but intruders will never see it. They can try to sneak through, but they'll get caught up and make a large ruckus trying to escape."

Zach's curiosity was piqued. "Why the tower, then?" Josh was having a guard tower—more of a large "Jenga-stack" of logs that would be about twelve feet high—constructed on the far side of the field where the main road from the lower range broke through the forest. It would get capped with a deck, roof, and some logs for cover on the front.

Good question, he thought, noting Zach was keenly listening to everything. "Very observant. You ever hear the expression…well, any expression, I guess, about the high ground?" Zach nodded. "The high ground is a tactical advantage. Someone up there with night-vision will be able to see almost the entire eastern side and provide covering fire to any of these positions."

He continued the lecture as he slowly led them back to their tools. About the time the group got to the tools, Josh's older brother and nephew, Eli and Jeff, came strolling out of the woods on the east side. Eli was carrying a bow, Jeff had a Remington hunting rifle, and they were each wearing a game pack with meat in it on their backs.

"Bagged one, huh?" Josh asked. "Doe, I take it," he guessed, based on the meat—or lack of it—in the packs the men were wearing.

"Yeah." Eli's face wore a frown. "Not sure how much longer this'll last. I think these woods will be over-hunted soon."

Josh had left the Horn men at their workstation and started following his brother and nephew across the field to take the road down. *Dadgummit,* he frowned to himself. *I guess hunting seasons only matter when the state can be out there, ticketing people...*

The three men were quiet for the ten-minute walk back to the main area near the kitchen. Eli finally broke the ice. "I sure wish we had a huntin' dog. I'd like to go look for a bear west of here, near the Mount Verde forest. Pretty sure I saw scat at least twice when we were on the rescue mission, and I wasn't even *really* lookin' for it."

That got Josh thinking. "Several members out here have brought their dogs with them. I've been thinking about how to put them to work. What breeds should I be asking about as I talk to people?" he asked his brother.

"Anything with hound, beagle, or ridgeback. If it's young enough, we can probably still train it."

"Roger that," Josh said, peeling off from his family to check the northwest watch since he'd wandered to this side of the range's property. He saw Payton in the kitchen door, glancing casually in his direction. He found her presence soothing, but his thoughts quickly dissolved into the unpleasant memories of two divorces and a post-war struggle with drinking. *This is home, now. Nothin' good can come from hurting her...*

2

Awe.

MOST PEOPLE DON'T HAVE A CLUE HOW PRISON REALLY WORKS. *BAD guys get guarded by good guys, right?* Not exactly. Smart bad guys figure out a couple of important things. For one, they have time to concentrate on their personal goals—like learning dead languages and teaching them to others. Whether Latin or the Language of the Birds, they now have a medium to communicate that nobody else knows. The term "jailhouse lawyer" comes from the fact that the brightest of them learn the law, oftentimes better than their public defenders. They also study the sciences, such as chemistry—for making better products and explosives—and physics. They figure out that not all leverage applies literally.

Prison staff, especially the guards, have to go to great lengths to hide their personal information. In the modern age, though, it isn't enough. Connected gang leaders behind bars feed the names to their unconfined networks, and in turn, those names wind up on a list. This applies to the lower-risk lock-up facilities and county jails, too. The guards are smart, too—they know the game. They go to work, scouting for that suspicious car that may just be waiting to take their family hostage. This is the harsh truth that the government at all levels hides from the public—*our respect for life—especially our loved ones—is our vulnerability.*

The day the hammer fell, a clock started ticking. For some guards it was immediate—*I'm never going back there again.* They knew that once they did, they would most likely never see home again. Some, like the divorcees and older ones whose kids had grown up, made that final trip. Some counties had planned for this by preparing shelter and food to house the guards. Others did not. Prisons need electricity to operate. The electronic gates and cameras serve as force multipliers, which reduced the number of guards needed. With the absence of electricity and half the guards not coming to work…well, it didn't take long for the foxes to rule the henhouse after that.

TAHOMA'S HAMMER, Minus 2 Hours.

GUESS IT'S a good thing I took the new schedule, Earl Garren thought. He felt a small victory over karma knowing he wouldn't have to deal with the I-5 traffic that evening. The retired Army Ranger, starting his third year as a civilian, worked at the Bass Pro Shop down in Tacoma. Back on active duty, he and his family had always lived near post. But the traffic in Western Washington was so horrendous, they moved up to Des Moines so his wife would have a short commute to her job. He hated Des Moines, but the smaller, cheaper home supported his true passion—their hunting and fishing cabin near North Bend, about forty-five miles northeast.

About twice per year, Bass Pro Shop would scramble the employee's schedules so that nobody got too used to having true weekends off. He didn't mind. The twenty percent employee discount was worth it, and trout had to eat on Monday's and Tuesday, too. This was the first Monday-Tuesday weekend he had on the new schedule, and he decided to forego the cabin while they figured out how he would support things like picking up kids from school. The earthquake that morning had reminded everyone how fragile things were. *At least it wasn't the big one.*

[Brrrt—Household 6: "Be home in 20. JL decided to close up and go home."]

[Earl: "K"]

Earl was a man of few words. The forty-two-year-old, 6' 2" former Sergeant First-Class loved his family and friends, but he detested using phones unless absolutely necessary. Victoria, known to everyone else as Tori, had fallen in love with that strength and had learned to tolerate the quiet. She was sometimes perplexed at how some of her friend's husbands could carry on active, hour-long phone calls with their wives. "It's all part of having a vagina," Earl would say, knowing his wife would pound him in the arm—hard—when he made sexist jokes like that.

Tori was truly the one person he would allow to boss him. She didn't know it, but he had entered her name as "Household 6" into his phone, a common GI Joe euphemism for a soldier's spouse. It indicated she was the unit commander. He may've been the SFC, but she was the CO. Tori was an Admin Assistant at a nearby financial planner's office, and it was relatively easy to shut up the store, when needed.

He remembered he'd forgotten to tell Tori about the kids. [Earl: "Got an auto-message. School's out. Kids should be home soon."] The 7.1 earthquake had rocked them, but Earl figured it was the plane crash that had solidified Des Moines decision to cancel school. All the local fire and police resources were assisting the airport, he guessed.

He was sitting at his garage work bench and decided that he

needed to get back to tying fishing flies. All this texting was wearing him out.

[Brrrt.] He ignored it and kept tying. [Brrrt.] Earl huffed and figured if he didn't check it, this would be the time one of his kids was hurt.

[Brrrt—Con-Man: "Dude. Answer your phone."]

[Earl: "What? Didn't ring"] Con-Man was Conner Moore, the yang to Earl's yin. They'd served together in the 75th Ranger Battalion at Joint Base Lewis McChord, but Conner got out after twelve years to tend to a divorce. He lived in Tacoma and was a heavy-equipment operator who worked wherever the union sent him, which for a few months had been to West Seattle.

[Brrrt—Con-Man: "All work suspended for state inspections. Should be off work in an hour or so. Beer?"]

Earl hit the "blue-thumb" of approval. [Earl: "Pick me up. Waiting for kids."]

As if on cue, he heard the familiar sound of the front door opening and a backpack hitting the floor. *Owen*, he thought. Owen Henry and Piper Elizabeth, thirteen and fifteen, were the entire world to Earl. He figured he'd give it until Tori got home before he sent out the search party for his daughter. *Maybe they'll say there's a cracked overpass so I don't have to go to Tacoma tomorrow,* he thought.

Tahoma's Hammer

THE SLAMMING OF THE 80" TV on the floor made no noise. That is to say, not any noticeable noise, as compared to the noise made by the range hood that had shaken off the ceiling and the three industrial refrigerators slamming into each other. Or the other noises, like the couches and recliners hitting the ceiling, or the windows shattering, or the alarm klaxons that screamed for about ten seconds before shutting off when the lights did.

The loudest noise, though, came several minutes into the event. It sounded like a freight train had decided to jump tracks and tip over, but it emanated from the ground and floor below. It didn't matter where someone on McNeil Island in Southwest Puget Sound stood—they heard it. They *felt* it. They *were* the noise, and it was them. As Tahoma sent her wrath towards space, the earth sent her sounds out towards the north and west. Nobody near Tacoma had to see the black and gray clouds billowing skyward to know Tahoma had erupted—she *told* them.

Forty-year-old Christopher "Sticky" Wood started laughing. By the time the shaking stopped, he was hysterical. If it wasn't for the sharp pain in his left elbow from landing on it when he first hit the tile floor in the dwelling unit's dayroom, he would've been having the time of his life. He enjoyed the looks of terror and concern on everyone's face, not just the guards and counselors, but the other residents. *Damn perverts are scared. Look at 'em!* He was beside himself.

He had no delusions that he was *not* one the perverts, but that didn't stop him from calling the other rapists and pedophiles that every chance he got. Especially when he figured out which counselors it pissed off. He was one of the forty percent of the island's 197 'residents' that refused to participate in counseling. He couldn't stand the thought of some granola-eating, feel-good psychologist trying to dive into his head. There was no room for himself in there —he sure as hell wasn't going to let someone else in.

Sticky had no love for the pedophiles, as even he had a code he'd never break. His hate was born out of being a child-victim himself, but his crimes were crimes of rage. The rapes and eventual murders—*they've never tied those to me*, he reminded himself—were just the shadow escaping. His victims of preference were women in their twenties who looked like his mother, followed closely by killing anyone who conflicted with the Risen Dead MC's interests. He didn't know what to call the shadow inside him, but he knew whatever it was, it needed to eat.

Sticky and his older brother were the sons of a professional meth-cook biker who'd spent most of his life in prison. Their addict mother turned tricks for cash and disappeared into her room for days at a time. There was that one regular, though, whose thirst was never quite quenched by the time she passed out stoned. That particular gremlin eventually went away for good, but the damage was done. Sticky earned his nickname when he was eleven, winning a dare and a bet by having sex with a sheep. His fourteen-year-old brother wasn't thrilled when he heard about the dare or the nickname, understanding it was a play on their last name. The kid all the other kids called Legion beat the living hell out of the one that put up the money for the bet, earning a seven-month trip to a juvenile detention camp in the process.

When the shaking stopped and the noise turned into a deafening silence, Sticky spent several seconds catching his breath and trying to stop laughing. He eventually got to his feet and started to look around. Everyone was dazed. *I don't suppose the fences fell,* he wondered. *Can't possibly be that lucky.* He figured the fences were for the public anyhow—*geez, it's an island, people.*

Nobody knew what to do. One of the very few ways this place differed from a prison is that the residents could go from building to building to courtyard to garden to ballfield at will, for the most part. Sticky made his way outside and saw staff running like a horde of headless chickens. *Where do they think they're goin'?*

Holding his left elbow near his ribs, he looked up through the drizzle at the battleship-gray fist growing skyward and smiled.

Tahoma's Hammer Plus 4 and 1/2 Hours.

. . .

It had been a much drier, fateful October day on the eastern side of the Cascade Mountains. The ash was settling, changing every-thing into a gray, gravelly lunarscape. This was the moment the sun was dipping below the mountains, but it had been "dusk" all after-noon. The city of Ellensburg was normally a picturesque town. Fairly flat and level, it housed a small university and the biggest hospital on the I-90 corridor between Seattle and Spokane. It situ-ated itself in farming territory on the north side of the highway, right where the south-easterly run off of the slopes veered due east.

The drier air meant the ash was taking its time, but the pebbles weren't. It started hailing pebbles in this part of the state about ninety minutes after Tahoma blew her top, and it was finally tapering off. The ash was taking the pebbles' place, settling down on everything—roofs, cars, storm drains...and the tent city that had started to spring up east of KVH Hospital.

There was just one block between Mountain View Park and the hospital, making it an ideal place for the triage to take place. When Cascadia played her music, the entire state of Washington and parts of Oregon, Idaho, and British Columbia had all danced to the shake, rattle, and roll. When Dr. Sorab Gupta picked himself up off the floor in surgery, he called out orders to have his department go set up triage in the park to the east. The head of the small college town's ER department had been through this before.

He finished up the elective, ventral hernia surgery as quickly as the back-up power would allow but was constantly flashing back to the June, 1991, eruption of Mt. Pinatubo in the Philippines. The Mumbai native was finishing his residency in Manila and recalled walking through ash a year later. Experience taught him that elec-tive surgeries became a thing of the past for a while.

There were really only two people in the ER department he trusted for such a task, and he'd made sure they were the two who always participated in the small city's emergency drills. The pair of women were both strong leaders and experienced in treating the typical trauma in this part of the state—farming and highway accidents. Dr. Sandra Tennant may've had rank, but Charge Nurse Natalie Grace was the backbone of the operation.

Natalie had arranged for the volunteer firefighters to get her some large, canvas tents and make sure the typical emergency-management triage tarps—green, yellow, red, and black—were lashed to the top. They needed to keep the ash and gravel off the patients, but still let people know where to take them.

Most of the patients were from auto accidents, being driven in by neighbors and Good Samaritans. There had been some older-building collapses, but most people fortunate enough to survive were doomed to die a lonely, frozen, dehydrated death a few days later. There just weren't enough resources to tend to everything.

The trickle of trucks and patients had been steady, but the flow was impacted by clogged air filters and fuel injectors, coupled with giant holes in the roads. Natalie's job was to sort the patients for Sandra by probable survivability. Green were walking wounded and basically expected to get off their bum and help. Yellow and red might have a chance. Nobody wanted to wind up in the tent under the black tarp. It was a cold, heartless decision, not unlike a military commander ordering her troops to perform a mission nobody would return from.

"We need push brooms," Natalie ordered a firefighter.

"Seriously?" the young volunteer questioned. Nobody had taken time for water, let alone food. Blood sugar was getting low and so was patience.

"Find some brooms," Natalie commanded. "Knock the roofs from the inside. Don't get it in the door. You wanna see a tent collapse?" *I'm gonna knock some morons out if I have to keep explaining myself...*

She shook her head and coughed some dust as she wandered over to the next person being carried in by civilians. They were using a sleeping bag as a stretcher. "Story?" Natalie asked the rescuers as she bent down to the woman and wiped some dust off her cheek. She was assessing the lady's shock level. The woman turned her head and looked at Natalie, dazed.

"I-90. We were—"

"Yellow," she said, pointing to the correct tent. In a matter of five seconds, she knew. That was triage—less taking vital signs and more experience-born instinct. Assuming there wasn't a massive hemorrhage or deformity, Natalie then looked for labored breathing and skin tone.

The lower layer of pebbles crunched under the now twelve-inch deep layer of ash as Natalie plowed through the dust, heading over to Sandra at the red tent. While it had been less than five hours, it had felt like one and she was tired enough for it to have been twenty.

"Look! Look where I'm pointing! Son-of-a—! Right there, Prospect!"

"Gotcha. When do you want us to start?" the senior prospect for the Risen Dead Motorcycle Club asked his State President.

"Be ready by dark. But I'll tell you we're going when it's time, so don't get stupid," Legion growled. "Now, grab that hang-around that showed up and get the utility closet prepped for the man. I want him separated from his ol' lady, so she'll go into the parts-area for now. I do not want our families knowing about this until absolutely necessary. Got it?"

"Every word, Legion." With that, the head-shaven prospect went to perform his chores.

Life in a "1-percenter" MC wasn't for the faint of heart in the best of times. Legion may have been born to be an outlaw, but that didn't make him stupid. Like any organization, the brightest and the Type-A's tended to float to the top. Prospects didn't generally get the luxury of having names, and hang-arounds usually didn't warrant any conversation from the man in charge of every chapter in the state.

The Risen Dead MC was by far the largest club in Washington State, known in that world as the "dominant club." No club—not even those clubs that dominated other states—flew their colors in Washington without Legion's permission. It was truly a caste-system operating in the world, right under most Americans' noses. The club had six chapters and almost seventy fully-patched members in Washington state. When prospects, hang-arounds, and "support clubs"—clubs that were directly tied to the parent club and usually flew some other variation of the colors, name, and patch—were added, their numbers grew by a factor of five. That's called an army, and Legion knew it.

Four of those chapters were on the west side of the Cascades and had standing orders to fall-in to the main clubhouse—Legion's home and business—in the eventual subduction zone collapse. Legion knew immediately this event was no normal event—getting everyone here would be luck. *Never expected the mountain to pop. That'll make it hard for brothers to get here...*Some would eventually trickle in, and he couldn't wait.

This was an opportunity. One of the things the smart outlaw knew was that unlike the ethnic gangs who dealt in the exotic vices, he would *always* be able to supply his customers with crank...and women. The other gangs would all take to the sex-trade, too, and he wouldn't fight that. But he would dominate the addicts, because the Black gangs would run out of crack, the Hispanics would run out of coke, the Asians would run out of heroine, and the Russians would run out of guns—*for a while, anyway...*

Like a smart leader, he knew he needed communications and was kicking himself for not taking care of this the dozens of times he'd told himself to. Legion started waking his crews up to prepping years earlier. They had a plan and enough stores to last them while they enacted it. He would round up the members' families for safety to start. Then they would start taking anything they needed, especially when the National Guard started to thin out in numbers.

Legion owned a hot-rod and chopper customization shop in the neighborhood north of Pacific Raceways in east King County. The front 2,500 square feet was his business, and about that much again in the back was his two-story clubhouse, which he and his woman and kids lived in full-time. The club was his life—it *always* came first. For everything. This was the distinction between hardcore 1-percenters and all the rest. Even if he stepped down as state president, he would always have a clubhouse in his home. In fact, it wasn't even truly his home. As part of the commitment, every member signed over the titles to their motorcycles to be club property. Legion had signed over his entire home and business—the only way he would leave the Risen Dead was in a body bag.

"What's on your mind, brother?" Trip asked him, noticing the prospect was making himself busy. Both men were standing on the elevated deck that overlooked the back parking area of the clubhouse. They could see houses in both directions.

"See that house with all the antennas on the other end of the block?" Legion said, pointing east about five homes down.

"Yeah. Dude must hate the cable companies!" Trip quipped.

"Not exactly," Legion answered. "Those are HAM radio antennas—a *lot* of them." Legion was no small man, at about 6' 2". He was fairly muscular, albeit with a whiskey gut. But he was noticeably smaller than his giant State Enforcer. Trip was the man that Legion trusted the most, with the lone exception being his brother on McNeil Island. Trip had one job—protect the state prez's interest. If chapters were getting pissy with each other, it was Trip's job to straighten them out.

His Enforcer wasn't dumb, either. "We need to grab all that stuff —and the dude who runs it."

"Bingo..." Legion said, trailing off for a couple of seconds. "And the houses on all sides of this property. We need to push our perimeter out and make room for the families." He did not break his gaze on the house with the antennas until he heard the sounds of two 103-cubic-inch Harley engines rumbling into the neighborhood. He looked at Trip. "We need to make sure the support clubs get word to get their butts in here, too." *We're gonna need manpower... Fast.*

3

"There is but one degree of commitment: total."
—Arnie Sherr

TAHOMA'S HAMMER PLUS 18 DAYS.

IT WAS SADLY IRONIC. In every major city west of the continental divide, citizens were experiencing rolling blackouts at a bare minimum. It wasn't just the obvious victims that had to adjust to life without electricity. When people around the eastern half of America talked about what was happening, they subconsciously thought about those poor Washingtonians. The sharper few realized that Cascadia had impacted Oregon, Idaho, and British Columbia, too. But out west, reality was much harsher.

The loss of power exports from Washington—followed soon via legislative action from the rest of the western states that sold electricity—had impacted every portion of every state in the American

West. Society had set itself for an eruption of its own for decades by conditioning people in the exact opposite direction of *natural*. Just-in-time delivery systems, all of the world's encyclopedic information on every phone, and year-round, sixty-eight-degree air conditioning had spoiled people—and made them lazy.

When smaller cities and counties began to comply with state mandates to induce rolling blackouts, the people weren't happy. When the blackouts quit rolling and began sustaining, they began to revolt. So many depended on power as an absolute must to their income that they started to get panicky. Instagram influencers, E-Bay resellers, and online vendors started to unite in their worry. The larger cities had pulled the long-straw for the moment—the banks' computer servers and the tourism dollars that cities counted on were going to be the very last thing to have their power cut. Los Angeles' residents were—ironically— "kept in the dark" the longest about what was in store for them.

It was difficult for someone in Utica to understand why the Seattle earthquake would cause power outages in Las Vegas—or so the media thought—so the riots out west were downplayed in the nightly news. That didn't change reality, though. The hammer's shockwaves were still rippling back and forth around the world and internet in ways most Americans would never even consider. The devastation to Amazon and Microsoft were just the start. Digital currency mining, enhanced AI research, micro-genetics—most future technologies were impacted and, therefore, the economies of the various countries that had been riding on the future success of those technologies.

Josh saw Payton near the range's big firepit at the intersection of Bay 4, the "school conexes", and the northern road to The Field. It was overcast but dry, and she was hanging laundry on the u-shaped clothesline they'd fashioned around the back half of the firepit, closer to the rifle line berm. *Wow, she looks good. Even pregnant,* Josh thought, and immediately chastised himself. *Stop!* The older he got, the more detached he became from the young man's game of gawking at women just for their looks. Still…there was just something about the way she…*hangs laundry? Just stop. She's still mourning the disappearance of her 'baby-daddy'…*

"Hey," he said as casually as he could. "What's up?" *What's up? Just stop, you idiot.*

"Oh, hi! Didn't see you coming up," Payton lied, looking in his direction. "What's the latest on the security improvements?"

"Tons going on. This eighty-something acres has a big perimeter. It's gonna take a while to get it to what I would call acceptable. I wish I could just snap my fingers or somethin'…Oh, what is this about an idea for the logs? Someone said to talk to you about some idea…" he trailed off.

"Follow," she commanded and started around the break in the rifle line berm.

Yes, ma'am! Josh did as he was instructed, still admiring the view despite his earlier self-admonishment. He caught up to her and they stopped a short bit later, smack in the middle of the settings for holding targets on the 100-yard line. They were looking back towards the covered line and benches to the west.

"For some reason, we've been filling in all the spots around the lower dozen acres with tents and campers except this one—the first forty percent of the rifle line," she said.

"Yeah, I guess I hadn't really thought about that," Josh admitted. The two were slowly strolling through the field. There was a small berm at the fifty-yard markers, but other than that, there was essentially a big flat football-field sized space not being utilized. "But we will still need to sight-in our rifles. We already have some crowding at the other end of the rifle range, tucked into the berms as they go up hill to the farthest cliff," he countered. "Putting stuff here would interfere with that."

"Yes, but you only need one shooting lane for sighting-in. Just sight-in one or two rifles at a time from Bench 24," she countered. She walked over to the edge of the field to get into the approximate spot between that bench and the down-range berm.

Josh followed her and started looking back and forth. "Yeah...I guess we could keep people from putting tents in this line of fire. Of course, we'd have to clear everyone out of the other tents anyway, for safety." He looked back at Payton. "What's all of this have to do with the logs?"

"So other than this line-of-fire, you agree that the first half of the rifle line could be better utilized?" She needed Josh on her side so they could team up if her father or the board objected.

"Let's say I do..." he said, cautious to commit too early. *She's good...* "Quit teasing me."

"I think with the horses and the logs and some ropes and pulleys, we could stand up a big log structure that could become almost like one of those old-timey revival tents. Roof. Open-sided. Big spot for meetings, meals, church..."

A smile started to form on Josh's face. He locked his eyes onto hers for a moment, then shifted his gaze to her strawberry-blonde hair when he realized she wasn't going to avert her gaze. *Beautiful and smart...* "Alright."

"Alright?" she asked. "It's frickin' genius, thank you very much!"

"It's...good...no—great. It's a great idea. I'll back you. But I save genius for things like curing cancer and picking winning lotto tickets twice," he joked.

Payton reached out and put her hand on his elbow, smiling. "Well, thanks anyway!" Then she switched her tone a bit. "Since I have your attention, I'd like to go over something else. Follow me back that way for a few?"

"Sure." They started heading back to the firepit. The youngsters —nine of them, all between the ages of five and eleven—were out there tending to the class homestead center in between the two conex boxes. They were learning to compost, help with meals, and tend rabbits. In spring, they would plant a garden. Josh and

Savannah waved to each other when they met glances. She'd taken to him since the rescue.

Payton continued to hang laundry. "I'm worried about the food. I mean—I'm grateful that Eli and Jeff and a few others are bagging what deer they can. It just isn't going to go very far."

Josh noticed that there were drying racks with some of that morning's kill positioned around the near side of the firepit. He figured the rest was in the several Dutch-ovens that were hanging over the fire itself. "Yeeaahhh...somethin' I've been thinking about a lot, too. I want to start working some patrols into the schedule, but I need to go over it with your dad and the others at tonight's big meeting first."

"Patrols?" Payton questioned.

"Well, that's just a simple way to describe it. I don't mean send people out to aimlessly look for bad guys. They'd go map the area, look for cargo trucks, see which houses are occupied, which ones look abandoned, scrounge for stuff people left behind, including food." He could tell by the look on her face she was skeptical. "What?"

"You mean steal," she said flatly.

"No, I mean procure. And get intel. Is it really stealing if we're sure people have abandoned it? I see it as a moral obligation over letting the tweekers find it first."

"But you can't be sure," she objected.

"Okay," he said, not believing he had to debate ethics with a woman who just admitted to being worried about the food supplies. "I'll give you a mathematical win—we can't with 100-percent certainty know that the owners are completely gone, *some* of the time. But the law of probability will be on our side."

"Meaning what?" she said skeptically. She was second-guessing her secret crush's moral code.

"Meaning that just like hunting for game, there are signs. Missing vehicles. House is boarded up tight but vacated. A lot of earthquake damage." *Natural deaths and signs of violence,* he didn't add.

Payton was thinking quietly. After a minute, Josh decided he had tasks to perform. He was going to talk to some of the dog owners about using them for hunting and guard duty. He also wanted their thoughts on killing coyotes and raccoons and using the meat to feed the dogs. He started to walk away.

"It's just a lot to take in," she said to him before he'd moved far. "I'm not saying you're right...but I'm not saying you're wrong, either." She paused while they looked at each other. "I just need to come to terms with it."

"With the fact you think we're stealing?" It was his turn to sound slightly put-off.

"No. With the fact that in 21st Century America, we have to scavenge to make it through winter."

PHIL LEANED ON HIS CRUTCHES, his left pant leg rolled up and pinned under his stump just below the knee. The informal jokes and conversation had gone on for the requisite amount of time. It was time to get everyone on track. "Alright, everyone," he said, a little louder than normal. They were all sitting around a large fire Phil had built in the flat grassy area next to the pond that sprang up every fall and disappeared every summer. They were across from the openings to Bays 7 and 8, near the base of the road that went up and back to The Field.

Small conversations died down and people began to shut up and listen. "Our guests will need to return to their homes as soon as possible, so let's get down to business," Phil instructed. It was only about six in the evening, but it was dark. The day had been one of several heavy days of torrential rains, but the rain had stopped a few hours earlier, which meant sitting by the fire was a pleasant necessity. Most of the people present were currently staying at the range. The rest were the men Phil had met that night at the off-road park, plus the leaders of some similar preparedness groups.

"Since the introductions were somewhat spread out and muddled, I'd ask that all of the key leaders of the different MAGs introduce themselves." MAG stood for Mutual Assistance Group, a common term for different groups of families and friends that may be of benefit in terms of self-defense, barter, and similar survival initiatives. "I'm Phil Walker. Yes, *that* Phil Walker," he said, deflecting the usual questions about his locally famous incident. He'd learned that even on crutches, people still felt compelled to ask. "I'm one of the board members and the day-to-day manager here at West Sound Sportsmen's Club," he said as he sat down.

The formal introductions went around the fire. The rest of the board and heads of range-families introduced themselves to Gary Stonefence, Kenny "Skinny" O'Brian, Lonnie Everly, and the leaders of five other groups. There were about forty people in all sitting around the fire, representing closer to five hundred people in their various groups, almost a third of whom were already living on the property.

"I'd like to start, if that's okay," Gary said, looking to Phil, who gave him the nod. "First off, it's not too many places that can sport an open-fire like this anymore," he commented, primarily to the various family-heads in the group. "If you haven't realized what a special place you have here, then you need to put some thought into it." He saw some heads nodding. "Seriously, the fact that you have an armed perimeter with natural barriers and a fence project that is improving every day…that's hard for us smaller groups to achieve."

Phil looked over to Josh, who was sitting to his right using a stick to doodle in the dirt while he listened. *I wonder if we should be taking minutes or something,* Phil thought. "We're very fortunate to have the people we have here. I haven't…" Phil started to feel the frog in his throat. "I'm…" *Damn.* He couldn't help but think of Crane. People could see the emotion creep onto his face.

"It's ok, Phil," Don Kwiatkowsky called out. A few others mumbled support, and some even teared up just seeing Phil get emotional.

He let out a big breath and choked it down. "Thanks, everyone. I'm fine." He paused just to make sure. "I've been a bit short with people lately as I deal with Crane's death. I'm just thankful that God has sent people like Josh, Eli...all of you. Sorry if I'm forgetting anyone..." With that, Phil started sobbing a bit as the tears fell.

"Hey, everyone here feels a hole in their heart," Gary said, taking the heat off Phil. He looked at Skinny Kenny, who gave him a nod. He changed the topic to get the spotlight off Phil's breakdown. "Some of us had a chance to link up on the trip over here today, and we have something you need to think about." Gary looked around to make sure he had everyone's attention. "You need to send a disproportionate response to the people that attacked you."

Josh looked up for a moment while the crowd started buzzing. Several "come again" type responses rang out as men and women digested what that meant.

"Easy to say when it isn't your lives on the line," someone called out louder than the rest. Murmurs and comments started to fly as emotions started to flow.

Phil stood up to signal to everyone to calm down. "Hey. Listen up—"

"Jerry and I have some things to talk about," Josh finally blurted out as he stood. Phil didn't normally take interruptions so gracefully, but he sat back down. Josh had earned some extra tolerance.

"Jerry, you first."

The HAM operator stood up. "I and my assistants have been hand-writing this for days." He walked over to Gary and handed him a stack of papers. "I want every group here to take two copies of this comms plan." Gary did as instructed and passed the stack along. Jerry continued. "First, if you don't have a good radio in the local bands with a decent wattage of power and an antenna as high as you can get it—you're failing." This earned a few murmurs.

"This plan assumes you can transmit in seventy centimeters and two meters, but there's some six- and ten-meter stuff in there, too. I've laid out standard times for regular comms checks four times a day. There's also a whole set of frequencies in there that everyone should program into their radios and set them to scan. That way we can still get each other's attention without waiting for the next calling window." Jerry could see the light coming on for most of them. "I can't say this enough—power and antenna height are your friends. We can easily talk from one end of this peninsula to the other, especially if we relay messages back and forth."

"What's this'n here list of codes?" Skinny Kenny asked.

"That's for Josh to answer," Jerry said, looking at his cohort.

"Phil told me about the posse idea," Josh started. "This will get it rolling." He looked around and noticed every set of eyes was intently paying attention. "We're going to start patrolling for supplies, mapping houses and activities, looking for resources. In doing that, we'll spray-paint the standard CERT markings on the buildings and trucks that have been vacated. Under that we'll put one of the code words. That way you know it's us, and we'll know it's you. In short, though—we all need to start conducting area intelligence assessments."

"I take it the codes are for our people to verify each other in the event they meet unexpectedly? Like 'flash' and 'thunder' on D-Day?" Gary said.

"That's half of it. I think we need some sort of physical mark, too. Double verification will be much harder to fake."

"Like a patch or something?" Lonnie suggested. "My sister has an old-school sewing machine. Big one, for leather and canvas. Making a simple patch would work."

"Until the scum-bags see it and make it themselves," someone yelled out.

"Keep it hidden," Josh suggested. "Only pull it out when the code-test is passed." This got a general round of agreement.

"I like it, Josh," Phil said, getting up on his crutches. "May I have the floor while everyone ponders that for a bit?" Everyone concurred. "Lonnie, have you all made a decision about moving out here?"

"We have," he said. "If you'll still have us, we plan on moving tomorrow. We have our stuff loaded in several trucks and three cargo trailers. I verified our route through the broken roads on the way today."

"Good," Phil said with a succinct nod. "Actually, great! That's some great news. We can use your help." He turned his attention to the other group leaders. "I know you all have your retreats established, but you can consider this a safe rally-point if something bad happens." This resulted in a few spoken thanks and smiles. "Now. What was this thing about a response, Gary?"

"You guys were attacked. If you want to reduce—greatly—the chances of that happening again, you need to find the home base of those people...and destroy everyone in it."

As the voices started to speak out again, Phil had had enough. "Stop!" he yelled. "He's my guest, and I want to hear him out!" He was starting to get tired of people cutting him off. *Holy Hell, people, just shut up for a second...*

Looking back to Gary, he said, "You know that is easier said than done."

"Actually, Phil, it's pretty simple. Do you know who did it?"

Phil blew out a deep breath, thinking again of Fred. "Undoubtedly, it is the Matthews clan, the Canal Vista patriarch family of meth-cooks and general, all-around white-trash."

"Then that's who you need to destroy."

"There's some real issues with that, and I don't mean the moral kind. I have no problem killing those animals," Phil said. "One is, what do we do with the kids?" This got a bunch of mini-conversations going. "The second is that this county is chomping at the bit to come confiscate weapons. That will surely draw their attention." More ruckus from the crowd.

Phil and Gary scanned the crowd a bit, each deeply thinking of their next counterpoint. Phil noticed Josh had gone back to drawing in the dirt with the stick. The rest of the crowd got into their mini-deliberations for close to ten minutes. Phil had finally had enough.

"Listen!" he commanded, trying to get everyone quiet again. "Josh, do you have an opinion here?" he barked.

Josh stood up and scanned the faces staring at him. He looked back and forth for several seconds, waiting for an almost-awkward silence to fall. Finally, "This." He pointed down in the dirt. Everyone looked at him like he had gone mad. "This," he repeated. "I mean it. Get up! Get up and come look." Slowly, butts started to get out of folding lawn-chairs and off of benches. He made sure they formed up and passed his dirt circle in the correct direction.

The crowd slowly filed past his inscription. They were staring at a circle with crosshairs in it, eerily similar to looking through a rifle scope. In the upper left quadrant was a volcano shape with a few steam waves coming off it. The other three quadrants were occupied by three letters— SPP.

"What is it?" Craig Wageman asked as he walked by.

Josh ignored him for a moment, looking at Gary and Skinny. "Will you be our ready reserve when we hit them?" The crowd was dead quiet.

Gary looked not just at Skinny, but at the leaders of all the other MAGs in attendance. "Yes. Each and every time. For any of you."

"Then the what-ifs will have to sort themselves out," Josh announced. "We hit them at 0330 the morning after tomorrow night." He looked at Lonnie. "Sorry to do this mere hours after you move in, but we can't do it without your help. Go, or stay back here and guard—but we need you."

With no hesitation, Lonnie said, "We're in. This is our home now."

Josh scanned around the crowd once more, finally ending on Craig to answer his question. "Then I present you with the mark of the Slaughter Peninsula Posse." This got a few nods and approving looks. "Now we just need a motto."

"Well, that's easy," Phil commented. "I've been saying it for years when people ask me why I prep or why my classes are so affordable." He looked around, realizing he'd actually had quite a few of the non-members in classes over the years. "Well, most of you have already heard this a time or two." The crowd was silent, waiting for him to say it like it was some sort of spell that would make it official. "Our duty is to be ready."

4

Road Blocks.

Tahoma's Hammer Plus 1 Day.

Natalie and the triage team were taking cat naps in the one tent set up for them throughout the first night. She and Doc Sandra had been taking opposite shifts, assisted by a couple of nurses and ER Techs and CERT and local Fire Department Volunteers. Sleep wasn't coming—it was mainly a form of eyes-closed rest. Everyone was too amped on adrenaline and worry. As First Responders, they had the same desire to go home and check on things as anybody else —without the liberty to do so.

Natalie's husband, Roy, had tried to come down and check on his wife the evening before, knowing her Kia would never make it home. He'd wound up with a slight goose-egg and a broken tie-rod when he drove right off an eighteen-inch tall shelf in the road. The old '78 Chevy short-bed already had a few spiderweb cracks in the windshield—running the wipers only made the sticky ash smear into streaks. Roy and his minor concussion hiked four miles home and slowly took the farm's yellow Cub Cadet utility quad the eleven miles into town. The dedicated nurse had shooed him away to tend to the kids and animals with instructions to come back early the next afternoon.

It was about 6:30 in the morning at this point. Natalie had spelled the doctor for her break about a half hour earlier. Mostly they were tending to the overflow of patients waiting for a chance to go to the hospital. The Ellensburg police, with some backup from the university police, had to start guarding the hospital to force people to the park's collection point the evening before. The ER department had been vastly overwhelmed, and most people thought they were the exception to the rule about victims checking in at the collection point.

A few had even dared to vent their frustration about it to Natalie. Most of them said some variation of, "But we were already there! Don't they know it's (insert loved one here)," to which Natalie would load her verbal shotgun with a full magazine of truth-slugs and open fire. *I haven't even been home yet!* She would exclaim each time. *None of us have! The ER could operate faster if morons like you would quit interrupting! We didn't put the signs up for our own amusement!*

The flow of new patients had slowed drastically around midnight. Natalie expected two things as the sun began to turn the eastern sky gray—the pace would pick back up and a large portion would wind up in the dreaded black-tarp tent. She knew from her turnover that Doc Sandra had been quietly administering morphine to those in the most pain. They had decided early into the event to halt the use of IV bags on those in this tent. *Doc's been giving them direct shots,* Natalie could tell from the simple band-aid. *I wonder how much? It is dark in here…If she accidentally gave too much, who am I to argue?* As the sun rose and more volunteers came back, she would have them start moving the expired victim's out to the morgue staging area on the other side of the playground.

True to her theory, she could see a Coca-Cola truck bouncing slowly up Maple Street, heading for the park. The roll-up doors were raised and there was a small squad of men and women holding on for dear life as they stood in the compartments and rode along on the sides. *Like a bunch of firemen riding on the outside in the old days,* she thought, momentarily amused. There was also a small contingent riding on the truck's flat roof.

The truck stopped and the mobile hopped off, helping the injured down. Natalie noticed that two men on the top used a blanket with ropes tied to the corners to slowly lower a victim to the waiting arms of several people below. While that was happening, a husky man in a filthy gray and red uniform made a fast jaunt over to her.

"These people were stuck in a mangled mess of vehicles out on 82 all night. Where do you want 'em?"

Natalie saw some of her team start to come out of the break tent to help with the fresh patients. "Put the one in the blanket here on this picnic table. The walking can go to the green tent, the rest go to the yellow for a moment."

With a piercing whistle, the delivery driver got the attention of the makeshift stretcher bearers. "Right here on the table, guys!" he yelled. He walked back over to the others to start giving directions.

Natalie reached into the pocket of her filthy-scrubs top, feeling for the flashlight that was supposed to be there. *Grrr,* she growled to herself. *Must be on the tent floor.* It was hard for her to see very well in the gray-dusk. Everyone was the same filthy gray, both in lighting and in actual ash on their clothes. The woman had collected at least two inches of ash on her during the drive over, except where the rescuers had kept her filthy, bloodied face covered with a hand towel.

As Natalie started her assessment, one of the men from the top of the truck made his way over to her. "She was in an older car, no air bag. She was only moaning at first, but she hasn't made any noise for at least ten minutes." It was obvious to Natalie that some of these rescuers were emotionally invested in these patients.

Natalie used her scissors on the woman's shirt to reveal deep purple—she supposed it was purple—blood pooling in the ribs and sternum. She did a quick check for lung sounds, and barely heard some air moving. "Black," she ordered the ER Tech who had strolled up.

Just then she heard her name. "Natalie…"

It wasn't a question, it was a statement. Almost instinctually she turned and saw who it was. She had actually turned her head back to the ER Tech for a moment before her tired brain caught up to her eyes and ears. *Monica…what are you doing here?* "Monica?" she asked out loud, looking back up at the visitor. It was her mother's best friend.

"I'm so sorry, Natalie!" the woman cried out in anguish. "I tried! I tried to help her!" She broke down wailing and would have fallen if not for the two rescuers helping her bear her weight. "I'm so sorry, dear!"

Natalie was confused. *Monica?* She asked her exhausted mind again. Then a deep, dark, looming sensation swept over her as a realization occurred. *Wait!—Where's my mom?* She looked back down at the ash-covered woman she'd just committed to the death tent. A blood-curdling scream that could be heard for two blocks escaped Natalie's soul as her tired mind caught up to her eyes.

"Tengo dudas, Reynaldo." *I don't know about this. How can you be sure it will work?*

Some probably thought it was luck that all three ships in Rey's fleet were in port and more or less deployable when the worst natural disaster in modern history hit America. Rey knew, deep in his core, that it was providence. The Americans had become a country rooted in laziness and greed. The hardest working people in that country, in Rey's mind, were born in Mexico or farther south.

"Nos cortara las dos cabezas si fallas," Rey's boss continued to press. *He'll cut both of our heads off if you fail.* Javier Ortiz was one of three second-in-commands in the Mendoza Cartel. He'd been elevated to that status in part because of the success of Rey's Fleet. If this massive gamble didn't pay off, they and the rest of their under-staff would find themselves hanging from a bridge en masse.

"Es una senal de dios, Jefe," Rey explained. *It's a sign from God. The Santa Maria had to come back to port for a repair to the desalinization unit, but she's fixed now. She should be in El Salvador this very night. La Nina just finished a two-month maintenance period. We just happen to have a fresh batch of foot-soldiers that have been trained.* Rey continued to press his boss. *This is the exact reason we've been building this fleet up all these years!*

"El plan es demasiado grande, Reynaldo!" *The plan is too big!*

They'll never see it coming, Jefe. The Americans have no idea how bad things are about to get. They have a massive panic every time they kill the electricity to fight wildfires. Just imagine them in two months...or six...I have already ordered the stores to be loaded. We can have the first ship at sea in a week and debarking the troops and supplies in two. I just need your approval.

"Esa es el comienzo," his boss countered. *That's only the beginning. Where will you land? What will you do when you're there? The army will wipe you out in a day!*

Look at these satellite photos, Jefe. The Mendoza Cartel had full access to the Mexican Army's military satellites due to a combination of bribes and threats. *There isn't an airport, seaport, or highway that is usable within 300 kilometers of Tacoma. There won't be any army in there for months! Their local State Militia will abandon their posts within days. I've already made contact with our Washington Captain—they are ready and willing to take this facility way up here near Blaine. See? The pier still looks usable. Jefe...they know full-well the costs for failure, and they're chomping at the bit to get started! Once we've secured the northwest, the army you've been building in Los Angeles for thirty years will be able to take over the rest of the west coast with ease. Especially once the other cartels are forced to join us.*

Javier Ortiz knew that merely proposing this was dangerous. If Mendoza thought it was foolish, he would lose all future faith in his judgement. It was a defining moment, the kind that forced him to figure out if they were in the game, or ready for pasture. "Vamos a verlo." *Let's go see him.*

"YOU GUYS TAKING CASH?" Nick asked the small-town clerk. He had pulled it all out of his gear-bag and stuffed it into a front pocket the moment he had to abandon his truck. He was on his way back from the west side of the Hood Canal, having gone up to the small town of Quilcene for a quarterly trek to a friend's house. She was a horse owner and outdoors-woman he'd met at a big sportsmen's show two summers earlier. What had started out as a friendly visit had evolved into a quarterly trip. He enjoyed both her company and the fact that she didn't pressure him for a deeper relationship than he was ready for. He was coming off a long weekend and was heading back to his part-time job driving auto parts to shops.

"Cash is king," the young gas station attendant said. "But we're closed, dude…"

The bridge on Highway 101 where it crossed a fork in a river had collapsed, but Nick wasn't going to let that stop him. He was on a mission. It would have been quick and simple to make his way back to his quarterly booty-call's ranch, but this natural disaster had just reset his life's meaning. Scaling down two hundred feet to a creek bed and back up to the highway was nothing but a small obstacle to the retired, light-infantry sniper.

With nary a second thought, Nick packed every usable item he had in his truck into his already full pack, which he never went anywhere without. A full career deploying to the third world had taught him to always be ready. *Better to have it and not need it than the other way around,* he always thought. Not caring that he had a seventy-five-mile trek ahead of him, he took that first slippery step down the slope and never thought twice about leaving his truck behind.

It was only a few hours into the second day until he'd made it to the Cove RV Park and Country Store. He was pleasantly surprised to see there was still an employee there. Looking around at the shattered windows and every item in the store that had migrated south to the floor, Nick said, "You sure? I buy it, and you *don't* have to pick it up. Right?" He could read the look—it was working. "No change, man. I'll round up. C'mon…"

"What're you lookin' for?" the attendant asked.

"Any food you got," Nick said. "Preferably nuts, granola, tuna, mac-n-cheese…"

"Back corner," mumbled the apathetic twenty-something.

Nick went back and dug through the piles to get every bit of food he could. He knew that hiking seventy-plus miles after an event like this could take several days longer than he was prepared for. It was raining and October, so he had no doubt he could find and filter his water along the way. He was set with high-quality gear. Carbs and protein were what he was really after.

He stopped at the counter and pulled out three twenties to slap down. "Thanks, man," he said. He stopped a step or two from the door, seeing a laminated map of the area that had fallen off the spinning rack. He picked one up and stuffed it into his back pocket, not caring if the kid said anything. He started heading south again, toward his home northwest of Olympia…toward his boat and his *other* gear.

Nick didn't believe in God anymore, but he believed that the universe was telling him something. The day before was his birthday —the hammer had to fall on *somebody's* birthday, after all. He'd just received the one present that no man could give him: the one chance that he'd wanted since the day that piece of human filth was committed to a secure island in the South Puget Sound. Nick was on his way to assassinate Christopher "Sticky" Wood.

NATALIE HAD SAT with her mother in the tent under the black tarp for several hours. She had cried herself dry, which added to an already growing dehydration effect. She continued to monitor her mother. Sandra had tried to override Natalie's triage call, but she wouldn't have it. Her mother had bled out internally and had a dangerously low core temperature to boot. She was gone, and the woman's heart and mind would soon shut down all systems for good.

In less than an hour, Natalie had once again been proven correct. All the other hospital staff and volunteers left her alone. Sandra relayed word to the police and her superiors at the hospital. While they couldn't spare anyone to go fetch Roy, they did put the word out to the HAM volunteers at the Kittitas County Sheriff's Office. Eventually a 4X4 Brush truck from Kittitas Valley Fire & Rescue was able to make its way to the farm and make a notification. Roy opted to take the Cub back to town in case the truck was needed elsewhere.

In all, Roy arrived an hour or two earlier than he would have anyway, but it was something. People helped him trudge through the two-foot deep paths in the ash to the correct tent. He noticed it sagging quite a bit.

"Hey, Honey-Bun," he called out softly when he saw her. He immediately noticed that there were still dead and dying in there. The sagging roof caught his eye again as he fumbled through the process of sitting on the ground. He took her extended hand. Seeing her husband had triggered a new round of sniffling.

"She suffered all night!" she exclaimed as her husband pulled her into his grasp and held her. He said nothing as he caressed her messy, ashy hair. Roy gave her a water bottle and she began to take tugs on it. They sat there silently for a long time, occasionally quietly interrupted as people carried out recently deceased. The influx of patients had slowed.

After about twenty minutes, Roy finally broke the still air. "I need to get up and knock out this roof, Honey-Bun." Nobody had been thinking about such things since Natalie went offline. He found a broom and went to work, which prompted Natalie to think about the present.

"We need to take her home," she said, grief still oozing from her words.

"Of course." Roy was glad their Cub had a bed and a pull-behind cart, but neither were big enough to respectfully carry a deceased loved one. "We'll need to arrange that. The truck is out of commission." He wasn't sure if Natalie had remembered that with all she'd been through. "Let me get you home."

"No! I need—"

"I'll come back—" Roy interrupted her "—and see to it. You need to get home and hold your kids."

The kids! Oh, God! "Did you tell them yet?"

"No. I wanted to wait for you."

Through eyes that had found enough moisture to wet themselves once again, she looked up at her husband's extended hand. She took his assistance getting off the olive drab canvas floor and fell into his hug once again.

Roy guided his grieving wife out through the flaps and ash to the Cub. He took the rocks off the 8' X 12' tarp he'd covered the Cub with and dragged it off the roll-cage. He threw those items into the small bed and trusted that the triage staff would tell someone they had left. Roy used a metal water bottle to wet a couple of bandanas, tying one around his head and neck to cover his nose and mouth. Natalie followed suit.

As the small, two-seat, utility quad slowly rolled north out of town, the pudgy balding farmer realized his wife was able to get her first glimpse of the destruction. "You should buckle up, Honey-Bun," he suggested. They both had a bad habit of not buckling in on the farm.

She complied when she realized how much jostling the gravel, ash, and cracks were truly causing. She took Roy's hand into hers. "How long do you think the ash will stay around?" She hollered through the makeshift respirator, trying to distract her own mind.

"Weeks," Roy hollered back, thinking. "Maybe a couple of months..."

Roy took it slow with the drive home, giving them time to contemplate the damage in Seattle, what the effects to next year's hay might mean, and how long until the government showed up with help.

5

Worry.

Somewhere in the United States Air Force a head or heads were going to roll. It would take a while for the guilty parties to be identified, but when they were, they would be made an example. Somehow, an official and encrypted message had been sent out. On several bases throughout the Air Force's supply chain, an official order went out to perform a sortie of air drops across the Pacific Northwest. Pallets upon pallets of parachuted goods were loaded onto C-17s and C-130s around the nation. Some of the goods had been staged as the relief efforts needed a place to park the food while a delivery plan was figured out. The rest had been triggered right out of the military supply system.

Rumor was that it had been Chinese or Russian hackers. Possibly, but more probable was that it had been a "hacktivist" with intimate knowledge of the USAF's supply system. That gave the FBI a place to start looking. Regardless of the how it happened, a large airdrop of food, medicine, and gear did make it over the Portland, Olympia, Tacoma, and Seattle metro areas. If only it had happened sooner. At almost three weeks into the event, the *strong* would decide who received any of those supplies. Those municipalities with some semblance of functioning government ordered that people turn in the goods that had landed in their neighborhoods. It was truly the funniest joke that had been told in twenty days.

What had been the reasoning for the delay? *They* weren't saying, but everyone on the inside knew why—there was a move internationally that was scaring the hell out of Washington DC. The Pentagon noticed movements in ports and on satellite photos of both China and Russia that caused them great concern within a few hours of the hammer falling. Activities were happening that could only mean Massive—*with a capital M*—military operations had begun. Sending the planes and the goods did not meet the "risk-threat" matrix when compared to defending the entire country if WW III were indeed about to break out.

"DADDY, I wanna go back to that other place," Kiersten Reeves told her father. "The one with the school."

It broke Charlie's heart to see his family hurting like this. "I know, Honey," Charlie told the seven-year-old. "But that may not be possible." It had been six days since he moved his family into the first responder's tents at the Bartlett FEMA camp. It was the largest of three such encampments on the peninsula, and any day coming, Charlie knew, they would fold the northernmost camp. There just weren't enough guards and cases of food to keep it open.

They were sitting on their cots, listening to the light rain, a welcome relief from the several days of pounding they'd been taking. The ground was soft. Tent pegs were coming loose, causing issues. Trees that had managed to stay up during the earthquakes were losing their hold and causing a new batch of transportation issues. Charlie looked at his wife, then back at his daughter. "I may take you guys to Uncle's on the Reservation, instead."

Charlie's wife, Melinda, hi-jacked the conversation. "You two go play with Danny and Seth for a bit," Mom commanded.

"But I don't wanna!" Kiersten protested.

"Yeah, Danny's kind of mean," Charles Jr. confirmed.

"Just for a few minutes," Mel reiterated. "Go on." She and the other spouses had worked out a privacy deal to watch each other's kids for a few minutes whenever a First Responder spouse had come in. Once the kids were out of earshot, she turned to Charlie. "I don't understand what happened between you and Phil, but you need to fix it!" she hissed.

"Look," Charlie started, but his wife cut him off.

"No! You listen!" She didn't normally talk over her husband like this, but it was time for him to see Mama Bear. "We're basically confined to this part of the camp. We are families of the 'government,' and it isn't safe for the kids to go down to the school and medical tents anymore!"

The thud of the rain on canvas was picking up, almost as if to mirror the perplexed look on Charlie's face. His wife continued. "People are bored, hungry...but mostly they're angry. They think we're living like kings up here." The first responders' tents were in the confines of the National Guard armory, but the larger camp with all the medical and dining facilities was established at the next-door soccer and softball fields. "You know the Rez isn't much better off. Why would you take us there when we'll be perfectly safe at Phil's?"

Charlie's brow was wrinkling as his face gave away his mixed emotions. He knew she was right, but he also knew something she didn't. "Listen, Mel—"

"You were the one who dragged us out there!" she said, raising her voice loud enough for a few other families to turn their heads. "You were right! Is that what you want to hear?"

"That's enough!" Charlie hissed through his teeth, trying to keep his cop-voice from taking over. "I know! But it isn't that simple!" He knew that the police and National Guard staffing levels were low, and more were deserting every day. He was thinking about it, too. If he took them to the Reservation, he was staying there himself. He wasn't ready to admit that the region had entered a point of permanent change. He took in a deep breath.

"I need to tell you some stuff, but you *cannot* repeat it! At all!" he said, letting the big breath exhale audibly through his nostrils. He had Melinda's full attention. Charlie went back to the low murmur most families tried to use while in the tent. "The gun range won't be safe much longer."

"Why not." It was a command, not a question.

"There's been a few instances that I can't discuss, but I can tell you that the Unified Command is going to start cracking down on the violence, and we won't be able to take sides. I've been watching the FEMA Director, the Police Chiefs...and especially Sheriff Raymond. There's rumblings of starting door-to-door home inspections, taking weapons and drugs...rescuing sex-slaves..." Charlie hoped his wife was starting to get the picture.

"Is that even legal?" she dared to whisper.

"They're using some language about martial law and confiscating resources from an old National Defense Authorization Act to justify it," he answered. "I'm no lawyer. I don't know if it's legal or not." He looked his wife in the eyes. "You have no idea—none of you family-members in here do—of the things we're seeing and getting reports about. This is the only place I can guarantee your and the kids' safety."

"Then tell me those things!" she quietly pled with her husband. "Let me in!"

Charlie's eyes filled with tears. "I can't...I can't tell you the worst stories." He was envisioning his family as victims in the scenes he'd seen recently—the burning victims, killed for their food—and he let the tears roll down his cheeks. "You wouldn't forgive me for telling you." He was turning his head so no other families would see the look on his face.

Melinda started to cry, too. "What does that even mean?" She could sense his fear, and she began to radiate it herself.

"It means it's going to be a hard winter," was all he could muster.

Melinda took his hands into hers and put her knees and forehead to his, respecting his wish to not talk about it, while also absorbing the fear of the future that was gripping her husband.

"I NEED you to fully understand what I'm saying. We have nothing to give. I wish we did, but we're in dire need, too. If we catch you trying to sneak onto the property, we will hang you. Clear?"

The beggars at the gate were in disbelief. "That's murder!" one woman screamed at Josh. "You can't threaten us just for asking for food!" Most of the group of a dozen men, women, and children were all crying out in offense.

Trying to steal our food is attempted murder, as far as I'm concerned, Josh thought. "It's not a threat, because I don't plan on doing it—unless you try to kill us first. And stealing our food is trying to kill us." The skinny, disheveled group was openly protesting again. "Red Rover, make your way to the front gate," Josh said into the microphone clipped to the top left corner of his hunting raincoat. "And bring a few people with ya'."

He and the two people on gate duty would need some back up if this group insisted on not dispersing. This was the third time in two days they'd had to repel beggars. He knew someone sneaking onto the property at night was an eventuality. *We'll need to discuss some sort of food dispersion program, if we can find some abandoned trucks that haven't been stripped clean yet.* Josh needed to make sure that the range's neighbors weren't starving, too, not just the families living on the property. Fed neighbors became part of the solution, not the problem.

The debate continued for another two minutes. The now-unusual hum of tires on cracked and broken asphalt started to reverberate down the Canal Vista Highway. About the time Tyler Wilson, call sign "Red Rover", showed up with three other people, the entire debate had come to a grinding halt to watch a convoy headed down the highway toward them.

"Ahh, Anarchy, this is the Northwest corner—the convoy is approaching," Josh heard the northwest fighting-position guards call on the radio.

"Copy, Northwest," Josh replied into his mic. "Help us get this crowd dispersed," he said to Tyler and the rest of his back up. Counting himself and the gate-guards, there were seven members. They began to walk the group back onto the road. One woman insisted on being shoved. She tried to dodge Tyler's grasp, but the starving people just didn't have the energy to put up much resistance.

Josh was keeping an eye on the people and the incoming trucks, which had started to slow down. "Rubber Ducky, we'll have the gate clear. Keep comin'. Slow down, but don't stop," he ordered Lonnie over the radio. He slid back to the secondary gate that led down to the rifle line and opened it up.

The beggars figured out they were losing the fight, and as a group, they slipped into the drainage ditch on the far side of the two-lane road to watch the vehicles creep into the property. Six SUVs and trucks—numbers 2, 3, and 4 towing trailers—slowly passed through the weak melee and turned left on the gun-club's property. Every vehicle had men, women, and older teenagers "riding shotgun," some in the beds, others in the cabs. Windows were down and rifle barrels were pointed out.

"CP, show the convoy on the property," Josh radioed up to Jerry at the Command Post.

He waited to see the group's reaction once the vehicles were through and the gate was being reclosed. "Move along," he ordered them.

"You can't make us!" one man yelled back.

"Move!" Phil yelled from the hilly brush behind and west of the group. "Now!"

The startled group never knew he was behind them, having come from the isolation of the western Listening & Observation Post in the woods on that side of the highway. Phil had opted to take a shift, just to have some time to himself and his thoughts.

The startled group's initiative had just been fully deflated by the appearance behind them of a camouflaged man with a rifle out of nowhere. They started walking south down the highway, knowing the battle had been lost. Phil looked at Josh for a moment and turned back into the woods to reman his post.

Josh stared at the brush where Phil had disappeared, worried about their leader. *I can't imagine what you're going through,* he thought, sending good vibes to Phil. *But we need you back to normal.*

SANDY STOOD at the window of her dark office, prying open two of the blinds to stare down at the rest of the National Guard compound in Bartlett. Past the fence and through two rows of maples that lined a road, she could see the tents and fences of the larger community camp down at the sports fields. Her office was cold. To save fuel, the heating and ventilation was only being used in the EOC to keep the humidity from building up to a level that would damage computers. The spot in the moisture she'd wiped off the window to look out was starting to get covered from her breath. She heard a knock at her office door.

She turned to see her trusted Number Two standing there. "Gerry, you look tired," she told Geraldine Johnson.

"Aren't we all, though," Gerry replied. "Anything interesting out there?"

"Rain. And the Guard trying to break up a fistfight down the hill. The usual," she replied.

"This morning's tally," Jerry said, handing The Godfather the latest data. Sandy noticed that there was some upside-down, unrelated data on the back. Gerry had expected the puzzled look. "We're down to a couple of cases of paper. Decided we should start using the second side of discarded paper on the daily stuff," she explained.

"Good catch," Sandy commended. "This is why I need you, Gerry. I'm a big picture gal. But you—you catch the little details that glue it all together…" Her voice trailed off, betraying that she was deep in thought, her mind elsewhere.

Gerry closed the office door. "Is there anything I can get you, Sandy? Are you getting enough rest?"

Sandy smiled the same way she might if one of her grandchildren—thankfully they all lived in California—had just asked about her day. "I'm fine, dear," she said. "Like everyone else, I'm painfully aware of the math."

Gerry nodded in understanding. *The Math* was how everyone at the Slaughter County EOC had started to refer to almost any logistical problem. The examples were everywhere—cases of MREs divided by mouths to feed, or gallons of fuel divided by amount used every day. The math had forced the Unified Command to start coming up with creative solutions.

The National Guard was starting to take their fuel trucks to the local gas stations and draft fuel from the underground storage tanks. It was an idea that they had as a result of a firefight the sheriff deputies had with some midnight thieves in the north end of the county several nights earlier. This had been the latest thing the citizens staying in the FEMA camp were complaining about. *How come you can steal, and we can't?* they wondered.

Because we'll eventually pay it all back, Sandy would think to herself.

It hadn't escaped her attention that those people didn't gripe at night while the generators kept their government-provided tents warm.

Sandy snapped herself out of it. "I've been thinking a lot about that Navy re-supply mission," she told her protégé. "I'm sure they'll have another one, eventually…" She paused.

Gerry caught on. "It *did* have a positive effect on everyone when those helos showed up—for a while, anyway…"

"Right," her boss replied. "Knowing how valuable these bases are to the Navy…knowing they'll be here again, eventually…" She looked for some sort of nod or face-twitch from her number two to let her know she agreed. "Maybe we can help ease some tension with a lil' dash of hope."

"Ehhh, I don't know about that," Gerry hesitated. "That has the potential to backfire."

"All things remaining the same, sure," Sandy mentored. "But they won't be the same. Food, medicine, and supplies are running out *looong* before winter is over. They're *going* to be pissed. We're *going* to have big riots on our hands. The end result *will be* the same." Gerry's face was showing the lightbulb come on. "We might as well get the benefit of the hope factor."

Gerry was still hesitant.

"And we can always just blame the Navy for being late when they start to catch on," Sandy added.

It was quiet for a moment as Gerry stared at Sandy's back while her boss wiped a spot to look out the window again. "We'll need someone from the radio room to be in on this, Gerry said.

"I've already thought about that," Sandy said. "Those boys know what it's like out there. If any of them don't play along, they'll just find themselves being escorted to the gate."

"THE INSULATION in here came out pretty good, Dad," Payton told her father.

"Yeah, not bad," he agreed. "You girls will be a lot warmer in here." He looked at Savannah. "And you won't have to listen to Grandpa fart at night anymore."

"Ewwwww! Grandpaaaa!" she screeched.

The three of them were in Phil's fourteen-foot enclosed cargo trailer. He had never gotten around to buying himself a travel trailer —he called people who used those "glampers." What he had done years earlier, though, was build some shelves that could double as bunk frames. He borrowed Craig's truck and went and retrieved the trailer after his watch at the LP/OP had ended. He wanted Payton and Savannah to have their own space.

The members had dismantled the small portable trailer that had acted as the restroom building before Cascadia dropped it. Everything was being reused in some fashion. The insulation from the walls was being used to line several cargo trailers. Some people used spray glue to hold it up, while others framed the trailers and sandwiched the insulation with cross-member framing or plywood. The destroyed trailer's metal siding was going to be part of the "common hall" idea that Payton had come up with.

"One good thing about moving to the trailer is that we'll be closer to the potty," Payton told her daughter.

"Well, sure," Phil said, "but you'll also have the privacy for a privy bucket in here so you don't have to go all the way there in the middle of the night."

"True," Payton said, nodding and looking around at how they would set up their stuff.

"Olive," Phil said, using his daughter's nickname, "I just want you to know how much I appreciate the things you're doing out here," Phil opened. "I haven't been very square in my head these last few days…since…" He started staring at the trailer floor.

Daughter and granddaughter moved in and formed a group hug. "I know, Dad," Payton said.

After a quiet moment, Phil decided to deflect. "Savannah, hopefully this room will allow you to sleep a little better." He didn't want to directly trigger any memories of the abduction, but he knew she was very restless most of the nights since. "And girls—I'm sorry if I've been a little temperamental with you. I haven't had much patience with people lately."

Payton just squeezed her dad harder. Neither of them would have ever guessed that this catastrophe would be the catalyst to start repairing their relationship. "It's okay, Dad. People understand."

I hope so, Phil thought. "I'm going to the tent to get a little rest. We'll be heading out around midnight." He saw the concern on his daughter's face. "I'll be okay, honey," he said, not realizing there was another man she was worrying for.

6

Contact.

TAHOMA'S HAMMER PLUS 2 DAYS.

"NAT? YOU OKAY?" Roy asked through the screen door on the trailer. It was an older travel trailer, one Roy had inherited when his father had passed away. It mainly provided a spot for the kids to have their friends sleep over—what farmer can just leave the animals and crops to go camping several times per summer? Natalie had suggested they move out to the trailer after a secondary quake around midnight. They were both a bit uneasy staying in the 1930's era, balloon-framed farmhouse.

As the morning crested, Roy and the kids went out to clear ash, evaluate how to get water to their chickens and goats, and most importantly—how bad the grass crops were damaged. Next to Natalie's job, their largest source of income was selling a variety of hays for export. It was now closing in on lunchtime and he hadn't seen her yet, figuring she needed the additional rest after her horrible two-day marathon.

"Migraine," came her one-word whispered reply.

Roy knew the protocol—silence and darkness were the only two things that would help her pass time. "I'll bring you a bucket and washcloth," he said, knowing the bad ones induced puking.

Natalie lay in the small bed with a t-shirt blocking out what light the trailer's shades couldn't. *Mom! I'm so sorry I wasn't there for you.* This migraine hadn't evolved into a puker yet, but it was the worst one she could remember because all she could do was physically lay there, hoping for sleep, yet she couldn't stop thinking of her mother's pain and suffering. *I just wish I could cut my head off and be done with it.*

The reality and bleakness of what had occurred was compounding the headache in a way she would have never expected. *I need to tell Dad.* Her parents had divorced many years earlier, and her father had never remarried. He was stubborn and crotchety, not unlike her brother, but she knew her father would still be heartbroken to hear about her mother's demise. *But how? How long until they have the phones up again?*

She heard the little trailer's door open. Roy was trying to be quiet, but he wasn't a thin man, and the whole trailer shook as he stepped onto the roll-out steps. "I brought you some water," he said with a quiet rasp. Water only—Roy knew any food smell would be bad for her.

Even with her headache, Natalie could tell his asthma was acting up. "Your chest," she said, using the code that comes with many years of marriage, in which sentences don't need to be finished.

"I'll be fine," he said. "Just a little ashy out there."

"I forgot to pick up our refills," she said worriedly.

"It's okay, Nat. I have close to a month's worth still." He was fooling nobody. They both knew that his lack of asthma medication could be a big deal in short order. "I'm keeping my face covered," was all he could think to reassure her with. "I'm going back into the house for our CPAPs and stuff." He figured that not using it half the night might have triggered her headache.

"I just need peace and quiet," she reminded him.

"Try to sleep," he said. "I'll come back in a couple of hours."

Natalie listened to her husband go back outside and start issuing chores to the kids. *I need to figure out how to check on Dad. Bubby*—her brother near Seattle—*can take care of himself. I wonder if Dr. Tennant or Dr. Gupta will hook me up with Roy's medicine? How long until the hospital gets overrun? How long until we run out of food or water?* Natalie knew the headaches were just beginning.

Several hours passed and the only time Natalie got up was to go pee. The thought of food made her want to throw up. Finally, around five or six that evening, she managed to sit up for a while. She felt like she'd been hit by a truck, yet the feeling that the headache was gone was somewhat enlightening. She put on some more clothes and ventured out.

She found Roy and the kids sitting in the lawn furniture around a campfire and eating hot dogs. "Mommy!" she heard Katherine yell excitedly.

"Hey, baby," she said, trying to muster a smile at her daughter. To Roy and the boys, she said, "Sorry you boys were stuck out here all day." She looked around at the piled ash, not believing her eyes. She started to tear up and turned toward her husband, seeing that he had already gotten off his chair and was walking toward her.

He opened himself up for a hug position in front of her, not sure if she was wanting that due to the headache. She leaned in and lazily threw her arms around his waist. "I need to go to work tomorrow and get us some meds," she mumbled.

"I'm not so sure that's a good idea," Roy said seriously.

"Why wouldn't it be?" she asked, not changing position.

"One of the volunteer fire trucks stopped by to check on our water situation. They said that there was a big riot at the hospital this morning—well, big by our little town's standards, anyhow."

"What? Why?" she exclaimed, picking her head up off his chest.

Roy just shrugged, mostly at a loss of words. "Just angry, I guess…"

What are we in store for? Natalie worried to herself.

"WHAT DO YOU WANT FROM US?" the man screamed. He was bloodied and had a large goose-egg that had formed overnight on the left side of his head.

"You don't need to scream," Legion said calmly. He was squatting in front of the man, who was handcuffed to the pipes under a deep sink in the shop's greasy utility room. They had left the man on the cold, concrete floor for several hours since the club commandeered him, his wife, and their food and radio gear. "The sooner you accept the new reality, the sooner you'll be able to live a functional life again."

The middle-aged balding man just glared at Legion in a mixture of fear and anger, not saying anything. He winced and gave a subconscious glance at his cuffed arm, which had grown numb hours earlier.

Legion caught the glance. "Let's not go taking crazy pills," he said, shutting down any notion of release. "What's your name?" Silence and lip trembling. After a quick moment, "Alright. You'll come around. You see—you're ours, now. It's real simple. You'll be our radio-guy, and in exchange—we'll protect you."

"I don't need your protection!" the man screamed in rage.

This caused Trip and Hoosier, who were standing near the door to the room, to bust out laughing. "Obviously not!" Hoosier said sarcastically.

Legion ignored the commentary but was smirking at it while he looked at the captured man. He stood up. "Sorry, Mitch, my knees just aren't what they used to be," he said stretching. The man's eyes grew wide. He recognized his own wallet as Legion pulled it off a shelf and started pulling cards out of it. He tossed them on the floor but stopped when he found the portrait of Mitch Witt and his wife. "Nice!" he said, flipping the picture over to see if anything was on the back.

This made the man start to cry. "Please don't!" he pled.

"Well, that's up to you, ain't it, Mitch?" Legion instructed. "See...you're gonna cooperate...and be fed and protected...and this will buy—Allison?" he said, squinting as he read the back of the picture. "Yes, Allison. This will buy Allison's safety." He paused for dramatic effect. "Right?"

"Y-yes," the man stammered through tears and the type of bad adrenaline that immense fear brings.

Legion turned to Hoosier. "Get 'im a blanket, would ya? Floor's gotta be cold." He turned, smiling, back to his new slave. "It seems we've had a breakthrough, Mitch. Atta boy! I'm gonna get you some chow, and in a while, you'll get to go set up your new radio shack in the attic." Legion turned and started to leave as Hoosier was returning with a blanket. "Get him some soup, too," he ordered.

"C-can I see my wife?" the man hollered to Legion's back.

"Baby steps, Mitch," Legion replied without stopping as he and Trip left the man in Hoosier's care. *It's your own fault for advertising yourself to me with all those damn antennas.*

They were transiting through the tipped over racks of parts and tools back toward the door that led into the clubhouse. "Get him up in the attic as soon as Sweet-T and the others have the new generators wired up and moved all the radio junk up there."

Trip nodded. "The families are going to see 'im when we drag 'im up to the attic," he pointed out to his boss.

"Yeah, I've been thinking about that," Legion acknowledged. "I'm sure most of them are fully aware of the new situation already. I mean—how many fires did Weasel and his ol' lady have to move through to get here?"

"True," Trip said. "But we should know what we're going to do when someone's ol' lady or kid starts to mouth off."

Legion stopped at the door and turned to his big Enforcer as he caught up. "Simple. Club first. Everyone knows that," he said, pausing. "If his family has an issue with how we provide, they can leave. But if any brother tries to leave, 'out bad' rules will be in effect."

"Agreed," Trip said. "But it would still be a good idea to have all the officers on board with this before it happens," he advised. He changed the topic. "And we'll probably need to get a few more houses when the other chapters and support clubs start trickling in."

"Yep, been thinking 'bout that, too," Legion agreed. *And about how we're going to get Sticky off that island,* he didn't say.

"Contact," Conner Moore mumbled to Earl. The former Ranger was watching his buddy's back, scanning in all directions. The thirty-nine-year-old divorcee was thinking of his kids in Montana— thankful for the first time in his life that they weren't around.

Conner had jogged all the way from West Seattle to Earl's Des Moines house with only two small breaks. He knew after the big one that his buddy would wait for him. He "Ranger-ed Up" like he did when he was in the Army, thankful he'd quit smoking five years previously. When he arrived a few hours earlier, Earl was in disbelief at the picture of the devastation that Conner painted. After a nap, he joined Earl on one last preparatory detail. He had no intention of trying to get to Tacoma. One look at the dark fist in the sky told him his life was tethered to his Army-brother's for the foreseeable future.

"One male, one female, approaching from the PCH," he said, referring to the Pacific Coast Highway to the east. The two men were topping off every jug and water bottle they could fit into their pull-cart. They were at Safeway just a couple of blocks from Earl's house. Earl knew the big commercial structure would still have plenty of water pressure left in its plumbing and that he could access the outside spigot with his little sillcock key.

"Let me know if I need to stop," Earl said. He knew Conner's experience and fully trusted him to be scanning for threats, but he didn't want to stop draining water from the building. *I want to get back and keep preparing for the late-night departure.*

"What's up, guys?" they heard the female say as they approached.

"Hey," Conner said in a voice that was a half-octave lower than normal. The natural comedian wanted to be all-business with his voice. He continued to scan in all directions one last time, lest these two be the distraction for the real threat. Despite the recent weather, his jacket was unzipped and ready to provide quick access to his holster.

"Could we possibly purchase or trade something for water?" the pretty but disheveled female asked.

Conner moved around Earl and the cart to have a better position in front of his partner. "Is it just the two of you?" he asked bluntly. He could see the girl's wheels spinning behind her eyes. Both were in dirty but nice clothes and had luggage, hers being a duffel bag.

"Yes," she said.

Conner did one last scan in all directions, moving his eyes in sectors and looking for anything that seemed like an ambush. "Looks clear," he said to Earl. "I think they're alone."

Might as well get rid of these two, Earl thought as he shut off the spigot and pulled the key out. He turned and faced Carmen Martinez and Stuart Schwartz.

He looked Carmen and Schwartz over for a good ten seconds before saying anything. "Alright. Get your bottles out." He pulled the sillcock key back out of his pocket and inserted it back onto the recessed valve-stem in the wall fitting.

"That's it?" he asked when the lady handed him a pair of the small disposable water bottles. He was all business and his serious tone shocked her.

The man piped up, trying to help his partner. "Look, sir, we don't want any trouble. We're just thirsty. We don't have much to offer..."

"First off," Earl replied, "I was an NCO. Don't ever call me sir again. Secondly, I wasn't scoffing at you. Sorry if that's how it sounded. That's just not a lot of container." He paused for a second, looking back and forth at the odd couple. "Where are you two headed?"

"Olympia," Carmen said. It was obvious to Earl she was lying.

"Olympia," Earl repeated incredulously. *We're done,* he thought. *Move along.* "Yeah. Okay. Olympia. Good luck," he said, as he turned around to fill his own jug again.

"Wait," she exclaimed. "Okay... Look, we just don't know you guys. Alright?" She appeared and sounded sincere.

"Lady, if we wanted anything you have, it would already be ours," Conner said. "But...we get it. You can't be too careful. Go wait by the corner while we talk." After the pair had moved to the corner of the building, he kept his eyes scanning while he addressed Earl quietly. "Thoughts?"

Earl had never been a very religious man, preferring to go fly-fishing on Sunday mornings over listening to lectures on morality from flawed men. But as the world had continued to digress in the years prior to the hammer falling, he had started reading his Bible again. As he aged, he found himself yearning for answers. He knew there was no way the universe was random. Choosing to believe there was a loving God, he knew the top two Commandments were to love God and to love one's neighbors as he loved himself.

"Let's hook 'em up. Soon the world will be full of a-holes. Let's try to keep the non-a-holes alive, if we can." *Lord, I hope you remember this deed on my Judgement Day...*

Conner waved the pair back over. "Tell you what," he said. "We know you two aren't your average scumbags. We're willing to sell you a water-filtering straw and four one-liter sports-bottles, filled, for a fair price. Say... sixty bucks?"

"Sixty bucks!" Schwartz started.

"Deal. Pay him," Carmen stated to Schwartz. "But I want our little bottles filled, too," she said to Conner.

"Agreed," he replied. He detected an annoyed look on the man's face.

"May I ask why you're being so generous?" Schwartz asked sarcastically as he pulled money from his pocket.

Earl had heard enough. *We're trying to help you, you little pip-squeak!* "Mister, you may not realize this yet…" He paused to look the man over. He was obviously not going to make it long in this world without some help from *On High*. "But everything is a resource. Water bottles. This little tool. Your shoes." He pointed at Schwartz's filthy expensive loafers. "If it has value, you can't expect it for free. Not anymore. Not in this world." *Don't you realize that I don't need your cash?*

He topped off their bottles, and Conner retrieved the rest of the items from the cart. Schwartz kept his mouth shut while Carmen retrieved the items from Conner. They turned south and started to move away, saying nothing else.

Help them, Earl heard his inner thoughts say. "Listen," he stated. The man and woman stopped and looked back. "I don't know where you're headed. But you're going to want to upgrade your clothing. And find yourself some leaf-bags. You can turn them into a poncho or collect some rain to drink." He watched the pair nod and continue south.

They spent the next several minutes filling jugs, but the pressure started to die off. It was taking a long time. Earl decided they were done. "Let's roll," he said, mimicking the saying made famous on September 11th, 2001.

The two men kept their heads swiveling on the trip back to Earl's house. "What made you say yes to helping them?" Conner finally asked. "It's not like the money will be worth anything in a week."

"I know…" Earl said, not knowing exactly how to say what he felt. "I guess…I guess I just don't want the rest of my human interactions to always be like when we were in Ramadi—constantly worried about people's motives. We both know what's coming." He went silent for another minute as they walked. "I don't want to harden my heart permanently," he concluded.

The normally talkative Conner was quiet but finally acknowledged his pal's rationalization. "I get that." After another ten steps and a left turn onto Earl's street, he asked, "What should we do with the cash?"

"We'll pool together every dollar we got. I want all of us, especially the kids, to keep some cash on them. If they get separated or someone gets the drop on us, that cash might just buy them out of a pickle."

7

Crossroads.

Tahoma's Hammer Plus 18 Days.

The hot-iron brand sizzled for almost two seconds against the back of the man's neck, just under his hairline. "Tu coraje no sera olvidado," Reynaldo told his companion. *Your courage will not be forgotten.* "Gracias, hermano."

"Para el futuro," came his soldier's reply, through a painful grunt and clenched teeth.

Reynaldo Hernandez insisted on doing this task himself. It was all part of a plan. He motioned for the orderly to tend to the burn with a head nod. As the woman with the burn cream and sterile dressing moved in to do her job, the soldier started to stand up. Rey looked down at the brand, staring at the burnt skin on it for a moment before tossing it back down into the farmhouse's fireplace.

"Jefe, los autobuses estan listos."

Rey looked at the messenger and acknowledged him with a nod, which sent him on his way. *The busses are ready. Good. We'll get those moving at first light. Need to keep the humanitarian mission moving forward.*

If there was one eventuality that Rey had prepared for, it was this one. This would be the thing that locked his place in la familia into permanency. There was a point in the cartel in which a man knew he no longer had to look over his shoulder, wondering when betrayal would come like a shadow at dusk, snuffing out life without warning. Once the upper echelon was reached, everyone in it died all at once—or not at all.

Rey was a master of winning hearts and minds, having been implementing the infrastructure for it in the Mendoza Cartel's North American market for the last four years. So many American movies and TV shows portrayed the cartel leaders as mega-wealthy buffoons with a mansion full of bikini-clad models. Extravagance had its place, but much of that money went into preparing for the future. His cartel alone had over 300 million dollars—almost all of it originated by American drug usage.

His cartel's warriors had performed flawlessly, standing up Mar de Paz services within days of the disaster. They had established a protected bus service, and now that two-thirds of Wave One's supplies and men were on location, he'd get started on *Operation Trueno*. While he did that, the ships would return to Mexico and load up for Wave Two. The beauty of the Mar de Paz's—*the Peaceful Sea*—mission was that it enabled them to sail right past the US Navy on a legitimate humanitarian mission.

The young, plain-looking orderly finished putting the dressing on the neck of the men who had been branded. "Vete," Rey said, ordering her to leave. She was fortunate for her plain looks, which enabled her to be…*less desirable* for some of the *prettier* lines of work. Rey took the brand back out of the fire.

"Hermanos, no te pedire que hagas algo que no hare," Rey said, handing one of the two men the brand. *I will never ask you to do some-*

thing I won't do. He unbuttoned his sky-blue business shirt, revealing a muscular, smooth chest under a simple gold necklace and crucifix. He slapped the spot over his heart, looking at his soldier, readying himself. The cartel member did as commanded and plunged the humanoid-shaped figure onto his boss's chest, sending smoke into the air for all to smell.

The man pulled the iron off his boss, looking at him in admiration. "Doy gracias a Dios que eres neustro lider," the man said. He thanked God that Rey was their leader.

Rey pulled both soldiers into his space and embraced them as if he were their father. *Heal,* he whispered to them. *I will let you know when it is time to go.* With that, the two men left the leader alone in his farmhouse office.

The day before Rey arrived, his local cartel branch secured several facilities near Ferndale, Washington. In addition to the arrival pier at the Alcoa plant, they commandeered two large farms and a church just a couple of miles east on Mountain View Road. This enabled Rey to house his army and their equipment while he brought everyone up to speed on the game plan. He had several operations planned, and all were important. Some were large in scale, such as the one with the large satellite photo of the Monroe Correctional Facility taped to the dry-erase board. Others required small units, operating independently. For these missions, he chose only former special forces operators.

He was extremely proud of his army, but he genuinely *loved* his special operators. All, like he, were true believers in their mission. And they were diverse—mostly from Mexico, but from a variety of other countries, too—a true grab-bag of races and languages.

As the fresh burn on his chest began to welt and weep, he picked up a sharpie and went back to the large photo on the board. There was a lot of work to do. *We must drive home the importance of laying low and providing aid to the locals while we gather intel! Winning hearts and minds is the key!* Invading the United States, while insane for even Rey to say aloud, was exactly what they were doing, albeit in an incognito fashion. To do so this far away from Mexico could prove to be either the most brilliant or fast-losing war strategy in modern times. Southern California had been so inundated with cartel in the two decades before this, that when the time was right, the entire West Coast would fall. Rey was operating not just on ambition, but on faith. *Our time has arrived.*

TAHOMA'S HAMMER Plus 19 Days.

"JERRY, IS THE CP READY?" Josh asked the Communications Lead.

"Yes," he told the group assembled in front of him. "I've made this as simple as possible." Josh was wrapping up a pre-mission brief. Its purpose was to ensure everyone knew the game plan. He had two regrets regarding this operation. One was that there was no time to get the cooperating groups there to hear the plan in first person. The other was that he had to do all the planning from maps. There was no time to scout from the woods, and they would've been too obvious going out there by vehicle. *At least our maps have contour lines.*

Jerry pointed to the dry-erase board he'd brought down to the rifle line. "Memorize this list of code words. These are your waypoints. Call these in to indicate a position as you pass it or a task as you accomplish it. You'll notice they're alphabetical to make it easier to memorize. I went with TV shows for pneumonics, but you'll still need to memorize the location or task the hard way." Jerry saw the forty-one people start to scan the board. "Questions?"

"Since we don't all have radios, do we all need to know this?" Emily Roberts asked.

"Yes," Jerry said flatly. "You may need to take over for someone injured. Any others?"

Jerry had done a thorough job explaining which groups would use which frequencies and how some radios would be using both.

He also explained where Gary and Skinny's groups would be positioned and how to trigger their assistance, if needed. They would be monitoring from a central location that had decent line-of-sight for the antennas, about fifteen miles away and ready to come to assist. There were no follow-on questions.

Good, Josh thought. *Everyone is serious and paying attention. They all know what this means.* "Phil? Final thoughts?"

The silent group looked at Phil as he used his crutches to assist getting out of the lawn chair. He slowly settled into a standing position and scanned the crowd. "It's a good plan," he affirmed, recognizing the worry on the faces. "Surprise is of the essence, if we want to overwhelm them and not lose any of our own. And we'll maintain the surprise by everyone knowing their jobs. I know it's a lot to ask. I had an old mentor who used to say this —slow is smooth and smooth is fast. I can't say it enough—you'll be amped on adrenaline. You need to control your actions, not the other way around." He looked back at Josh. "You've done good, young man. You have my every confidence in this operation." Phil sat back down.

Josh could see a hand go up just a bit, like the person wasn't sure if they wanted to ask a question. "Yes?" he asked the man whose name he didn't remember.

"I'm still wondering why I'm going and not the doctor," newly arrived chiropractor Thadeus Werner said open-endedly. "I want to be clear—I'm happy to go, and I'm not trying to make him go. I'm just curious about the logic of it."

This caused Phil to scramble back out of his chair as Josh started to answer. "I get it, Doc," Josh told the man. "I hate to say it like this, everyone," he said looking around, "but we're not risking the surgeon on this." He could see a few faces get wrinkled. "And remember, he's kind of a guest here. He hasn't actually asked for residency." *Yet,* Josh told himself.

"Your role will be to assist Tony and Sheila with field trauma," he said, pointing toward the Manners couple. They would be staged a few hundred yards away from the assaulting force, prepping any wounded for transport via pick-up truck. A total of four young men and women would act as a team of stretcher-bearers if they needed to move any wounded assaulters back to the triage station. Tony would be ready to drive them back to Schwartz and Alice at the range.

Thad Werner and his wife had arrived at the range as part of Lonnie Everly's group just a few hours earlier. She was a physical therapist, so their combined skills would prove to be quite valuable to the group. "Got it," he said.

Phil reined in the rest of the skeptics. "I'd like everyone to think about this perspective. We lost Fred. We have a baby on the way, and there will be others of both. And if you think a flood of disaster-related illnesses isn't on the way, you're fooling yourselves. I said it once, and I'll say it again—political correctness died with the volcano. Despite how any of us feel about it, some people's skills are more valuable than others, and doctors and nurses are near the top of that list." Most everyone started to do the slow, small head nod in agreement.

"Friends," Phil continued, "I need to make sure everyone gets just how serious this is. Some of you may not make it back." He looked around and saw at least a couple of hypothetical lightbulbs coming on. "Combat is life changing, even if you get through it unscathed. Taking life is something you need to start squaring away in your souls, now, ahead of time…" He studied the faces. "This is the last chance. If you *don't* understand why we need to respond with an overwhelming show of force, then just head on up to Fred's grave and get reminded." The group was deadly quiet and attentive. Phil slowly sat back down and nodded to Josh to indicate he was done.

After ensuring there were no other questions, Josh ended the meeting with an order for everyone to go rest before the 2330 assembly time. As people were filtering out of the rifle line area, he and Phil cornered Jerry. "Remember, you're in charge here while we're all gone. Is the CP going to be functioning if some other crisis pops up?"

"J.R. and James can handle it," Jerry said confidently. In actuality, he'd started training more people than he could remember. Communications training had suddenly become something everyone wanted to know.

"Good," Phil said, looking at Josh and then back to Jerry. "What about the mods to the drone? And the Gotennas?"

"All A-Okay," Jerry affirmed.

"And our little experiment?" Josh asked.

"It'll work. They'll all work. Just remember—timing is key. The fuses aren't guaranteed to be consistent."

TAHOMA'S HAMMER Plus 20 Days.

THE DRONE CAME BACK to hover over Jeff. It made sense to let the young man operate it—youth were just naturally better at using joysticks then the vast majority of the older men and women in the assault force. Once he was done with both halves of this task, he would become one of the stretcher-bearers.

He's a natural, Phil thought. *Hmmm—this is twice that I've been glad this kid played video games. What's that mean?* The device's little green and red lights had been disabled, so Phil had to squint to see it, finally catching sight when it was a mere thirty feet up. It was 0300, and the assault teams were making their way to various positions around the Matthews' clan main homestead. Jeff landed the expensive asset on the ground in the clearing 120 meters northeast of the objective structure.

Planning the operations—primarily Josh's task—was the easier thing to do. Phil and the other board members had the tougher task —developing their rules of engagement and desired mission statement. People were no longer in denial—it had been nearly three weeks since the events, and it was more apparent with each passing day that society was shifting. In many ways, the Dark Ages had returned to the 21st Century. Everyone had mixed emotions about entering a facility as the attacker. *We aren't,* Phil reminded them. *We're defending ourselves from attacks, both past and future.* Still, though, there was the temptation to round up the one's that gave up and drive them down to Bartlett. *That will only result in our arrests,* Phil reminded.

After the meeting had broken the night prior, Tony had made one grim suggestion to Phil. "Brothuh, it pains me to say this, but there is one solution…"

He was extremely hesitant. "Go on," Phil prodded, not patient for bush-beating anymore.

"Well…we could hang 'em," Tony suggested, not able to conceal the disgusted look at even muttering those words. "Cut the head off the snake, so to speak."

"You mean, like…'Judge Roy Bean' hang 'em?" Phil asked, shocked.

"I'm not crazy 'bout it, neither," Tony said, just as shocked. "But you said yourself they'll come arrest us all."

Phil was silent for a bit. "I know the world's gone sideways, but…wow. Are we really talking about hanging them like horse thieves?" Phil couldn't believe the conversation—and the fact he was taking it seriously.

"Well, I never studied the Wild West or nothin'," Tony started, "but…uh-huh. I guess so. I mean, think about it. They did that back then because stealing people's horses and cattle was basically threatening their lives an' livelihood."

"That's a line we can't uncross," Phil replied. "I'm not saying you're wrong, by the way. But…as long as there's an elected sheriff, I'm going to have to rely on the law that was."

It was enough of a seed, though, and Phil took the idea to the board. They knew there was still a functioning government down in Bartlett. They deliberated half the night before concluding that any of the opposition not killed in the raid would be arrested and dropped off close to town. Knowing that survivors may be revenge seekers in the future, the group was still having a hard time coming to terms with the rules of the New World—that there *were* no more rules. For better or worse, the group decided to maintain an old-world view of murder and take their chances with possible arrest.

Phil watched Jeff and two others remove the camera from the bottom of the drone and go to work attaching the makeshift device to the bottom. A solenoid from a radio-controlled airplane was being mounted under the drone. When commanded from a different controller, the little electric gizmo would rotate, opening a claw. Jeff knew from the recon flights what direction he needed to fly at max speed and for how many seconds. *Timing is key,* Phil caught himself repeating Jerry in his mind.

Minutes earlier, Phil had radioed the assault teams in the positions of the sleeping guards on the north and east sides of the property. If there were any on the west or south, he hadn't seen them. The target property was a run-down horse ranch in the extreme west end of Slaughter County, close to the Hood Canal. There were three fairly open acres in the middle with a large home and shop in the northwest corner and a barn south of that. The teams would be approaching from the east and north, cutting through other properties, the majority of which were wooded and undeveloped.

Many of the assaulters were now using a variety of night vision optics on their rifles or helmets, courtesy of many of the older range members who had acquired them over the years. Each four-person team—six, in all—had at least one radio operator and one person equipped with a suppressed rifle or pistol. Two teams each would attack from the north and east, taking down the house and shop under Josh's command. One would clear the barn. The last team— Phil's—was the commanding squad, ready to surge if the plan turned to garbage. *Murphy. He undoubtedly will show up at some point,* Phil thought.

Phil looked to Jeff and the rest of the stretcher team for one last confirmation. When he got it, he led the command squad through the last stretch of trees and brush to their overwatch position. "All units, this is Six," he said into the microphone. "Status of the sleeping guards."

"Sleeping permanently," he heard Josh report back. *The suppressors worked well,* Phil thought.

"Copy. Stand by."

"Light 'em," he told Charlotte, Lonnie Everly's wife. Charlotte and her brother Bob started lighting several homemade smoke canisters albeit several seconds apart. Jerry had made them using a mixture of potassium nitrate, sugar, and baking soda. He put the mixture into cardboard tubes topped with the heads of several matches and a fuse. All of this was stuffed into a soda can and taped up to contain everything but the fuse.

Phil switched to a special AR-15 that had been repurposed with a device he'd purchased just for this kind of reason. The "can-cannon" operated on blank cartridges—they had no bullet, just gas—and would launch any soda can or tennis ball sized item out of a tube that served as a barrel. He dropped the first lit smoke device into the cannon, aimed up about fifteen degrees, and squeezed the trigger. *Whoompf!* The can launched as predicted, leaving a slowly increasing trail of smoke. It landed twenty meters from the house. "Fred. Fred. Fred," he said into the radio, letting everyone know the operation was commencing.

Upon hearing that, back in the clearing, Jeff lit a fuse of his own. It was a sixty-second fuse, and Jerry had spent a lot of time making sure it was accurate to within a second or two. The drone took off, trailing a lit, one-pound sparkler bomb with it. One of the members had discovered some sparklers in their travel trailer, left-over from an Independence Day campout. While not intended to do any real damage, it would put off a noise and flash that was sure to wake and confuse the dead. A small servo, receiver, and battery from a radio-controlled plane had been placed under the drone, along with a modified piece of hardware. With a separate radio-control, one of Jeff's team would release the sparkler bomb on the west side of the house.

Whoompf! Whoompf! Phil had continued to launch the dozen smoke grenades as fast as he could, in a variety of angles and distances. Within forty-five seconds, the area around the house and shop was starting to fill up decently with smoke. Five assault teams started to run in fast and stage themselves around the entrances to the structures. At sixty-four seconds after calling out the signal, the sparkler bomb exploded—*Ka-Boom!*—and twenty men and women entered the three buildings.

Here goes nothing, Phil worried. Most of the assaulting force were experienced, amateur practical shooting competitors. Most had also taken at least a couple of the tactical training courses the range offered over the years. Josh and those few that were combat veterans spent the day running everyone through "no-shooting" movement drills. They had built an assortment of rooms with the shooting props so everyone would get refresher training in muzzle control around other people. Avoiding friendly fire in close quarters was Josh and Phil's biggest concern.

Ka-Ka-Krow! Phil and the command squad kept a close ear on the radio and eye on the action. He started to raise his rifle when he saw an armed scumbag crawl out a bedroom window of the house, only to lower it back to low ready when three shots rang out, causing the fleeing drug dealer to go limp in the window frame. *Pop-Pop! Ka-Ka-Ka-Ka-Krow!* Phil could hear a variety of shots ringing out in all the directions. It occurred to him he should probably take a slightly better position behind a tree before a stray round found its way to him. He stood behind a tree, impatiently waiting for a clear signal from each squad leader.

Over the next few minutes, he did indeed get each of his status reports. Bob Huddlesten had received a bite wound, of all things, when he was jumped from behind by a tweeker-chick. One other member reported a sprained ankle during the run-in on the house, and two reported that the scumbags managed to get off some pistol shots, but they missed their marks.

The smoke cleared from the property while Phil and his squad started to light several oil tiki-torches they had brought with them. It cast an odd, orange glow that contrasted with the lingering smoke and smell of gun powder. His stretcher-bearers came forward to pull guard duty when it became obvious that they had received no casualties.

Phil was headed toward the house to make his own check on the enemy KIA when he heard some radio traffic. "Six, this is Squad Five. We found something in the woods on the far side of the property you need to see ASAP."

"HOLY..." Phil murmured, at a loss for what this meant. He was staring at a semi-trailer full of goodies. Mostly it was a huge cache of fireworks. There were some more weapons, mostly pistols and an assortment of rifles that had most assuredly been stolen. He even saw a few customized semi-auto shotguns in the pile. There was a bunch of ammo, too. While there were lots of two and three-inch mortars, the fireworks were mostly the professional grade six and eight-inch shells.

"Where do you think it came from?" Josh asked.

"Wellll...if I had to guess, probably from..." Phil looked up, in his mind's eye searching for the name. "Shoot, I don't recall the name, but there's this company around here based out of West Slaughter. He's the guy that does all the big fireworks shows for several of the smaller cities here in West Sound." Phil thought for a moment longer. "Actually, I bet there's more trailers than this."

Phil decided he wanted to scramble up into the semi-trailer to take a closer look. He stepped up onto the bumper and placed his butt on the trailer's floor. First he swung his good leg up, and as he tried to follow it with the prosthetic left leg, the heel of his boot caught a piece of the bumper's structure and sent him reeling sideways to the ground. "Crraaappp!" Phil cried on the way down.

Josh scrambled over, trying to hide his grin. Phil's left shoulder was buried in the soft mud and grass. He looked up at Josh's face and started cracking up. "Bwa-ha-ha-ha!" This eased the tension for the others, who started chuckling, too. "Josh, the look on your face trying not to laugh was almost funnier…" Phil said as he slowly picked himself up. All the magazine and gear pouches on his battle belt and plate carrier were covered in mud. "Guess I didn't need in there *that* badly," he said, stretching his back and knocking mud off himself.

"If it matters now that you've been slimed, we've only found the one so far," Josh told him.

"Hmmm," Phil hummed. "Could be hidden anywhere on any of these properties."

"Or some other up-and-coming crime-clans got 'em," Lonnie said as he walked up.

"Hey, Lonnie," Phil called out, sticking his handout for a shake. "Glad your assault went smoothly."

"Glad you think so," Lonnie said, a little edgy as he shook Phil's paw. "We made some mistakes. I think we got plain lucky."

"I concur," Josh said, looking back and forth between the two men. "But considering what we're working with, this little victory will motivate everyone to improve, if we hot-wash the mistakes without sounding like we're chewing butts. I think a good 'After-Action Report' is called for."

Over the next hour, Phil and his Posse started their collateral duties. Everyone knew what they had to do, and time was of the essence. He wanted to be back on Salal Road and headed toward the range before the sun started to come up. *At least we can take the road out.*

His team acted as if they'd been doing this for years. Some gathered the dead from the opposition. Counting the two guards, they'd killed twelve and left none wounded, probably because Josh and Phil taught everyone that in combat, shoot your enemy three times to ensure you remove the threat, with five shots being even better. They found drugs everywhere, mostly crystal meth. It was so predominant, even with children in the house, that Phil second-guessed himself on the "no hanging" decision. *Animals.* He looked at the seven women and thirteen kids that were now their prisoners. *Will I have to put you down, too, some day?*

Eli fired up the semi they found in the barn and was able to hitch the trailer up. "We need to convoy this thing as if it is all the gold that used to be at Fort Knox," Phil quipped to Josh. He thought about torching the structures but decided against it. He stood back, watching his team secure prisoners and pack vehicles with captured loot—much of it already stolen from its rightful owners, Phil was sure. *At least we don't have to hike back through the woods.* With that, Phil said a little prayer of thanks, wondering if they would get so lucky next time.

8

"Face reality as it is, not as it was or as you wish it to be."
—Jack Welch

Tahoma's Hammer Plus 3 Days.

Early in the wee hours of the morning on the first Friday after the hammer fell, a young family plus one slipped into their Chevy Suburban and started to bug out. There was a common 5' x 8' open utility trailer—the kind someone gets for hauling lawn mowers or a motorcycle—towing behind it. Everything that had the most value was in the Suburban, while the utility trailer had bicycles, a pull-cart, tables, chairs and such. Earl had left the headlights operational, though he had no intention of using them. He dimmed his dash-board light. It was an older Suburban with analog gauges, not the more modern digital variety. He was wearing his bump helmet with his Armasight night vision binoculars mounted, which caused him to slouch while driving. Clan Garren and Uncle Conner were bugging out of Des Moines, Washington.

After the move to Des Moines and the purchase of the river cabin near North Bend, Earl had started taking the bulk of his camping and preparedness supplies and leaving them on his weekend trips. The family would assuredly be okay through winter, even with Conner along, as he would help fish and hunt his own needs. *If we cut calories, we can even support the family, if they come over,* Earl realized. He wasn't too worried about that. They lived well east of the mountains—he couldn't see a need for his extended family to come closer to the devastation.

Earl's mind did weigh heavily with how his kids were dealing with all of it. Fifteen-year-old Piper Elizabeth had been doubling-down on her usual amount of angst and drama. She had threatened to go stay at her bestie's house "until it all blew over." Earl had just about lost his cool. He was *not* enjoying the age of insolence. Owen Henry, two years her junior, was obviously worried, but he was also full of the bravado that came with being in an outdoorsman's family —they would be fine. "This will be like camping, but without cell phones, right?" *Not exactly,* Earl had told him. Earl was keeping a close eye to be ready when reality hit his kids in the face like a Mike Tyson punch.

The small family had made it about one-and-a-half miles before they were forced to make their first major decision. The overpasses at I-5 and 272nd St. had collapsed.

"What ya' thinking?" Conner asked.

"Tough one," Earl said. "We could chase flattened bridges for miles in both directions." He went silent again.

"I'm really wishing you hadn't left the quads out at the cabin right about now," Tori said, concern in her voice. It was eerie dark but not quite pitch black due to overcast skies with mixed rain. "But we need to do something besides sit here in the open," she concluded.

Earl had been scanning his memory and the blackened horizon

where the treetops met the dark gray skyline. "We know the elementary school is right there," he said, pointing south, "but I think we should go into the big park-and-ride lot on the north while we think."

The family unit made their way into the big parking lot, which despite being covered in a foot of ash, showed several cracks and shelves. This kept them close to the entrance. Earl and Conner made a security check, sensing that there were a few camps in the woods around the big lot. They decided not to stray any farther and made their way back to the vehicle to begin deliberating the options. Travelling at night seemed attractive, but it was not without its own hazards. Only Earl had night vision. It would be easy for simple ankle sprains and complex ambushes alike to become a problem. After forty-five minutes of discussion, they decided to switch to a daytime bugout.

"HHHuuummmpphhh," Piper huffed. "Seriously? Why didn't we just stay in our beds?"

"Shut up, Piper!" Owen said, defending his dad.

"That's enough," Earl said. He didn't need to yell. Over the years, he'd found that by consistently giving them one warning and then upholding whatever discipline they'd earned, that his warnings went heeded on the first try most of the time. This was something Tori blamed on the length of his deployments. *They never listen to me on the first warning,* she'd complain to him. Earl decided to review the new plan.

"All four of us Garrens have laminated maps in our bags that I made explicitly for a foot bug-out."

"Really?" Tori asked. She had never been much into preparedness, and Earl hadn't pushed it. She figured any time and money he put into it was about hunting and fishing.

"Yes. Really," he said with an ever so slight "why don't you trust me" tone to his voice. "Most people don't realize that when they use Google maps, there's a little walking-person icon. It will give you a much different route than the standard car version. I printed that and laminated it when we moved here to Des Moines." Even in the dark, he could tell that his intelligent, strong wife was looking at him dumbfoundedly. "I told you all this like two years ago!"

"Sorry, Sergeant Grumpy-pants," she said. Conner let out a little snicker. "I'm just not into the prepping thing," Tori chastised.

You're about to be. Earl looked in his rearview mirror at the grinning Conner. "Not a word," he ordered his old battle buddy.

"Of course not, Sarge…" he said, before quietly adding, "…ant Grumpy Pants." Owen and Conner burst out laughing, joined by Tori. The boy and the uncle in the middle row were high-fiving. The back-bench pop diva known as Piper just groaned in annoyance.

Once the little distraction had quieted down, Earl went back to business. "Con-Man, you slept most of the day. You good for first watch?"

"HUA," came the familial Army reply. It meant *Heard – Understood – Acknowledged.*

"Thanks, brother. Wake me on the split. Clan Garren, get comfortable and sleep. We have a lot of biking and walking ahead of us."

"Why can't we just go home!" Piper pleaded.

Because I said so, Earl thought. "Too much commotion. We've left that place, and it will be a long time before we go back. You're going to have to face facts, Princess." He received a massive huff in return. Piper was down to three percent charge on her cell, and she used it to once again see if her friends had texted. *I believe when that girl can't listen to her music anymore, we are all in for a new level of spoiled brat.* With that, Earl took his bump cap off and donned his tan Ranger ball cap for his nap.

TAHOMA'S HAMMER Plus 4 Days.

.   .   .

SHE'S SCREAMED HERSELF HOARSE, Sticky thought. He felt weird watching—not at all sexually arousing for him. *I'm wondering after most of a week where her mind is? Maybe she's invented a happy place...*He was growing tired of the nuts running the cuckoo farm.

Immediately after the hammer dropped on Tacoma, the staff and counselors had begun guiding residents through the process. *Remember—we're here to help you. Don't panic, everyone. We'll get through this.* "Denial ain't just a river in Egypt!" Sticky heard one of the serial rapists say to the Chief of Psychiatry for the facility, Dr. Lillian Gomez, right before he punched her in the side of the head hard enough to knock her out. The lone male staffer in the counseling center at that moment was hopeless, once the residents figured out that the security office's electronic lock had turned off. It was a safety feature intended for a structure fire. In some form of unspoken rule, almost the same way that giant flocks of birds all turn together instantly, every non-resident was free game. The males wound up being beaten to a pulp and handcuffed in the boiler room. The residents had different plans for the female staff.

All staff within the confines of the fence were unarmed—these weren't *prisoners*, after all, but *confinees*. Even the double fence line had no guard towers—just electronic sensors that had suddenly become worthless. There was a small armory in the chief security office outside the main gate. Once the shaking was over, the nine guards on duty began to deliberate the proper procedure. There should have been twelve, but almost every day, a few guards had to escort a few residents to medical or attorney appointments in Tacoma.

The security staff geared up and made entry into the facility, not sure what to expect. They had to come in through the manually-locking personnel gate next to the electric drive-thru, which wouldn't open. That meant it was just them and their riot gear—no heavy vehicle to use as a fallback point.

Within hours of that fateful Tuesday's main event, the first guard had been murdered, freeing up an M-4. This quickly led to the demise of the rest—197 to eight were not fighting-odds, espe-cially when the 197 had prisoners as leverage.

Here it was, four days later, and Sticky had been brewing an idea. With the lone exception of the lack of wells, this island would be a perfect stronghold for the motorcycle club. And it rained plenty —between rain collection, boating over supplies—*and offing 200 psychopaths,* Sticky thought—there would be no water issues. It had been several days in which he'd wanted to give his left arm a good rest before he started making moves. *Break-time's over!* Sticky moved through the pile of men, shoving a few out of the way. He stopped just behind the sixty-two-year-old Level III rapist who was currently on top of Dr. Gomez in the middle of the dayroom, hearing some vocal complaints about cutting in line. Using a piece of twine from the gardening shed, he dropped it over the rapist's head and began to strangle him from behind.

As several of the cheerers started to move towards Sticky, two other residents dropped kitchen knives out of their long sleeves and began to violently stab those who were trying to stop Sticky. Two others with captured firearms held the rest of the crowd at bay. He was a biker, first—a man from an organized criminal enterprise. He knew who the *real criminals* were. He'd slowly been building an alliance, with Legion's help. His MC had been caring for the fami-lies of several residents, making sure that harassers were dealt with and ensuring that they had food on the table when money was tight. Now it was time to call in the favors.

The large, out-of-shape man assaulting the doctor was scratching his own neck violently, trying to get the little rope off his windpipe. Sticky could hear the cartilage cracking as he pulled. His own fingers were ghost white from the several wraps of rope around his hands cutting off circulation. The man tried to flail, but Sticky had a wide base for his stance and was leaning backwards. This wasn't the first time he'd done this, after all. After twenty-two seconds, the man slumped. Sticky kept yanking. Dr. Gomez rolled over to her side—shrieking and afraid to see what would happen next.

After one minute, the circle of men had shrunk considerably. Those who had no criminal training other than rape—especially the pedophiles—knew *immediately* that they'd better disappear. After close to seventy-seconds, Sticky let the fat piece of human waste fall to the floor. Sticky was panting a little. He slowly turned and looked at his new crew, smiling. They all were. At their feet were four bleeding bodies, wails and moans still emanating from some of them. He approached the closest, not-yet-dead rapist. As he plunged his own knife into the man's heart, he screamed, "I'm in charge here now! Anyone else feel like dyin'?" while his four accomplices began high-fiving each other with bloody hands.

TAHOMA'S HAMMER Plus 5 Days.

EARL KNEW that he and Conner could have rucked the forty-five-plus-mile goal in three days, and that allowed for extra time navigating obstacles and scouting threats from a dead stop. But as a family, he was starting to doubt they would make it in a week. They were now halfway through the third day of hiking the foot route to his cabin on the North Fork Snoqualmie River north of North Bend, Washington. The untrained unit did indeed have to stop for threats and obstacles…and to tend to a few blisters and emotional outbreaks. Princess Piper was starting to realize the full extent of what had happened. And she had refused any moleskin for her feet's hot spots until the blisters had started to form, which was too late. She had been so sure that she wouldn't get blisters peddling a bicycle.

Thanks to the jet stream, the ash was only about a foot thick. The rain was turning it into a sloppy paste. They stuck with riding and walking in tire ruts. The ash even showed them the way people had figured out over and around obstacles.

They had just left the roughly due-east travelling on major thoroughfare Kent-Kangley Road, for a less travelled Summit Landsburg Road. Up to this point, the obstacles had all been made by the disaster. Earl was expecting to round a bend at some point and face a roadblock. Their travelling had been hindered a bit by the population density—it took quite a bit of time before the mid-autumn dusk to find a good place to hang hammocks and pitch the one tent. They wanted out of sight, off other people's private property, and close to the road—all at the same time.

On the first day of hiking, the kids and Tori had learned the value of the pull cart and the over-fender racks that Earl had installed on their bikes. They were able to keep their packs on the bikes to save their backs. Tori and Earl were mostly pushing their bikes, mainly because Conner was setting the pace with the cart. He and Earl would swap every hour. It had taken a couple of scoldings for Earl to get his kids to quit riding ahead. Every once in a while, Piper would try it again, reminding her parents she was practically old enough to vote and move out.

On the first night, the three family members were rudely introduced to the joys of camping in the rainy October weather without a fire. This went over with Piper much like a fart goes over in church. Owen also found out that MREs can be eaten cold when his water-activated heater failed. Earl made sure that his and Conner's MRE heaters went to the family to act as hand-warmers once they were done heating entrees. He had them put them in their armpits so as to warm the blood closer to the skin's surface.

On the first day of hiking, the mix of foot traffic was going in both directions. There was some vehicle traffic, but they often caught up to trucks and cars that had passed them when those vehicles came upon downed bridges, trees, billboards, and flipped over vehicles. By the third day, the foot traffic was noticeably eastbound

—everyone was employing their *I'll just live off the land* prepping strategies.

"I ever tell you kids 'bout the time your old man went swimmin' in a plastic room?" Conner said, breaking the ice of boredom after a particularly long quiet spell. He'd heard enough bike tires and wet footsteps for a while.

"Stop." Earl calmly stated an order that he knew was about to be ignored. When Conner got started, it was a losing battle. His best bud suffered from what he jokingly called "center-of-attention-deficit-disorder."

"No!" exclaimed Owen excitedly. Piper pretended to ignore the whole conversation.

"We were in Yakima, qualifying for deployment—what was it —'06?" He was starting to giggle as he spoke.

"Stop," Earl said, just a little louder.

"And there was this one fella…Muldoon, was it?…who just could *not* say no to a dare."

"I dare you to shut up," Earl challenged.

Con-Man was grinning at the kids, trying to get some morale going.

"Aaaanndd?" Owen asked. Tori was staring at her warrior, smirking.

"And *somebody*—I don't recall who—dared Muldoon to run into the outhouse while your old man was…talking to a man about a horse, let's say."

"Huh?" Owen queried.

"Somebody," Earl repeated his buddy's innocent tone. "Some-body? Or you?" he said, the amusement not exactly showing itself.

"Not important," Conner brushed it off quickly. "Dropping the kids off at the pool," he explained to Owen. "Pinching a loaf?" The kid still had a blank look. "Takin' the browns to the Super Bowl—"

"Enough!" Earl almost yelled. Tori started laughing openly.

"Ewwwwww!" exclaimed Piper. She started to ride ahead to get away from all the embarrassing adults.

"That's far enough!" Earl yelled when she was only twenty meters ahead.

Conner continued. "But what *somebody* didn't realize was that the pallet on which this porta-potty sat was broken on the far side. When Muldoon hit it, the whole stupid thing went flying onto its side!"

"No way!" Owen screamed elatedly.

"Guh-ross!" Tori stated, her face making the sympathetic puke response.

Earl just stared at the road ahead of him. He knew what was happening. Conner was playing the court jester at his expense, but for five minutes his family had forgotten the world was ending. He could live with that.

"What happened?" Owen wanted to know, staring at his dad.

"Whatever you think—it was worse than that," Earl said calmly. The little family continued to march on slowly, taking on the huge voyage one step at a time. *I can only hope that what lies ahead does not make that seem like a cakewalk...*

9

"I had reasoned this out in my mind, there was one of two things I had a right to, liberty or death; if I could not have one, I would have the other."
—Harriet Tubman

Tahoma's Hammer Plus 20 Days.

The various impacts to the world's economy were becoming very apparent. Markets had tanked overnight for fear that the trade in and out of the North American West Coast was going to come to a grinding halt. The cost to replace the infrastructure alone would cost trillions. Most people just assumed that the government would reach into the pocketbook and work miracles. What they didn't pay attention to was that the United States had entered a point-of-no-return on its debt years earlier. Even without the largest, natural disaster in recorded history, the U.S.' tax income was not even enough to pay the interest on its securities, let alone the actual loan.

This was complicated by other factors, too. The world operated in a "derivatives bubble" that was going to burst eventually. For years, markets had operated more on predictions about future earnings than on actual money. The markets traded an amount of fake money nearly ten times over the actual money that existed in the entire, actual world. The day after that wet, October day, the bubble popped. Stock markets around the world began to take record losses. It took two days for China to demand that the trillions the U.S. had borrowed years earlier to bail out the auto and real-estate markets be repaid. As everyone knows, what doesn't exist can't be repaid.

Portions of the internet were affected by the hammer. Amazon and Microsoft were the heart and lungs of the e-commerce world. Even Silicon Valley was affected by the severe power outages. This brought about accusations of meddling by the U.S. from foreign states—and vice versa. Rhetoric of WW III started to be thrown around like an old baseball. Only in this game, the baseballs were being tossed by angry kids with nuclear weapons.

"WHAT DO you mean it sounded like a war zone?" Sandy demanded of her staff member.

"That's what they're reporting, director. Would you like me to get the HAM who took the report?"

"Yes," she commanded as the staffer took off for the communications center. "Gerry?" she yelled across the EOC to her number two. She was already headed that way as Gerry looked up and moved towards her.

"Ma'am?"

"Where's the sheriff?"

Gerry glanced at her watch and started flipping through her

clipboard. She stopped on the sheriff's standard plan of the day. "He's probably at the deputies' roll call over in the apparatus building," she told her mentor. "Should I send a runner?"

"Nope. Follow me," Sandy said curtly, not meaning to unleash her wrath on her friend. As they made their way out of the EOC, she saw the HAM coming out of the communications room. She waved a finger at him, commanding him like a dog to follow.

Sandy brought her number two up to speed on the two-minute walk to the big building nearby. She could move fast when she was motivated. When she made it inside, she could see various National Guard units doing rig-checks on their HumVees. "Where's the sheriff?" she barked at a soldier, not caring who he was.

"Back corner, Ma'am," he answered, pointing. She made her way through different units of men and women with her two attendees in tow. She finally saw the khaki and brown uniforms she was looking for and approached the group. A lieutenant was giving a tactical update. The sheriff looked around when he noticed many of his deputies and sergeants staring behind him, and he turned to see what the issue was.

That's right, you friggin' idiot, Sandy thought as she smiled at him. *Come here!* The sheriff smiled back and was thinking similar pleasantries himself. He broke off the line of senior leaders behind the officer giving the briefing and made his way over.

"Mornin', Director," he said flatly. He was tall and skinny with a full head of silver-tipped brown hair. "To what do I owe the *pleasure?*"

"Sheriff Raymond, we're getting reports of a big gun-fight out in the western portion of the county. Have you heard about that yet?"

"No, nothing yet." He was genuinely caught off guard, something he didn't like, but especially in any conversation with her. "Do you have some details?"

"Tell him," she ordered Dillard Hawkings, the lead operator for the comms team.

"Several HAMs have reported a large-scale conflict over the last few hours. At first it was hard to pinpoint a location, but it's sounding more and more like way out in Cranston. There was an explosion at 0330, followed by a several minute firefight. It was—" The HAM was cut-off by the commotion of several soldiers nearby who were slowly starting to buzz. Something on the Guard's radio network had started to wake them up.

The foursome exchanged glances and made their way through the various vehicles and Guard members to the offices near where they entered the building. Before they could get to Major Matsumoto's office, Sandy saw him following two of the unit members into their communication center. Her little entourage followed her as she tried to catch up.

"What's going on?" Sandy asked as she entered.

"Director…" Adam Matsumoto said with not even faked enthusiasm. He made his way past her back out into the apparatus bay before her entire group could squeeze their way in. Sandy could hear some radio chatter that caught her interest. The major was trying to keep them out of his people's way. "One of our patrols just found a bunch of women and children tied up to a light pole on Slaughter Avenue, near the bottom of Canal Vista Highway."

The group all wore concerned looks as they each evaluated the responses of everyone else. "Come again?" Sandy asked.

"We're bringing them in through the usual holding process," Adam noted. "We'll know more soon." By this time, the sheriff lieutenant had ended roll call and had dispersed all the day-shifters to start their thirteen-hour shift. They were now in double pairs everywhere they went, which didn't afford them much area. The department wasn't that large to begin with, and with the staffing level slowly dissolving each day, things were looking bleak. They were down to less than forty members per shift, and that was including the corrections officers who became available after the jail was emptied.

Sandy noticed a large portion of the on-coming shift had drifted over to hear what they could of the new events. She looked at Sheriff Raymond. "Your department is starting to get thin, Ward," she said loud enough for all of them to hear.

The career lawman turned politician tried to control the situation. "Perhaps we should go into the major's office?" he suggested to the group.

"Yes," Adam agreed, exchanging glances with the sheriff. "Let's." He made his way towards his room before Sandy could manipulate the situation anymore.

As THE SMALL group of leaders disappeared into the major's office, a small contingent of deputies had been keenly observing from the other side of the apparatus bay. "I have two burning questions in my mind," said Deputy Matty Wildman to the group. "Who did it? And how long until they turn on us?" The rumors of the night's events and the news of the arrested women and children had spread through the soldiers and deputies faster than a case of Montezuma's Revenge.

Charlie shot the young peace officer an annoyed look. "Those aren't the questions we should be worried about, Deputy." Charlie knew Matty was fishing for a story about Phil. He turned his head back toward the closed office door.

"Then what is?" Deputy Wayne Luzon asked from the other side of the gawking group.

Where is Sheriff Raymond's line in the sand with the FEMA lady? Charlie didn't say out loud. *How long until this no longer feels like America?* "Get to your rig checks," he ordered as he left the group to file a shift-plan with the Operations Chief.

He made his way out of the large motor pool building and crossed over to the main facility, but instead of heading into the EOC, he turned right down a dark hallway until he found a half-lit room labeled "Operations." A variety of officers from most of the police and fire agencies and National Guard unit were addressing a number of maps and dry-erase boards.

Upon seeing him, one of the few remaining officers from the sheriff's department greeted him. "Reeves." She gave a nod for Charlie to come over.

"Mornin', LT," Charlie said. "I assume my plan is in the middle of changing? Maybe you guys can let us know *before* we head out, today…"

Lieutenant Shara Murphy ignored the subtle sarcasm. "What's all the scuttlebutt?" Even the civilians in a Navy town used the lingo.

"I'm sure you know as much as I do," Charlie told her. He could see by her face he wasn't getting off that easy. He let out a frustrated sigh. "Just something about the mother of all battles and a bunch of women and kids being brought in by the Guard. They were found not too far from here—should be here soon."

"Did this happen in your sector?" Murphy asked.

"Yes, I'm hearing way out near the canal. Hence why I figured my shift-plan was evolving as we speak," Charlie said. He was tired, and it was getting hard to hide it.

"You figured right. Check it out. Talk to the Guard Liaison over there and get yourself a squad for back up," she ordered flatly, looking back down at her papers.

"Since I'll have them, can I release Luzon and Hornet to join another unit?"

She was skeptical. "Who's that leave you with?"

"I'll still have Wildman, and those two will be able to back up either of the other two units in the east sector," he explained.

"Approved," she said. "Now get 'er done…"

"I'm surprised you're not asleep," Payton told Tony. The pair were scouting the start of the log-house project, joined by Tony's wife Sheila and their twin daughters, Talia and Tasha.

"Yeahhh, well, I didn't have quite as much post-adrenaline-crash as most o' those other folks did," Tony said. "Plus, I wanted my baby girls here to know I'm alright. I can make it 'til some of them get up."

"Sooo…what is it you're trying to build here?" Sheila asked Payton. She was staring at the big pile of logs somewhat skeptically.

"Hopefully," Payton began, emphasizing *hope*, "a large, open-walled but roofed common area—for dining, church, meetings, and such."

"Just with logs?" Sheila asked, not following.

"Babe," Tony began, but Payton cut him off.

"It's alright, big guy! Let the ladies talk!" she said, smirking.

Tony began to smile. "Awww, daaannnng! Am I gettin' it from both sides now?" he played along.

"Dadddd," Tasha said, embarrassed.

"I could be in bed right now! It's all I'm sayin'. All I'm sayin'!" They all had a good chuckle. Moods were elevated after the success of the midnight-raid and bounty they had captured.

"Anyway," Payton continued to Sheila, "one of the members out here brought a couple of chainsaw mills to turn these logs into lumber," she explained. "But, from what I'm learning, we want to season that lumber before we use it. So, in the meantime, we're going to build smaller log stacks for the corners and occasional spots to bear weight, and then put a log roof on it."

"What's a mill?" Sheila asked.

"From what I hear, a regular mill is a big piece of equipment. The roads and downed trees may make it a bit tough to get one of those, but for now, they're gonna use a fancy cutting device that just guides a chainsaw to cut straight lines."

"Sounds big," Sheila said. She was staring intently at the open spot in the middle of the rifle range, trying to visualize it. "How are you going to get them up there?" she wondered.

"What the Kubota won't be able to reach, we'll use the horses," Payton said.

"Say what?" Sheila was thoroughly confused. "How on Earth are horses going to put logs twenty-five feet in the air?"

"Mommm!" It was Talia's turn this time. Tony was smiling and enjoying the show.

Payton grinned a little. "With block and tackle," she answered. "Ropes and pulleys," she said, cutting off the next question at the pass. Sheila started to look embarrassed because of her confusion. "Don't worry!" Payton said. "I didn't know any of this stuff, either."

"And I come into this," Tony jumped in, "because Payton and I will be the co-chairs of running this facility. She's in charge of the kitchen and hall's schedule, and I'm in charge of organizing the storage we'll use some of the space for," he said proudly.

"And I'm still in charge of you," Sheila reminded him with *The Look.*

Payton excused herself and headed for the kitchen. She occasionally caught some of the older women—*and one man,* she reminded herself—getting a bit stubborn and passive-aggressive with each other about how things should be done. She walked into the middle of a conversation about the influx of deer meat they'd all be consuming.

"All I'm saying is that it's dry and hard to chew!" Teddy Wilson was explaining. Payton quickly figured out that he and Donna Gladstone were in a friendly squabble.

"It beats starving, doesn't it, Teddy?" Donna countered.

"I never said it didn't!" He saw his new bestie walk in and tried to get Payton to ally with him. "Would you please tell her I'm not unappreciative?"

Payton replied with the same sass she would give anyone, in true Walker style. "Fight your own battles, pal. It sounds to me like you two are just looking for something to argue about because you're bored."

Donna knew that when Payton figured out someone was bored, she would have them do dishes. "No, no. Not at all, young lady. I know what will happen if we agree," she said winking at Teddy. "We're just having a conversation, right, Teddy?"

"Yes—about how bland deer meat is. It's too lean for my tastes."

"Exactly," said Payton. "We're out of spices." *Spices!* It occurred to her that Josh had better prioritize that on his 'shopping list.' "Fat is what we need," she continued. "Usually butchers cut deer sausage and ground deer meat with a small percentage of pig to add some fat."

"Well then, we need to figure out how to do that!" Teddy agreed. "My palate can't take this survival stuff much longer!"

Having worked in the Safeway deli for several years had taught Payton a few things. "If we can grind and blend in some high-fat nuts, maybe…Good luck finding those. What we need to do is start trading for some butter or avocados—even cheese would work. We're running low on the canned, clarified butter that Dad had stocked up." *Fat! Who'd 'a thunk how important that would be when we were storing up all those carbs and sugars.*

IN ALL, three Hummers with a dozen Guard members had accompanied Charlie and Matty's patrol rig out to the west end of the county. They had a pretty large area to check. The EOC's radio operators were able to eliminate quite a bit of it by noting where the reports were coming from on the map. It was a rough form of triangulation based on, *"Bill said it was coming from the east, but Pete said it was coming from the north."*

A few people had come out of their homes when they saw the authorities. Most of them were hoping it was some form of food delivery. *After three weeks, these people still think the food fairies came and delivered stuff while they were sleeping,* Charlie thought. *Amazing.* Most didn't want to talk about what they heard. *Are they scared? Or protecting someone? Or both…* Charlie couldn't tell.

After being out and looking for close to two hours, someone

finally opened up. "Pretty sure it was the Matthews' place," he said. "They been out here robbin' everyone. No thanks to you," the skinny man said bluntly. "As far as most folks are concerned, they had it comin'," he summarized.

"Had what coming?" Charlie asked pointedly. *I bet everyone out here already knows every detail. Shoot! I bet they've already picked the place clean!* The man hesitated. "C'mon," Charlie nudged. "You already spilled it. Just finish."

"Hmmph. A'ight…" he paused, looking around. Charlie just kept staring. "They say that a whole army attacked 'em. Killed 'em. Every man—dead. Even a couple of the women. Made the rest of the women and kids march out to a truck."

"Did you go out and check?" Charlie asked. "The Matthews ain't but, what, a mile from here? Mile-and-a-half?" The sheriff's department was well acquainted with that family.

"No way! Not me, man!" the man exclaimed.

Of course not. "Thanks. The last hummer will stop and give you a couple of MREs for helping." Charlie gave Matty the nod to get going and called in the order to the last rig. In less than three minutes, they were slowly rolling through the woods onto the property. Matty came to a stop about thirty feet in front of the house. The Guard rolled in and parked. The soldiers started to set up a perimeter, while the staff sergeant in charge walked over to Charlie and Matty.

"We're just going to maintain the perimeter and stay out of your way. We'll call you if anything comes up."

"Roger that," Charlie said. He exchanged glances with Matty, and the pair started to move towards the house. They were moving slowly and watching where they stepped. "Well, bullet holes aren't in short supply here, are they?" They continued towards the front door. "What are these soda cans?" Charlie asked out loud, more to himself than his junior partner. He stopped and used a pen to pick one up by the pour-hole. He peeked in and sniffed it without getting his nose too close to it. "Smells burnt," he said. "Like food or fire-crackers, though, not drugs."

He stood back up and they continued towards the house. "Blood," Matty called out. Charlie looked at where he was pointing, at a broken windowsill on the end of the house.

"More soda cans," Charlie observed. "Look around, there's a bunch of them."

As they arrived at the porch, Matty called out, "Brass. Lots of it." There were shell casings galore, mostly in 5.56 caliber, but a few others, too. He looked at Charlie with a questioning look.

Charlie read his face. "We'll walk the rest of the property and then call the Guard in for a much tighter perimeter when we go inside." He spied some deep ruts in the ground running between the house and barn. "I want to see where those go."

The two deputies started tracking the fresh, deep tracks in the mud. The property had been covered in fresh tracks and footprints, as it was, but these belonged to a semi. They were deep and wide, and the treads were for a highway, not a construction site. They went around a couple of crudely constructed fences. There didn't appear to be any animals on this small property in quite some time. They stopped at the dead end inside a tree line in which there had been recently cut low branches. Those were thrown into a pile in the brush.

"Looks like a trailer was here," Matty stated the obvious.

"Yep. Makes me wonder if this was some sort of payback from whoever they stole the trailer from," Charlie wondered as he squatted at the muddiest set of prints. "Lots of people walked through this."

"Or maybe the attackers just decided it was victors' spoils," Matty counter offered.

"What's this?" Charlie said, spying some plastic in the muck. He stuck his gloved fingers down and started to pull, but it was taking its time with a small suction. He eventually pulled out a polymer rifle magazine. He stood up and handed it to the junior deputy. "See if you can wipe that off in the grass while I clean my glove."

Matty wandered back out into the field and made for a grassy spot. He spent a few seconds trying to wipe the magazine clean and eventually stood up. "PEW?" he said, reading it. He flipped it over and was able to eventually make out the other side. "Anddd...the number 17," he finished. Charlie had finished wiping off his glove and came over to take a look. He knew immediately what this piece of evidence meant, but he didn't say anything. Matty finally broke the silence. "Want to go clear the house?"

Charlie just stared at the magazine, silently. Finally, he said, "Sure. But we won't find any survivors."

10

"The best laid schemes o' mice an' men…"
—Robert Burns

Tahoma's Hammer Plus 6 Days.

Cedar Falls Road, Earl thought. *The home stretch.* Though they had a good fifteen to eighteen miles still to travel, he was starting to feel pretty good about the trek. Everyone was wet, cold, and tired. Now they were contending with real slopes, too. The gradual elevation increase had given way to no-kidding hiking trails on the western slopes of the Cascade Mountains. *I don't miss this part of rucking,* Earl thought, reflecting on his Army days. Fort Stewart had some hills, but not slopes like these.

They weren't actually on the road for a good portion of this leg but a forestry access road that roughly paralleled it. Earl knew the four-legged threats would avoid them, and the two-legged threats would be easy to spot. They had to get onto the actual road for the last push around Rattlesnake Lake and through the towns of River-bend and North Bend before they made their way to the cabin.

Earl, Tori, and Conner had been engaged in a planning meeting, discussing things like meals, getting the neighbors organized into a defensive group, and the state of Seattle when Earl noticed his daughter had quietly started to increase the gap between herself and the nerd-herd. She was at the farthest reaches of yelling to get her attention. Earl was pulling the cart—it was Conner's turn to ride the bike. "Piper!" Earl yelled as she rounded a curve and kept going.

Without a word or hint, his old partner took off. *I'd forgotten how much you can communicate with just a look when you've trained thousands of hours with someone,* Earl thought. He looked down at the rifle cases in the cart and suddenly realized they had probably entered the period of time where they needed to start wearing the rifles slung. He watched Conner slow down and start hugging the shoulder on the right side, which was the inside of the curve. He was probably two hundred meters ahead. The road was fairly rural, with household driveways every quarter mile or so.

Suddenly Conner took off at full speed and completely disappeared around the bend. "Get off your bike!" Earl ordered his son. Owen knew by the tone not to argue. "Get into the bushes right here!" he told Victoria. "You guys stay put until you hear from one of us!" He looked at the nearest landmark, which was a mailbox stand. He unzipped his rifle case and slung it on his front, pulling the adjustable strap tight to keep it from interfering with peddling. He jumped on Owen's bike, taking off as fast as his tired legs would peddle.

Pop-Pop! Pop-Pop-Pop Pop! the gunshots screamed. *Dammit! Hold on, Princess! I'm coming!*

"Big Mac!" Legion hollered out in glee. "Great to see you, brother!" he yelled as he bear-hugged his just-arrived Kent Chapter President. The exhausted, chubby biker, his wife, and their two kids had strolled in on foot. He didn't say much at first, but the relief on his face was obvious. Legion moved on to Ronnie and the kids, giving them all hugs as a welcome.

Big Mac was average in size and a bit portly. His road-name was a play on his real name—Sam Burger—more than a reference to size. He dropped a heavy looking pack off his back—they all did. His face was both grimacing from the toll and relieved to be rid of the weight on his back. "Glad to finally be here," he mumbled. It was rainy, but Legion could see the man was sweating heavily once he started to pull his high-dollar biker's raingear off.

Weasel and Shorty had started to help scoop the Burger family's gear off the floor. The hang-arounds and prospects were all on various assignments, primarily working the perimeter and guarding the radio operator in the attic. Shorty was the Kent Chapter's V.P. "Glad to see you, bro! What took you guys so long?"

Big Mac was already looking for a low-ball glass behind the clubhouse bar—three fingers of Crown Royal was called for...a couple of times. "Ronnie and I were on the way to Sammamish to visit her mom for the day when this lil' quagmire started with the first quake." He took a long pull on the glass, nearly draining it in the first drink. He nodded to his wife to move the kids to wherever Weasel was dragging their gear. Once the kids were out of range, he continued. "It's hittin' the fan out there," he said with a look of concern.

"Depends on how you look at it," Legion said. "But go on. Where's your bike?"

"In a ravine somewhere along 900. We figured it wasn't rainin' too bad, and we wanted to get a ride in. After that first quake, you'd have thought we went home. 'Might as well keep going' we thought. 'Aftershocks won't be too bad.' Quake flipped us like we were on a carnival ride. We both got banged up real good. Took through the night to get home, which turned out to be demolished. Luckily one of the kids' friends took them home from school with 'em." He had everyone's undivided attention, so he finished his tale. "So…we dug our camping gear out of the rubble and rested for a couple of days. Then walked here." He looked around. "Surprised she's still standin', honestly…"

"That's cuz I built her strong when I remodeled a dozen years ago," Legion said. "Why do you all think I've been pushing the prepper paranoia all these years?" he asked the whole room. "Brothers, it ain't the end of the world. It's the beginning! Everyone get in here for a shot!" The few members in the room at that moment strolled over and complied.

"We do need to bring you up to speed on some things," Legion told Big Mac.

"Like what?" he asked, with a look of concern.

"Like the fact that I called for a meeting with the brothers, the Russians, and the rest. Seems that some of our supporting networks"—he was referring to the informal array of people he used to distribute and sell the meth they cooked— "have been gettin' hit. We can't allow that. Rather than start a big war, I called for a meet to see if we can come to terms for real estate."

"And?" Big Mac asked.

"The Mexicans didn't show up."

"I still say we wax those turds!" Shorty exclaimed. This elicited a general sense of agreement from around the room.

"Me, too," agreed Weasel, who'd returned from showing Ronnie and the kids where they could rest. "Need to send a message." The consensus was starting to build.

"Due time, brothers…due time," Legion placated. "But, first things first. Everyone knows we're the crank dealers. Everyone knows the Russians got the AKs. And everyone is figurin' out that the coke and heroine will stop rollin' in soon."

"Natalie? I think you'd better come look at this!" Roy called out from the barn. While not a dairy farm, they did have their own small herd, like a lot of farmers. They weren't dairy cows—they used them for grass control in the pastures that were taken off-line after being used for commercial grass several years in a row. They were also a source of meat for the family.

Natalie was in the house's side yard retrieving every usable apple she could from their three trees. She heard Roy call and plowed her way through the ash. When she got to the barn, she removed the N95 paper dust-mask she took from the hospital on her very last trip there three days earlier.

"What's goin' on?" she asked her husband with a slight concern. "Why aren't you wearing your mask?" she immediately said upon seeing him. "Your asthma!"

"Stop," he said calmly ignoring her. He pointed to the third stall down on the left.

Natalie saw one of the cows laying on the ground, hyperventilating. "Ooooohhh, nooo," she said sadly. "I was afraid of this! I figured it would be dehydration, but the ash must be killing them!"

"That's what I figured, too."

"It could actually be a combo of both," Natalie surmised. "We just aren't going to be able to keep them watered and there's definitely nothing we can do about the air. They stir it up when they walk!"

"I'm going to take the Cadet and go visit some of the others," Roy said. "I think releasing them to fend for themselves is the best option."

Or just putting them down, Natalie thought. "Okay. Drive carefully. And wear your mask!" she commanded.

"A couple of dudes found an outboard motor and small john-boat in the maintenance shed down by the main pier," Georgie Coryell told Sticky. Georgie had proven himself to be his closest ally, one of the men the Risen Dead had paid for. The fellow serial rapist had been a resident of the island for seven years.

The two men had just enjoyed a session with their new, involuntary partner, Dr. Gomez. They were in one of the residential structures on the island, the former home of the recently tortured and deceased chief of security.

"We need to get down there, then, before everyone wants to take off," Sticky said.

"You want them all to stay?" Georgie asked, confused.

"Naw...I don't give two licks if any of these perverts live another second. But they'll take off and we'll be at the mercy of Mother Nature to find another boat. No. We send out smart men— men we trust, and they bring us back an actual *boat.*"

"Got it," Georgie agreed. "You think O'Reilly and Kilgore?"

"Naw, I trust them *too* much. We all need to watch each other's backs for a while, ya know?" Sticky answered. "How 'bout Brady, Watson, and White?"

"Sure."

"I also want to check out that large garden on the southwest corner of the island."

"Except it's fall, right? We ain't growin' squat..."

"Plans, my friend..." Sticky thought. *I gotta lot of bikers to feed next year.* "Always plannin'."

As they made it to the front door, Georgie asked, "What about her?" They'd left her handcuffed to a radiator in the old house. A motivated person could easily escape if noise weren't a factor.

"Where the hell's she goin'?" Sticky said with a laugh. "It's an island!"

11

Mission Statements.

"TWELVE!" Slaughter County Commissioner Sean Fox asked incredulously. Charlie had just been brought into the Unified Command's mid-afternoon meeting at the sheriff's insistence. The Sheriff knew he would be peppered with questions, and he wanted the lead investigator to be there to answer them. He had just given the report on the number of dead at the latest shootout. They had pockets of violence every night throughout the county, but this was the first time the death toll from one incident had broached ten bodies.

"And you said they were all men?" the Bartlett Police Chief, Brandi Farrly, asked.

"Mostly, Chief," Charlie answered. "There were two women.

That makes us think they were probably engaged in the actual fight —that the attackers were not shooting everyone, just those with weapons."

Looking at the rest of the command council, she stated the obvious. "That just validates the stories of the women and children brought in this morning."

"Walk us through the scene with these photos you took, Sergeant," Commissioner Fox said. As long as the command council had gas station fuel tanks to commandeer fuel from, they would be able to enjoy big screens in their meetings.

"Well, sir, these pictures of the house show a number of bullet holes, mostly coming from the inside-out." This drew a number of puzzled looks as Charlie kept going. "These cannisters were some sort of homemade smoke device. The attackers obviously have some tactical experience." The slides kept going. "This scorched spot in the back yard near the bodies was some sort of sparkler bomb."

"Bomb?" Sandy interrupted.

"Not for fragmentation, Director," Charlie explained. "Very similar to the flash-bangs we use to enter a building."

"How'd it get onto the middle of the property?" she asked.

"Not sure," Charlie said directly before continuing. "Once we did our initial walk-through, we pulled the Guard unit in and had some of them help us process the evidence." *If that's what we're still calling it.* Charlie thought. *It's not like we're still trying cases...* "We found a total of 179 cases. Most of them in the .223/5.56 caliber. Blood patterns seem to support a theory that the majority of the deceased were shot as they had just gotten off of the floor or a bed. That tells us this was well-coordinated and a lot of people attacked at the same time." He paused to see which photo he was on. "We think between three and five of the deceased died in the nearby shop."

"You mean victims," Sandy corrected.

"Director?" Charlie said quizzically.

"You said deceased. They're victims, Sergeant. Right? They were attacked in their own home?"

"Perhaps I should've mentioned the large pile of drugs that had been set on fire in the backyard, ma'am," Charlie said. "And the piles of stolen clothes and jewelry. These people were one of the county's most well-known meth-syndicates."

Sandy decided to let it go. "Go on," she directed.

"These photos show some makeshift huts that the Matthews household was probably using as some sort of guard shack. We found 22-caliber casings near those. I'm guessing they used a suppressor to take out the guards first." This drew mostly grimaces as well as a few audible gasps. In addition to the large body of politicians, police, fire, and Guard personnel on the command council, there were also a number of aides at the meeting.

"Sounds like professional mercenaries to me," Sandy observed, really ramping up her fake Southern drawl. "This was no doubt about one group of thugs trying to steal from another."

"Let's not jump to conclusions," Sheriff Raymond said.

"I concur," Chief Farrly said. "It was a lopsided victory, for sure, but the fact that the women and children were spared may support a different conclusion about motive." This caused a few small conversations to buzz on both the council and the audience.

"Order!" Commissioner Fox said, trying to rein-in the noise. He looked at Charlie. "Anything else, Sergeant?"

"Uhh, yes. There was a picture of a rifle magazine. It had some stuff inscribed on it. That's a lead I'd like to follow." *How much do I tell them?* Charlie was hiding it, but he was stressed...torn between supporting his oath as a peace officer and trying to keep Phil out of trouble. *I need to get ahead of them on this.*

"What was on it, Sergeant?" Sandy asked. "Some sort of racist propaganda, no doubt."

"No, ma'am, it had a number and the word 'pew'," Charlie half-lied. "Many people who train in firearms etch some sort of markings"—he chose *not* to say initials—"on their magazines so they know whose are whose when they're all on the ground."

That triggered Sandy's full attention. "Where?" she asked, being mis-directional on purpose.

"Where…what, ma'am?" Charlie asked confused.

Sheriff Raymond knew where this was going. "I think the director wants to know where do you want to follow the lead, Sergeant?"

Crap! I walked right into that! Charlie was kicking himself inside his head. *I hate bureaucrats.* "There's a firearms training facility in West Slaughter that might be able to help me identify what 'pew' means," Charlie said, trying to recover. "They're a valuable asset."

"Or the perpetrators," Sandy said, squinting her eyes at Charlie. "Very well. Conduct your investigation, Sergeant. Thank you for your service and this great report." She looked directly at the sheriff. "Sheriff, I think the council could benefit from every detail you can scrounge up on this firearms training facility."

JOSH SAW Payton and Savannah giving Maya Jorgenson and her mom hugs near the horses. He decided now was as good of a moment as any to go see how phase one of the common project was coming along. Pam Jorgenson owned the three horses the range had started using for various tasks. Not only were they helping with hauling logs and plowing, but they were grazing down grass in the future garden area, which saved on fuel. They were helping haul things like firewood wherever it needed to go. Payton was giving the ladies the grand plan when Josh walked up.

"Hey, everyone," Josh said, politely interrupting.

All four smiled at him when he approached, but Payton's and Savannah's smile had a little extra something in them. "Hi," Payton said. "Josh, have you met Pam and Maya yet? We go way back."

"Don't think so," he said, extending his hand. "You were Crane's friend, right?" *Moron,* he thought, seeing the sadness appear on her face in an instant. "Sorry. I'm not that bright sometimes."

"It's okay," she said.

"We can't pretend he didn't exist, right?" Maya said. Pam looked at her daughter with an empathetic eye.

After all the introductions were finished, Payton explained, "I was just going over the plan with them. Pam's been wondering why they were dragging all the logs down here."

"Yeah, I can see you got some groundwork done while a lot of us were sleeping today," Josh said. He was looking at what used to be a slightly bumpy and unlevel field in the rifle line was now graded with the blade of the Kubota's loader bucket. There was mud and tracks everywhere.

[Brrrt—Lon: "Got something to show at CP"]

"Sorry to be rude," Josh said, checking the text. *Love this mesh network!* "Duty calls," he said, smiling as he turned towards the southern perimeter road.

"Wanna eat with us tonight?" Savannah yelled at him as he started to walk away.

Josh turned back and walked to her, putting a weathered hand on the back of the little girl's head as he looked at her affectionately. "I'd love to, but sometimes I get distracted doing stuff. If I'm not there by 6:30, don't wait on me. Deal?"

"Deal," she said.

Josh looked at Payton and smiled, heading off once again. *If a man were looking for an insta-family, he could do worse,* he thought to himself. Quickly, the thought of two failed marriages and a bout with problem drinking returned to him. *Stop!* He scolded himself. Deep in his psyche, he thought of a promise he made to himself when he cleaned up his act. It would be a long time coming before he set himself up to hurt yet another woman he cared about.

Six minutes later he was entering the CP tent. The enclosed canopy had been retrofitted with interior wood walls, both to cut down on wind chill and provide places for maps and other sheets to be stapled up. There was a workbench with battery chargers for the various devices. What was now absent was the actual working radio gear.

The CP had been augmented with a small, U-Haul enclosed trailer that someone had procured for their one-way trip to the range. It was only five feet tall and about forty square feet, but it worked for a small desk, radio gear, and a seat for two operators. The equipment had been moved into the trailer because it was much more durable against the large branches that were bound to get blown off the weakened trees during the fall and winter windstorms.

"Hey," he said to the assembled group. "What's up?"

Lonnie Everly showed him some patches he had in his hand. "My sister used to make extra cash doing patchwork, mostly for motorcyclists. She has an old manual sewing machine, big needles, leather, etcetera," Lonnie explained. Josh had taken one of the patches and was eyeballing it as Lonnie went on. "Anyway, she found an old, faded, brown canvas tarp here on the property and decided this would be easier on her needles if she was going to make dozens of these things."

A big smile crossed Josh's face. "These are awesome!" He was looking at the sewn version of the simple logo he'd come up with two nights earlier. She had installed the circular emblem with volcano shape and SPP into the quadrants, and she'd hemmed the edges to keep it from fraying. "How many of these has Patricia cranked out already?"

"About twenty. Give her a couple of days, and it'll be a hundred."

"Really..." Josh commented, his face showing surprise. "That's pretty impressive! I'd like a patrol to take a batch to at least Gary and Skinny's groups tomorrow, if we can arrange it."

"That we can," Jerry chimed in. "The comms signal instruction is working pretty smoothly. Several groups are participating with check-ins every six hours. One of the things I included on the list of code words was a set of training duress words."

Josh quickly knew what he meant. "Ahhh, so we can call out for duress at any time, but the word will tell them it's a drill?"

"Precisely. But we've all agreed not to use one of those for a couple of weeks, while we work out the bugs."

"I'd also like to go over everything for the patrols tomorrow," Lonnie said. The plan was to have the first two patrols conducted by those who would then be the leaders as the squads grew and travelled farther away.

"Right," Josh agreed. "Yep, let's dial in the final mission statement, goals, and marking system now, before the actual pre-patrol brief tomorrow. You're right, sorry. We've all been so busy, it slipped my mind." The group concluded with agreement to meet later that evening, allowing Josh to grab some papers from Don Kwiatkowsky's RV. The whole family had been crammed into it since they had to make the last leg of their trip on foot.

On the way back down to the main area, Josh got another text from someone manning the front gate. *Now what?* When he got there, he saw Phil had beat him meeting the pair on watch. "What's up?"

"More beggars," Phil explained. A few other range members were drifting towards the gate in a show of force.

"Go on!" Tyler Wilson told the crowd. "Move along. You can't stay here," Josh and Phil could hear him directing.

Tyler is showing some real decisiveness. I think he should be leading one of the scavenge and intel patrols. "This is getting worse," Josh commented to Phil.

"Ummm-hmmm," Phil acknowledged. "The question is what to do about it..."

"No easy answer, there, but you might want to make sure that everyone is fully aware of it at the morning meeting," Josh suggested. "I think some of the families out here have gone out of their way to avoid the perimeter so that they can avoid seeing this."

Phil looked at Josh. "Maybe," he concluded. "I hadn't caught on to that, but now that you say it..."

"My real concern is wondering what night we start getting night raids. I think it's a matter of 'Not if, but when'," Josh continued.

"If what we did last night isn't a deterrent, I don't know what will be," Phil responded.

"From organized attack, sure. What I'm talking about is something more primal. Not an attack, but people slipping in one or two at a time to steal. Hungry people will do anything."

"Hmmm," Phil said. "Like the Bedouin when I was in Desert Storm. Those crafty dogs came right in through the perimeter and stole all of our water one night."

"Yep, exactly like that," Josh agreed with a nod.

The pair watched the beggars start travelling south down the highway for a few minutes, then decided they could disperse. "Have you noticed more people getting a cough?" Phil asked before they parted directions.

"Matter of fact, yes," Josh thought out loud. "I'll go down to the sick-bay and talk to the doctor." He made his way down to the enclosed facility they had built at the end of the rifle line. He'd noticed that someone had framed in an even larger area in the last few days and used Tyvek paper to make a wind-breaking wall.

"Doc?" he called out as he wandered into the space.

"Back here," he heard Stu yell. Josh could see the light of a candle dancing out through the crack around the mostly closed door. He slowly pushed it open and saw Stu laying on a cot, writing a letter. The candle flickered a bit as the door opened.

"Hey," he said in his familiar greeting. His face went quizzical. "You staying warm back in here?"

"Cozy enough," Stu replied, remembering sleeping next to a wet log under a holey tarp. "You offering better?" he asked with a twinge of sparkle in his eye.

"Uh—no." The two men chuckled a bit. "It wasn't why I came back, but I'll see if someone has a small propane camping heater or something…"

"That sounds good," Stu said, "but I just appreciate the roof. What can I do for you?"

Down to business. I like that. "Someone just asked me a question that made me realize I know nothing about the potential medical issues we're facing. Is there anything contagious going around?"

Stu sat up and slipped his donated house slippers on to keep his socked feet off the bare concrete. "Have a seat," he said pointing to the small, rolling mechanic's stool that doubled as his exam chair.

Josh fully entered and closed the door most of the way again. "We need to rig up something for people to get a hold of you that doesn't require you to leave that open."

Ignoring the side-bar comment, Stu asked, "What's on your mind, Josh?"

"Well, Phil and I have both noticed that more and more people are coming down with the flu. Should we be worried?"

"Oh, I see," Stu said. "The short answer is no, except for those already sick or in the higher age brackets." Stu caught on. "Ohhh, yes, there is quite a large number of elderly here, huh?"

"Exactly," said Josh.

"That's something to watch for sure, but it's the long-term effects that we should probably worry about more."

"Meaning?" Josh prodded.

"So, the weather is forcing us all into tight confines, right? People aren't washing their hands very often now, or covering up when they cough. Yes, we could be in for a rough cold or flu season. That's not what I'm as worried about."

"As worried," Josh parroted. "What does that mean?"

"It means with the number of older people here, yes, we could see some of them get sick enough to have complications. A few might even die. But it won't be an epidemic. What will be problematic, though, are the diseases that normally pop up after natural disasters. Dirty water, lack of hygiene, and poor nutrition—those are the things that lead to diarrheal diseases. Things like cholera and TB are springing up in the more populated areas by now." Stu thought for a moment longer. "If you can improve handwashing and find vitamins and minerals, we'll all be ahead of the game. I mean *really* get on everyone to wash their hands multiple times a day. Keep some water on the fire at all times just for that."

"Guess we need to add soap to the shopping list…" Josh mused.

"Sure. But tell them just to find a good dish soap, like Dawn. We can blend it with water to make that foamy stuff in a hand pump, which will last a lot longer than bar soap."

Josh thought about that for a moment and then changed the subject. "Should we build you some sort of quarantine?"

"I'm just the hired help," Stu said, lifting his hands. "You all know better than I what the facilities here are capable of. But it wouldn't be a bad idea—especially if you can procure an RV that already has insulation and a bunch of beds." Looking around, Stu added, "Then we could dedicate this space to people with injuries."

"Thanks, Doc. Come up and get some stew," Josh suggested.

"Now that's funny," Stu said, chuckling.

Josh didn't remember the doctor's first name and didn't quite get it, but he smiled anyway. "Thanks, Doc." He started to head out, then turned back, hesitating. *I wonder if he's ever delivered babies…*

"Something else?" Stu asked.

Josh changed his mind. "Another time, Doc. Good night," he said, slipping up to the chow trailer to find two special somebodies to sit with.

Reynaldo inspected the healing scars under the bandages of the two soldiers in his New World Army. "Sanando bien!" he exclaimed. *Healing nicely.* He hoped that the healing would be completely over by the time the soldiers needed them to be authentic.

Before him in his farmhouse operations center were several pairs of operators, along with his various unit commanders. They were being fully briefed on the high-level views of the plan. True to the nature of his multi-racial/multi-lingual army, he had before him not just Hispanic warriors, but Black, White, Asian, and Russian, too. Each two to four-man team was garbed in attire that would help them blend in with their operational surroundings.

"Amigos, Dejanos rezar. Padre nuestro…" *Friends, let us pray. Our Father. Offer your protection over these brave men as they fulfill our mission. Should they fall, oh, Father, shower them with blessings in Heaven. We will provide for their families until the ends of the Earth. Amen.*

With that, Rey excused the soldiers and held back the commanders. After his special operators had departed, he made sure the unit commanders were aware of why he'd been sending the soldiers out in the form of humanitarian missions for the last two days. *If all eight hundred of us were travelling down the broken highways together, we would draw their attention. But escorting busses of citizens as they travel south? That is just a civic duty.* Of course, they had been conscripting needed skills at gunpoint—forcing "hired labor" to start clearing obstacles from roads with bull dozers—since the first day they were operational. Some of the busses actually did carry citizens, starting the process of endearing the local populace to whomever could provide for them. They were delivering them right to the feeding tents they were setting up in the more populated areas. The other busses were stuffed with their army and special tools, though.

Rey pointed to the maps and photos hanging on the boards and walls around them. "Alguna pregunta?" *Any questions?*

"Solo uno, Jefe." *Just one, Boss.* "Cuan lejos esta de Monroe?" *How far is it to Monroe?*

"Hermanos…" *Brothers. We're eighty-seven miles from doubling the size of our army.*

12

The Point of No Return.

TAHOMA'S HAMMER PLUS 6 DAYS.

EARL FLEW AROUND the curve on his son's bicycle and hit both sets of brakes as tight as his grip would allow. The bike started to skid sideways just a bit as the tires had locked up on the wet and ashy pavement. Instinct took over as the skid neared its completion, as Earl pushed the left peddle down and leapt off on that side, flipping the bike towards his right as he did. The slung rifle had been held fairly close to his left abdomen area, and considering his pistol was holstered under his rain gear, it was the obvious choice. It came up in a flash. He had a Holosun optic, and the battery kept the device powered for years on end—true to its reputation, the little site held a red reticle directly on the head of the walking dead man who was holding his daughter hostage.

Earl was walking sideways to the left, careful not to cross his legs as he navigated to get a second position that wasn't directly behind Conner. Between Conner and the stand-off lay two other soon-to-be-dead meat-bags, bleeding in the sloppy ash. Conner had placed two pistol headshots on number one, and in his haste to get rounds on the other two, had shanked his third and fourth shots. *You can't miss fast enough* had been drilled into him in the Army. He concentrated on his trigger control and front sight, and shots five and six found their marks. Unfortunately, the knife wielding scum had managed to close the gap on Piper. The four people now found themselves in a stand-off, right in the middle of the road.

Piper was clutching her assailant's arm around her throat, crying hysterically. Earl wasn't having any. As soon as he had a good angle and fully realized the perp had a fixed-blade knife to his daughter's throat, his choice was made. The perp was trying to walk backwards, maintain control of Piper, and pivot to keep an eye on both armed defenders. It was too much, particularly as Conner began walking at an opposite angle as Earl, to the right. This was increasing the amount the perp had to pivot his head to keep an eye on them. The tension in the man's swearing was obvious by the increase in pitch and desperation. It was a matter of moments in which he made the fatal mistake of letting too much head get exposed from behind his human shield's head.

Earl was close enough that he knew he could aim an inch to two inches high—the rifle was sighted for fifty meters, which meant for closer shots the bullet would hit lower than was aimed. The offset he practiced at three meters was between three and four inches. He figured for a twenty-meter shot, the needed adjustment would be a small part of that. He squeezed the trigger. *KA-KROW!*

Piper screamed in sheer terror as the would-be terrorist's gray matter exploded out the back of his skull at almost 3000 feet-per-second. The shot had even made Conner flinch. The standing corpse loosened his grip around Piper's throat, and she fell to the ground in a terrified heap. Earl rushed in to double check for a case of possum—that what he thought he saw wasn't just a trick being played on his mind out of the fear for his daughter's life. He saw the damage and knew the threat was down for good.

Meanwhile, Conner checked on his first two targets—the first was expired, but the second had received torso shots and was still quite conscious. "H-Help"—*POP!*

"Nope," Con-Man said coldly as he ended the man's suffering. He scanned the woods on both sides of the road as he did a magazine change. Surely there were more rats in the pack. Finally, "Looks clear."

Earl was kneeling on one knee, holding Piper close. "I need you to go fetch Tori and Owen," he said to Conner. "They're hiding near those mailboxes." As his best friend hopped back onto the bike and rode west, Earl scanned the scene around him. *I can't believe this just happened,* he thought in shock.

Piper sobbed uncontrollably, squeezing her father with all she had. Earl tried several times to calm her. A few minutes later, Owen and Tori came flying up on the bikes, while Conner was jogging the cart down as quickly as he could. Tori screamed her daughter's name when she saw the three corpses still oozing the red stuff into ash. Earl suddenly found himself holding and trying to calm all three of his kin in a mass huddle.

Conner finally arrived. "We need to get moving," he reminded his old boss. For the next several minutes, he busied himself dragging corpses into the woods while Earl tried to compose his family.

Unlike in his combat deployments, this Immediate Threat Action had completely shaken Earl. It was different when one's family was in danger. *We're on what...day seven? And it's already come to this?*

TAHOMA'S HAMMER Plus 7 Days.

. . .

"YOUR LUNG SOUNDS ARE HORRIBLE," Natalie told her husband as she removed her stethoscope from his back. She didn't really need it. Anyone could hear his wheezing. The ash was everywhere, kicking up as a dust anytime a person moved. The Cascades were holding the autumn storms to their west, keeping the wind and rain from pushing the ash east or down into the creeks that led to the mighty Columbia River. "You need to start using that albuterol I scored on the last trip down."

He was in the little trailer, sitting upright in the bed the way asthmatics do when they can't seem to get the elephant off their chest. "I know, Nat. I don't know what to do." *Wheeze*. "It's not like we have the power to run a humidifier," Roy pointed out.

"Good thing for you we have some essential oils. I'm going to get some water boiling for tea."

"I don't want tea!" he said in a somewhat child-like voice.

"Eucalyptus," she said, ignoring him. "And peppermint, I think. Those will help. And, yes—we can run the generator tonight to power the humidifier. Peppermint oil in that will help, too."

"Nope." *Wheeze*. "We haven't been running the CPAPs, and you've had two migraines. No fair to you," he objected.

"The difference is that asthma is much more likely to kill than sleep apnea. Who's the nurse here?" She'd won, and they both knew it. "Think about the kids." *Got ya'. Now shut up and obey.* "I think we need to think about going to Bubby's," she said to change the subject.

"*Closer* to Seattle? You're kidding, right?"

"Not at all. And…I need to tell Dad about Mom."

"Nat, we live on a farm. *This* is where your brother and his family should be coming." *Wheeze*. "Not the other way around!"

"There's like two feet of ash out there!" she exclaimed. "The PH will be all jacked up next year. We'll be lucky to feed ourselves—not even thinking about crops to sell! We just let our cows go loose, for crying out loud!"

"No," he countered. "We have hay and oats for the winter."

"But the surface water is all tainted. We can't live on a generator for months on end! Think about it. Bubby's place has plenty of water and it's isolated." She could see he was thinking. "And *protected*," she added.

"I guess we could take the Cub that far," he conceded. "We'll need to bring as much gas as we can." *Wheeze.* "I don't think I can walk over that pass this time of year. What about the hospital?"

That was in a past life, she thought. "It won't last much longer. I think Sandra and Doctor Gupta are about done. Once they're gone, the hospital will be done for. Nobody there knows when more meds and supplies will show up because the highways are unusable." *Nope. We're going to Bubby's. He's much better suited for this crisis.*

I_T WAS EARLY AFTERNOON_, and the Garren Clan was finally strolling and riding up the small lane to his riverside cabin. *The last mile is the longest*, Earl thought. Some of the thirty-three residences—twenty-three on the river side, ten on the mountain side—on Coho Spawn Road were site-built homes. Most were framed cabins, and some were log. Each had a good spacing between the nearest neighbor, but not so distant as to forget they're there. The Garrens' log cabin was about two-thirds of the way down the road on the river side. The roar was loud, as the fall rains had it swollen and running fast —*too fast for wading for a while...Looks like we'll be bank fishing.* As he eye-balled the river, he could see it was much murkier than usual. *Probably all this ash.*

"Finally here!" Owen said with a groan.

"Arrrggg! Shut! Up!" Piper yelled.

Tori was about to get on her when Earl shot her a look. *Let her process it*, he said with telepathy. He wasn't sure if Tori read his mind, but she read his face and didn't say anything. In Owen's youth, he knew what had almost happened to his sister the day before, but the true impacts to her psyche were lost on him. Earl had board games and cards staged out there, but he figured it might be a while before she was up to doing anything with anyone that required patience.

"You see that?" Conner asked him.

"Huh? No. Lost in my own thoughts. What?"

"Curtains on that house flickered. Like we're being watched."

"I noticed that we just strolled right up the road," Tori added. "Almost like they think they're safe out here…"

"I think once those closest to us see us go into our own place, word'll get out," Earl concluded. After a moment, he added, "Still, I've met those closest to us a couple of times. Can never remember their names, but we should get 'em together and try to organize some sort of civil-defense plan."

The five-some strode the last five minutes quietly. Piper let the bike hit the gravel driveway after she removed her stuff from the fender rack. She made a beeline for the front door. It was locked, of course. "HHHmmmpphhh!" she said without words.

"You didn't seriously think I just left it unlocked, did you?" Earl asked, smirking.

"Well, what if you had died or something?" she said, annoyed.

I'm so glad 'how you will get into the cabin' would be your biggest worry in that scenario, Earl thought. He was biting his tongue to give her some time to process her ordeal. *I'm about done with this attitude.* "Mom knows where the hidden key is," he said evenly. After picking her bike up and putting down the side-stand, he walked over to the front door and unlocked it.

"Wait here," he ordered his family. He and Conner took a minute to clear the small cabin before allowing everyone to enter. It had been a couple of weeks since he'd been in there. *Needs some airing out.* "Brother, would you get a fire going?" he asked Conner. *Thank God I built up the wood pile this summer.* Earl went and opened a few shades and windows while Tori and the kids hauled their bags into the cabin. It was basically a three-room cabin with a loft serving as one big room, the space under serving as another, and the kitchen and common area on the river side of the house. There was a cast-iron woodstove in the far corner. Earl would have loved to have a big river-rock fireplace, but at that moment he was thankful for what was there.

Owen tried to flip a light switch. "Really, bud?" Earl asked.

"I was just checkin'," his son said, bummed.

Now that's optimism, Earl thought. *We just walked over forty miles and killed three people in self-defense, and he thinks the power might be on out here.* "Son. You know you're going to have to share the back-room with your sister for quite a while...right?" The thirteen-year-old still held the dejected look. This got Earl thinking. "Tell you what. Give me five minutes and we'll get the quads out of the shed, hook up the cart, and haul a bunch of firewood up from the farthest stack."

"That sounds fun, and all, but, uh..."

"Cabin aint gonna heat itself, son. Better get used to chores taking the place of your video games." He looked towards the woodstove. "Any water left in that can?" he asked Conner.

Conner looked into the old coffee can. "Bone dry." This made him suddenly realize something. He'd been out here at least twenty trips and had never thought to ask this. "You on a well out here?"

"Yep. And one of the first things I did when we bought this place was see how deep it is on the state's website. When I saw the water table out here was shallow enough, I installed a hand-pump on the head. Bring the can. We'll fill the water-jugs while Big-O gets the quad warmed up."

Tahoma's Hammer Plus 8 Days.

"I need you two to do me what I would consider an un-repayable favor," Legion said. Shorty and Trip just looked at him stoically. *I knew they'd be up to it.* "I want you to go rescue Sticky from exile."

The pair looked at each other. "Just the two of us?" Trip finally asked. "I mean—yes. Hands down—yes. But it'd be nice to have a couple of prospects with us."

"Can't spare 'em, brother. You know that. Still waiting on the other chapters and the support clubs to file in. With a lot of the overpasses pancaked, it could take weeks."

"No sweat," Shorty replied. "Consider it done." He looked at Trip. "We can just get over to the Sound and find a boat, I'm sure... Right?"

"That's what you'll need to do, for sure," said Legion. "But it could take a couple of days to get there, and a couple to find one that didn't get wiped out." He looked back and forth. "You two up to this?"

"Of course!" Trip exclaimed with confidence. "We'll ride as far as we can. There's a bunch of marinas. My cousin took sailing lessons somewhere over there when we were kids." Trip changed the subject. "Who's gonna be Enforcer while I'm gone? There's a lot of people here now."

"We'll be alright," Legion said. "You two get ready. Just leave tomorrow since today's half-over already." He turned to leave them in the bedroom he'd dragged them into for the conversation. "Oh— and take a little 'party product' with you. Sticky's earned it. So, have you guys." With that he headed to the attic to find his radio operator.

"What's the news, Prospect?" he asked the man he'd assigned to guard and play student to the kidnapped HAM.

"Things're startin' to get sketchy all over the place," he said. "It's kinda cool to sit here and listen to stuff all over the state, but at the same time..." He drifted off.

"What stuff?" Legion demanded.

"I dunno. It's almost like one of those end-of-the-world movies. We actually heard a couple of gun battles between the cops and someone on the radio this mornin'."

"Well, did you map it?" he asked, pointing at the big map on the wall. "Never frickin' mind!" he said, annoyed when he saw it was unmarked. *Stupid prospects. Sheesh...*

"When we can, boss. They need to drop street and neighborhood names and stuff. It's not like I can Google it anymore," he explained.

"Yeah, Prospect, I get that. Just get what you can—but listen up. It's called 'intel.' And we need it. I need to know who's fightin' who, where, why, when. Pretty much all the damn W's. Got it?"

"Copy that, boss."

Not too much longer and our quasi-pact with the Russians and Blacks is gonna fall apart. We need to be ready.

13

Hope and Hopelessness.

Tahoma's Hammer Plus 21 Days.

"Wait here," Charlie told Deputy Matty Wildman, who had just parked their patrol rig with the engine idling in front of the sign and small flagpole at the main gate to the West Sound Sportsman's Club. Charlie got out and approached the sandbag wall under the brown plastic tarp as a man and woman stepped out from under it.

"The club's Executive Officer is on the way up," she said.

"I figured as much," Charlie said. There was a second patrol car idling still out on Canal Vista Highway. Charlie and the two gate guards stared at each other in awkward silence for about four minutes until Phil finally showed up from the direction of the secondary gate that leads down to the far end of the rifle line and action bays. He opened it enough to just pass through it and re-latched it behind himself.

"Sergeant Reeves," Phil said.

"Really, Phil? It's gonna be like that?" he asked his supposedly best friend.

"Last time you were out here, you made it pretty clear how things are," Phil replied bitterly.

You mean the time before that, Charlie said in his own head. He remembered holding Phil up under the weight of the world crashing down on him on the last visit. "I think we can both agree that things are complex now," Charlie parried.

"Sure," Phil agreed. "Is there something we can do for the Slaughter County DEM?"

"Seriously? We're gonna keep up this little game?" Charlie was starting to get annoyed. "Fine." He keyed up his lapel microphone. "Zeus, you guys stay in your rig. Matty, bring up the evidence bag." Matty walked up to Phil and Charlie about thirty seconds later with a plastic bag, though Phil couldn't tell exactly what was in it.

"Can we come in?" Charlie asked.

"Got a warrant?" Phil countered.

"Do I need one?" Charlie retorted.

Phil stared at him for about five seconds and finally turned around and opened the lower gate. "You're getting good at this, Charlie," he stated as the two deputies started to travel in after him.

Oh, boy. "What's that?" he asked, knowing he would receive some sarcastic answer. Best friends are figuratively family that people get to choose, and nobody knows how to pull a person's strings like their family.

"Serving the crown," Phil said flatly.

Charlie stopped and then looked at Matty. "Why don't you stay here." It was an order, not a question. Matty complied without resistance.

The two men strolled down the gravel road slowly, and Phil finally asked, "So, what's in the bag, Charlie?"

"In a minute," Charlie said. "First, what did you hear about a big firefight out in the west end, night before last?"

"You might have to be more specific, Charlie," Phil said. "There's all kinds of danger out here at night." Neither man was enjoying playing this game of mental chess, and both were a little angry that it was with someone they cared for. "We're constantly sending beggars along their way—will be any night now that we're arresting them and calling you guys. Non-violently, of course," Phil said, adding the dig to draw a reaction. "Wouldn't want our guns to get confiscated."

You're being a jerk, Charlie said with his stare. Phil understood it. "Enough games, Phil! What happened out there? I know you were there."

"If something happened somewhere, *brother,*" Phil said, thinking through his words as if they would come back at him in court some-day, "I'm sure it was self-defense." He was doing his best to remain calm. He remembered learning, once, that he who loses his cool first, loses the debate. It was a lesson he rarely remembered.

"Could be, I guess." Charlie was choosing his words, too. "But usually the self-defense argument goes to the people who were attacked, not doing the attacking."

"Well, Deputy, since I have no idea what you're talking about, I'm going to have to keep speaking hypothetically—unless you give me some specifics."

You asked for it. "You want specifics? Okay—remember that kid you arrested here the night after the quake?" He was observing Phil's face. He thought he saw the pupils widen just a bit. "His entire family and several other people were obliterated the night before last. Funny, though. He wasn't with 'em."

"The Matthews? That's what you're talking about?" Phil deceit-fully asked. "World's better off without them!" he said emphatically. The two men stared at each other for another ten seconds before Phil finally pushed, "What's in the friggin' bag, Charlie?"

Charlie couldn't help but let the corners of his mouth curl up ever so slightly. He barely took his gaze off Phil when he pulled the AR magazine out of the plastic evidence bag, still full of ammo and covered in dried mud. Phil looked at it, and his face went blank, but he said nothing.

"How many classes have I taken here, Phil? Only shooter I know whose initials spell 'pew'," Charlie said. *Boom goes the dynamite!* "Nothin'? You all out of sarcasm, Phil? Smart-ass tank empty?"

Phil's face was turning beet red. He just stared...and stared... Finally, he said, "What's this mean, Charlie? You all here to arrest me?" he asked, waving towards the highway.

"No, Mr. Walker," Charlie said, returning to the fake niceties, "I'm here to deliver a message—well, two messages, I suppose." Phil just kept staring with a face that could no longer hide his anger. Charlie continued, "One—the Slaughter County Unified Command is the authority in this county, whether you like it or not. They're the ones who will decide how justice is dispensed, not private citizens. We can't allow vigilantes to take over, Phil."

He waited, but Phil was lock-jawed—afraid anything else he said would be so insulting that it would indeed get him arrested.

"And two—you have a friend who was shot in an altercation last night. I thought you would want to know."

"Who?" Phil demanded, intense anger still radiating from his face.

"Reverend Sherman Robertson."

STU PULLED the seamstress-style measuring tape off Payton's belly. "I'd like to see this grow a bit," he said. "Are you getting enough to eat?" They were in his little room, evaluating the state of her pregnancy.

"Is anyone?" Payton wondered aloud as she sat up and pulled her shirt down.

"Touché," Stu replied, smiling softly. "But, seriously—you

need it. This baby's chances of starting his or her life healthy increase dramatically if you get enough good food. No sharing your portions with your daughter. Take seconds, even. Doctor's orders."

Payton smiled. Having Stu at the range was a big relief, though she knew he could decide to leave at any time. "I'm glad you're here, Dr. Schwartz."

"All things considered, so am I. Three weeks back feels like a lifetime ago."

Three weeks? Is that all it's been? They both fell silent for a moment until Stu got it rolling again. "I talked to Josh about trying to get vitamins. I know they started their foraging patrols today, or whatever they're calling it. You and a few other patients get first dibs on whatever they bring back."

"Cool. What about you, Doctor?" Payton asked, trying to find a way to plant seeds. "What does your future hold?"

"Well, I have a couple of parents up in Sequim I need to go find," he admitted. Payton noticed the worried look cross his brow ever so slightly. "Though my Jewish mother is probably too stubborn for the disaster to have affected her."

They both knew he was deflecting, but Payton had the sense to let it go. "I'm sure they're managing, Doctor," she said. *Now isn't the time to ask him...*

"Please—call me Stu. I—I..." He started to choke on his words as his eyes turned moist. He missed Carmen.

"Stu." Payton put her hand on his arm. "Whatever it is..." She paused and smiled until he looked back up at her. "We've all lost someone...we've all had to grow up—fast. It's okay."

"Thank you, young lady," Stu said, composing himself again. He was starting to enjoy medicine again, especially when there was no rush to get the next paying customer onto an operating table.

"And you're welcome here as long as you want, as far as I'm concerned," Payton said. *Seed planted!* "Now, if you'll excuse me, I need to go check on things."

"Of course," he said. As she stepped past the patient bunks out in the rifle-line area, he called after her, "And get more rest!"

"Will do," she hollered back. Once past the windbreak wall, she turned right and started moving towards the construction site between the fifty and hundred-yard markers on the range. She was making a beeline for Tony, who was helping two other people muscle a notched log up onto a stack.

Tony saw her wobbling up to the worksite. "'Sup, girl? How'd your appointment go?"

"Says I need to gain weight. Not exactly rocket science. But he's right, I guess."

"Course he's right, Payton! Everyone knows you're workin' too hard!"

Payton grinned. She enjoyed the big man's husky, Virginia drawl. "Pregnancy is no excuse to slack," she said. *But it would be nice if my feet weren't swollen for a change...*

"Never said it was," Tony replied. "Whatcha think?" he asked, changing the topic to the progress of the common.

"Coming along. Why you guys moving these logs the hard way?"

He looked over at the far end of the layout and pointed. "The Kubota's taking over after we get the first couple o' rows up and plumb and level," he explained.

Unlike a traditional log cabin, this structure was going to have a much larger footprint and be open sided. They were building up the corners and key load-bearing points with traditional notched logs, about six-feet long, in either an L or a T shape. In the middle and tops of the stacks, they would occasionally use an additional piece to be the "hypotenuse" and hold the stacks square. They wanted this facility to be at least eight feet tall on the open sides. When finished, they would have a 70' x 120' common area with a log roof. There were even plans to get rocks from the nearby salmon stream and make a fireplace at each end.

"Your man make it back from the patrol yet?" Tony dared, smiling. He just threw a big rock in the pond.

"What?" Payton jumped. "What man?" She blushed. "I don't know what you're—"

"Nope! Nope! Nope! Ain't buyin' it, girl. Tony ain't buyin' it. Everyone knows you and Josh got a thang— 'cept you and Josh," he added for fun.

Payton just let out a big huff to go along with the jaw that had fallen to the bottom of her neck. Tony started busting a gut. "Maaaannnn—the look on your face!" He walked over and wrapped her up in a Big Tony bear hug.

She huffed again, smiling and still speechless. Finally, "W-what else are people saying?" she asked as Tony let her out of the loving hug.

Tony slowed his laughing and took on a more fatherly tone for a moment. "It's a good thing, Payton. Your baby...love in the air...it gives people hope," he said with a smile.

"I saw the worst fight I've ever seen today down in the main camp," Melinda Reeves told Charlie as they laid on their side-by-side bunks. They were speaking in hushed tones while Junior and Kiersten played Uno for the seven-hundredth time. Charlie was unwinding as best as he could. The shift wasn't just about his showdown with Phil —he, his peers, and the Guard had been involved in containing a large riot at the mall in Sylvan. Charlie really had no interest in hearing about the FEMA camp, except for needing to stay abreast of any threats to his family.

"I thought you guys didn't go down there anymore," he said.

"We went and stood in line for vitamin shots. There's a crud going around, and I want the kids to be as protected as they can be," she explained. "I and three of the other spouses all took our kids down as a group. Safety in numbers."

"Heh—yes, Mel," Charlie laughed. "I get the concept." He turned his head and saw she wasn't laughing. "What was it about?" he asked to smooth his quip over. He knew Melinda was itching to talk—once she got started, he would only have to grunt every minute or two.

"Well," she started slowly, "not that people need a reason to fight anymore…but rumor has it"—the rumor mill ran any and all news, fake or otherwise—"that the Navy is supposed to be here in a week with more supplies. Some of the conspiracy theorists called that 'fake news,' which pissed off some of the others. Soon everyone was throwing out racial and political insults. It got ugly real fast. It looked like a flash mob, but scarier. I hate to see what happens when food starts running out."

The talkative Melinda continued for a few more minutes, knowing full-well her husband was passively listening. The topic usually didn't matter—her chewing his ear off was part of their routine. She didn't mind, because she knew it helped him relax. She considered it part of helping him rid some stress.

Charlie noticed her wrap up a description of how the MPs came in and got things under control before she went silent. "Sorry, honey. I'm listening, I swear."

"I know you are. I'm just trying to help you relax."

"It sounded a lot like my day in Sylvan."

"Want to talk about it?" she asked, knowing the answer already.

"No." He went silent on her. *What I want is for this living Hell to be over. I'm tired of drinking rainwater through filter straws. I'm tired of getting bruised and sliced breaking up fights. I'm tired of finding the aftermath of the worst crimes imaginable. Mostly, I'm tired of knowing what's coming and not being able to do anything about it.* "It would just sound a whole lot like the story you just told."

14

Starting New Chapters.

TAHOMA'S HAMMER PLUS 8 DAYS.

"THANKS FOR COMING," Earl said to the small group. It was around noon, and the two closest homeowners were people that Earl had said hi to enough times that he decided to see if they were home. Both couples were home and agreed. "Like I said, I'm Earl. That's my wife Tori, and my brother, Conner." Sometimes it was just more natural to tell people that. "And Owen. Our daughter Piper is resting. I'm retired Army—was working at Bass Pro Shop when all this went down."

"I was an admin assistant," Tori added.

"Heavy equipment operator," Conner mentioned. He looked at the next pair.

"Hi," the woman said. "We're Chopper and Dorothy. Good to meet everyone!"

"Chopper?" Owen asked gleefully.

The old biker carried a very friendly, smiling persona, which revealed several holes where teeth belonged. "Name's Windell, but everyone just calls me Chopper" he said, laughing. The man's attitude was infectious in a good way.

"Cool!" the young man said.

"Hi, ya'll. We're Jack and Diane," said the next man, a southern twang making his words almost musical.

The bait just hanging there was too much for the large-mouthed bass named Conner to resist. "Jack and Diane? You guys grow up in the heartland? Doin' the best you can?" Tori slapped her forehead.

Jack just said, "Yep! Ne-e-ver heard that one, before…"

There were a few chuckles, and Earl chimed in. "You'll have to excuse my brother. He has this…condition. Idioicitis. It gives you diarrhea of the mouth." He shot his buddy a discerning look. *This is why you were never gonna make it the full twenty,* he said with his glare.

"Sorry," Conner mumbled to Diane.

"You're just lucky she doesn't kick your butt to next week!" Jack said. The whole room broke out laughing. Conner had a couple of more one-liners about football stars and chilidogs that he wisely let go.

After everyone reined themselves in, Earl continued. "To clarify, Conner is my Army brother. We served together through several deployments and have a lot of experience in security." He scanned the other couples. "Which is why we're wanting to talk to everyone…"

"Yes!" Diane exclaimed. "Finally!"

"Oh, yeah?" Earl said, somewhat surprised by the enthusiasm.

"Yes. Dear, God, yes. I was just telling Jack yesterday that I can't believe nobody has set-up a roadblock or anything!"

Jack was nodding and ready to add his two cents. "Yes. Problem is, we both worked in software. We have no idea how to get started. I think everyone out here is waiting for someone else to do it…"

"We were thinking the same thing!" Dorothy announced. "But…" She looked at Chopper.

"But," Chopper picked up, "I'm sixty-two. I have high blood pressure. Just don't know how much good I'd do. I was a Machinist's Mate in the Coasties, but that didn't translate into any real security experience."

"Do either of you live here year-round?" Earl asked.

"We do," Dorothy said.

"Not us," Jack contributed. "This was our weekend getaway."

"That's alright," Earl said. "Dorothy, do you think you could take us around to meet everyone you know this afternoon?"

"I suppose. That soon? Don't you guys want to settle in?"

And get murdered tonight? Earl thought. "No. I think we should have a bigger one of these meetings tonight, if possible."

This got the other couples to start chirping up a little more. Earl shot Conner a glance and could see his buddy already thinking it, too—*we're going to have to teach everyone from scratch, aren't we?*

TAHOMA'S HAMMER Plus 9 Days.

IT HAD TAKEN Natalie and her misfits the entire next day to get ready. It wasn't just her husband and kids—there was a predominantly black lab mutt named Tomfoolery, two goats named Jerk 1 and Jerk 2, and a reinforced lumber chicken tractor hitched to the cart that was hitched to the Cub. They had started the loading with gasoline, water, and chicken feed to let Natalie know how much room was left for food and gear. Creative packing, meaning a lot of rope, straps and bungees, ensured that both Cub and cart were tall and top heavy. *Looks like the Grinch's sleigh,* Natalie thought. She was letting no space go unused. She even had small gardening tools tethered to the wire fence on the chicken tractor.

The Cub had two seats, which meant the four adults and teens were taking turns walking. She tried to arrange it for Roy to have the most driving time—she didn't want the uphill and off-road journey to blow all the moisture out of his lungs. The ash was already doing enough damage. Four-year-old Katherine would get to ride, mostly. Natalie didn't want to deal with the inevitable blisters on a tyke.

Roy was keeping a close eye on the Cub's engine. He'd rigged up a t-shirt as a pre-filter over the air intake that he shook out every chance he could. The engine was buried under the bed, which made it difficult to access when loaded up. He had also covered all the loads in both beds with plastic. Being mid-Washington farmers, they were all decked out in a mix of winter-lined outdoor gear. It was October, after all, and the chance of encountering snow in the mountains was pretty high.

Their first destination was Natalie's father's house near Cle Elum. They would be making a steady uphill path along Old Highway 10. She remembered reading a local hiker's blog article that taught her about the trail that paralleled it. At times, this would take them several hundred yards away from the old highway and a few miles away from the main interstate. *Fine with me*, Natalie thought. *The less people, the better.*

At a few points the trail got very close to the Yakima River. "Go try this thing out," she told Wesley and James, handing them the never-used back-packer water-filter pump. "Wes, keep an eye on your brother." It was a little agreement that she and thirteen-year-old James had made a couple of years earlier—to pretend his autistic brother two years his senior was watching out for him. James shot her a look of understanding and wandered the two hundred or so feet over to the river's edge with his brother.

"I'm going to stretch, too," Roy said. He unstrapped a lawn chair from the side of the stack. "Here, honey. Sit."

"I think I will," she agreed, smiling from under the damp hood. It was starting to drizzle. "And I think it's Wes's turn to walk."

"Heh, we'll see how *that* goes," Roy said, stretching. He pulled the Remington 700 from behind the driver's seat. "Be back in a few," he said as he wandered down to the river to find his sons.

Natalie looked over at the other barrel sticking up behind the passenger seat. It belonged to their only other firearm, a cheap Winchester Defender shotgun. They usually used it to scare coyotes away with birdshot. Roy had found four rounds of buckshot, and they were the first four rounds to get fired if it came to that. After that, the birdshot was all they had. Whereas both guns were kept in gun-socks at home, Roy had left them well-oiled and open to the elements, minus taping some nitrile gloves Natalie found in her scrubs, over the barrels. *Nurses aren't supposed to think this, but…why in the world don't we own an AR-15?*

RETIRED ARMY SNIPER Nick Williams could only hope that he wasn't too late. His venture back took way longer than it should have, primarily because it turned into a full-on cross-country hike for most of the route down the west side of the Hood Canal. The entire hillside had slid into the canal for close to twenty-five miles, taking with it every home, road, deer, tree, and insect. Nick's first thought was to go try to bargain for a boat and navigate through the mess. Then he used his binoculars.

He could see that the canal had been literally destroyed on the south end. It was technically still a mappable waterway, but there was so much mass and fill from the unimaginable mudslide that all he could see was murk and treetops as far down as the binoculars would scan. It took him four days just to climb up the rest of what used to be the hill, down into the next valley, and south through the brush to a point where he was back out of the wilderness.

As badly as he wanted to get on with his mission, he'd spent the day before resting and triple checking his gear. This was a long-range, no-resupply mission that would fail to launch if he couldn't even get his boat in the water. He was relieved when he got home to find the house standing. It was trashed, as the foundation had split in several places, allowing the roof and windows to leak badly. But at least his stuff was relatively secure. More importantly, no trees had fallen on his boat.

He talked a neighbor into letting him use his truck. They had to craft some ramps out of fallen trees with chainsaws. The road into the park where the boat launch was located had split, with the half closer to the water now fourteen inches lower than the rest. Nick and his neighbor both knew that going back up the makeshift ramp would be the real challenge—something the neighbor was happy to do to earn a free AK-74 and 600 rounds of ammunition. *I'm never going to need that thing again,* Nick thought. It used a different ammo than the two most common semi-auto rifles—a person was less likely to find that ammo when times got lean.

After running his mind through a few hundred items in his mental checklist—Water? Batteries? Ass-wipe?—he decided it was time to shove off and head out. Anything else of real value that Nick owned was hidden as deeply into the broken crawl space as he could get it. As the small amount of daylight dissipated from the gray sky and evolved into night, he crept the boat along slowly toward McNeil Island. He landed right in the spot he'd planned for after his countless practice runs over the years. He was on the north-side of the island, away from as many structures as possible. *Time to send some pedo-rapist souls to hell.*

15

The Trek.

"YOU'RE MAKING A BIG MISTAKE," Josh warned Phil.

"Probably," Phil admitted, putting a hand on the side of Josh's shoulder for a second. "But my mind's made up. I'm going alone. We can't afford to lose two gunfighters here, especially now that you've got the scavenging and intel patrols started." Josh started to protest, but Phil kept going. "I've made sure the board members know that you're in charge of all things security while I'm gone. Whatever you say. You have my complete confidence, brother." He could still see Josh's skepticism. "Other than this last week, the Reverend was there for me in the worst moments of my life—I have to at least try."

No! What we can't afford is to lose you permanently. Josh thought about his choices. *Try one more time? I think it'll only piss him off.* "Alright. I get it...And, I've known you long enough to know I won't win this." *But there are alternatives to winning.* Josh stuck his hand out for a shake, which Phil took firmly. After the handshake, he turned back toward the midnight blue Jeep that was Crane's pride and joy.

Phil double checked that his pack and tennis racket case were secure in the passenger seat with the seatbelt. He was wearing cargo pants and a hunting raincoat, not the multicam battle dress he'd kept on pretty much since Savannah's abduction. Payton was nearly at the point of knocking him out with something so she could wash those clothes. Phil wasn't wearing his plate carrier or battle belt—he was back to an inside the waistband holster for the tan Glock with several spare magazines on his person and in the orange tennis racket case. Also inside it was a fully assembled AR pistol and several magazines, ready for action, but not drawing the wrong kind of attention.

As Phil turned left off the club's property and started slowly driving south down the Canal Vista highway, Josh called out, "In case I didn't say it, you're making a big mistake!" Phil gave him a backwards wave over his shoulder and kept going. Josh could hear weird noises from the jeep and couldn't decide if it was due to all the cracks in the asphalt or Phil's prosthetic leg interfering with his ability to clutch.

I need to find Eli and Lonnie, Josh thought as he started walking back through the main gate and the sandbag vehicle trap. *I think Lonnie was about to take a patrol out. No time to waste.* He saw the green John Deere Gator utility wagon near the office and jumped in. Three minutes later he was pulling up to the CP up on the hill. He could hear the generator running. *Must be charging batteries.*

Sure enough, when he stepped in, he saw eight men and women —two four-person teams—reviewing the maps from the areas around the club's property. "Lonnie, got a second?" He waved Lonnie outside with his head.

"What's up?" he asked, instinctively pulling his rain hood up.

"Can you have Tyler run your squad today?"

"I dunno about that," he said hesitantly. "That makes it three, and four is already a bare minimum number as far as I'm concerned."

"We'll take the east fighting positions down to one person to back-fill, then." Josh's mind was already made up. He wandered over to the tent and yelled for Tyler to join them. Josh was right to the point when he showed up. "I need you to run today's intel patrol."

"O-o-okayyy..." he said slowly, looking at Lonnie, who just shrugged.

Josh caught the look. "I need him for a special assignment. I was already thinking about culling you into the leader of a future squad. We need to expand anyhow, if we plan on scavenging enough stuff for winter. What I really need to know is—are you ready? Will the others listen to you?"

"Yeah, I think I can manage." The insurance salesman was an Air Force logistics officer a dozen years back. He'd been a practical shooter at the club for several years. "I mean—Gene's a bit preachy. As long as he and I can maintain a system of respecting each other's differences, we'll be fine."

Huh—guess I missed that, Josh thought. It dawned on him that even after all they'd been through, not everybody was going to have the same ideals and values. People were going to have to get a lot more tolerant of others who disagreed with them. "You think he has a problem with you 'cause you're gay?"

"Uhhh...not yet. I don't think he knows. Don't get me wrong, we get along. It'll just be interesting to see his reaction when he figures it out."

"Okay. Let me know if I need to mediate. I'll find you another body or two in a bit. I have to get Lonnie and Eli going on this other thing."

Tyler excused himself to go back into the tent, giving Lonnie the opening he wanted. "So why all the mystery?"

"I need you guys for a special task."

"What's that?" Lonnie's curiosity was piqued.

"Let me go grab Eli. We'll be right back. See who you can grab from the mid-east foxhole to fill in for you." With that he jumped into the gator and took off for the northern road to find his way to their trailer. Eli and Jeff were preparing to leave on a much longer hunting trip into the state forest to the southwest. "Eli!" he yelled out, not even getting out of the Gator.

"What?" he heard from inside the trailer. Older brothers were never going to answer to the younger ones without a fight.

"New mission. Grab your gear and hop in."

Eli looked out and could tell by his younger brother's face and tone that it was serious. "Alright. Don't get your panties bunched up…"

They made their way back up to the CP and ran into Lonnie, who was coming back from the eastern perimeter. "So, what's all the excitement?" Lonnie asked as soon as the rig shut down. He didn't like having to bail on his little squad now that they were starting to gel.

Jeff threw a nod in his brother's direction as he said, "I know he can ride." He looked back to Lonnie. "Can you ride a horse?"

THE CARTEL HAD MOVED themselves down the passable highways and by-roads over the course of two days in busses that had been stolen from the City of Bellingham's school district. They had spaced themselves out, choosing to hide in plain sight as they travelled. The evening destination for the last night before the first major operation was a series of fields west of Highway 2 between Marysville and Monroe. Rey had dispatched several teams to steal as many Jeeps and trucks as they could from the auto lots in Marysville. It was almost midnight, and he was overseeing the last-minute preps.

"You did good, anticipating roll cages on some of these Jeeps, Armando," he said in English.

"Si, Jefe. I figured there would be a few. I like the way these clamps are working out for the 50-cal mounts and Mark 19s."

Within a hundred feet, sparks were flying on a few of the freshly stolen trucks. "And the welded mounts? They'll hold?"

"Si, Reynaldo. Every vehicle will be outfitted," Armando said enthusiastically.

Rey went over to the crates that had been dragged off the nearest bus, and imagined what it would look like in a few hours, when the 50-caliber, belt-fed machine guns and 40-mm grenade launchers would turn these vehicles into Somali-style "technicals." *The only technicals in the world to have new car smell*, he guessed.

"Keep it up, Armando. You do the cause proud!"

He moved back to the SUV he was using to move his personal gear and battle plan materials around. He watched as a large tow truck with a snowplow blade pulled into the field and parked. Three of his men hopped out of the cab and went to check-in with a superior. In Mexico, there would have been cheers, music playing in the background, probably some drinking. Up here, though…Everyone knew the consequences of failure. They were all acting like professionals. Most were working by lantern. They would probably attract some curiosity from locals but were far enough off the beaten path that Rey didn't anticipate any law enforcement threats. They had still established a violent security plan but were trying to keep things as low-key as possible.

One of the men who had returned in the tow truck walked over to Rey. "Estos son para ti, Jefe," he said. *These are for you.*

"En Ingles, Geraldo," Rey commanded gently. *I need you all to be able to understand the locals.*

"Sorry, Boss. These are your keys."

"You keep them. I need a driver tomorrow morning." Rey studied the tow truck a bit. "A snow plow?" he inquired.

"We thought it would stop bullets," his man said in broken English.

"Good thinking, Geraldo!" He and the cartel soldier stood and talked for a few minutes, until another man came up.

"The overwatch is all set up, Reynaldo. Are you sure you want to use the big missiles?" The man knew that they would definitely send a big, expensive message.

"You'll decide that in the moment, Sergio. The second unit will set up along the highway, but the timing with mortars will probably be off a bit. If too many of them make it through, the big missiles will have a much greater effect on more of them. The idea is to bottleneck them into one, big, fiery pile."

Reynaldo counseled more and more unit leaders throughout the night. The next day would be a big test. There was more on the line than just dying in a simple battle. This was about establishing dominancy in a new world without rules—or laws.

PHIL HAD FINALLY BEEN GRANTED access to the section of the large FEMA camp in Bartlett that contained the mobile hospital. The main civilian hospital was just too isolated on the wrong side of the one intact bridge to make guarding it practical with dwindling staff levels. At first, the protection was specifically for the narcotics and antibiotics. It eventually became for every type of supply. Ultimately it was about employee safety—someone had tried to kidnap a doctor and a nurse a week earlier. Apparently, a highly valued skill could be a detriment if those who possessed it didn't also have a protection plan in place. Moving all hospital operations to the FEMA camp also made for improved fuel savings.

When the Jeep had finally made its way to the correct street where Phil would need to turn to enter the complex, he saw a large volume of Guard members manning a barricade and conducting bag searches on the civilians trying to enter. *That won't do...*

He weaved the Jeep a mile farther south, passing an apartment complex on the other side of the road. He figured most of the residents would be at the FEMA camp—*or dead or bugged out*—by then. He regretted not finding some big chain to at least make the steering wheel un-steerable before he started the venture. *Oh, well. It is what it is…*

Phil cinched up his pack, took the tennis racket case into his left hand, and started walking. He couldn't be sure he wasn't being watched, but he had no choice—he darted into the woods for about a hundred meters and hid both bags in some brush next to a log. *No way am I not keeping at least the Glock on me…*

Fifteen minutes later, he had to stand in a line to be run through a metal detector. He triggered the electronic beep—barely audible over the sound of generators—and was stopped by a Guardsman. "Sir, I'll need to wand you," he stated, starting to move toward him. Phil turned so that the man could see his left side and hoisted his left pant leg, showing the bottom of the prosthetic.

The soldier looked up at Phil. "IED?"

"AK round," he said. *Hey, I'm not lying. Lucky me if he thinks it's because I was in the sand box…*

"Carry on, sir," the soldier said.

Phil continued on, thinking, *There isn't that much metal in this thing. It's mostly carbon fiber and polymer. Better to be lucky than smart, I guess…* He went through several other processes over the next hour trying to find his way to the medical sector. He discovered four large, green inflatable buildings. They each had generators running air blowers that fed large ribs almost three feet in diameter. The giant tents were about 60' x 100' in size and nearly thirty feet high. *What we could with one of these…*

He followed the signs and waited in yet another line. After a half-hour, "Yes?" came the un-thrilled response to his presence by a young Guardswoman.

"I'm looking for Sherman Robertson. Woulda been brought in the night before last."

Clickity-clack-clack.   Silence.   *Clack-clickity-click-clack.*   Silence.
Clickity…

Computers? Really?—*even after the start of the apocalypse…*Phil was
starting to get irritated.

"I'll need to get one of the nurses," she said after reading her
screen for a moment.

After a minute, a man came up to Phil. "Sir, you're the one
asking about Sherman Robertson?"

Uh-oh. "Yeah…"

"Are you immediate family?"

"Kind of?" Phil was a horrible liar. The Reverend was black, for
starters…

The nurse smirked ever so slightly. "Look, let's just say you are,
okay?" His face returned to business. "Mr. Robertson passed away
from his wounds in the late evening yesterday. Sorry."

Phil was dumb struck. *When will it stop?* He was at a loss for
words.

"Is there anything else I can help you with?" the nurse asked.

Phil read his name badge. "Y-yes, Sal…Is there anything you
can tell me about what happened? All I know is he got shot in some
sort of altercation. Do you still have his clothes or anything?" Phil
was having a hard time accepting yet another death to contend
with.

"Sorry. His remains were interred here, and his clothing and
effects were returned to his family down in Bartlett. Maybe you
should go see them…" the nurse suggested.

"T-thanks," Phil mumbled as he wandered out of the facility. He
was too dazed to take a good look around and see just how many
tents there were. People were milling about in all sorts of directions,
too, without much to do but wander in the light rain.

As he slowly made his way towards the main gate, he had
another idea. He spent three hours trying to track down whoever
was on patrol that night. He wasn't going to be allowed anywhere
near the barracks. He had tried three times to get someone with

clearance for entering that section to take a note to whoever patrols in Bartlett at night. Each time, the wait grew longer. He figured the people were just tossing the note as soon as they were out of sight. During the middle of all of that, Phil noticed a procession of vehicles head out—a forest green MRAP, followed by six HumVees.

His presence at the interior gate to the barracks had not gone unnoticed. A HumVee pulled up and stopped, and two MPs approached Phil.

"Sir, I'm going to need to see some ID," he ordered. Phil couldn't lie and say he lost it, as he had to show it just to get checked in earlier. He dug it out of his wallet and handed it over.

"What's your business, Mr. Walker?"

"Maybe you guys can help me with that. I'm trying to talk to whoever found my friend shot while on patrol the other night."

The two cops looked at each other. "We encounter that multiple times, every night. You're going to have to be more specific."

"Sherman Robertson. Night before last. East Bartlett. Somewhere within a couple of blocks of Allandale Baptist Church. Some sort of gang shootout." He looked at the two disinterested MPs. "You guys aren't gonna write this down?

The two soldiers looked at each other once again. "Look. We can't bother the patrol guys every time someone comes to the fence."

Phil grew agitated. "Then why bother asking for specifics?!"

The junior partner said, "I got an idea. Let me pull up the night-blotter and see if we can find something." The senior MP kept Phil in check while his partner opened the rear passenger door of the HumVee and started digging through binders. He returned after a couple of minutes.

"Report says they heard a firefight. It was over when they got there. Four dead, one wounded, all shell casings on sight were 9mm and 40-caliber. They brought the wounded party back here for treatment."

Phil looked at the ground, trying to think of any more questions.

The senior MP wasn't having any. "That's all we got—and you need to leave."

Phil looked up at him. "Thanks for your service," he snarked as he walked past them.

After Phil had made his way back to his gear, and ultimately to the Jeep, he decided to try to make it to the church and see if he could learn anymore. The ride over was eye opening for him. Trash was strewn everywhere. The storm and sewage drains were clogged —every low spot was a large, stinky pool of God knows what. The big billboards by the highway had fallen into a heap, as had many of the business signs along the city roads. He was forced to drive over some large steel plates that the DEM had laid out over large pieces of road that had dropped off. It was much like driving an obstacle course at three miles-per-hour.

He noticed he couldn't make the left at 17th street that he wanted to. It was blocked off. The road was on a hill, and it was about eighty feet higher in elevation than most of 17th, and the point where his current road and 17th met was basically a large bridge structure that had collapsed. This forced him even closer to downtown, near the shipyard. He noticed that the big stack that used to be a cooling tower at the shipyard's powerplant was conspicuously absent. *After I check on the Widow Robertson, I might as well camp. Tomorrow I'll see what the Feds will tell me about Crane.*

Phil saw fires in barrels with people camped around them right in business parking lots. It was ironic, since many of them were in front of the remains of burnt up buildings. He detected what appeared to be crude checkpoints on most of the side streets. *People 'bringing the fences in', just as I figured.* He remembered from Crane's and the Reverend's visit that he would have to use the bridge on the far side of town. He had an uneasy feeling the entire trip, as if he were being watched. *I am being watched,* he reminded himself. *And like a fool, I have nobody riding shotgun.*

After forty-five minutes of slow zigzagging, Phil finally managed to pull up to the Reverend's church on the far east side of Bartlett.

He was greeted by several men, a couple of them openly armed approaching the Jeep. He got out with his hands up. He noticed that group was an even mix of black and white church members. "Peace!" he called out. "I come in peace."

The man who seemed to be running the watch spoke up. "Not too often we get a rig rolling right up to the front door. When it does happen, nothin' good comes with it."

"I'm just here to pay my respects to Martha," Phil said.

This eased the tension a little bit. "What's your name, friend?" the leader asked.

"Jerome O'Malley!" they all heard a small, old lady's voice call out. The whole group and Phil looked up the stoop at the old church's front door. "Don't you know a celebrity when you see one?" The whole group turned back to Phil, not giving a crap who he was.

"Hello, Martha!" Phil said, smiling. He looked at Jerome to see if he was going to give way a bit.

"What—never seen a black Irishman before?" Jerome asked as he stepped aside.

As the small guard detail began to open up a little bit, he made his way up the ten stairs and into Martha Robertson's waiting arms. The two embraced like long-lost siblings, though to Phil, she could've been his mother. "I'm sorry," was all he could think to whisper during their hug.

"Me, too," she said back to him once the hug had broken.

It took him a second to think about it as he and Martha went into the church and closed the door. "Oh...you heard then?"

"Oh, yes, dear...everyone in town knows about what's happening at the shipyard."

Phil felt a wave of tears slam into the front of his eye sockets out of nowhere. He let out a shuddering breath as he tried to compose himself. "A-and here I was trying to comfort you!" he said, laughing as he had to wipe his eyes. The pair moved deeper into the dark-ened building. First the smell told him and then his eyes confirmed that there were dozens of people living on the pews. The building's windows had been completely boarded up with 2" x 4" lumber and scraps of plywood to protect the interior from small arms fire.

As they sat down, Martha told him, "It's alright, dear. I'm old, an' God will reunite me with my better half when He wants to."

"I don't know how you're holding up so well, Martha," Phil sniffled.

"Well, I'm still human, Phil. I get mad and sad…and all those things you supposed to get!" she exclaimed.

"They said they buried him up there?" Phil queried.

"Yes, that's what they told us, too," she sighed. "At least he was buried, unlike all those poor people that died a thousan' diff'rent ways on Reckonin' Day," she said matter-of-factly.

Reckoning Day…Is that what this is?

16

_____

Rude Awakenings.

TAHOMA'S HAMMER PLUS 11 DAYS.

"REMEMBER—GO west, first. We'll try north on another day," Sticky instructed the rag-tag crew of pirates. _Piracy...that really is what this is, ain't it?_ Another idea was being born. _Forget the sex crimes—people'll start moving goods by water and there'll be no cops to stop the piracy. Others are gonna do it. May need to establish dominancy in that quickly..._

"We got it, Sticky," said the man, somewhat annoyed by the micro-managing. "We brought the boat back, didn't we? If you don't trust us, get your own butt on the boat!"

Sticky knew that like himself, these men were real killers, not just rapists. He decided to tread carefully. "Not distrust, Chris. Just making sure you all don't waste your time in Tacoma again. Lessons learned and all that."

"Don't worry. Just leave this to us. You figure out how to get that MC of yours involved, or we may need to rethink this deal."

Oh, no, you didn't. Without so much as a word, Sticky raised the captured AR-15 up to his eye—*Ka-Krow!* The man standing on the stern of the cabin cruiser suddenly felt his jaw and throat explode. It caught everyone else off guard. He screamed in pure agony as blood began to shoot out of the hole in his neck. Sticky was close—he'd been aiming at the spot between the man's eyes but shot low.

The screams were intermixed with gurgling and choking as blood started to take the path of least resistance down the man's throat and windpipe. He dropped to his knees, clutching his throat with terror in his eyes. Sticky had aimed at the next man over, just in case he had any bright ideas.

"Holy hell, Sticky!" Gary White screamed. He pulled the gagging and struggling man over to the cruiser's wall and hoisted his torso onto it. The bloody deck of the boat was getting downright slippery. Gary pulled a pistol out of his waistband, chambered a round, and shot Chris Watson right through the temple. The body fell back onto the deck. Gary looked up and immediately raised his hands when he saw the rifle aimed at him. "Whaddya doin', man?!"

"You two dip-wads got any ideas about changin' plans, too?" Sticky asked him and Anthony Brady. "I thought not," when he saw two heads clearly shaking no. "Now, go get a little of everything on the shoppin' list—women, girls, boys—and bring 'em back. We need to keep the creatures on this island fed, right?" He looked over at Georgie. *Do we have to do everything ourselves?* his look silently asked.

"What about him? You guys need to come get 'im and bury 'im," Anthony suggested.

Sticky looked at the meat pile. "Give him to the crabs."

"Dad?" Natalie said loudly as she opened the front door to his small house. *Don't want to get shot.* "Dad?" she repeated.

"Natalie?" she heard the old man's voice call out. "Is that you?"

"Yes!" She could hear some rustling back in the bathroom. *What is that stench? Oh, no!* She knew immediately what the accumulation of human waste smells like. Her father suffered from congestive heart failure, high blood pressure, and emphysema, all courtesy of smoking his entire life. He was only sixty-four, but she knew he was having a hard time getting around as if his body thought it was fifteen years older.

She bumped into him as he closed the bathroom door in the tiny hallway, heading out to see her. "Hi, Grandpa!" they both heard as the kids were making their way into house.

"Ewwwwwww!" said the always honest Wesley, still not making eye contact, but definitely calling out Grandpa for the weird odor.

Katherine followed her oldest brother's example. "What stinks?" the four-year-old yelled.

"Roy?" Natalie said, giving him the look to get the kids under control.

As soon as he stepped in and smelled it, he knew there was no way they would be staying in there for the night. "C'mon kids. Let's move the stuff into the garage." After all the kids hugged and greeted Grandpa, they complied.

Once they had the room to themselves, Natalie asked him point blank, "Dad, have you been using your toilet?" She was starting to worry about him.

He looked at her eyes for a moment and then looked down at the ground. He hobbled past her and went to the old, worn-out recliner that had his butt shaped into the flat cushion. "I don't wanna talk about it."

"Dadddd..." she started.

"It's none of your business, Natalie Rose!" he insisted.

She started to tear up, not for being yelled at, but out of sympathy. *He used my middle name!* "Dad, I'm just worried about you. Have you been getting enough water? Do you have your meds?" She looked around for pill bottles as tears started to flow. The old man started to cry, too.

"You shouldn't have come," he said through small gasps. "I never wanted your kids to see me this way!"

She knelt on the floor by his feet and grabbed his hands. "We had to, Dad," she said. "We're going to Bubby's. You need to go with us."

"No! No, not that," he objected.

"You two need to bury the hatchet and start talking again," she demanded.

He looked at his kneeling daughter's eyes. "It's not that, Sweetie." He paused.

"Well then, what?" She was confused. "Why not? You can ride in the Cub! I'll walk——"

"Listen! Just give me a second here," he said to shut her down while he chose his words. "This is my home. This is where I've made my life since your mother and I got divorced." He looked out the front window. "I wouldn't even leave if I could, and I can't." He finished by looking down at his severely swollen ankles.

Her eyes followed his. "The edema…Dad, I can get you some meds. You just need——"

"No. No. Natalie?" He paused until she grew quiet. "Just…no. I'm glad I got to see your kids, again. But you all can't stay here and see me end like this!" He started crying again, sticking his wrinkled hand over to the empty tissue box and finding nothing.

I still have to tell him about Mom! Natalie's heart was breaking for her father. She started to bawl, too. "I have to tell you something about Mom."

THE ENTOURAGE of trucks and SUVs being led by one bright yellow civilian Hummer H2 rolled north and west towards Seattle, taking the same zigzag detours that any police or National Guard rigs would. In every populated area, there had subconsciously sprung up a certain few paths that had no civilian-run tolls or checkpoints. Those that profited from them didn't set them up on main thoroughfares, mainly as a way of not having law enforcers stopping and asking questions. Legion and several of his extended club members were on the way to another meet near Seattle. The roads had been cleared of the largest obstructions—trees, billboards, flipped over vehicles. Any stranded cargo trailers had been long ago stripped of goods, leaving behind empty shipping containers.

"Stop here," Legion commanded his prospect driver from the lead vehicle. The whole convoy stopped behind him. "What's up?" he heard Weasel say over the radio from the next rig back.

"Just running a little litmus test," Legion replied in the radio. To his driver he said, "See that?" He was pointing towards the front end of a dirty police cruiser, parked in a Jack-In-The-Box parking lot. "Whaddya wanna bet he takes off in the next minute?"

"Nothin'," the prospect wisely said. As if on cue, the squad car drove off and turned at the next intersection.

"Told ya," Legion boasted, not particularly impressed with himself. "It ain't exactly rocket science. The rule of the wolf pack is returning." Before his prospect could crack a joke, he looked at him and said, "You make one joke about that stupid movie, and I'll beat you senseless. Got it?"

"Crystal clear, boss," said the wise nobody.

"Keep going," Legion ordered. As the procession started back up, he scanned the road the cop turned down. *Nowhere in sight. Cowards. Won't be long before they don't even leave their compound anymore. Not when the wolves are roaming.*

THE ROOST WAS PERCHED on the military crest of the small hill east-southeast of the main compound. It wasn't much of a hill—maybe thirty feet higher than the compound itself. From there, he would have 500 to 600-meter shots over a field and between buildings. Nick had used 3D imagery on various apps to study this island for years. He knew where every structure, intersection, and field was. He would've preferred the view into the courtyard between the buildings offered by the north profile, but he wanted to be able to move south in a hurry—*just in case they make a break for their boat*. He'd parked his own boat in a small cove on the north shore and covered it with branches. It took quite a while to skirt the island and find his favored position, but he wanted the boat on the opposite side of the island's pier.

Nick had been on the island for over thirty hours at this point. The day before, he had set up two backup sniping positions—one near the primary one and one overlooking the pier—*just in case I need to chase them down. I'm here for you*, Nick told Sticky Wood subconsciously. *But I'll kill every last one of you pieces of dung if I get the chance.* Earlier, just as he had found a decent spot for his roost near the head of the pier, he caught sight of a van travelling north and a thirty-something-foot cabin cruiser departing the island. He used his spotting scope for the wider field of view to glass down and see two men dump a third man's body into the water. *Not my concern*, he told himself.

Currently he was in his primary position, looking into the courtyard, observing. He decided that if he positively identified Sticky, he would take him out immediately. After that, it was *game on*. He didn't want to die, but he figured there was no purer reason to die in battle in the entirety of human existence, than to eradicate sexual predators. He could occasionally see men milling about. He wasn't about to open fire on just anybody. *C'mon, you son of a whore. Where are you?*

17

"A fondness for power is implanted, in most men, and it is natural to abuse it, when acquired."
—Thomas Jefferson

TAHOMA'S HAMMER PLUS 22 DAYS.

THIS IS SURREAL, Charlie thought. *I feel like I'm in a bad movie.* He and seven deputies were stuffed into the back of an armored MRAP, rolling up the Canal Vista Highway as part of a convoy. They were backed by two squads of National Guard and were on the way to the West Sound Sportsman's Club to "serve warrants." *Warrants...I can't believe that's what they're calling them.* The big Native American was starting to wonder how bad things were out at one of the coastal reservations.

Their vehicle came up to the front gate area of the club's property and ground through the gravel to a halt as the deputy driving hit the brakes. It had been a bumpy ride, with major cracks in the road to avoid, coupled with the horrible suspension in the giant IED-resistant-rig. Charlie and Zeus opened the back doors and climbed out, leading the deputies on a fast walk.

"Get me Phil," he coldly barked at the man and woman on watch at the front gate. The southwest corner fighting position had been so mesmerized by the site of the rigs that they had failed to call it in. The front gate only had the sound of big tires rolling up the broken asphalt as a thirty-second warning.

"Josh to the front gate immediately!" Donna Gladstone yelled into the radio, scared.

Charlie could look onto the parking area and a little bit through the woods at the rifle line and see people scrambling. "I said Phil!" he barked. "And open this gate!" None of the sheriff's or soldiers had their slung rifles up in any kind of shooting position, but every one of them had one or both hands on their firearm, ready to use them if need be. They were all fully-kitted, as if they were about to raid a drug-house.

Josh was running across the parking lot at a full sprint, hands on his rifle to keep it from bouncing. "What the hell *is* this?" he demanded. The site of his sprint caused a couple of Guardsmen to begin covering him with their own rifles. He maintained his cool and didn't return the action as he slowed to a stop at the metal gate.

"Get Phil up here, Josh," Charlie demanded. "And get this gate swung up or that big old truck is going to roll right through it and over those sandbags." He wasn't playing.

Josh nodded at Vic and Donna to comply with the demand. This wasn't the moment to play Butch and Sundance—they'd be slaughtered. After they raised it, the deputies and soldiers began to trickle onto the property. "Phil's not here," Josh said coldly, giving Charlie a pissed off look.

"That's a load of bull if I ever heard one."

"Personal matter. Wouldn't say where he's going," Josh lied. "What is this, Charlie? You guys here to arrest someone?"

Charlie sized the former 11-Bravo combat vet up with a stare and then reached into the map pocket on the front of his plate carrier. "Here," he stated as he slammed a stack of papers into Josh's chest and passed him. "We're under orders," he began yelling out to the crowd of residents who were gathering in the parking lot, "to serve warrants of intent and confiscate firearms that are *out in the open!*"

Josh flew back around to Charlie's front. "What do you mean by 'warrant of intent'?!" he screamed, crushing the papers in his hand before he threw them at Charlie.

Charlie let the stack bounce off him and hit the mud. "It means that evidence exists that multiple residents of this property attacked and murdered residents of another property—" Charlie was interrupted by the rapidly-growing protests and vocal displeasures. This made him start to raise his voice over the crowd as he continued. "—based on physical evidence found at the scene! You are to surrender your arms! Nobody is to leave the county without checking out of the DEM's Command Post in Bartlett first!"

"This is tyranny!" erupted from the crowd, in several formats and colorful metaphors.

"What evidence?" Josh demanded

"It's all in the warrant," Charlie replied. He yelled out to the crowd once more. "You all should consider yourselves very lucky that we're not chipping you per the new protocol. We're only taking firearms that are openly carried," Charlie told the crowd as he stared directly at Josh. *And not searching your trailers and conex boxes.*

Josh didn't break his stare with Charlie's eyes as a junior soldier began to remove the slung rifle from Josh's front. His nostrils flared and his face was beet red with rage. "This is illegal!" he announced, trying and failing to regain his composure. "You're triggering things that can't be undone!" he said through clenched teeth. There was no mistaking his look—he wanted to throw a hard punch right into Charlie's Kool-Aid-hole.

That's what I'm afraid of, Charlie thought. "You would be smart to let this go."

"You tell your sheriff to bring his own butt out here and do it himself next time!" Josh dared.

Next time will be a bad day for all, Charlie thought.

"DEEPER INTO THE HILL," Josh demanded the man digging with the tractor. *We'll be ready next time.* He was directing cache construction in several spots around the property. "This is one of the ones that will only have dirt covering it, so it needs to be deep into the berm."

Burying caches was something he'd been thinking about anyway, but the confiscation they'd just been through drove home a need to prioritize it. He wasn't just burying firearms and ammo—he was safeguarding some of anything that had value: food, medicine, batteries, radios, much of the new fireworks haul—lots of things. All caches were meant to be hard to find, but some had to be quick to access. This meant a combination of techniques.

In the kitchen and office, drywall was being removed and repaired so that items could be stuffed into the insulating space. In the rifle line berm, holes were being dug with the Kubota. They used hot water tanks they'd scavenged from nearby abandoned houses. They used a small grinder to cut an opening into the end that would be nearest the opening of the long, slender, horizontal hole it was stuffed into. In the woods in various spots, darkly painted PVC of varying diameters was being lightly hidden in the brush and given paracord handles to grab onto and yank it back out in a pinch.

One of the key details was to ensure that the caches would offer decent weather protection, but the items inside would still need to be weather-tight independently. This meant a lot of cans, jugs, plastic bags, and tape. For firearms, they were coating them heavily in axle grease and then wrapping them in plastic sheeting. The water tanks and old, holey barrels that served as shooting barricades for competitions were given false wood floors to keep the items out of any puddles that formed.

Josh was still irate at the loss of a decent number of good firearms—they'd lost over half of their night scope enabled rifles—but they weren't screwed by any means. Most of the range's residents still had several in their trailers and tents. *Part of me wants to believe Charlie swayed the light search in our favor on purpose,* Josh thought. They also had the firearms they had collected from recovering Hope Braswell's body, as well as those they had confiscated after the two battles. *To the victor goes the spoils,* Josh thought glumly. *Only, there is no victory in all of this. Just lesser degrees of losing.*

TAHOMA'S HAMMER Plus 23 Days.

PHIL HAD A HARD TIME SLEEPING. *How can they be snoring?* he wondered. The church pews were packed—even the floors had a lot of people sleeping on makeshift pads. He had his gear and had been tempted to set up a hammock but decided against it. He didn't want to seem rude to the people who were probably living here for the unforeseeable future. He was trying to use his gear as a pillow while on the floor.

The evening before had evolved into a two-hour storytelling of sorts, as Phil asked people about what had happened to the Reverend. None of them knew for sure. The rumor on the street was that the National Guard had killed him, not the gangs.

"In fact, we think one of the gangs was escortin' him home," Jerome revealed.

"Hmmm," Phil said. "I take it some of them used to go to church here?"

"Yeah," Jerome told him, nodding. "He was loved and respected by everyone around here."

They sat silently while Phil pondered his next questions. "Any chance the local gangs are going to start comin' after all of you?"

"Why d'ya think we guard the stoop?" Jerome countered. "Man is by nature sinful. An' when people get hungry, they forget stealing's a sin."

"And murder," Phil said quietly, as an afterthought.

"Pardon?"

He cleared his throat. "They forget that murder is a sin, too. And that murder and killing aren't necessarily the same thing." He wasn't thinking about gang members when he said it. Directly to Martha, he gingerly asked, "Would you mind if I see the clothes he was wearing that night?"

She was a bit shocked. "Why, dear? What good could come of it?"

"Honestly, probably nothing," Phil said. "There's just this nagging thought in my head…" He hoped that would be enough and was rewarded. Martha went into one of the rooms at the far end of the church and came back out a minute later with a box.

She had tears in her eyes when she handed the box to Phil. "I haven't really even looked at it myself."

"Thank you, ma'am." He couldn't think of anything to say that would comfort her. He opened the lid and pulled out the reverend's pants. "Looks like they laundered everything," he said softly. He had Jerome and several other's full attention. Phil pulled out the shirt and coat and laid them out on a pew. After staring for several seconds, he opened the coat and put the shirt in it to see where the man had been shot. Then it dawned on him…

"Jerome," he said, asking with a nod if he would follow him outside. To Martha he said, "Would you mind if I stayed here tonight?"

"You'll always be welcome with me, Phil, and I'm sure the Lord don't mind you bein' in His house, neither!"

"I'm going out to grab my stuff, then." He gave her a quick hug and then headed out the church's main entrance followed by his new friend.

"What'd you see?" Jerome said.

"Something I didn't like. What do most of the gangs around here carry?" Phil asked.

"Nine-mil, just like everywhere else," Jerome answered with a quizzical look.

"Hmmm. That's what I thought," Phil said, not believing what the facts told him.

"What?" Jerome asked, his voice lowering a bit as his face turned even more stone-like.

"Those holes are less than a quarter-inch," he explained. "Could be a common .22, but more likely .223 or 5.56 because of the damage it caused." He wanted to test Jerome's deduction against his own.

"You sayin' the streets may be tellin' the truth??" Jerome was pissed.

"Only way to know for sure is to ask someone who was there and decide if they're lying," Phil answered. *And I got a feeling the Guard has already lied about it.* "But, yeah, that's what I think."

Phil decided to wait the night out. Jerome and some others helped him get his Jeep around to the back—the church's public lot was much too likely to be robbed on a nightly basis. He'd spent the night there, getting a true sense of foreboding as they heard gunfire, yelling, screeching tires, and screams most of the night. There were no lights to cast shadows, even when cars drove by. Everybody had figured out to disable every light on their vehicle when they drove at night. Nobody wanted to say, *Hey, everybody, here I am—rob and kill me.* Anyone driving was probably on gang business, as it was. Fuel had become much too valuable to waste. At one point, Phil thought he even heard a couple of wild dog packs wandering around hunting. *Mama never called me smart,* he thought, as he decided he needed to talk to that gang when the sun came up.

Snohomish County, Washington had been preparing for at least one aspect of a massive natural disaster for several years. As one of the counties that houses a state prison—the Monroe Correctional Facility —they had been pushing the state for extra money and people ever since 9/11, most of a generation earlier. They had prepared for the capability to ensure that should the state fail, they would be able to provide for the guards and their families for up to four months. Indeed, the foresight had become invaluable. Despite some structural damage, the newer buildings in the facility had withstood the quakes. They released the least violent twenty percent of the inmates within two days.

The county had implemented their various emergency responses, including building a tent city for the prison guards at nearby Monroe High School. Without the ability to feed the prisoners for much longer, though, the prison officials themselves had to make a quiet decision. They released another forty percent of the prison population, retaining only the worst offenders, most of them members of organized gangs. In essence, they allotted some of the food that had been stored for guard staff and used it to be able to retain the worst-of-the-worst for a few months until the relief started to trickle in.

The guards that had actually come to the prison had known they could bring their families to be protected, which was a powerful remover of leverage from the criminals inside. They had been corralled into much tighter confines so the guards could be closer together. At just over three weeks into the post-disaster efforts, the prison and county officials had started to feel that all of their planning efforts were starting to find an equilibrium. If only they'd planned for RPGs and mortars.

One rocket-propelled grenade would probably not have completely breached the main gate at the prison—which is why Reynaldo chose to employ three at every guard tower along the back of the property. He also had mortar teams targeting the main gate and front side towers. The hardened structures were not intended to repel small bombs from directly above. Once the perimeter was breached, a few more RPGs shot into the main building convinced the remaining staff to give up. Reynaldo rewarded them with a relatively quick firing-squad death.

A mere fifty minutes after their initial attack and he was standing on the back of a tow truck with a bullhorn in hand, addressing the remaining 779 former prisoners. "My friends," he said in near-perfect English, "you may be surrounded by my army now, but at your feet is the moment you were born for." He let that linger for a moment or two. "Not all of you are cut out for my all-star team...but most of you are." He looked around. There was a soft hum of silent conversation drifting from the men corralled on the softball field.

Rey continued. "Many of you were enemies. That will end now. Close that chapter. Start the next one." He gave a small wave to a unit of men who had contained a large percentage of the white prisoners—not every white prisoner, but those who openly sported white supremacist markings. All of them had been forced at gunpoint to lie in the mud in front of all the rest. Ka-*Ka-Ka-Ka-Ka-Ka-Krow!* His men started to shoot them in the back of their heads. A few had tried to scramble to their feet when the shooting started, but they were vastly outnumbered. In all, sixty-seven white racists had been killed in a matter of three seconds.

Every prisoner had some sort of reaction, regardless of their ethnicity. "Brothers!" Rey yelled into his hand-mic to get the loud buzz to die back down, "I've been advised by my leaders that I cannot trust the Blacks, the Whites, the Asians... Is this true?"

A raucous course broke out, as men emboldened by this new vision all cheered out, hoping for an opportunity. The vast majority were thrilled just for the chance to escape, but almost all of them recognized what was happening—this Mexican Army was going to take over the Pacific Northwest, one city at a time. *Better to join than die,* most of them thought.

"Los policias ya casi estan aqui," Rey heard in his earpiece.

"Hermanos…Brothers…the time to stop killing each other is here. Join us! Help us rebuild a society for the strong! The pigs and the Army are moving in. Now is your chance to join us in the fight for our New World!"

Rey began firing a rifle into the air, and hundreds of new members of his army roared in unison. He watched his men back a truck into the crowd and begin issuing weapons and orders to their new soldiers. They had anticipated a response from the local police and National Guard. He had an overwatch poised to launch two javelin anti-tank missiles right down Highway 522 into the column of response vehicles. *They have no idea what they're up against,* Rey thought as he smiled.

18

Cleansing Breaths.

TAHOMA'S HAMMER PLUS 12 DAYS.

NICK HAD a choice to make and plenty of time to think about it on that long hike home. He had qualified with a few different platforms in the Army, and in the years since, had purchased the civilian equivalents. He knew immediately he didn't need his Barrett 50-caliber. *Don't need that distance on that island. A lot of weight, considering I might need to fight my way back to the boat.* He truly loved his Remington 700, most similar to the M24 he started his career with. The stand-out choice for this mission had been the Knights Armament SR-25. It was chambered in .308, and he trusted it out to eight hundred meters, even in the crosswinds he expected.

This twenty-inch model was fairly new—it had been purchased for him as a retirement present, and he'd spent the years since tricking it out for this mission. On the front was a quick-disconnect suppressor. He had folding bi-pod legs and a dual-system scope mount, which held an expensive Leupold sight and in front of that, a clip-on PVS-30 sniper's night sight. He preferred very light triggers on his work platforms in the Army, but for the expected dual-role of this model, he kept a heavier, two-stage trigger that would be forgiving in engaged combat. He also had a standard sixteen-inch barrel AR-15 in the boat as Murphy insurance. Other than those two rifles, he had brought with him only a Glock 17 with an RMR red-dot sight and an Esee fixed-blade knife.

He looked through the spotting scope one last time to check the wider field for last minute surprises. After two-and-a-half days of waiting—*several years, actually,* he corrected himself—the reason he still lived in Washington state was in front of him. They were having some sort of assembly in the common area between all the buildings. There was a pretty hyped up crowd ranting and worked up over something. *Could have to do with the van that came from the pier this morning. I wonder if that boat came back?*

He'd buried the better of the two roosts that covered the main compound a little farther back into the trees. The back-up roost was farther east—it still covered any escape toward the pier but had much less angle into the center courtyard. His range finder was hanging around his neck, as was a back-up pair of binoculars. He had to be ready if he needed to abandon the spotting scope. *627 meters.* He did some quick math and figured out the bullet would need three-quarters of a second to lob to its target—plenty of time for the crosswind to push it right-to-left.

He started deep, cleansing breaths, breathing in through his nostrils and slowly out through his mouth. *Slow the heart rate.* This one was personal. The rush reminded him of the first few of his career. *Breathe…Slowly exhale…*He had his body positioned directly in line with the rifle, feet spread apart and flat, toes pointing out. *No parallax in the site? Check. Good solid pull into the shoulder? Check. Cheek weld? Check. One last breath in, exhale it half-way...squeeze…*

THE GRACE FAMILY had stayed in Natalie's father's garage for the night. Roy had found an old propane camping heater and a couple of one-pound bottles. He'd found the twenty-pound bottle for the home BBQ, too, but he doubted the old man had the cheap cable and adaptor to enable it to hook up to their camping stove. Nevertheless, he added the big bottle and a few tools to their kitty. Roy had also reminded his wife that her father owned a .357 revolver, which she asked for and was gifted. She had mixed emotions on that, knowing that as dark as the thought was, leaving it might be the more humane alternative to the death that was coming for him. Ultimately, she remembered something that had helped her cope with her mother's death—*God chooses when, not us.*

On the evening of arrival, Natalie and Roy had busied the kids with getting the chicken tractor onto some grass and tying up the goats while she told her husband the entire scoop. He was no fonder of the idea of leaving the old man behind than she was, but they both knew that getting their kids to Uncle Bubby's was the first priority.

The next morning, the drizzle had finally evolved into rain. Everyone was buttoned up tightly. She made sure the kids and Roy had an adequate goodbye with Grandpa. *I think James understands that this will be the last time. Wesley will, too, but he probably won't show emotion about it. Katherine won't even remember him!* This made her tear up again as she watched the farewells.

Animals tethered, Roy shepherded the kids and "wagon train" to the end of the driveway to give his wife some space. He knew she was the toughest member and leader of the family but that she would be fragile for a while.

"Dad," she said through tears as she leaned in to hug him and kiss him on the cheek. "I love you so much!" The water works started. "I feel like this is the last time I'll ever see you."

"No, honey. We'll meet again," the old man said, smiling

through his own tears. "I love you, too. I'm so sorry you had to see your mother suffer. I think you're old enough to get that despite being divorced, we still loved each other."

"Yes…I get it," she nodded.

"Tell your brother," he started, pausing to collect himself. She waited patiently. "Tell him I'm sorry." The memories of a painful past of regrets he had as a father made him start bawling again.

"I will," she said through her own emotion.

"Tell him," he continued, "that I wish I'd gotten to know his family better, and that I'm proud of him for standing up to me and making his own life!"

Natalie embraced her father for a while longer, finally letting go and turning. She chose not to look back, preferring to close the painful chapter and start moving forward into a scary and uncertain future.

THE BARRICADE HAD BEEN BUILT with the nearest resource in large quantity—downed logs and river rock. At the head of their road on the south side of the river, Earl and Conner had instructed the residents in how to construct a zigzag pattern out of logs that would allow cars and trucks to work their way through slowly. They used the quads to haul river rock up and reinforce the gaps from the logs to the forest hill on the south side of the choke point and build a wall to the bridge on the north.

The bridge was on the crossroad and led north to a similar road on that side of the river. Like theirs, that road was sparsely populated with homes every three to five acres. After working with the various residents in the principles of watch-standing for a few days, Earl had decided to go check on that road. He and Conner were slowly walking across the bridge, armed, but elbows bent up a bit to show their hands.

"You gettin' that sense?" Conner asked. He was referring to the feeling they'd had in Iraq when they knew they were being watched.

"Yep," Earl said.

The partners subconsciously spread themselves apart. Whereas in peace time they would walk next to each other like anyone else, in alert-mode they had spread out about fifteen feet. As they crossed and rounded the bend where the road went along the river, they saw an elaborate chokepoint crossing it. They were surprised to see several men and women, all of whom were well-armed. There was a teenager pushing a garden-cart behind two of the women and one man, who didn't seem to be part of the guards. Those four were on the near-side of the intricate gate and walking toward Earl and Conner, smiling.

"Don't be alarmed!" the older of the women said.

Earl could see a few other people still on watch on the far side of the gate. They were using the big plastic jersey barriers that could be filled with water for weight. The barriers had been spray painted a camo pattern. Their zigzag had two, parallel lanes. At the far end of those lanes was a huge log tethered to an old pickup with chain. It looked ready to be pulled in front of the lanes to allow for an instant cut-off. There was a decent-sized wooden shed kit with an asphalt shingle roof that had been constructed. *Makes a rainy night on watch quite tolerable,* Earl figured. He saw that the cart had a big jug and some supplies in it.

"We brought you guys some coffee!" she said. "Please—come in and have a seat!"

Earl and Conner looked at each other as they closed their own gap and approached. They both knew that if there had been danger, they would've died having never seen it coming. "I'm impressed," Earl opened, looking around. "You all didn't just happen to throw this together. I'm Earl."

"Conner," his wingman introduced himself.

"I'm Vince," the graying-man in his early seventies said. The mother-daughter combo introduced themselves as Erin and Lacey as they all went into the little shack on the other side of the gate. Earl noticed the men and women still on watch and the teen with the cart had maintained their sense of alertness to the outside world, even as they passed through. Everyone was armed—even the teen— and well-equipped. *Serious folks,* Earl thought. Lacey brought the coffee urn and stuff in from the cart.

The shack was about eight feet wide by twelve feet deep. It had a table, chairs, lantern and radios being charged by a bank of car batteries. *Must be solar on top.* There was a large map on the wall that showed every property by address. Earl started studying it.

Erin saw his gaze. "Just a quick reference. We don't want to give away too much detail to any invaders," she explained.

"I'm *still* impressed," Earl said. "I'm retired Army. That's hard to do. And, you all were expecting us, which tells me you have a good perimeter and communication system running. I didn't see any antennas on this building, but I'm guessing you have some in the trees…maybe even a mesh network."

"Go on," Erin urged as she sipped some coffee.

A test…MMM-kayyy…"Coffee to spare. I'm betting that won't run out for months. Maybe years. Those barricades were already out here, somewhere…" He looked at Conner. *What am I missing?*

"You didn't just know we were coming," his bestie took over. "You knew we were worthy of a sit-down. That means you've been reconning our side of the river." He nodded his head towards the door. "The junior high kid outside is strapped. That means you all are not only highly trained, but your kids are, too. And, everyone trusts each other's kids to have firearms. You aren't just neighbors. You're family. Some of you anyhow."

Vince chuckled. "Just cuz I'm Hispanic doesn't mean I can't be part of the family!"

The usually flippant Conner was caught off-guard. "I—I… wasn't—I'm not…"

"Relax, Con-Man, he's screwing with you," Earl said, taking his brother off the hook. Everyone but Conner and Lacey were laughing. "I'm guessing you were a Joe, too," he said to Vince.

"That was long ago. I was a Huey 'Slick' crew chief. Took that trainin' and became a full-fledged helicopter mechanic."

"HUA," Earl said with the familiar Army groan. "We gettin' warm?" he asked Erin.

"Baby!" Erin exclaimed, who was probably in her mid-fifties. "You guys are on fire! You Army, too?" she asked Conner.

"75th Rangers. Vet, not retired. I've been an equipment operator for several years."

"What brought you guys across the bridge?" Vince queried.

"Well…unlike you all, the south side of the river is occupied by well-meaning but ill-trained folks," Earl explained. "We have a basic check-point set up. Conner and I decided to see where this road went." He looked back and forth at all three of his hosts. "I guess our northern flank is secure." This elicited a small chuckle from Erin and Vince. Earl looked at Lacey. "I noticed you don't say much."

"I speak when I got something to say." The look on the young woman's face was set in stone.

Got ya, Earl said with his look. "Roger that." To Erin, "We'll get out of your hair. Thanks for the cuppa joe. Doubt you all need anything from us, but…maybe we should set up some sort of comms strategy to alert each other…"

"You said what I was thinkin', Earl," Erin agreed. The group as a whole went outside and prepared to separate. Lacey loaded the cart and started heading east. Erin turned back to Conner and Earl. "My daughter's been through a real rough patch."

So has mine. "No explanation needed," Earl assured her before changing the topic. "Can I ask you how long you all have been preparing? I gotta admit I'm just a bit jealous. It's like you hypnotized your neighbors and ordered them to be preppers."

"Years, darlin'," Erin said. "Vince and I are just the reception committee. Some of us are related," she said, answering Conner's guess, " but mostly we're all just friends that've been working together on this for a long, long time. Eventually someone bought a place out here. Rest followed suit as life allowed 'em to. People around here know us all as Phalanx."

Like the Spartans, Earl realized. He stuck his hand out for both of them to shake. "I've got some radios. Let me get a few other people from my side to come back this time tomorrow. There's a few like me an' Conner that aren't completely helpless. You should meet them." *And help me train them,* he didn't add as they left.

KA-KROW! The lower brainpan of a man fifteen feet in front of and to Sticky's left dissolved as if it were a flesh-colored water balloon filled with red paint. Blood and brain coated everyone between the two. Almost simultaneously, Chuck O'Reilly's chest to Sticky's right caved in. That three-quarters of a second for bullet-travel had been enough time for the walking man to literally be in the wrong place at the wrong time. The thin bone of the face was not enough resistance to skew the bullet's trajectory very far...but it was enough to deflect it into Chuck. Fate had saved Sticky Wood.

Ka-Krow! Ka-Krow! It wasn't conscious thought that drove Sticky straight down to the ground like an eight-penny nail—it was the subconscious survival mechanism that triggers fight or flight. Not everybody possessed it. *Ka-Krow!* Another chest exploded. Then two more heads. But Sticky's mind was in full-alert. *Body parts don't explode,* his subconscious mind said. *Lower yourself to the ground rapidly. Here, let me help.* His knees went limp, and after two full seconds of staring at the five—*No! That's six!* —victims on the ground, he started low-crawling like mad. Any drill sergeant would have been proud. No butts were sticking up in the air *that* day. Seeing the flyswatter up close was a powerful motivator.

Most of the resident-perverts had run into various buildings. Sticky had crawled back into the main rec facility. *How many of them are there?* It took him several minutes to work up the courage to crawl around in the building. The sniping had slowed and then ceased after the targets had all disappeared. *Holy crap! Double crap! Cops? No! Maybe...naw! That's someone else...He's a...* Sticky actually smiled when he caught himself getting ready to think it. "Up yours, Predator!" he yelled to nobody in particular. Just like the day the hammer fell, Sticky started laughing uncontrollably. The rest of the men sheltering in that building just looked at him as if he'd gone mad.

Look at 'em all. "Dealers of death and destruction" until it's their neck on the chopping block! Sticky reveled in the opportunity. His first instinct was to start helping the sniper. *I could take all the pedos out, for sure,* he thought. He ultimately decided against it. Numbers were safety. *There's just one or two guys out there. Why would I reduce their number of targets?* He looked around at the terrified residents. *Shoe's on the other foot, now, ain't it, perverts?* He decided he would make someone go out and "play canary" after dark.

19

"The two toughest kids on the block, I guess. Sooner or later, they gonna fight."

—Lt. Col. Andy Tanner

Tahoma's Hammer Plus 23 Days.

In the weeks since the events, both China and Russia had been making motions. Each was motivated by the intense desire to feed its population. Each also had ulterior motives. For Russia, it came down to proving after the thirty-plus year gap since the *first* Cold War ended that they had been right all along. For China, it came down to the fact that they felt they were due. It was their turn to be the world's provider, protector, and dominating superpower. Their *system of government* was less than a century old, but their *culture* was almost five thousand years old. *It's. Our. Turn.*

The former biggest kid on the block—the U.S.—now had a

broken arm. Russia and China, while both establishing aggressive foreign policies towards the U.S., were now eyeballing each other, squaring up. Trains in both countries were starting to load up with troops and gear and move toward their mutual border to conduct exercises. Navies started loading ordnance and food onto ships. Both bullies figured they'd better fight each other at full-strength and get that broken arm kid afterwards. The trickle-down effects of Tahoma's Hammer were getting dangerous for the entire world.

"YOU'LL NEED to pay a toll 'bout two blocks that way," Jerome told Phil. "Once through there, about four to five blocks north ought to get you the audience you seek." He gave Phil a concerned glance. "I still think you need to reconsider this."

That'll put me a couple of blocks from the house Crane was renting, Phil thought solemnly. "You're the latest on a growing list of people to tell me that," Phil told the big man with a small smile. He stuck his hand out. "Take care of these people, my friend. Come summer, I'll make sure some of our yield makes its way down here." The church had fed Phil some soup, and Martha had insisted he stay for their daily prayer vigil. It was already late morning by the time he made ready to leave.

Jerome gave him a firm handshake and a respectful nod and stepped back from the jeep. A month earlier, these two men from different worlds would have hardly looked at each other at the gas station or grocery store. That distinction was not lost on people from different cultures who had to start earning trust with actions, not words. Phil figured that most modern racial strife was probably more about cultural differences rather than skin tone. In the grand scheme, Phil didn't care what the scholars decided—he just cared if the people around him shared the same core value—*treat others well.*

With the clunkiness of a half-sized clutch leg, he caressed the Jeep to the intersection and turned east. Just as Jerome predicted, he rolled up to a series of cars and lit barrels forcing him to stop. The three young men and women staffing this checkpoint approached the jeep with caution. They weren't openly carrying firearms, but Phil was sure he was in someone's sights at that moment.

"Turn around. Leave," he was ordered by the tallest one. He looked of Islander descent and had tattoos on the backs of his hands sticking out from under his raincoat. He started to eyeball the jeep with the look of a wolf.

Phil was scanning the other three as they started to surround him. *Don't get tunnel vision.* "I'm trying to set up a meet with the Terrytown Kings," Phil said. "I can pay the fee."

"TK don't want to meet you," the lead guard said. "An' you can't afford the fee."

"Bet I can," Phil said. He nodded towards the tennis racket bag on the passenger seat.

"Slowly, brah," the man said.

Phil could sense their unease. He unbuckled the far seatbelt and pulled the bag toward himself. He barely unzipped the side pocket, pulling out a sandwich bag with a hundred rounds of 22-caliber ammo and fifty rounds of 9mm. He lightly tossed it to the man.

He scanned it and looked back up at Phil. "What else is in the bag?"

"There's a hefty fee to find out," Phil said coldly. He kept his eyes locked on the man's eyes. *If I'm going down, you're the one I'm killing in the process,* his eyes said.

After a tense moment, the man nodded the rest of his crew back to their post. "Go north until you can't go no mo'," the man said.

Phil cautiously snaked the jeep through the fiery barrels and cars and slowly drove north at the next intersection. Many of the older houses in this part of Bartlett had been shaken off their foundations. Some had collapsed. Trees were laying on others. The entire area reeked of human waste, as every low spot was a pool where the rain kept pushing stuff. There were fires in the front of some houses. Phil deduced those were probably a marker for the ones that were intact.

There were boards over windows and wind-damaged tarps flapping from broken roofs.

He was five blocks along when a gray Chevy pick-up with five armed men in the back pulled in front of him and came to a stop. He slowed down and checked his mirrors, which confirmed the same thing happening behind him with an older blue truck. *Ambush 101…If I make a run for it, my clutching alone would let them catch me. Here goes nothing.*

On the slow drive up, he'd pulled the AR pistol out of the case and slung it around his neck, leaving it in his lap. As he put the rig in neutral and set the parking brake, he slowly unbuckled the seatbelt and stepped out. When he did, the AR yanked down with a motion, revealing itself to the locals. Phil had his hands up just high enough to be above his elbows. He'd left the jeep running for obvious reasons. He scanned around. The men in the truck to his rear were still in the back of the pickup. He figured that truck was poised for the chase, should he decide to rabbit. The five men to his front were slowly spreading out, and the one in the center was approaching.

He was a tough looking Filipino in a brown trench coat and leather plateau hat. *He looks like an Asian Stevie Ray Vaughan,* Phil thought. "You made a mistake coming here," he said. "Bad mistake, dead man."

Phil knew there was only one way out of this pickle, and it involved both luck and earned respect. In one swift motion he grabbed the pistol, flipping off the safety as he raised it to the firing position aimed at the man ten yards to his front. He could feel the blood start to pound in his temples as the adrenaline started to surge. He waited for the impact of a bullet to his skull. *One second. Two seconds…*

"I'm here to talk. Tell them to stand down," Phil said coolly. The man before him was a cool cat with crazy in his eyes. He just stared at Phil, smiling as if deciding whether or not he was going to pick that day to die. "It's about the Reverend Sherman Robertson!" The man's delay had spooked Phil into thinking he needed to keep trying. "I know the soldiers killed him!" Pandering wasn't beneath Phil when he was outnumbered ten-to-one.

This was enough to spark curiosity with the gang leader. "You first," he told Phil. Phil scanned the others and all four of them were still squarely beaded on shooting him. He slowly lowered his weapon to low-ready. The leader looked at the others and nodded, causing them to lower their weapons. "So...whatcha want, dead man?"

"I want to hear the story about how 'the man' shot the Reverend from those that were there," Phil replied.

This seemed to genuinely surprise the gangster. "Gonna cost you, bro. That jeep," he said smirking and nodding at the vehicle. Phil knew they were going to take it anyway. It pissed him off, but he knew he had to bury that for a time when he was out of danger. He nodded at the man. This was the moment he realized he might just get to see Caroline and Crane again, very soon.

"Spring?" Stu asked. "I don't know, Josh...I know I can't string you guys along, but I need to go check on my folks."

"I get that, Doc, but I'm thinking about Payton. She's well past half-way on this pregnancy. It's mutually beneficial for you to stay here with us, too," Josh explained.

"Oh, I know," Stu said. He'd had enough life experiences in the prior twenty-four days to appreciate the people around him—and their capabilities. The arrogant Stuart Schwartz was dead, and the new one didn't particularly miss him. "And I truly appreciate you all for putting me up here. If it weren't for needing to get to Sequim, I'd be committed to the cause..."

"What if our radio guys can get hold of someone up there. Do a welfare check." *What if they find out your folks are dead,* he didn't add.

"That's something to consider, for sure," Stu confirmed. "But in reality, they're going to need me. They're in their seventies, after all."

"Sure, Doc, I get that." Josh was silent while pulling up the words for his Plan B. "How about this—go get them and bring them back."

This caused the light bulb to come on over Stu's head. "That might be worth thinking about..." He discarded the idea fairly quickly, though. "Except we're moving toward winter. I don't know if I could get there, convince them, and get back that quickly. I mean, we both know that this will be on foot. It literally takes an army to drive anywhere now-a-days."

He's got me on that one, Josh thought. *And we can't spare the people to take him...or could we?* "Tell you what, Stu. Let's both agree to think some more before any decisions are made."

"Sure thing," the good doctor agreed.

Josh left Stu's little cubby hole and headed toward the front gate. As he passed the end of the rifle line structure, he looked at what was the back wall of Stu's office. *This is like fifty feet from the gate. Need to line this wall with sandbags!* When he got to the gate guards, he talked to them while they all watched a couple of wanderers. He could see Tyler's daily patrol slowly driving down the road from the north in a pick-up truck. They opened the lower gate and let them drive down. *Looks like they scored quite a bit of canned goods and gasoline today...*

As the patrol members piled out, a few other range members came over and started helping unload. Josh helped with the chores. As the group eventually dispersed, Tyler and Teddy Wilson started towards their tent holding hands.

Gene Hackett just stared. Then he looked at Josh for a moment, then looked back. "Those two brothers sure are close," he mused.

Josh almost laughed out loud and could see thorough confusion on the man's face. *Might as well get ahead of this...* "You mean husbands," he corrected him.

"Huh?" Gene was a bit slow on the uptake. "What?"

"They're married. Pretty much everyone knows," Josh explained.

"Oh, for Pete's sake! Does Phil know?"

Josh wasn't sure, but he knew it wouldn't have mattered. "Yep. Why? What's the matter?"

"I'm just surprised, I guess," the middle-aged man said. "They don't seem gay."

"Not all gay people act queer, Gene. Most of my gay friends don't." *I thought everyone understood this by now.* "Is this really a problem for you?" Josh was a little concerned.

"No. Not as long as my Christian beliefs are equally respected." He could see the doubt on Josh's face. "Seriously. Recent history is full of examples of Christians having the viewpoints of others crammed down their throats, usually in court. I respect those two, because I know I'm no better than them. But I won't cause any drama as long as they don't."

"Judging by the fact that you *just learned* about them being gay, it seems that they've already proven they won't. Right?" Before Gene could answer, Josh headed off to find Payton for some quality time before he got trapped into a philosophical conversation. *People are in for some tough conversations as this thing plays out. People need to learn to respect the ones they don't necessarily agree with.*

"You got balls, dude. I'll give you that," the older man seated across from Phil said. "Giant, hairy ones."

He had been taken to a house one block north and two blocks east. He was sitting across the dining table just off of what used to be the living room in the older home. Phil presumed the man to be about his own age. He was also of Filipino heritage. Phil noticed that the entire group was Filipino or Islander.

I need to connect with this guy. "Reverend Robertson was my friend.

I just want to know the truth about what happened. Word is that you guys were escorting him that night."

"That's true."

"So…was that just for general safety, or was there some threat on the Reverend? Another gang…"

"All of the above, homes," the man said. "This heavily medicated society is fresh out of their stock. Plenty of crazies out there. 'Specially at night."

"All of the above…" Phil repeated. "So, he had some sort a threat against him?"

"Word is that some of the others weren't happy with him feeding and helping people clean up," the man said matter-of-factly.

"Who actually shot him?" Phil said, getting to the point.

"Why, brah? You won't accept it anyways…"

"It was them, wasn't it?" Phil said, already knowing the truth.

"What's it matter?" the old mad asked again, laughing. "The people in charge always been shootin' whoever they want. Just seems you white dudes forgot that for the last hundred years. Some friend o' yours gets shot and now you care?"

"So why did you guys protect him?" Phil asked, unsure what he might hear.

"Most of us are Catholic," he said, looking around. "But all the black and white kids 'round here grew up going to that church. Robertson was a good dude. Not a pedo. Cared equally for the whole flock, you might say." The man paused and looked up, searching for his closing words. "He was old. People like him aren't gonna make it long in this world."

"Old people?" Phil asked, appreciating the moment and hoping he still had a way out of this. *Need to connect!* "You and I are old compared to the rest of these guys."

"No, homes, I mean nice people." The man made a small nod toward The Hat, who with a second man, swooped in behind Phil and grabbed his arms and shoulders. He struggled to use his one full leg to stand, but they were too strong and fast. They hauled him out of the chair and tried to force him to his knees. As he succumbed to the force, his below-knee prosthetic became askew a bit and turned awkwardly.

"Yooooo!" The Hat said. "Dude has a fake leg!"

Dammit!!! Phil was screaming in his head. He was scanning with his eyes, both arms still under the full control of two powerful men. Counting the old honcho, there were six of them. *I'm in deep kinchee here!*

"You shoulda never pointed my new gun at me!" The Hat hissed into Phil's ear.

The honcho had stood up by then, slowly moving around his men to see the fake leg. "Hmmpphh. You a vet?" he asked Phil.

Phil was breathing heavily from the small struggle and stress. He tried to calm down, but said a very pissed off, "Yeah!" *Try to connect,* he told himself. "You?"

"Uh-huh," the man said. "But stuff like that just don't matter no more, brah."

20

Cat and Mouse.

TAHOMA'S HAMMER PLUS 13 DAYS.

NICK'S ALARM woke him up as the cloud-blocked sun was lowering. It was turning the wet, nasty day into a dark gray instead of a light one. There was no need for a radio, so he left it in the hidden boat. This freed up his ear for an earbud. *Guess the phone was still handy for something. Glad I put it on the small solar panel.* He had a career's worth of experience to know how deep he could catch some Z's out in the field. Logic told him that the initial volley would hunker all of them down for at least a couple of hours. He knew it would be a long couple of days, so he got some rest after moving to the back-up roost.

Nick left his helmet and mounted night vision in his pack, relying only on the night vision mounted on the rifle to watch the field and structures before him. At about one-and-a-half hours after dusk, he saw movement. *Predictable. One fat perv. Must be a child rapist. Shame to let him go.* He was going to let as many single runners go as it took to convince Sticky that the coast was clear. *He'll be in the middle of a big pack.*

The fat rapist made it all the way from one building to another. Ten minutes later, Nick saw another leave the first building and start running for the trees across the wide open field. *Headed for the pier. C'mon, little mouse. Draw them all out.* He waited. He checked his six to make sure he wasn't being sneaked up on himself. When he reacquired his zone, he saw four more running to the southeast. Patience. *They'll start flowing soon—just like the time in Ethiopia.*

Ten minutes later, *Bingo! Looks like a zombie horde. Must be fifty of them. Look at 'em all run! Most of them are out of shape—they'll be too tired to run back once I start.* He let the front of the pack get two hundred meters from the building—almost halfway across the gap to the next tree line—when he started plinking targets. *Ka-Krow! Ka-Krow!* The SR-25 used twenty-round magazines. By the time he emptied one, the pack was too scattered to keep an eye on without a spotter— especially at night. *Shoot…I'd better get to the pier roost and get that boat out of commission. No telling if I got him yet.* He stood up, threw off his ghillie suit, threw on his pack, and started a speed-run through the forest.

He got to his pier-roost about twelve minutes later. He was breathing heavily, which meant his one-shot kill-ratio was going to drop significantly. *You got soft in retirement,* he kicked himself. He could see a few of the younger ones trickling in off the road. He had a choice to make—open fire on the boat's engine compartment and send everyone scurrying or let Sticky flush himself. He hoped that he'd already gotten him and that all he needed to do was kill them all to verify it. He knew his luck wasn't that good, though.

Wait, his instinct told him. He knew the boat wouldn't fire up until whoever the top dog was had ordered it. *What the… Well, dang, scumbag's smarter than I gave him credit for.* Entering the area that fed the pier was a tightly-packed group of men all holding a large amount of brush and branches next to their part of the mob. It looked like a giant bush with about two dozen feet. *Nothin' a little infrared can't fix...*

Nick calmly pulled the battle helmet out of his pack and removed the mounted night vision. He pulled the little FLIR monocular out of its case and mounted it onto the helmet. He swung it down in front of his non-dominant eye after he donned the helmet. The walking bush had made it another thirty meters in that time. Through his FLIR, he could clearly see the men's individual body heat. He picked the one in the middle of the pack and opened fire.

Whoever that was dropped like a bad habit while the rest scurried. He flipped the FLIR back up since they dropped the cover they were holding. He resisted the urge to shoot at will, scanning the crowd for the face he'd memorized years earlier. He heard the boat fire up. *Crap!*

He looked on the pier and saw a flurry of activity as seven or eight men were trying to board the vessel and cast off lines. He saw Sticky dive into the cabin of the boat and splintered the helm panel with a shot that was a milli-second too late. The boat lurched forward. He shot the rest of the men he could see, but whoever was throttling was hiding behind a bench that he couldn't see around. *Ka-Ka-Ka-Krow!* He started opening fire on the engine compartment by shooting through the boat's transom. *I could sure use that Barrett right about now!* What he lacked in grain-weight with the .308, he made up for with volume. He switched mags and kept dumping rounds into the engine compartment. Smoke started to roll out of it. *Yes!*

Nick Williams was in full combat mode. He started packing up his gear, ready to run the three miles down the back roads of the island as fast as possible. Their boat was wounded with a head start. They wouldn't make it far. *Need to get to my boat!*

· · ·

Tahoma's Hammer Plus 14 Days.

Nick got back to his fishing boat and dragged the branches and brush off it, trying to flip it uphill into the woods so that it wouldn't become caught in his prop. He untied it from the tree and shoved off, dropping his pack and setting down his rifle. It was dark and rainy. *Take a breath. Another minute won't hurt. Make a plan.* He started the engine and let it get warmed up while he continued to drift out a few feet, engaging it into reverse and letting it slowly pull him out a bit more. *Maps…*

He went to his pack and pulled out his Garmin full-screen GPS device and put it into its holder above the steering wheel. He turned it on, memorizing the shape of the shoreline for the next island to the northeast and the main body of Tacoma to the south. *Engine's warm. Need to make up time.* He hit the throttle and started to steer for due east.

He was hoping to see something obvious, but visibility sucked. As he started to clear McNeil Island, he took the throttle down to troll for a few moments, listening for sounds. The rain and wind were too loud—they also had made any smoke trail break apart. *Son of a—!* Nick was pissed that the one person he was after may have slipped past him. He powered back up and decided to speed over to the most likely land mass that they would've headed towards—Tacoma. As he headed south, he kept playing the scene over and over in his mind—they had an easterly trajectory. Something in his mind said to turn east, and he listened to it. *They must be trying to get across the Sound…*

He consulted the Garmin and started to head northeast, shooting for the gap between Fox Island and Tacoma. In desperation, he slowed one more time, pulling the binoculars up. He could see nothing on Fox Island's shore. *I wonder…* On nothing but gut instinct, he put on the helmet from his pack and flipped the FLIR down. There it was, glowing like Homer Simpson's fuel rod. *Gotcha!*

The boat's engine-fire had been too small for its light to break through the rain and fog, but it shined like a beacon in infrared imaging. They had taken the stricken craft to the south end of Fox Island.

He jammed on the throttle and banked hard to port. *Need a plan. This monster is too crafty.* He decided he would keep a few hundred yards off shore when he got close and try to land to the west side of the island. He didn't want to be counter-ambushed. As he got closer and closer, he started to slow and veer off towards his destination away from the wrecked cruiser. *SNAP-Whirrr...* He hit the throttles and ducked. Anyone who has ever received incoming hypersonic bullets knows exactly what they sound like when they pass by. *So... you think you can take me, huh?* Nick asked his adversary with his thoughts.

He cruised north-northwest for a couple of minutes at full-speed and then cut power to one-third and started heading for shore. He wanted to be close enough to find a trail, but far enough away to land safely. Once he tied up to a tree between two large, spacious mansion properties, he donned his gear and rifle and climbed ashore. He looked at the boat—he was running some risks not covering it, but time was too critical. He checked his G-Shock watch. *Almost midnight.* He started pushing his way through the brush. *Ding-ding—Round two, you human waste-of-space...*

THERE'S a lot of patrols on this island, Nick thought. *Either they've had training or something's got them scared.* In the fifty-five minutes he'd been trying to sneak east-southeast, he'd had to hide in the shadows three times. The lack of proper gear and procedure that these rich people had, showed they were being reactive, versus proactive. *Something has them spooked to be out in the rain like this.* He could hear them discussing something about bikers. They were yapping as if nobody was listening, but he could hear it all from quite a ways off.

He decided he needed to be proactive himself. *These people need to know what just hit their island. Must be some sort of command post somewhere. They can help me trap the animal. I'll do the dirty work for them...* He slowly started following the latest threesome of men, armed with two hunting rifles and a golf club. The pack took him north, but he figured that Sticky Wood would be heading that way anyhow. He kept a good 150-meter spacing so that he could counter-surveil to see if Sticky was watching them, too. They slowly made their way up the main north-south road on the long, slender island. They occasionally stopped and shined a flashlight in between properties, never once moving into the area to check more closely. *They're afraid of something, for sure,* Nick noted.

He'd heard a few generators going along the way. People were running every light they could around the properties. This just validated their reactiveness in Nick's mind. As the team he was trailing neared the center of Fox Island, they walked into a well-lit canopy with two generators running along the side of the main road. *The command post...here goes nothing.*

Nick used his FLIR to look around for heat signatures. Satisfied he wasn't being stalked, he slung his rifle backwards onto his back and walked up to the lit canopy. It alarmed him to know that he got within three meters and had to announce his presence. *Some of you are bound to die,* he thought bluntly. He put his hands in the air. "Ahem!"

"What the—?" he heard about five different men and one woman say. One of them immediately leveled a shotgun at Nick.

"Whoa! Whoa!" Nick said loudly. "My hands are up!"

Two of them almost tripped on each other trying to get out of the canopy. "Stop right there! Who are you?!" the taller one said.

"Retired Army Master Sergeant Nick Williams. You people are in worse danger than you thought." His full tactical attire and hands-up approach had given itself a certain air of legitimacy. Regardless, his inexperienced captors were confused and nervous, a dangerous combination.

"How'd you get here?" the tall one demanded.

"Can I get you to lower those muzzles? I'm here to help."

A cooler head prevailed as a pudgy and short man came out. "Forgive us if we don't trust you, Nick. We've had some devastating news lately. If you agree to step back a couple more paces, you can put your hands down and we'll lower our weapons a little." Some of the men looked at him as if he'd lost his mind. "I'm Michael. What's your business?"

"Michael...Folks...I'm tracking a sexual predator whose last known location was on the south end of this island. Member of a motorcycle gang—" Nick stated, getting cut-off before he could finish.

"We know," Michael said, showing a level of relief. "Your worries are over, friend."

Nick was confused. "I'm...not...sure what you're referring to, Michael, but the animal I'm hunting just landed on this island less than two hours ago."

The entire group made a strange noise collectively as some of them gasped and the rest erupted chaotically. "What—" The noise was disruptive. "What—" Michael couldn't hear himself talk over the panicked commotion. "Hey!" They all shut up and stared. Michael turned back to Nick with a worried look. "What do you mean? Please explain," he almost begged.

"Look, no offense, but it's obvious you people don't know much about this. As you can see, I have two firearms that I haven't used. I'm going to ask for a little trust here. You first. What did you think I was talking about?" *I'm in charge here. You just don't know it yet.*

Michael looked around and got nods of approval from a couple of the others. "Two nights ago, two of our residents on the south end were viciously murdered in their home. A couple other victims managed to kill the two thugs as they were escaping. Now—I need to know what you're talking about." Michael was all business.

How to say this nicely... "You know who the residents on the island to the southwest are, correct?" The air became still as realization slammed these people like a wrecking-ball. Thanks to the shop-style floodlights scattered around, Nick could literally see them turning pale. "This evening, a boat with about three of them crash-landed on your southern shore." *These people will die if I try to use their help.* "I need all of you to get indoors and barricade yourselves into the deepest, safest part of your home."

The commotion started back up. "We can help!" Michael said. "First the bikers, now this. Tell us what to do!"

Bikers! Nick saw a connection that he hadn't picked up on earlier. "These guys are armed killers. I can guarantee that if you help, most of you will die." He looked around at their stunned faces. "Or all of you." The silence was broken only by the generators. "If you're indoors, then I have greater confidence that I won't be shooting at one of you. Get it?"

"We get it," Michael affirmed. "But just realize we have another patrol of two men down on the south end right now!"

"You got radios?"

Michael held up a little handheld radio. "Just this cheap kind from the sporting goods store," Michael explained. "But they haven't been replying for the last forty-five minutes." He started to hyperventilate.

"There's nothing you can do now. I'll look out for them."

"W-what are you going to do by yourself?" Michael asked.

Nick pulled the sniper rifle off his back and re-slung it to his front. "My job, Michael. Now—tell me what you did with these bikers."

21

Guardian Angels.

TAHOMA'S HAMMER PLUS 23 DAYS.

PHIL'S FACE, neck, and scalp were getting hot. His body was coursing blood to all of his senses, enacting nature's reaction to extreme danger. *I'm not dying like this!* He kicked his right knee up, trying to throw his one good foot onto the ground. He'd used the upward momentum to try and break the grasp of the two people holding him down. It was no good. Both of them tightened their grips and shoved him back down, yanking his arms farther behind his back. He turned his head and glared at The Hat, who just smiled.

"Up yours!" Phil screamed angrily.

The old man pulled a nickel 44-magnum with a six-inch barrel out of an old U.S. Calvary holster on his hip. He walked a bit to get squarely behind Phil. "Look, brah. Nothin' personal. We mighta even been friends in da old days…" *Thump!*

Something heavy hit the front door. Phil didn't even catch it at first. He was panting heavily and squinting, trying to say one last prayer. The old man, The Hat, and the four others all looked at each other. The old man used the magnum to point at the front door. The Hat moved over and yanked it open, ready to yell. "What the—"

A body—the man who had been guarding the front porch—had been pinned to the front door through his skull by a carbon fiber arrow. He slid off the arrow as The Hat yanked the door open, landing on his boots. It caught them all off guard. In that moment of surprise, Phil finally looked up and behind him. *What's happening…?*

The front window exploded into a thousand fragments as the old man dropped where he stood. *Ka-Krow!* echoed into the house. *Ka-Ka-Krow! Ka-Ka-Krow!* The controlled, rapid bursts of two semi-auto rifles was unmistakable. Two more men dropped from multiple, well-aimed shots.

As The Hat and the last two men both began to seek cover behind the same bookshelf, Phil couldn't believe it. He flipped over to his butt, straightening the prosthetic. The sounds of a legitimate gunfight were emanating from the front of the house. *Rival gang!* Need to get out the back. He slowly crept backwards toward the kitchen. He kicked a dining chair as he was nearly there, getting The Hat's attention. The Hat turned—*Pop!*—and tried to fire off a rapid shot at Phil, who managed to get around the fridge. He flew across the kitchen, grabbing a skillet off the stove as he passed it. He yanked open the back door and jumped the three steps down to the concrete. *Pop!*—The Hat tried another shot that splintered the doorframe right next to Phil. The run for his life had begun!

He scanned left and saw a small, detached garage. He just rounded the corner by a bush when The Hat—*Pop!*—took another shot. Around the corner, he ducked so the bush would obscure his rival's view. *No choice! Cover too far away!* The Hat's lack of training revealed itself when he rounded the corner full speed and right into Phil's swinging skillet. *Clang!* It was a dizzying shot, for sure, but it wasn't a knock-out blow. The inertia and excitement caused Phil and The Hat to tangle and tumble together, with Phil winding up on top. The Hat dropped Phil's Glock, which scattered toward the house about ten feet and went under a different bush. The Hat lost his hat when they hit the ground and started wrestling. They both looked at the Glock and then at each other. The Hat tried to shove Phil off, and Phil grabbed the loose skillet. *Clang!* He swung at the same moment The Hat had gotten his feet on Phil's chest and kicked off.

Phil landed upright and on instinct, turned and started running. He shot between the garage and the house next door heading for the back yard, tossing the trash cans next to the house down as he flew past them. He wasn't sure what kind of lead he'd built up, but by the time he got to the far end of the fenceless back yard, he heard The Hat trip over the cans. He thought that maybe the skillet, the dropped gun, and the cans had bought him a hundred feet. *Goose egg or not, he's younger and faster. He's gonna kill me! Just need to make it to the next block!*

There! Phil limp-ran for a big RV in the driveway across the street. As he rounded it—*POP!*—he heard another rushed gunshot come his way and splinter into the rig. He ran down the conceal-ment of the RV and through the next gap between two houses. He plowed right through an old wooden fence with his shoulder and tumbled into a backyard. Dogs were starting to bark, but the gunshots had guaranteed nobody would be coming to his aid. *Nearly there!*

Phil ran right up onto the back porch of the old house on Marilyn Dr. and plowed into the back door at full speed, fracturing the frame as it gave. He fell once again and scrambled up. He saw a flash of The Hat coming through the gap in the smashed fence. *Hell!* He darted through the tiny dining room of the sixties era

rental home and shot up the hall looking at the ceiling. *Son-of-a—!*
Where's the stool?

Out of shear desperation, he went into the bedroom and
grabbed the small bedside table that his beloved son Crane had used
his entire life, dragging it into the hall under the attic access cover.
He heard The Hat scrambling onto the back porch as he braced his
arms onto the walls of the hall to assist the right-leg squat up onto
the table. He shoved the drop-in access cover up and over, feeling
with both hands. *Yes!*

He yanked one of the rifle cases down in such a hurry that he
fell backwards into the room he'd fetched the table from. He could
hear The Hat shoving a chair out of the way to start up the hallway.
From his knees, Phil pulled a loaded magazine out of the side
pocket on the soft case and frantically unzipped the main compartment, grabbing the AK-47. With the muscle memory of thousands
of magazine reloads to draw from, he inserted the mag and chambered the well-tested battle rifle. Just as The Hat got to the corner,
Phil leveled off the AK from the hip, shooting right through and
next to the doorframe. *KA-KA-KA-KA-KA-KA-KA-KA-KROW!*

*THANK YOU, son...*Phil thought. *I miss you so much.* He looked at the
gasping man in front of him. He could see the life leaving his eyes as
rapid blood loss drained his life with it. "That's why you always keep
a ready-mag with your gun cases!" he yelled as a release for the
stress.

After the ringing started to dissipate from his ears, it occurred to
him that he may still have others on his tail. The AK rounds were
sure to let any trailers know exactly where the action had happened.

Phil got back up onto the table and grabbed the second rifle
case. It was one of the hard, foam-filled kind. He knew it would
have Crane's shotgun and two pistols in it. He also pried his own
pistol out of the cooling, dead hands of The Hat and put it back

into his empty holster. It had taken lives all those years ago, and now it had almost ended his. "Have fun reaching room temp, you piece of garbage!"

I want my crap back. I want Crane's Jeep. Something deep in his mind was telling him to let that stuff go, but he didn't always listen to that voice like he should.

He slung the AK around his neck, checking its case for anything else of value. He picked up the other full case and walked to the end of the hall. He caught movement outside and dropped the case. *Hell's bells and shotgun shells—here we go again...* He heard the back porch creak under someone's bodyweight.

"Jarhead?" he heard a familiar voice call out his radio callname.

Whew! Phil sighed in a big way. "Papa Bear?" he replied. He saw Eli slowly look around the broken frame of the door, big compound bow in his left hand and rifle slung around his neck. Phil smiled. "I don't know what angel sent you two," he said, catching sight of Lonnie, "but I owe him a steak dinner!" Phil picked up the rifle case and headed out back to meet them. He was taken aback at the sight of three horses hitched to the porch's post.

"How'd you...?"

"Josh," Eli cut him off, as the two men had a big handshake. "Figured you were a fool for coming to town without help. Looks like he'd be right." Phil detected a tone and knew he had no reason to be angry about it.

"Look, guys—"

"Save it," Lonnie said, coldly.

Phil's elation at being saved had just been replaced with shame for putting these men in this position. Whereas his natural instinct was to be defensive, in this case he realized he'd let foolish pride endanger all of them.

Eli caught the tension and changed the subject, glancing at the house and the cases Phil was holding. "Whose place is this?" he asked quizzically.

"Crane's," Phil said. "I remembered the last time we spoke he mentioned hiding his guns inside the attic access."

Eli's eyes grew a bit and he shook his head. "Lucky!"

Or maybe not, Phil thought.

"Let's make tracks," Lonnie urged.

"He's right," Eli agreed, looking at Phil. "It's already dusk. We'll need to camp, and it should be nowhere near here."

"There's a lot of heat where we came from, plus the cops and the Guard'll be patrolling around here," Lonnie pointed out to Eli. "Not to mention these guys' families. I know it's the long way, but what's your thought on going around Orca Inlet?" It was becoming apparent to Phil he would have some damage control to do later on.

Lonnie looked down and thought about it. "Yeah, I think you're right. We can find cover at the county fairgrounds." With that, the three men saddled up on borrowed horses and headed north out of Bartlett.

REYNALDO'S ARMY had made it to Seattle. When he arrived at the Monroe Correctional Facility the day before, he knew he didn't need all of his several hundred soldiers for that operation. He had planted an ambush along the highway. After the two anti-tank missiles wiped out the front two-thirds of the responding Guard units and police, killing and capturing the rest had been easy. The first rule of an ambush is to push through. Multiple vehicle fires prevented that. Retreat was cut off by an encircling cartel army. Rey had planted units on both sides of the highway in a textbook ambush.

A few of the captured were enslaved and kept alive for their knowledge of which bridges and roads were navigable. The Mar De Paz army rolled west into Seattle, setting up camp in the multiple ballpark facilities at the University of Washington. There was no hiding it now—they were an army of nearly two thousand, and they were taking over. The Seattle Police, Washington State Patrol, and National Guard tried to approach the campus, knowing what had happened to the prison the day before. They were targeted with mortars, which the initial wave wasn't prepared for. A communication down to the state's EOC at the makeshift Camp Crandall near Vancouver revealed that nobody—not the National Guard, the U.S. Army, or the Washington State Patrol— had any intelligence whatsoever on what was happening.

"We start by carving out Seattle," Renaldo had told the bosses before he departed Mexico. "When they realize they can't take the city back, they'll try to bargain. The fools will hold onto the notion that their states and cities will somehow return to the same borders and operating principles as before." *Carve them up like a roasted pig,* he was told. *We will attack California from within when the time is right. The entire West Coast will be ours.* The Cartel had proven time and again that even the Mexican Army was no match.

"Jefe, tenemos algunas noticias," a runner told him.

News? News of what?

The Risen Dead Motorcycle Club has formed a coalition, our sources say. Them, the Blacks, the Russians…even the Asians.

Rey had anticipated this scenario. He wasn't worried. "Gracias, amigo."

Reynaldo stared down from Husky Stadium at the burning police and Guard vehicles on the quake damaged Montlake Bridge. He was enjoying watching some of his new recruits down there mopping up the wounded *Americanos.* Rey then pondered his multiethnic special operators, confident that at the correct moment the next day, all of those amateur gangs would fall to his masterful plan. *Soon, we'll be the only providers in this entire city—protection, food, drugs, medicine, whores—it'll all be run by us,* he thought, smiling to himself.

22

Close But No Cigar.

TAHOMA'S HAMMER PLUS 14 DAYS.

"ARRRRGGGHHHHH!" the old, white haired man cried in excruciating agony. "Why are you doing this?" he cried out at Sticky. He'd just had a toenail yanked out with a pair of his own pliers. He was tied down flat and naked to his dining table.

"Well..." Sticky paused. "What's your name?" he asked calmly. He was puffing on one of the man's cigars, savoring the moment.

"D-Don. Don Kemper!" the scared man cried.

"Well, Don, a few reasons," the psychopath said, almost in a teaching manner. "For one, my friend in there wants some...shall we say 'quality time' with your missus..." Don started to scream at Sticky, which drew a scolding from the psychopath. "Now, Don... don't you go interrupting me again. If you cooperate, I'll see to it the end goes quickly for both of you." He let that dangle for a bit. "Then, there's the other way…"

Don just stammered. He could hear his wife being brutalized, and there was nothing he could do about it. Sticky continued. "Now, there's a guy out there about a half-block over—something Smith, I think… He and his pal just died, by the way," Sticky said matter-of-factly. "Surprised me how good of a fight they put up! There *were* three of us. You got lucky, Don! They took out one of my men. Anyhow—Smith told me that two Risen Dead members were murdered next door two nights ago. He told me that you were the one who helped—" He paused to scan the letter and business card in the light of the sole, flickering candle—"Doctor Stuart Schwartz leave the island after he killed my brothers. You see, I just found this here signed confession from the doctor in the house next door, and I'd like very much to speak with him." Sticky was angrily serious. "After all, Don, I saw the blood. My brothers were butchered like cattle."

"Y-y-yes! They did it! Him and the girl!"

"Keep talkin', Don," Sticky encouraged in a sinister tone as he moved the pliers towards another toe. "What girl?"

Don was trying to talk and watch the pain procession, which caused him to really ramp up his pitch. "T-they t-took some gear and left the island! Please don—Arrrrgggghhhhhhhh!" as another toenail slowly and painfully ripped itself from the toe.

"You're doin' great, Don! Really! Keep goin'."

"I d-dropped them off about a mile o-off the island. That's all I know!"

Sticky grabbed the fresh, throbbing, fleshy part of where Don's left big toenail used to be with the pliers and squeezed hard. While his prey was screaming, he yelled, "I don't think it is, Don! You want me to start yankin' nails off the wife? Keep going!" Sticky was screaming directly into his face.

"G-Gig Harbor!" Don screamed. "They wanted me to take them! I wouldn't g-go that far. She was trying to get to the Navy base in Bartlett. He s-s-said something about Sequim! Oh, God! Please stooooppp!" Don yelled as Sticky put the glowing end of the cigar on one of the old man's nipples.

"Sequim, huh?" Sticky asked. He laid the pliers down right on Don's exposed private parts, sending a big message in the process. "Business card says L.A."

"Y-yeah! His parents live there! T-that's really all I remember!" He started sobbing. "P-p-please!"

Sticky listened for few seconds. "I believe you, Don." Sticky sighed. "What'd you all do with my brothers' bodies?"

"Back!" Don shouted. "We buried 'em in the backyard over there!" He was bawling for his life. He saw Sticky move over to the kitchen and get a big butcher knife. He started to beg again, but Sticky went to work.

"Now, Don. A promise is a promise." He started stabbing Don in the chest and belly repeatedly. After nineteen blows, he stopped. *And I promise I'm going to find Stuart Schwartz…*

Sticky went upstairs to find Georgie in the process of flipping the old lady over and re-tying her up. He looked at Sticky as he walked in and smiled. "Kinda like to finish in the back side, ya know? Kinda my thi—"

Ka-Krow! Georgie dropped dead from the leaks that had suddenly sprung on each side of his head. A second shot put Mrs. Kemper out of her pain and suffering. *Sorry, pervert.* Sticky thought. *Don't need to keep fueling your habit every day or two. This thing is all about me, now…*

NICK HAD SWITCHED BACK to the night vision device on his helmet. He'd spent forty-five minutes moving most of the way down the island to about where he thought the boat had been stranded and another half-hour slowly searching for it. The FLIR caught a mass of odd-shaped heat. Nick switched back to night vision and quietly made his way to what turned out to be three cooling dead bodies. He figured the third body could either be an escapee or a different resident. *Well, Sticky obviously found the patrol. No evidence as to who this other one is. Still have to assume it's 1-on-3 right now.* From cover, he scanned with both devices, but all he could see were the large lawns of waterfront mansions. He found the address he'd been given and slowly made his way around the property.

Another fifteen minutes scouring inside the mansion had revealed the scene of the killings and not much else. He went out to the fresh graves in the back—three of them. Michael had told him that the Sorensons had been given a proper service and burials in the heart of the grand lawn, while the brutes that killed them had been lumped together in one grave close to the garden house. Nick found one of the shovels that had been used on the patio and went to work uncovering the bikers. *Any clue might help...* He was hoping for some sort of message or communique that would reveal how they and Sticky had wound up so close together.

Whew! He'd seen plenty of grotesquely dead and bloated bodies in his career, but it did not prepare him for the smell. He was almost glad to be looking at the whole scene through his "nods", as it gave it a "watching it on TV" vibe that helped his mind. He dug through each man's pockets, pulling out anything he could find. Michael had told him about the drugs, so he was taking his time, careful to avoid getting hit with a dirty needle. He collected two wallets that had nothing but cash, a Zippo lighter, two pocketknives, a glass pipe, and an expensive looking watch. It had something inscribed on the back, but he couldn't read it.

Nick took a knee in the tree line to think for a moment. *Obviously, Sticky hasn't dug up these bodies.* He knew of Stuart and Carmen's existence because Michael had told him the whole story, but he didn't have a name. *Why would this biker have a Mariner watch in his vest pocket?* He decided to make a light-locker with his rain-poncho by draping it over himself while he knelt. He turned on his flashlight to take a better look at the watch's inscription. "Hand-crafted by Mariner for

Dr. Stuart Schwartz," it read. He scanned the rest of the items but felt the watch might actually be a lead.

Nick packed up the rest of his gear and hunkered down to wait for Sticky. *He killed that patrol not five hundred meters from here. He's close...* Nick yawned. The pre-dawn glow was just starting to break through the rain and clouds to the east. He popped a couple of caffeine pills. After another twenty-five minutes, he thought he heard the pop of a gunshot. *What?* He listened intently, scanning his head in the direction of the next mansion to the north. Just as he convinced himself he was hearing things—*Ka-Krow!*—he heard it again, just as the wind died momentarily.

Nick picked himself up and left his pack on the ground, sprinting. His heart started pounding. He had close to 250 meters to sprint to get to that structure. As he approached, he slowed to a muzzle-controlling combat walk that allowed him to keep his muzzle up for an instant shot. He approached the back door of the mansion from a very wide angle, slowly peering into the building as sharply as he could to the far side. He then walked a slow semi-circle about six to eight feet out, around the door, keeping his eyes inside the entire time. Finally, he tried to push in the door. *Locked!*

He proceeded to stroll around the building as quickly as he could without exposing himself any more than he had to. From cover between two windows, he slung the large sniper rifle onto his back, suppressor up, and drew his pistol. He kept his muzzle on the front entry as he approached the door. It opened, and he entered. He began the slow, steady process of clearing a large facility without back up. As he was on the south side of the mansion, he heard an engine come to life on the far side. *Shoot!* As he sprinted back across the formal sunken living room, he heard a large crash come from the four-stall garage. Tires barked as the BMW made a sharp J-turn in reverse while hitting the brakes.

Nick finished sprinting out of the building and across the covered entry to see a BMW peeling out and fishtailing down the driveway. *Pop! Pop! Pop! Pop! Pop! Pop!* The rear window shattered and the BMW swerved wildly as it veered off the property, heading north. Nick began to sprint up the driveway, changing the pistol's magazine as he ran, and trying to get to the road before Sticky was gone forever!

Retired Master Sergeant Nick Williams came to a screeching halt when he got a few feet into the road. He slammed the pistol into its holster as he lifted the nod off his face and back above the battle helmet with his other hand. With fluid speed, as he finished those tasks, he pulled the SR-25 off his back and fell to his knees. He continued the lunge down to a prone position, falling in behind the implement of precision and death as fast as he's ever dared. The BMW's taillights were like rapidly shrinking beacons, waving back and forth as Sticky drove wildly away at rocket-speed.

Ka-Krow! Ka-Krow! Nick began to pour his fire into the zig-zagging car as best as he could, remaining calm as the car approached a curve in the road about 400 meters away. The tinkled of .308 brass complimented the sound of the suppressed shots and acrid gunpowder. On his seventh shot, the car's wild waving intensified. It lost control and slammed into a tree! Nick clambered to get back up off his tired, bruised knees and began to sprint. "Arrrghh-hh!" he yelled in frustration as he punched the rifle's mag release. As the mag was clearing the well, he was already slamming a full one into it. He re-positioned the night-optic over his eye as he sprinted, trying to see any movement down the road.

He reached the car about ninety seconds later, finding it still idling up against a Douglas fir in front of a house with a private pier and boathouse. He took cover behind a tree, scanning for movement. He approached the car cautiously, peering in and not seeing any signs of blood. *Figures.* He looked around, seeing the boathouse. *That's where I'd go!* He started trying to speed walk down the property quickly, keeping his rifle up as he went.

As he got near the rear corner of the main house, he had a decent view of the boathouse in his nods and could tell the door was forced open. In a repeat of events a few minutes earlier, he heard an engine fire up. *Not again!* He began to sprint.

He began to "slice the pie" again on the broken door to the boathouse. He could see the big powerboat with nobody at the helm. In the exhaustion that had accumulated, he made a mental mistake. He was right next to the door as he began his pivot to see inside. *He's right here! Can't let him get away again!*

Suddenly, a pair of hands reached through and grabbed the barrel, yanking it inside and dragging Nick with it. Sticky used leverage to pull the barrel and attached body past him and throw Nick directly into the water at the boat's stern. Nick began to sink under the weight of all the gear and rifle. *No!* He could tell by the chop that he was dangerously close to the boat's propeller. *Ka-Ka-Ka-Ka-Krow!* The biggest luck factor was the pitch black—Sticky didn't have night vision. Nick exhaled all his air, sinking to evade the rifle fire.

This caused a negative buoyancy, and at eight feet down, he unslung his rifle and let it go. He stripped off his plate and magazine carrier, too, ditching it to swim under the pier directly under Sticky. He slowly surfaced and gasped for air. Sticky had already cast his lines and boarded the vessel. He gunned it and drove straight out of the boathouse. Not only had his quarry bested him, he'd lost half his gear and was watching him motor away.

NICK OPTED to run north to the Command Post. *Of course! Vacant under my own orders!* He saw that one of the sporting goods store radios was laying there and hoped for a miracle. "Michael! This is Nick! If you're out there, I need your help!"

After an excruciating nine seconds, he heard a response. "Yes, Nick. I'm listening."

Nick told Michael about finding his lost patrol dead and had Michael come back to the command post. He asked Michael to drive him back to the south end via car. On the quick drive down, he grilled Michael about the events of two nights earlier. "Who'd you say killed the bikers?"

"A doctor and a girl. Why? What's that got to—"

"What do you remember about them? Any detail."

"When Don Kemper took them off the island, we took their photos and names, just in case we ever found them sneaking back on. Will that help?"

Yes! Finally, a break. "Absolutely."

First they checked on the dead patrol. Michael confirmed that the other man was not an island resident he'd seen at any of their meetings. Once they parked at the Sorenson's, Nick ran down to the woods for his gear. As they started heading north again, he pointed out the house next door which the chase began. "Wait—stop. I'm in a hurry, but I need to check out this house." *Why were you in there?* "This is where the chase began."

"Oh, no!" Michael exclaimed. The man was wearing a lot of worry. "This is the Kempers' house. They're the ones who helped the doctor and the girl off the island." The retired litigator was starting to feel the pressure of the mounting body count.

Nick stopped him after they got out of the car. "Why don't you let me check first, Michael? Take a breather."

"I-I'll be okay. I'd rather not stay out here by myself…"

Suit yourself, but it won't be pretty. "Alright." Nick drew his pistol and led the way into the house. Their flashlights led them around multiple pieces of garage door that were thrown all over the driveway. There were muddy tracks in the lawn.

Nick stopped after they were in the living room. "However bad you expect it to be, it'll be worse. Last chance." Michael just nodded Nick to lead on.

They eventually found their way to the formal dining room. Nick smelled the large volume of blood before his flashlight beam caught Don Kemper's body. It was twice as horrifying looking at the gore in the pitch black and flashlight shadows. Surprisingly, Michael held his food. Nick proceeded to clear the house with the assistance of his helmet and nods. *Thank the stars I had my chin strap in place when he dunked me.* He went upstairs, leaving Michael behind to compose himself.

When he found Mrs. Kemper and the other body, the gunshots made sense. *He took this guy out so he wouldn't slow him down. He's even smarter than I thought. But...it truly is 1-on-1 now.*

He caught Michael at the bottom of the stairs. "You don't need to go up there. Just wait 'til daylight," he warned. "There's another dead scumbag, too."

Michael was sobbing. "What did they do to him? Why...How could he do this?"

"They had info, and he wanted it."

"What info?" he demanded.

Nick pulled the Mariner watch out of his pocket. "He's going after that doctor." *And that poor girl...* "Look, Michael—we need to go. I need a copy of the picture and anything else you can tell me about them. They're the only lead I have."

Michael took his laptop out of the backseat of his car, pulling up Doc and Carmen's photos. "Oh, yeah. He left a couple of more of these business cards, too. They were both very traumatized and ready to assist with the authorities when things return to normal."

Nick suppressed a skeptical laugh and took one of the cards. "Anything else?"

"Just that they were trying to get to Bartlett—and for him—to his parents' in Sequim."

Nick climbed into the car. "I need you to take me to my boat, please."

"Are you going to Gig Harbor?" Michael inquired.

"Yes." *Eventually. First I need to get home and re-arm. You win this round...*

23

Tension You Can Cut.

TAHOMA'S HAMMER PLUS 24 DAYS.

THE U.S. NAVY's response to the destruction zone was highly publicized in the national media, though their actual mission priorities were not broadcast. Part of Task Force Truxtun finished up its objectives and headed back to Southern California for re-supply. The Feds intended on sending them back—not only for national security efforts, but for civilian relief, as well. The Pentagon even highlighted the Air Force air drops—it wasn't until hackers leaked the info that the U.S. populace learned those air drops were never supposed to happen.

What was tightly controlled, however, were the other operations. The Department of Defense was highly aware of the growing tension between Russia and China and why. A submarine that was specially outfitted with the most secure and secret spy capabilities in the entire U.S. Military limped into Pearl Harbor with battle damage, and another one was flying a Jolly Rogers flag, using crossed torpedoes instead of bones. The first submarine was normally homeported with the ballistic missile boats at the submarine base in Washington State, not the attack fleet in Pearl, San Diego, or Guam. The Navy sent her to Pearl for two reasons—the facilities at Bogdon were in the largest bug-out in American Military history, and they knew the sailors that lived off base would go "UA"—Unauthorized Absence—rendering the boat inoperable.

On top of the ocean, Battle Groups on deployment were being extended, and others that had recently returned from missions were being told to stand down their leave and training cycles. In other words, "be ready to deploy." The Pentagon was shuffling ground forces from the East Coast to Southern California, Hawaii, and Okinawa. Food and supplies were being re-routed. The President issued an Emergency Executive Order, declaring that companies that produced ammunition and MREs could only sell to the U.S. Government for the next 180 days. As these actions were noticed, the American citizens added it to their frustration and reasons to organize not so peaceful protests. The war-drums were starting to be heard by governments and civilians alike.

THE CLIPPITY-CLOP of horse hooves on broken asphalt announced their presence to the northwest fighting position. It was just past noon. The wayward cowboys had rescued their lost sheep—three tired men were finally home. *Home,* Phil mused. *We passed my house back there, but this is my home...*He was going to have to eat some crow. He wanted to give Lonnie a little more cooling time, but the lack of a Jeep was noticed by everyone immediately. By the time the three horses walked into the lower gate and down to the rifle line, half the range's population was walking over to them.

They got off the horses on the side road. Phil stopped and hugged Payton. "Your building is looking sharp!" he said to her as he waved at Tony.

"Don't even! Where's the Jeep? What happened?"

"Hi, Grandpa!" yelled Savannah as she and the rest of the school-aged kids came running up to see the fuss.

"Peaches!" Phil said enthusiastically. He picked her up and held her for a bit, looking back at Payton. "Later, Olive. Right now, I need to find the board and Josh and have a chat."

She gave him a skeptical look. "You're holding out on me. I can always tell when you're trying to hide something."

"Just like your mother...I know, honey. We'll talk later. I promise." He set his granddaughter down.

The crowd was murmuring. Maya and her mother walked over from the bay that had the chickens and took custody of their horses. "Any issues?" Pam asked Lonnie.

"Not with the horses," Lonnie said in his usual straight-shooting fashion.

As the commotion started to die, Phil went around and assembled the range's officers, Josh, Eli, Lonnie, and a few key family leaders. They all crammed themselves into the office.

Most were still quite talkative. "You going to regale us with the tales of adventures in Bartlett?" the always happy Don joked.

"Not exactly," Phil said with a serious look. He scanned the room, waiting for the last of the banter to die down. He was leaning against the counter, pretty much in the middle of the room. He saw that Lonnie was still wearing the pissed-off look and noticed that Josh had been conspicuously silent. "I owe everyone here an apology. Lonnie, I'd like to start with you."

Lonnie looked out the window for a second. It was not in his nature to keep silent about something that was pissing him off. He looked back at Phil and nodded.

"I figured out why you won't talk to me," Phil said.

Lonnie didn't believe him. "Why's that?" he challenged. He figured Phil's apology was coming from the place of a bruised ego.

"Because you rolled the dice, trusting me and my leadership… my judgement. And right after you move your family here, I get you involved in a battle and then make you come rescue my dumb butt."

"The retribution fight I got no problem with," Lonnie acknowledged, still annoyed.

Several guffaws shot up around the room. "What are you talking about, Phil?" Alice Huddleston asked.

He looked at her directly. "I let my ego get the best of me." He scanned the room again. "Josh tried to talk me into taking help, and I thought I didn't need it." Silence. He took a good breath and blew a bit out. "You know—I'm 'Phil Walker', like that's supposed to mean something. I should've been dead for the last eighteen or so hours. These two saved me," he said openly, pointing at Eli and Lonnie. "Well, them and Crane. Lonnie…Eli…I'm sorry I put you two in that position. I hope my sincerity will convince you that I've learned a big lesson about myself." He saw a weight lift off both men's shoulders.

For the next thirty minutes, Phil told every detail he could remember about the whole trip, finishing with a warning. "I think it is a matter of time. Very soon, the National Guard and Sheriff will be out here to arrest me."

"Speaking of that, we got something to tell you, too," Josh said, finally breaking his silence. He brought Phil up to speed on the authorities' first visit and the actions they'd been taking since.

"Do you think Charlie was favoring us by not inspecting every square inch?" Phil asked.

"Maybe," Josh admitted. "I was pretty pissed, so I might have missed some non-verbal cue."

"Either way," Eli chimed in, pushing off the merchandise rack he'd been leaning on. "We need to figure out the next steps. This ain't no game of chess. I say hunker down." He leaned back against the rack to indicate he was done.

"What's that mean, exactly?" club officer Joe Santillan asked. "Like—resist?" He looked around. "Are we actually talking about fighting the National Guard?"

"Whether there's a fight or not is up to them," Phil said. "But next time they come out—and they will—they're taking every gun we have. They may even try to tell us we have to move to their camp...for our 'own protection'. I agree with Eli. We need a plan, and everyone has to be on board with it." He went silent for a few seconds, but when nobody spoke, he added one last thought. "We need to let the rest of the Slaughter Peninsula Posse know what's happening, too."

"LOOK AT THE LOG ENTRY!" Sandy yelled at Sheriff Raymond and Major Matsumoto. "While you were supposed to be arresting him!" —she pointed at the Sheriff— "you were letting him traipse around this supposedly secure facility!" she finished by pointing at the major. They were in the meeting room surrounded by a couple of dozen other people.

"We had a communication lapse, Director. Those things are only going to get worse as we both continue to suffer from AWOLs," the sheriff said rationally, looking at Adam. "Perhaps if you had gotten some more people and equipment from Camp Crandell, like you promised..." This caused an eruption that everyone who witnessed it would later refer to as "Volcano, Part Deux."

"What...the...*hell* did you just say to me, you old miserable son of a dog?" the Godfather screamed. She started up from her seat at the head of the conference table and marched down that side of the table. "Why—you two-bit, cereal-box tin-star, poor-excuse of a politician! Me and my folks are still here doing our jobs!" The fake-southern twang was long gone. It was replaced by flying spittle. "Don't you *daaaarrre* blame your shortages on *me*! You neither, Major Screw-up!" she said, stabbing at the air in Adam's direction. "A Grand Canyon mule train has less asses than your two staffs!"

Some of the rest of the Unified Command started to interrupt due to her demeanor, but she walked right over them. "Gross incompetence! That's all I've seen from you two and your whiny departments." She pointed at the mayors, commissioners, and police and fire chiefs, as she made points about all of them. "Bartlett's had riots on the Navy base fence for days on end! Firemen! Hmph! Those lazy boys ain't done nothing but eat MREs for the last three weeks!"

Wham! The table shook and people jumped as the sheriff pulled his collapsible baton off his duty belt and slammed its handle down. "That is enough!" he yelled after standing up. "Sit down and shut up!"

The room exploded into chaos as the policy-planners and front-line leaders began to argue. *What on Earth,* freshly promoted Lt. Charlie Reeves thought as he watched from one of the chairs around the outer wall. *We're screwed with these clowns running the circus.* He stood up, put the whistle hanging around his neck into his mouth, and blew the little noisemaker hard enough to make his cheeks hurt.

Charlie made sure they were all looking at him. The people closest to him were just starting to uncover their ears. "You people done being jerks?" the handsome Native American said bluntly. Some composed themselves, while others were silent, but they all turned their seething glares at him. "You all are arguing about things that just don't matter! Why don't you talk about the things that we can actually affect?" *Bureaucrats! Sheesh!*

The senior leaders seethed for a few more seconds. Then the sheriff broke the ice. "What *lawful* action do you propose, Director?" He had emphasized the L-word.

"Was Phil Walker involved in the massacre of that Filipino family in Bartlett last night? The ones that killed his friend?"

"We believe so. An AR pistol and Jeep found there were registered to him and his son, according to our databases," the major answered. "Plus some other gear with his name on it."

"Then, Sheriff," Sandy said with a snarky sneer, "go chip and de-arm that law-breaking vigilante, just like every other criminal!"

Tahoma's Hammer Plus 25 Days.

It was about 0200 when the Guard vehicles came roaring up Canal Vista Highway. Some of them veered to the right and through the gate on an old piece of federal property that the Navy and Marines used to use for training. There was a clearing for them to park and begin to hike north, where they would find themselves on the range's eastern perimeter. The next vehicles flew past the range and came to a stop at the round-about a half mile north of the club's property. They started beating a trail east into the brush and forest to find the club's northern boundary.

The rest of the procession had yet more Guard, as well as a combined task force of county deputies and Bartlett police. They came to a stop all along the road, right where it bordered the gun range on the west. They had the club and all its residents surrounded...or so they thought.

About a hundred meters on the west side of the highway, twenty-year-old Shay Bryant, Eli's only daughter, had been on the observation post watch. Her primary connection to the range was the radio earbud in her left ear. She quietly buried herself in the brush, trying to become one with the mud. She heard the heavy-duty zip-lock bag that held her phone and radio vibrate. She checked the phone and saw a mesh-text from Phil, telling her to stay quiet and feedback anything she could see.

The arresting force had rolled in so quickly that most of the range residents were still getting dressed when they heard Sheriff Raymond's voice come over a loudspeaker from one of the MRAPs.

"This is Slaughter County Sheriff Ward Raymond. You are all ordered to lay down your firearms and come to the front gate with your hands in the air."

I can't believe this is happening! Charlie thought. He'd been promoted to Lieutenant when Shara Murphy had disappeared and never returned. This allowed him to be part of the commanding squad. None of this sat right with him, and he felt that most of the others felt the same.

The sheriff and Major Matsumoto looked around and then at a few others, including Charlie. "Reeves. Get over here," Sheriff ordered. In some counties, the sheriffs were still active peace officers. This wasn't the case for most of the counties in Western Washington. Most of the serious sheriff candidates figured out about halfway through their careers that they were actually politicians. By the time they were under-sheriffs, the job was entirely about budgets, personnel management, and networking. Sheriff Raymond hadn't been on an actual arresting force in over a dozen years.

"Sir?"

"You know this man. What's he going to do?"

Now you want to know? Charlie thought angrily. "My guess is that we're going to have to go in by force, Sheriff." *Why didn't you ask me this two hours ago!*

The sheriff's face was strained. He looked at his watch, stalling.

"Let's give Walker a call-out by name," suggested Major Matsumoto. "Get him to the gate and talking to us. That'll buy some time while my troops are getting set on the rest of the perimeter."

"Good thinking," the sheriff agreed. He reached into the open MRAP door and pulled the corded microphone back out. "Phillip Edward Walker. You are ordered to the front gate by a warrant issued by Judge Rudolph Floor. You have five minutes to comply."

"I don't recognize Commissioner Floor's authority, as he is not a duly-elected judge," they heard Phil say on their radios.

Phil had proceeded up to the command tent as soon as the

blockade had started. He knew Jerry had every conceivable frequency the local emergency departments used. He figured they would be scanning all their normal tactical frequencies, so he gave it a shot. This had shocked the sheriff and some of the others. Charlie would have smirked if he wasn't so worried about the very real threat of violence at play.

Sheriff Raymond threw the PA-mic back into the rig and took the radio off his belt. "Did anyone catch what channel he was on?" he yelled angrily.

"Tac-8, sir," Charlie heard one of the other deputies say.

The sheriff changed his output to the proper channel. "It doesn't matter what you recognize, Walker. You need to comply, or we'll enter by force."

"This is illegal, Sheriff. Do you see my two gate guards under that tarp?"

"Yes," he answered, not knowing what to expect.

"We have a signed answer to your demands. Please send Sergeant Reeves over to retrieve it."

The sheriff didn't reply to Phil. "I can't send you, Reeves," he said to Charlie. "He needs to know who's calling the shots."

"Understood, Sheriff," Charlie said. *Besides, I can guarantee that you won't be happy with whatever it says.*

"Wildman," the sheriff barked. "Go get it."

The young deputy got about halfway from their line of departure to the gate when Phil's voice came to life. "You're not cooperating, Sheriff!"

"Neither are you, Walker!" the normally collected sheriff barked. "You want me to read it? Then *I choose* who goes up!"

After several seconds of nothing, Buddy Chadwell stepped out from under the tarp and behind the sandbags with a big envelope. Phil had ordered him to pass along the proclamation on their own frequency. He flung it like a frisbee and it did a big, curving, flip-flopping arch and landed in the mud near Matty Wildman. He picked it up and took it to the sheriff.

He wiped the mud off the golden yellow envelope and opened it, pulling out a stack of papers and a small book. Charlie saw the sheriff's face sour while Matsumoto's eyes rolled. He leaned in for a look. *The U.S. Constitution...Ohhhh, boy. Here we go.* He started craning his neck to see the papers.

The sheriff's face turned red and he glared at Charlie. He slammed the stack in Charlie's chest, pacing past him and exhaling a stressed breath. "What's your friend thinking, Reeves?"

Charlie looked at the papers. Several of them had signatures—dozens upon dozens of them. The very top one was the one that had set the Sheriff off. In big letters, it said, "Nuts! – General Anthony McAuliffe, December 22, 1944."

24

Investigations.

"You're crazy if you think we're giving you all of our chickens!" Roy said, raising his voice in anger but not quite yelling.

"You wanna add them goats to the cost?" the scraggly looking service station attendant said, looking back and forth between Natalie and Roy. Roy's face was flushed.

Natalie, with Katherine in her arms, looked at the man while pulling on her husband's arm. "Give us a minute," she ordered the man, dragging her husband from the dirty, small shop-bay back out the front where the Cadet had been parked with Wesley and James guarding it.

They had limped it into town as slowly as they could on a flat. They had no spare tires and wheels for the small utility vehicle. Roy had brought a little 12-volt powered air pump and the battery from the truck. With those tools, they had been able to keep the tire inflated enough to keep the bead from popping off the rim. It was taking longer to fill each time, as the battery was losing its oomph.

Out of earshot from the opportunist, Natalie said, "He's got us, Roy. We need the Cadet fixed. We're hosed without it."

"I know, I know," he mumbled. "It just pisses me off! What'd we ever do to him?" he exclaimed, casting an angry look back toward the smirking worker.

"It pisses me off, too, but I'm going to be really pissed if he jacks the price up! Let me talk to him," she encouraged.

Roy huffed. He knew his wife was right, but he was too upset to say anything. He nodded, and the pair and toddler went back in. "You get the whole chicken-tractor, but not until the tire is fixed. And—we want our spare battery charged. Deal?" she said squarely.

"No problem," the middle-aged grease monkey said like a fox.

Natalie wasn't sure if he owned the small town gas and service station or was just the last worker to keep coming to work. *I can't believe this is where we're at,* she thought. *This would've never happened at a Firestone or Les Schwab.*

Roy scowled at the man as they went back outside and unhitched the small trailer and chicken tractor. As they moved the Cadet into the building, Natalie heard a small generator and air compressor fire up. Natalie and James took Katherine into the woods behind the shop to find a spot to go, and then Roy and Wesley took their turn. By the time they were all done getting a bite to eat, the Cadet had been fixed.

Forty minutes later they were back on the trip, passing through the small neighborhood near the town of Snoqualmie Pass. They had only been averaging four to five miles per day, due to someone always being on foot. The tire issue had slowed that down even more. The trail they were following was going to take them quite a way off the highway for a few miles. It would follow some power lines up the worst of the slopes before they were on the longer, downhill leg of the venture. Because it was a powerline run, it resembled more of a barren ski-slope than a small trail through the forest.

Over four hours and two uphill miles had gone by when Roy commented, "Brrrr. I was afraid of this. I think we may have snow on the way."

"You think? I mean, it's still mid-October…" Natalie replied.

"The temp isn't just dropping because were climbing," he explained. "See how dark the system has gotten?" he asked, pointing up at the clouds crossing the Cascade Mountains.

"Maybe we should go back to town and stay on the highway's shoulder," she suggested. "The highway pass is cut through a lot lower than this trail."

"I disagree," said her husband. "We'd be doubling back, travelling on the highway—*and* back in town with that shady mechanic." He was instantly pissed again.

"Well, then let's at least find a good spot to camp," she advised.

"Now *that* I agree with," Roy said, smiling. They were just rounding a bend where the powerlines made a slight turn toward the southwest when Roy hit the brakes. About three hundred yards ahead of them was a wagon and team of horses that wasn't moving. "Hello," Roy said aloud to himself. "Who are you?"

Natalie looked ahead, scanning. She could only see one man and one woman. "Hon, where's the binoculars?"

"Bastard!" Roy said, chastising himself. "They're in the truck!"

This is why I told you to write a bug-out checklist! Natalie yelled in her head.

"Bastard!" Wesley yelled. His autistic mind always took advantage of when the funny-word rules were suspended. James started to laugh. "Bastard!" Wesley yelled again.

"Not now, Wes," Natalie said in a short tone.

Four-year-old Katherine was sitting in Natalie's lap. "They said bad words, Mommy," Natalie heard slip out from under a tiny, camouflaged rain-hood.

Natalie shot Roy a look, who had a look of his own. He wasn't so much worried about the cussing. The hairs on the back of his neck were standing up at full attention. He looked at his wife. "What do you want to do?"

Good question, she thought.

TAHOMA'S HAMMER Plus 20 Days.

"YOU GONNA LET ME IN, LOUIE?" Sticky asked the heavyset, graying biker in the doorway.

"Sticky?" The man couldn't believe his eyes. "What's happenin'?" he said excitedly, pulling his MC brother from another mother in for a bear hug.

As the two embraced, Sticky said, "Fate led me this way, bro. I need shelter."

"Get in here," his comrade ordered. The man looked like garbage—gray, pasty, and breathing heavily.

In the six days since he'd barely escaped the chase from his unnamed predator, Sticky Wood had been resting and laying low. The boat he'd stolen got him to Gig Harbor to investigate. He'd discovered the bus service to Bartlett run by Mar de Paz Services. Other than raping and killing a middle-aged woman for a house to rest in, he had maintained a low profile. He was trying to see if his stalker was going to show himself.

On Day Plus 18, he bartered himself a bus ride to Bartlett, using the Doc's photo on his business card to try to track them down. A couple of new-homeless near the bus station remembered them passing through just the day before. Since the bus route went no farther north, he had to weigh his options, landing on needing to see if any of the Slaughter County Chapter of the Risen Dead was still around. *It is good to have a network,* he reminded himself.

He ditched his stolen pack and raingear in the entry to Lame

Louie's house. After an unusually beautiful day on his arrival, the rain had returned. "You the only one?" he asked the retired welder.

"Soup took the crew to Legion's, like the standing order said to," he explained. "I'm not going," the sickly man said.

"What's going on?" Sticky asked, concerned.

"I was in the middle of chemo, brother. Lung cancer," he said rolling his eyes matter-of-factly. "Started smoking when I was nine, so not exactly a surprise, right?" He laughed, which triggered a round of coughing. "And—I been out of smokes and oxygen for days! Truth be told, I was thinking about sittin' in the bathtub with a toaster. 'Cept the power's out!" More laughing and coughing. After he'd gotten his spell under control, he told Sticky, "But it's weird. You know what I'd actually kill for more than anything right now?"

"A big joint?" Sticky guessed.

Louie shook his head no. "I want a no-kiddin' Reese's Peanut Butter Cup so bad I can taste it." That got a good chuckle out of Sticky, but the mood turned more serious. "So, what's your story? Why did fate bring us together, brother?"

Sticky went into the long rendition of riding out the earthquake on the island, plans for turning it into a secure site, and the massive hunt that shoved him north against his wishes. "That little turd killed Trip and Shorty, bro. I can't let that go." *It seems like if I could feel emotions, this would be a good moment for them.* "Once I make him pay very slowly, I'll link up with the club."

"Understood, my man. I only wish I could help." Lame Louie looked around his house. "I got nobody left. Consider this your place. Take what you need. All I ask in return is for you to…" He couldn't find the words.

Sticky's face soured. "What? No, no! Don't ask me to do that."

"Sticky…Brother, it's okay. You'd be doin' me a solid. And I don't mean right this second. We'll do it when you're ready to resume your hunt. So," Louie continued by changing the subject, "any idea who the dude after you is?"

"Not sure," he mulled for a bit. "But I'm guessin' he's *her* brother. The one in the Army."

"Who?" Louie asked, but then quickly remembered the trial. "Ahhh. Yup, that makes sense."

Sticky had a realization. "You know anyone in Sequim? Friends of the club?"

"Sequim?" *Cough-cough-wheeze-hack.* Once Louie's latest spell lapsed, he said, "Why would you want to go up there?" he asked, smirking. He saw that Sticky wasn't returning the sentiment. "Oh... uh—I know a couple of cats in P.A." He was referring to Port Angeles, the "big" city on the Olympic Peninsula's north coast. "These guys are plumbed into anything shady that goes on up there." Louie went back to hacking.

"Do me a favor, bro. Jot down anything you can that will help me find them. I'll probably need some help finding where the doc's parents live."

Listen to that cough. Yep. I need to put this dog out his misery, all right, Sticky realized. He thought a bit longer while Louie found a charter fishing company's business card and started writing on a notepad. After Louie was done, Sticky stood up from the recliner he'd been parked on for story hour.

"Where you been pissin', brother? I don't want to make a mess." He started walking past Louie toward the hall.

Louie looked at his friend's eyes and saw no soul hiding in them. "Buncha Gatorade bottles on the back porch, brother. Keeps the smell down." He didn't turn around to keep looking at Sticky. After several silent seconds— "Thanks, Sticky. We'll meet up in Hell, brother."

Sticky pulled out a pistol and said nothing as he killed for something other than the demons for the first time in his life.

"THIS IS the fourth time in a row, people. We can do better!" Earl said, trying to pump his team up after yet another loss in a training exercise very similar to capture the flag. "Phalanx may have years of training on us, but they aren't ninjas. How'd they get past us this time?" He knew the answer. He wanted to know if *they* knew.

"They floated down on the river," Tina Howard suggested "Something we were never looking for."

"Exactly," Earl agreed. "We're stuck in our own paradigms that they're coming from that road or over the hill."

"So what's the answer?" Larry Jacobs asked, somewhat annoyed. "We can't always have people watching the whole river. This road is almost two miles long!"

"This is why I've been lobbying for a foxhole at the dead end of the road," Earl advised. "Terrain can be taken advantage of, but you never assume it is impenetrable. Once you do, that is where your enemy will enter. Take the hill, for example," he said, pointing toward the steep slope on the south side of their road. "If you're starving and the only food is owned by the people in the next valley, would you go to their front gate, or would you cross over that sucker because they aren't watching it?" He saw a few heads bouncing.

The crew before him was comprised of most of the security volunteers from his road, almost thirty in total. That represented the bulk of the able-bodied older teens and adults. They were on their fourth of five days training with a cadre from Phalanx, whose leaders knew that having a well prepared and allied neighbor could only help them. They were providing the training gratis. The training cadre had already departed for the evening. Conner, Chopper, and Jack maintained the guard station at the head of the road and were not participants.

After the first two days of basic security, movement, and communication principles, Phalanx had started running them through drills. Their goal was to stop the entering team from getting to an objective. Both groups were using small branches spray painted orange as rifles because there were no paintball guns. That was done so that nobody took the enemy as a real threat. Each time, the objective was changed up. This time, Phalanx had to smash a rotting pumpkin next to a road cone that had been staged near a house by Earl. For this drill, he and the invaders were the only people to know where it was—he didn't want his defenders to camp on the spot and cheat the game.

"That isn't fair!" Diane Naud complained when she heard the rules of this round.

"War isn't fair," Earl countered a bit too bluntly. "Your enemy knows who they're trying to kill. You don't. We have no idea which direction they're headed, or why, until after the battle."

They would run two more drills on the final day. Earl hoped they could have a win on the fifth game, because then they would get one chance to be the attackers.

"It's getting dark, and I'm sure we're all hungry," Earl said as he went around collecting his small contingent of radios that he'd been lending for the drills. "Don't be too hard on yourselves. You're all getting better with each game. Tonight's homework is to reflect on what you learned. And your push-ups and sit-ups," he said, grinning ever so slightly. "Don't forget those."

With that everyone broke loose. Some of them would be back out to relieve Conner and his team in a few hours. Earl decided to go check on them.

He jumped onto his quad, aware that at some point he would need to go procure some replacement gasoline. A half-mile later he pulled up to the make-shift gate where Chopper was standing. He gave Earl a little wave. Conner and Jack were sitting under an improvised structure that had been built out of branches, paracord, and a tarp. Occasionally one of them would get up and pace the entry control point out of sheer boredom. Earl strode under the tarp structure, un-slung his rifle, and took Chopper's empty seat. From day one, he decided he wouldn't go home until the bored guards had been relieved.

"What'd they learn today?" Conner asked.

"The importance of watching the entire perimeter," Earl said frankly. *And I learned that I wish I'd built a trustworthy retreat-group years ago.* "They came in over the hill again this morning. Then they floated down the river this afternoon."

"Sneaky devils," Jack commented. "Did we even see them?"

"Nope," Earl replied. "I expect tomorrow they'll cross the river upstream without drifting down and attack from the east."

"Here's to hoping that our team figures that out on their own," Conner said.

"Yep," Earl agreed. *We can't be everywhere to do the fighting for them, can we?*

After a longer silence, Conner opened up again. "What happens when we need to put together a larger unit? Something like what that town had to do against the biker-horde in the book *One Second After*? I mean—we both know that eventually the bad guys will morph into something big and hard to fight."

Good question. "I don't rightly know. I get the feeling Phalanx may have already networked for something like that."

"Really?" Jack wondered. The software engineer couldn't fathom that some people had been preparing for a day in America when the authorities could no longer protect them. It still felt like science-fiction to him. "What about the Army? Wouldn't they just obliterate a horde?"

Earl just looked at him. It took a few seconds for the urge to treat him like a Private passed. Once it did, he calmly said, "What Army? Most of the guys Conner and I served with are deployed or got covered in mud three weeks ago. I ain't seen the rest of the Army show up. Have you?" Jack turned his head with a slightly burnt look. "Sorry," Earl mumbled. "Your question just made me realize that people are still stuck in the fantasy that things will be normal again."

"You think they won't?" Jack asked.

"I think 'normal' will be redefined," Earl said. The whole group remained silent in thought after that.

Just an hour or so after dusk had given way to rainy black, Nick Williams tied up to a large, broken tree laying on the shore at Sequim Bay State Park, east of Sequim, Washington. The sleepy town was just a few miles as the crow flies from the Strait of Juan de Fuca, which connected Puget Sound and the Pacific Ocean. It had been a fast six days since he'd nearly been chopped up by a propeller.

When he left Fox Island, he knew his adversary had too big of a lead. He also knew he needed to hit the reset button. A rookie error from being tired had nearly cost him his life. He motored home and ate five chewable melatonin pills to jump-start what was fourteen restless hours of sleep. It was filled with nightmares. His entire being —body, mind, soul—was completely wired to this mission. His failure thus far was haunting him. It took two more days of rest to feel fully ready.

Down into his crawl space he went. He replaced his missing sniper rifle with a Lapua chambered in .338. It would have the range and speed to make up for the notorious winds pushing around the Olympic Mountains, but not weigh as much as the Barrett. This meant needing to carry a separate battle rifle, which turned out to be his HK 416. Most of his magazines were for 5.56, so he stuck with what he knew best. The one thing he learned on the first, failed mission was that his quarry was crafty—nothing would go according to plan. He brought his back-up plate carrier, which was older and heavier. *Still beats getting shot.*

An experienced sniper knows that his best advantage is being set up where his target *will* be. *Playing catch up sucks.* All signs pointed north—*Sticky's tracking the man who killed his brothers.* Nick knew his one chance was to get to Sequim, find the doctor's family home, and set up for the long game. He had also consulted every set of notes he'd ever built on the man that raped and—ultimately, in his mind— killed his sister. He knew there was a chapter of the Risen Dead

Motorcycle Club in Bartlett where Sticky could lick his wounds. *The biggest gamble in all of this is that Sticky finds the doctor somewhere on the trail to Sequim.* Nick couldn't control every factor—some things were up to the universe.

After his recovery, he stopped in Gig Harbor, but the trail was cold. *Needle in a thousand haystacks.* That was when he decided to trade a case of ammo for a full tank of fuel. He wanted to travel at night, but even with night vision, the marine hazards were too numerous. It was sheer luck that he hadn't run straight into a tree during the high-speed chase that night. Nick travelled a moderate speed during the day. He noticed that the few craft out in the open were full of armed people. *I wonder how long until piracy comes back? One worry at a time.*

As he surveyed the wave-damaged beach, Nick had three immediate concerns. First was making sure his supplies would last. He opted to spend the night moving his stuff into the woods in a particularly hilly and brushy area, covering them with a tarp and bushes. If he lost the boat, he could recover. The mission was a bust, though, without food, ammo, and supplies. Operating without the support of the pencil-pushing Army was quite different.

Secondly, he needed to find the doctor's family home. It might be as easy as looking in a phone book, but he was doubtful. Once he found the home, his last concern was finding a good roost to watch the front without drawing attention. A different, abandoned house would be ideal. *Gonna have to cross that bridge when I get there.* All of Nick's eggs were in this one basket. The intel and analysis were the best they could be—*he should track that doctor up here.* After hours of unloading and moving supplies, Nick set up his hammock and tarp, settling in for more restless sleep.

25

"The basic tool for the manipulation of reality is the manipulation
of words. If you can control the meaning of words, you can control
the people who must use the words."
—Phillip K. Dick

Tahoma's hammer Plus 24 Days.

"What chapter you say you're with?" Legion asked the two men
suspiciously. RDMC was the biggest, baddest motorcycle club in the
northwest part of the U.S. There were a few hundred full-patched
members plus hundreds more of the prospects and support clubs.

"Eugene," the taller one said. "But we're trying to make our way
back. We were on a detail in Spokane when this thing hit." A patch
on his "cut" identified him as "Bad JuJu."

"Ohhh," Legion said, nodding. He'd never met these two, and

he had no way of checking with the Oregon State hierarchy to verify. "Who's your chapter prez?"

"Pipes," he said, giving the man's road name.

"Pipes...Pipes..." Legion was searching his memory for any of the rallies, wondering if he'd ever met Pipes. *Sturgis? Laughlin? Our Snake River campout?* "What's his real name?"

"Nelson Pettit," the shorter one, who went by "Fireball", replied.

The two men were in the middle of the clubhouse. They had walked in, wet and ill-prepared but otherwise healthy. "Look," said JuJu, "I know you don't know us, but it's all legit."

"It's not that I don't trust you boys," Legion said, smirking. "It's just that...well...I don't trust you...boys." He nodded, and several of his own men grabbed the two and shoved them to the beer-stained throw-rug next to the pool table. "Check 'em," he ordered.

The two didn't go down without a fight. A couple of guys took elbows in the nose before they had them secured. "They got the brand," Hoosier said. "Looks pretty fresh, though."

Legion hadn't expected this. "Really? Check it again. Make sure it's *right!*" he emphasized that word because the RDMC branded every member on the back of the neck with the zombie and rising moon symbol. What most people didn't know, though, was that the moon was off set more on the brand than it was on the patch they wore. That was a tightly held secret to help verify narcs and posers.

"They got the right brand, brother. They're good."

"What about ink?" Legion demanded, walking over to scan them for himself. They were covered in plenty of old and fresh ink, some of it prison symbology, but only JuJu had club ink. It looked a couple of years old, at least. "Huh..." *You're getting too paranoid, old man,* Legion told himself. "Let 'em up," he ordered.

As the two began to pull themselves off the floor, Legion stuck a big arm out and helped yank them up. First Fireball, then JuJu. "No hard feelin's," he said, almost more of an order than a question. He gave each of them a welcome hug. "Welcome, brothers. Prospect!" he yelled at the nearest lowlife. "Get them some water and food!"

The two men wore looks of relief. "Thanks, Legion. We get it. Stuffs gettin' hardcore on the road."

"So—where's your bikes?" he asked them

They looked at each other. "Some of the overpasses along 90 just dropped where they stood. There's pileups all over. It looks like a zombie movie out there. We walked most of the way," JuJu informed him.

"Right," Fireball confirmed. "I actually laid mine down when the rear tire caught a big crack and threw me off the high side." He picked up his shirt to reveal road rash.

"Geez," Big Mac sympathized. "That explains those bandages. How fast were you goin'?"

"Like...fifteen. You gotta go slow, now. That's the only reason I ain't dead!"

Big Mac told him about getting thrown into the ditch. Slowly the two newcomers were being accepted.

Zombie movie...Ironic, Legion chuckled to himself. "You look like trash! Why don't you two go in back. We got hot water, women, whatever you need...

As the two men disappeared down a rear hallway, he nodded for Big Mac and Sweet T to come over. "I think they're legit," he almost whispered. "But keep an eye on them. Remember that Mexican Army that hit Monroe. Anything goes now."

Little did Legion know that at that moment, the City of Seattle and University of Washington were getting well acquainted with what an organized and motivated cartel could do.

"But they're white," Sweet T said. "Chill-ax, old man! They're patched members."

Legion reached out behind the man's shoulder and gave it a friendly squeeze-n-shake with his hand. He looked around the room. "It's a great time to be alive, ain't it? I'm so glad all of you are here!" He was the leader, and paying those little kudos went a long way. *Now...where the hell are Sticky, Trip, and Shorty?*

. . .

TAHOMA'S HAMMER Plus 25 Days.

THE MORNING SUN was starting to peek through the forest. The lingering, tropical system had finally blown completely east. Josh and his team felt the temperature drop rapidly in the pre-dawn as the lack of clouds allowed the earth's crust to cool. There was a light fog enveloping everything. About 150 meters east of the club's eastern border, a small fighting position had been hastily assembled the evening before. When the meeting had broken up, Josh had proposed to Phil that they have a few surprises planned.

The four-person team had been texting the info about the troops on the eastern perimeter for almost four hours. *Those little Gotennas are worth their weight in gold,* he thought. Phil and Jerry in the Command Post had a decent idea of the number of Guard surrounding their property and where they were hunkered. At about 0530, Josh had heard what sounded like a shotgun come from the highway. He learned via text that the Guard shot down Jerry's drone.

The brush in this area was very dense. The little trails the hunters had been blazing for the last few weeks were the only place people could walk and *maybe* not be heard. *These guys are rank amateurs,* he thought. *They haven't once sent anyone up this trail to see if we're here.* He could hear them talking, and it seemed to be getting a little more intense. He looked at his team, who had been working hard the last few weeks to learn everything they could about infantry basics.

Josh was taking point, due to his experience. He had the father/son team of Theron and Stephan Middenberg, and John Horn as his other teammates. In a small column that couldn't stagger very well due to the noise it would make, the four men very slowly proceeded west on the small trail, heading towards the range

—and the troops in between. Each was decked out in camo clothing and tactical gear. *I still can't believe I'm in a combat situation in Slaughter County.* His mind was taking him right back to Iraq.

He called for a stop and they all went from crouch-walking to kneeling. Like he'd trained them, the other three covered a different direction, setting "360-degree security." They were probably thirty meters from the nearest troops, just around a sharp bend and definitely exposed more than he liked. They seemed like rookies, and he didn't want to startle them into shooting. *It sounds like a couple of them are arguing.* He gave the signal for the others to stay put and proceeded to the last tree that would offer him both cover and concealment. He turned up the microphones on his electronic hearing protection, which had a decent chance of letting him eavesdrop.

"...up for this, Sarge!"

"I know, Jacobs, but what choice do we have. We're under orders!"

"We got the same choice everyone else has been makin'! Just leave!"

"I can't desert," a third voice said. "Not after all this time."

"All's I know is—I ain't shootin' people who haven't done anything wrong! And what this county's tryin' to pull is BS!"

"Maybe," said the sarge, "but that ain't up to you or me to decide. We're grunts. We follow orders. That's how we get back to our families without bein' court martialed."

Josh turned the volume back down a bit and cautiously retreated to his small squad. He gave a hand signal and they slowly made their way back to the prepared fighting position—a set of logs near the top of a small dell that they had made a primitive branch roof over. Everyone had a firing lane that they had spent the evening making with pruning saws. It would be easy for anyone paying attention to see all the fresh cuts. Josh just hoped the little unit between them and the range kept bickering amongst themselves.

"Keep those smoke-cannisters dry but accessible." He double

checked that the small butane torch was staying dry, too. That was the best way to light a bunch of fuses all at once.

SANDY SHOWED up to offer 'encouragement and support' about an hour or so into the afternoon.

"You shouldn't be here," the sheriff said without even looking up from his map.

"Feckless as usual, I see," she said nonchalantly. "Why haven't you boys entered yet, Sheriff?"

"Look, Sandy," he said. "Despite what we may think about each other, I don't think either of us wants to see bloodshed. Right?"

"Well, of course not, Ward. You make me sound like a tyrant when you ask it like that."

"Then let us do our job. This is not a twenty-person gang in Bartlett. Good people on both sides will die for no reason if we just go in guns blazing. So, please—get back in your HumVee and go home." He looked over at the major. "We don't need any more people in charge out here."

"Nice try, Raymond. You're not getting rid of me that easily," Sandy countered. "Major—you're in charge, now," she ordered.

Adam Matsumoto's face twisted with irritation, while the sheriff flushed with anger. "Absolutely not! No offense, Adam. This is a county issue, not a state or federal one." He looked at Charlie. "Reeves! Get her back to her HumVee!" he barked.

"If you like living on the right side of the bars, Lieutenant, you'll ignore that order!" She turned back to the sheriff. "The Unified Command passed a resolution this morning, giving me the authority to put the major in charge of this operation. Judge Floor approved it. After all, ninety percent of the men out here are his. Step aside, Sheriff. Or get arrested. I really don't care which!"

Sheriff Raymond looked at all the faces around him. *Confused fool needs time to think!*

"Judge Floor? You mean the judge who was a county commissioner three days ago?" Sheriff Raymond yelled. He found the whole situation extremely *iffy*.

"The law is the law, Sheriff!" *And that would be me!* "Major? What is your plan to arrest Phillip Walker?"

Adam was not happy with the situation. Like everyone else present, he was buying moments, trying to think things through. But she was pressing. "We have people surrounding the entire facility. We'll enter from here and keep them contained to their own property." He was lying—he had another plan, but he didn't want her to know.

There was an awkward silence while Adam thought he was done and Sandy didn't. "That's it? Great. Get started. Go on, Major." *What's the problem with these weak men? We need to wrap this up and be ready for that cartel!*

"Director, I'll need to perform some last minutes checks and tasks. I need you to go wait in your HumVee for your own protection."

The irony of what the major was doing to Sandy was lost on her. "I'm fine, Major! I'm in charge, now. Let's get this show on the road!" she said, clapping her hands with her last words like some sort of basketball coach.

"You said the resolution placed me in charge, correct? Specialist?" Major Matsumoto called to a young soldier. "Escort the Director to her HumVee. Ensure the crew of that rig knows she is to stay put until I give an all-clear." He looked back at Sandy when he said, "For her own protection."

"Yes sir," the young lady replied. "Ma'am?" she said to the director, trying to passively push her with a force field.

Sandy glared at Adam Matsumoto, but the frown eventually turned up into a knowing smirk. *Good to see your balls finally drop. Don't try it again...*Sandy complied and moved back into the rig she showed up in.

Adam looked at the sheriff. "Why don't you monitor from the

back of the MRAP so she'll stay out of the way?" The stunned sheriff nodded and moved back there quietly. "Charlie," the major called out. "Did I hear your friend on the radio say something about talking terms?"

Charlie was confused. "Uh, no...I didn't hear..." Then he caught the look on the major's face. "Ooooh—Yeah!" He pulled the cell phone from his pocket.

"How ya doin', Princess?" Earl asked his daughter. They were on the river, attempting to fish. They still hadn't caught anything. Earl figured the ash runoff had killed off a lot of them. *No need to tell her that. Just happy she's starting to integrate.*

"Alright, I guess," Piper said. She had opened up to her mother, and even to Conner, about the attempted abduction. She was reluctant to talk to anyone very much.

"Piper, I'm going to ask you something, and I want you to be straight with me."

She had just finished casting. They were floating flies in a quieter pool not too far from their cabin. She finally looked at her dad with tears in her eyes. "Yes, I know it's my fault," she said passively.

"Princess..." Earl said sullenly. "I'm sorry that's what you thought I was going to say." They fished for a bit more. "Are you mad at me for taking the shot? Do you think I would've killed you?" Piper started crying. Earl reeled his line in and set his pole on the bank. "Baby..." he said, at a loss for words. The father and daughter embraced for a bit. "Let's go up. They ain't bitin' today."

When they got near the cabin, Owen was coming out. "Dad!" he called when he saw them, oblivious that his sister had been crying. "Conner called on the radio. Told me to drag you to the gate."

"What's it about?" Earl asked.

"He didn't say, but he did say to hurry."

"Alright. Go on in and help your mother, Princess," he said to Piper. "Big O, could you secure this gear for me?"

"Yes, sir," the teen said. He got busy, and Earl jumped on one of the quads to scoot up to the gate. When he approached, he could see Conner, Dianne, and Jack as well as two youth. His jaw dropped as he stopped the machine. Before him were two tired, grungy, worried, familiar faces. They had depleted backpacks and one shotgun with them. He almost thought his mind was playing tricks on him.

"Wesley? James? What's going on, boys?" He looked around, confused. "Where's your mama?"

James started to sob a bit. The autistic Wesley wasn't going to cry, but he was rocking at the hips with stress. "Uncle Bubby!" James said, running to Earl and grabbing the big Ranger. That's when the boy really started sobbing. He was gasping too much to talk.

Earl looked at Wesley. "Wes? Can you tell me what happened?" Wes just added heavy exhales to his rocking and his face crinkled even more. "Buddy, it's okay if you can't. Calm down."

"Bad. Bad. Bad! Bad!" the fifteen-year-old started to repeat. His rocking intensified until tears finally started to come.

Earl dragged James with him and went over to wrap his arms around his older nephew. *What. The. Hell. Happened!* "James. I need you to calm down, now. What happened? How'd you get here?"

"Th-th-they killed my dad!"

"Who did? What happened to your mother and sister?" Earl was using his entire career in the Army as a foundation of calm, but inside he was exploding. "Talk to me, son. Where?"

"Way east of here!" the boy exclaimed. "Up near the pass. We've been walking and hiding for days!" Earl had finally looked at Conner, and his best friend's face was as concerned as he had ever seen it. James finally composed himself enough to finish. "We were on the way to here," he said. "We stopped at Grandpa's first."

"When was that?" Conner asked.

James looked at him. "Like about two weeks ago." He looked

back at his uncle. "It was going slow 'cause the Cub got a flat. We were staying on hiking trails south of the highway, mostly. We made it to Snoqualmie Pass about a week ago."

"Go on," Earl nudged.

"The trail cuts through some homes and then follows power lines across the mountains. We were quite a ways off from the highway. We came up on a team of horses and a wagon. Mom and Dad made me and Wes hide in some trees a little bit away!" The boy started getting anxious again. "They got jumped by a whole bunch of men! They killed my dad, Uncle Bubby!" The boy yelled, grabbing onto his uncle again. "W-we couldn't bury him! We had to just leave him there! Th-they took M-mom and Kathy!" he screamed into Earl's coat.

26

———————

"What?"

Tahoma's Hammer Plus 25 Days.

"What?" Legion yelled.

"The law and soldiers had to retreat in Seattle last night," the kidnapped radio operator repeated in his attic dungeon. "Plain as day. They were outnumbered and outgunned. Not only did I hear it on the local freqs, but that is *the* story being talked about on the HF channels all around the country. I even heard a conversation from South or Central America. *They're* talking about it."

Unacceptable, Legion thought. *This is our territory—it's our time!* "How many?"

"No idea, but the cops were guessing at least two thousand."

Two thou— "What?!" Legion repeated. *How is that possible? It's only been four weeks! Less than, actually!* "Keep listening!" he barked at the man and the prospect guarding him. He flew downstairs. "Praetorium! Five minutes!" he yelled loud enough for everyone to hear. Members of the support clubs started scrambling to go let people in the other houses know. Family members were put on lock down. Something bad was going on.

Praetorium. It was sacred to the club. More than a meeting or church, it was where brothers were made and business was handled. Members and invited guests only were locked in chambers—no guns, no phones, no grudges or beefs. If someone had something to say against another brother, it happened there. If a brother was being put "out bad"—kicked out of the club—Praetorium was where they had their club ink skinned off with a knife and lost an eyeball. It was balance—war and peace…yin and yang…heaven and hell.

The chamber wasn't meant for more than the normal compliment of members and guests, maybe twenty people. With invited club's officers there were almost fifty crammed in, all with a concerned look. There was a nervous buzz.

"Seal the chamber!" Legion ordered.

The two men closest to the door did as ordered. Legion sat in his big, padded chair, looking over at where Trip and Shorty should be. "I appreciate how you all have rallied, and how we've been able to go about conducting business here in the valley." He looked around. "You all need to keep it zipped when I say what I got to say. Feel me?"

There was a chorus of agreement. The room was heating up with all the bodies, made worse as nerves were starting to swell. Legion continued. "There is a no-kiddin', two-thousand-man Cartel Army that took over North Seattle last night." Despite his orders, the room exploded with comments. *What? Are you sure? No way!*

Legion rubbed his temples for a moment, then picked up the big battle hammer that he kept on the floor next to his chair. Big Mac had been quiet. When he saw the hammer, he plugged his ears. The big chair went flying backwards as Legion stood. *Wham!* The eight-pound maul came down and splintered the thick, oak table where he slammed it with all his rage. His most trusted brothers were absent, his plans were falling apart, and these knuckleheads couldn't follow a simple instruction to shut up. It had all added up.

"Quiet!" he screamed. Some of the members of the subservient clubs were not happy being treated like that. Men quieted, but nostrils were flaring and foreheads were darkening with anger.

He looked around the room. If he caught any attitude, the hammer was getting bloodied. "We need to get hold of the others —all of them but the Mexicans. They obviously knew this was comin'. This is real. They had rocket launchers and mortars. Get it?" He paused. They were all paying strict attention this time. "We got one choice. Find the Russians and the Blacks and form an immediate alliance. I'm not even puttin' this up for a vote! Anyone got a problem with that?" The room was in stunned silence.

"Now's your chance," Big Mac said, backing up his state president. "I will personally de-patch any brother who whines about this after Praetorium is over!"

Nobody felt like losing skin and an eye. They all knew Legion was right. If all they were being told was true, it had become a numbers game, and a real shooting war was on the way.

THE STANDOFF WAS ENTERING its fourteenth hour. The sun was starting its November descent and the shadows in the forest were all growing. Phil was coming back from the north perimeter when he got a few texts from the guys at the gate, and from Shay. He learned that some lady had arrived and essentially emasculated the sheriff. He texted back to Shay.

[Phil: "Hang in there, kiddo. You'll be having company soon. Approaching from the west. You should see them any minute now."]

He pulled the old piece of tarp out of his pocket and looked at the circular stitching. *If this doesn't work, it's going to be a bad night…*

THE MESH NETWORK! Still plugged in! Phil had given Charlie access during the stint that he and his family were staying out there. He shot Phil a text, hoping.

[Charlie: "We need to talk. Let me come in. Just me."]

After a long three minutes, he felt a phone vibrate for the first time in weeks. *I knew keeping this thing charged would come in handy!*

[Brrrt—Phil: "Meet you halfway down the rifle line. Proceed."]

Charlie hoped that he didn't get shot approaching the gate. He had his hands slightly up and walked slowly. Buddy Chadwell unlocked the secondary gate that goes to the rifle line and let him through. Charlie could see a few people lining the trees as he walked down the road. *Yikes.* He couldn't help but look at the big log structure that was nearing completion. *That's pretty impressive. Especially the rock fireplaces.* He made it to the far end of the structure near the slots for holding targets at the hundred-yard marker.

The bright, blue November day was chilly, especially in the long shadows of autumn. The morning fog had burnt off many hours earlier. Finally, he could see Phil approaching from the north, coming up the cross-range road. He was walking somewhat slow and painfully. When Phil was just a few yards away, Charlie broke the ice. "What's up with the limp?"

"Hmmm," Phil mumbled, not expecting small talk. "Been on the prosthetic way too much lately. Think I'm getting a rash. Hopefully that's all it is…not cellulitis or something worse." They went silent. "So, Lieutenant, huh?"

Charlie chuckled ironically. "Battlefield promotion, let's say," he joked.

"Interesting choice of words," Phil countered softly.

"Yeah, except I'm not the one comparing this standoff to The

Battle of the Bulge," Charlie replied. "Yes, I've read a history book or two."

"What's happening here, Charlie? Why does the sheriff want to de-arm us so badly? We're not the bad guys."

"It's not the sheriff, per se, Phil—it's the system."

"What does that even mean?" Phil asked, slightly annoyed. He was trying to keep his voice calm. "Systems don't make decisions—people do."

"It means that the leaders of the local government during this state of emergency have made a decision to disarm people who commit crimes. We have evidence that you've been at two shootouts in just the last few days. You all don't have to like it—most of the cops don't like it—but it's the law."

"That's where you're wrong, pal," Phil said. "First off, laws are written and passed by legislators, not commissioners and directors. They write codes and regulations—"

"I know, Phil. Semantics and technicalities. We've had this discussion a dozen times. I already know what you think. Remember?"

"And secondly," Phil continued a little more firmly, "any regulations, codes, or laws that are in disagreement with the superior forms of law above it are null and void! Those orders don't have to be enforced." They both paused for a bit. "Let me put it a different way. There are something over three thousand counties in the U.S., right?"

"Sure," Charlie agreed.

"And the top law enforcement official in each and every one of those is the sheriff. He or she has the power to kick the Feds out, if he wants to! That's what the Constitution's Tenth Amendment gave us. 'The powers not delegated to the United States by the Constitution, nor prohibited by it to the States, are reserved to the States respectively, or to the people'," Phil quoted from memory. "*The people*, Charlie!"

"What's your point, Phil?" *You can get quite repetitive in your law sermons...*

"That the sheriff can decide! It's that easy! He is the chief peace officer for Slaughter County. Not that FEMA lady!"

"Except he's more worried about his career than your rights," Charlie said. "You know that. Besides, there's a point here you're not even considering."

"What's that?" Phil asked skeptically.

"Like the fact that the gangs are getting ready to run everything. Do you know that a huge cartel army hit Seattle last night?"

This caught Phil off guard. "Well, *that* I didn't know. But I am *keenly* aware of what the gangs are up to. What happened in Seattle?"

"Hundreds, if not thousands, of cartel members wiped out an entire sector of police and Guard near the university," Charlie explained. "You see—we can't be wasting time like this, Phil."

"Perspective, my friend. If what you say is true, you don't need less armed citizens—you need more! Work with us, Charlie! You know how good the training here is. Find the good citizens in this county and deputize them! We'll train them!" Phil could see Charlie's wheels spinning. "Bring the sheriff in here. Let me talk to him."

Too little, too late, Charlie thought. "Sheriff's been relieved," he finally said. He knew he shouldn't have, but he felt peace would only hold if they were fully honest with each other.

Phil's face turned red. "By whom?"

"The Unified Command just put the major from the Guard in charge. I don't think he wants to push this, either, but I'm sure he'll do it if I fail to talk you guys into giving up."

"The Unified Command? Or *her*?" Phil asked angrily. Just then his phone vibrated, and he checked it.

[Brrrt—Shay: "They r here, will spread out @ signal"]

"Problems?" Charlie asked.

"Quite the opposite, my friend." Phil sent a quick text to Craig Wageman just a couple of dozen yards away. "May I suggest we go into this log structure?" the old Marine said.

"Why?" Charlie asked very suspiciously. "What's goin' on, Phil?"

Just then, the *Whoompf* of very large firework mortars went shooting skyward from behind the rifle line's left side berm. "Just a little distraction," Phil replied, dragging his friend into the new shelter.

Boom! Boom!

"What the—" Charlie started to yell.

Boom! Boom! Boom! Boom! In all there were twenty of them that erupted over the next two minutes. It was still too light out to make for a very good show, but the noise was deafening and the sparks were distracting. *Perfect!* Phil thought. The mortars had a slight angle toward the highway and were exploding over the Guard units.

Charlie's radio squawked. "Reeves! What just happened?!" he heard Adam Matsumoto yell. "We were just attacked! I'm ordering you to stand down and exit the facility immediately!"

Charlie seethed as he looked at Phil. "What—was—that?"

"Sorry, brother. I wasn't sure if your people were going to start shooting, so we came in here for cover."

That answer wasn't good enough for Charlie. The big deputy got in Phil's face. "Tell me everything! Now! If you ever want to salvage our friendship! What's happening?!"

"I'm proving my point, my friend. And if your Major is smart, we can all get out of this alive."

27

Hope For The Best.

TAHOMA'S HAMMER PLUS 25 DAYS.

"YOU THE DUDE in charge 'round here?" Sticky asked the man. He was in the small city of Port Angeles, west of Sequim. It was the main hub of anything that might be considered remotely industrial along this part of Washington State. Sticky was surrounded by no less than eight men, most of them wearing some form of flannel shirt, logger-style dungarees, or heavy-duty fisherman's raingear. They were in the second floor loft about six blocks from the piers, where many of the facilities and boats had been ripped to shreds by the incoming tsunami. The wave had travelled due east, sparing the city from major devastation only a few blocks in from its waterfront.

Sticky had utilized what he'd learned from Louie. He knew that the men he was looking for either operated or flat out owned a charter fishing service. They also happened to be occasional meth distributors for the Motorcycle Club. Once he got to town, it was as simple as going to the wharf/marina area and asking around. They were in what used to be a small office and apartment above a local watering-hole.

"The name's Shotgun," the grizzled looking fisherman in his late fifties said through a gray and dirty beard. He was sitting behind a desk fooling around with a battery and a marine radio. He gave Sticky only the slightest of looks. "Just who are you?"

"I'm with the Risen Dead. I'm on a quest to avenge a couple of slain brothers," Sticky said coolly.

This got Shotgun to look up. If it were true, he didn't want to disrespect the man. Shotgun was no fool—he knew that the RDMC had been preparing for a world without the rule-of-law for a long time. "Really?" He looked Sticky over. "Forgive me if I don't just take your word...It's not like you're wearing a cut. And you're by yourself." *He ended with a look that said care to explain that?*

Most of the men around the room remained still, though Sticky could hear a couple of the younger ones become restless. He stood up and removed his coat and shirt, revealing several pieces of club-related tattoo work. "My name's Sticky," he said about as calm as any man could be. He was completely within his element.

"So, *you're* Sticky Wood, huh?" Shotgun had always gone to great lengths to maintain a positive, working relationship with any organized crime that might *actually* feed him and his family to the fish. He knew prison and gang tattoos, and he knew criminals—he had no doubt this man was who he said he was. He also knew that at some point, he would have to cut the crime syndicate in on his recent piracy booty. "I thought you were locked up?"

"I seriously doubt too many people are locked up by now," Sticky countered.

Shotgun gave out a hearty laugh while he was pulling a vodka bottle off the bookshelf behind his desk. "You guys relax!" he called out to his crew. "This guy's an honored guest!" He found a couple of dirty glasses and poured them full, handing one to Sticky. "What can we do for you...can I call you Sticky?" Shotgun had owned a few Harleys and camped at a few biker rallies over the years. He knew better than to assume anything with a full-patched one-percenter. Respect was a huge part of their culture.

"Of course, Shotgun!" Sticky said, half-downing the glass in one pull. "I have a feeling we're gonna be pals by the time we pass out tonight!"

As Shotgun's crew meandered out of the room, the pair of men swapped stories and downed shots for close to an hour. Sticky learned that Shotgun had set up a coalition of the owners of boats that had survived. Once he learned that the local Coast Guard Station had been completely wiped out by the waves, he knew that nobody would stop him from robbing relief ships as they cruised east on the Strait of Juan de Fuca. He didn't need to hit them all—just enough to feed a black market that had sprung up in the foothills of the Olympic Mountains.

"You know," Sticky said under the wisdom and insightfulness of a good buzz while he stared at his glass, "you guys are pirates—you should be drinkin' rum...."

"Bwah-Ha-Ha-Ha-Ha!" Shotgun exploded in laughter. After the raucous noise had died down and they both grew silent for a bit, Shotgun finally asked, "So, who are we looking for?"

"There's a future-dead-man on the way up to Sequim to check on his folks. He somehow managed to kill two of my brothers in their sleep. I'm going to make him suffer—and I mean for a loooonggg time...." Sticky's eyes had dilated so much that they appeared black and colorless, which scared the drunk right out of Shotgun.

"Don't worry, Sticky," the new ally said. "I got contacts in Sequim that can find *any*body."

JERRY and his assistants had spent a lot of time making sure everyone was proficient at using the little cheap Baofeng radios. They could monitor two channels automatically, but with programming they could scan a few or many—it all depended on what the operator wanted. He had programmed his, Phil's, and the new listening post team leaders' radios to not only scan the range's two tactical frequencies, but all the county's as well. The new posts had been hastily built off the range's property the evening before. They couldn't listen to the guard, but they could hear anything that the civilian police and sheriffs were transmitting. The range perimeter was using one channel and the new, hidden LPs were using another.

"Contact northeast!" Josh heard someone panicky yell into their radio. He was less than three hundred meters from that position, with a lot of trees and brush in between.

"Contact southeast," he heard a slightly calmer voice say. "They're pushing in from both east and south."

Josh heard Phil's voice. "All eastern perimeter positions, 'wheels up'. I say again 'wheels up'. LPs, commence Plan Alpha. *Do not engage first!*"

Wheels up was code for them to light off the Catherine wheels style of fireworks they had hung in the trees about twenty feet up and eighty feet out from their foxholes. Those were large circular fireworks, in this case about three feet in diameter, that spun and threw out a large volume of sparks in a huge, circular design for about forty-five seconds.

"Everyone drop your field packs and check your safeties," Josh ordered his team. "Grab the smokes and torch," he said directly to John. When the man had shouldered the special bag, Josh gave them the signal to form up behind him and stagger as best they could on the thin trail. The sun was dipping west, in the direction they were travelling, making it difficult to see. Josh knew that two other teams were making similar approaches on the north and south sides.

Ka-Krow! A slight pause...then—*Ka-Ka-Krow! Ka-Ka-Ka-Ka-Ka-Ka-*

Krow! The sounds of a firefight started up on the northeast corner. *Dangit!* Josh sliced-the-pie on the big tree from earlier that morning and noticed the squad was gone. He scanned into the orange glow to the west and thought he could see bent brush swaying. *Forward!* He gave the hand signal to his team. He could smell and see the smoke being created by the circular fireworks up ahead. Suddenly the sounds of a firefight erupted from the southeast corner. *We need to hurry! I think these guys can be reasoned with.*

It was late in the club house, and many of the men were having shots to help them sleep. Most had drifted to their various rooms in houses nearby. Those with women were looking to fill more primitive needs. The next morning was a big trip to Seattle—the meeting they had sought was easily attained. All the other gangs knew what had happened. The alliance was practically formed already. They just needed a battle plan. None of them noticed the fresh bandages on Fireball's arm—or the fact that he and JuJu had been drinking from their own bottle of whiskey.

The olive green rohypnol pills—commonly called roofies—had been hiding under a very realistic-looking scab on Fireball's arm, part of a professional moulage kit that make-up artists use for special effects. Legion himself had provided a great opportunity to spike the alcohol. The two infiltrators never even went to Praetorium, choosing to hide in a closet until the chamber was sealed. They poured several bottles out, thereby forcing everyone to drink from only six bottles. They put enough drugs into them to knock out an elephant.

Pretty much everyone had had *something* to drink. The effects started within twenty minutes, taking quick effect on some and longer on others. The powerful tranquilizer did its job. Grown men started to lie down, feeling woozy or nauseated. Their cheeks became flushed. They all assumed they were just too drunk from not eating enough food. JuJu and Fireball were both experienced operators. They had kept track of who slipped out without drinking a lot. Once the room started to pass out, they pulled their aluminum water bottles out of their packs and went to work.

Out of each bottle came a rag. Each one unrolled to reveal a suppressor and threaded barrel for the otherwise standard pistols they were carrying. They stuffed spare magazines in their pockets and went to work. Once they had killed everyone in the main building—except for Legion—they went out to start clearing the rest of the buildings, one at a time. The most dangerous part of all of it was the women and children. They hadn't been drugged, and it took a bit of coordination when a few of them tried to shoot back.

Legion had been tied up and force-fed additional alcohol to ensure he would pass out while they wrapped up the operation. After they finished clearing and double checking everything, they went back to the main structure. They cut Legion's clothes off and threw him on the pool table, naked. They double checked his bindings and commenced taking turns catching naps. There was a big day coming.

28

Prepare For The Worst.

TAHOMA'S HAMMER PLUS 25 DAYS.

AFTER PHIL TOLD Charlie the full plan, Charlie knew he needed to get back to Major Matsumoto. *This'll be a bloodbath if I can't stop it!* He ran back across the range and out the gate at about the moment he heard gunfire erupting on the eastern side of the property. "Stop!" he yelled at the major.

"You had your chance, Charlie," Adam said. "I don't like this any more than you do, but it has drug on long enough!"

Charlie was still catching his breath from the sprint. So far no engagement on the west side had erupted, but everyone was taking cover...on edge... "W-What are you doing?" He pointed east towards the building firefights. "People are about to die!"

"That's something Phil Walker will have to live with, then!" the

major exclaimed. He turned his attention to one of his junior officers, who was trying to queue up the helmet cam footage on a
tablet. Everyone was taking cover behind vehicles. The plan had
been the exact opposite of what the major had told Sandy McCallister. The box-in would be performed from the three forested sides,
with the highway team serving as the pressure point to drive
everyone toward.

"More than you know, Major," Charlie yelled. "They have you
outnumbered! It's a trap! You need to call this insanity off!"

"They *don't* have us outnumbered, Charlie!" Adam said,
confused. "I don't know what you're up to, but my number one
priority is to my people. We need to wrap up this op and start
preparing for the cartel. Now—out of my way!" He brushed past
Charlie, just as upset about the whole situation but committed to
seeing it through.

Sandy McCallister just couldn't help herself. She looked
somewhat silly in her wrinkled pants suit, flak jacket, and old military helmet that swam on her head. She jumped out of her protec-
tive HumVee and strolled over to the major and Charlie. "You're
relieved of duty!" she yelled at Charlie. "Major! Have this man
detained!"

Charlie had finally found his breaking point. He wasn't sure
what the future had in store for him and his family, but his career
with the Slaughter County Sheriff was wrapping up in the next
moment. "You can go to hell!" Charlie grumbled through clenched
teeth. Sandy started to yell back, but she wasn't a 6' 2" deputy with
Command Authority. "Shut your stupid pie-hole! I'm not done! You
claim power and authority you don't have, and now people are
dying! You hear that?" he yelled, pointing in the direction of the
firefights. "Huh?! *You* caused that!"

Charlie's mistake was coming up for air. The Godfather had her window. "If people die, *Sergeant* Reeves" —implying his new promotion had just evaporated— "then their blood rests squarely on the shoulders of that criminal in there! Just *whaaat* on Earth were you doing in there? Selling him fireworks?" The not-so-subtle dig at Charlie's heritage caused Adam and a few others to twist their faces and look away.

"Kiss my hairy brown butthole, you racist witch!" Charlie screamed directly into her face. He'd never been tempted to punch a woman so strongly before.

Sandy smiled a vindictive sneer. "You're done!" She looked around at the shocked audience. Instead of paying attention to the range's western perimeter, they were all gawking. "Listen up, all of you! And listen good! This isn't about guns! It's about *compliance!* The sooner you all come to terms with that, the better your lives will be!" She had everyone's full attention. "We are the authorities! We have to deal with the crises as they unfold. If we can't control one man, then just how do you think we're going to beat that gang of mercenaries!" She was practically frothing. "It's *plain* and simple— they *need* to obey us or pay the consequence!"

JOSH SPRINTED in three second bursts, using the old soldier's montage, *I'm Up! They see me! I'm down!* as he ran. If they had been in the open, he would've been hitting the ground each time. In this brush he was only taking a knee every time he got to *I'm down* in his head. His team did their best to keep up while maintaining cover. *Ka-Ka-Ka-Krow! Ziiiippp-whirrr!* The engagement between the perimeter post and the troops to his west had started. He dropped to the ground and his team followed suit.

"Keep low! We're just as likely to get hit from friendly-fire as them shootin' at us!" He started low crawling up the trail, trying to see the Guard squad's rear. *I sure hope their inexperience means they aren't watching their six.*

Just then Josh's radio exploded with excited, panicky chatter. "This is the north-central foxhole! We need the runners up here! Craig and Emily have both been hit!"

Crap! We need to get this locked down! Josh knew that once those with no combat experience started seeing their friends get shot, casualties would sky-rocket—or the Guard would overrun them very quickly. *We can't afford to lose the initiative!*

He finally caught a glimpse of two of them, hunkered behind a fallen log and occasionally taking shots to the west. His eyes finally caught the other four. *They got caught in the tangle-foot!* he thought excitedly. *The snare actually worked! We need smoke!* He gave John the hand signal. John pulled the materials out of the pack and lit the fuses, while Theron and Stephan maintained their eyes in the south and north directions. All of them looked frightened, but everyone was behaving decisively. *These guys are holding it together,* Josh noted. John scooted up and started handing the lit smoke cannisters to Josh. "You throw northeast, I'll get the rest!" Josh hissed. They both got up on one knee and started tossing the energy drink cans as far as they could.

When they were done and waiting for the smoke field to build, Josh keyed up on the perimeter frequency. "East-central, this is East LP. Shift your fire northeast or southeast! We'll be on the east side of your engagement in one mike. If you hear them stop shooting, then cease fire! How copy?" He heard an acknowledgment in his ear protection speakers. The firefight was building in intensity. *I just hope to God everyone is keeping their heads down before this gets out of hand!* "Remember—I want to try to capture and talk to these guys! Instead of bounding each other, I'll keep the lead." He started to crouch and move forward. *I can't let one of these newbs get killed making contact.*

The smoke was doing a very effective job. *They think it's coming from the fireworks!* Josh approached the two scared Guard members, and they never heard him coming. "Cease fire! Drop your rifles!" he yelled from behind a tree eight feet away. The two members froze.

He could see the others freezing, too. "You're surrounded. Put your rifles down and your hands on your helmets." The sounds of the firefight slowed along the north perimeter.

All six of the Guard members unslung their rifles and placed them on the ground. A couple of them kept their bodies turned from Josh and their hands low. "Look, chumps! I served in Iraq! I know what I'm doing. Put your hands up! You're only in danger if you don't!" All of them began to comply. Josh and John covered them while the other two came up and started securing rifles.

"We gonna zip tie these guys?" Stephan asked.

"Naw. There's a hundred YouTube channels that taught everyone how to break out of those, and we don't have any of the actual handcuff zip ties. I got a better idea."

Josh had his team set 360 security while he radioed in to Phil and the perimeter that the position was secured. He could hear the action cease on the northeast as well. He then had all the soldiers sit on their butts along the log that the two had been using for cover. "LP3," he called into his radio. "Do you need us to push from the flank?" He waited a few seconds.

"Negative, Lead, we'll have this secured shortly," he heard.

"Roger," he told the southeast squad leader. He then let his slung rifle fall to his front. "Look dudes…and gal," he said after taking a more thorough look. "We were listening to you all discuss your loyalties this morning." As if on cue, the last of the gunshots died out. "Hear that?" he asked, pointing in that direction.

A few of them looked at each other, murmuring. "Don't say a word to him," the sergeant ordered.

"I don't expect you to talk," Josh said, ignoring him. "You all are in timeout. I just want you to sit there and think about the one— and only one—way this plays out. We can't have Americans killing Americans like this. We had you dead-to-rights. We chose not to shoot. You can, too."

THE MAJOR HAD BEEN RECEIVING reports and helmet cam footage. His head dropped. He had tuned her out moments earlier, no longer caring what Sandy did or thought. His attack was not going according to plan. He heard the engagements slowly die off, which verified what he was seeing on the tablet. "Director," he said, trying to interrupt her diatribe. "Director!"

"What, Major? What! Spit it out!" She was still looking around at everyone wildly.

Just then, a few of the nearest soldiers started pointing and talking. Everyone looked at the gate. There was Phil Walker, walking through it, with his hands up and waving a dirty, white towel.

Here goes nothing, Phil thought nervously.

29

"The honor of a nation is its life."
—Alexander Hamilton

Tahoma's Hammer Plus 25 Days.

The crowd grew silent as Phil walked through the gate. He paused at the sandbags and tarp that served as a guard shack, looking in. "Great job, guys. I know you both must be tired and hungry. Hang in there just a bit more." They both nodded.

Phil walked out to the edge of the driveway and highway with his hands in the air. He paused and looked around. Every person had stopped in their tracks to watch him. *Guess I don't need this anymore.* He let the towel hit the ground and proceeded to the officers standing next to Charlie. He looked at Matsumoto. "I'm Phillip Edward Walker. I demand a trial by jury, and I want to speak to the elected and sworn sheriff." The major's face was shocked, and Phil knew why—the club had gained the upper hand. *He's confused as to why I'm turning myself in,* Phil thought. *Good.*

What Phil and the major both knew was that several of the squads had been captured, and the vast majority of the rest had laid down their arms voluntarily. Despite some casualties on both sides, the club members had risked their advantage and momentum to capture rather than kill the Guard members.

Adam went over and personally removed Phil's Glock from the holster. After removing the magazine and chambered round, he handed it off to a subordinate. "You may put your hands down, Mr. Walker. Follow me." He headed for the open back of the nearest rig. Sandy was approaching with a pleasantly surprised look on her face.

As the two men and Charlie and Sandy converged near the back of the rig, she said, "I hope you know that you've been an arrogant donkey, Mr. Walker." She was trying her best to invoke a scolding any mother would envy. "All this has done is waste our resources and endanger lives. I will ensure the law is applied to you to the fullest extent!"

"I'm only dealing with the sheriff," Phil said coldly as he stared straight down, towering over her. "I wouldn't let you lick the sweat off my stump if you were dying of thirst in the desert."

Sandy was livid. "Why, you—"

"Oh, shut up, McCallister!" everyone heard from a new direction. It stunned many of them—everyone had nearly forgotten Sheriff Raymond was still around. He descended the steps on the back of the MRAP. "Nobody wants to hear you bark anymore! You're under arrest." She guffawed and started to protest, but the sheriff yelled over her. "Wildman! Luzon! Place the director under arrest for…sedition sound about right to you?" the sheriff said to Phil.

"Sedition!" she screamed.

"We'll find some other charges, too, I'm sure. Usurpation of power not authorized and such." Sandy screamed bloody murder as the two deputies dragged her to a squad car three vehicles south and threw her in the back.

"You know she's connected, right?" Adam asked. "Still...*whew*... that was pretty awesome!" He was still shocked like most everyone else.

"I'm not too worried about that, anymore, Major. It'll be a long time before we need to worry about politics the way we used to. If those days ever come back, I'll just quit anyhow. Now—" he said, looking at Phil. "What made you give up after three-quarters of a day?"

"If I'm truly guilty of a crime, then try me in a legitimate court, Sheriff."

"You know darn well we won't be able to do that for a long time," the sheriff replied.

"Kind of like not worrying about politics," Phil countered.

The sheriff chuckled. "I...guess you got me there," he said, smiling slightly.

Phil looked at Charlie, who nodded for him to proceed. "You know what you need, Sheriff?"

"I can only imagine what you're about to say, Phil..."

"A posse." Phil let that hit him, noting his skepticism. "Seriously. This cartel thing is just the start. Wait until they start feeding people. Or giving them health services. It ain't just about drugs and human trafficking, Ward. They'll be providers."

"And you think if I form a posse, that'll help with...what? Our staffing? You really proposing that I send out civilians on patrols, Phil?"

"We already are. And in a much bigger way than you realize."

"I know, I know. You've been busy out here. Still curious about the East Bartlett thing, though..."

Phil could see it was time to let them know exactly how the Slaughter County slaughter would have played out. "The major may not have told everyone yet, but we stole the initiative. We captured your troops or enticed them to lay down arms. You are in over your heads. The Slaughter Peninsula Posse is reliable and effective, Sheriff."

"You mean you had the forest squads surrounded," Adam corrected.

Phil knew it was a time to speak with actions. He pulled a chemlite out of his pants pocket, giving it a crack and shake to get the two chemicals to mix. The little plastic rod started to emit a dark, pastel red that contrasted with just about everything out there. Phil wandered away from the small group at the back of the MRAP, stepping towards the west side of the vehicle behind it. He held the glowing stick over his head, slowly moving and turning as he looked at all the surrounding deputies and Guard members. After a good thirty seconds, he stopped, facing the forest to the west, which was several feet higher than the freeway itself. He dropped the glowing stick to the ground. There wasn't a person out there who wasn't watching—even Sandy, screaming with no noise at the glass that imprisoned her.

Everyone except Charlie dropped their jaws at what came next. Out of the woods came flying a solo, green, glowing stick. Then another, followed quickly by two oranges and a yellow. Suddenly it was raining glowsticks, not just from the woods to the west, but from the strip of forest along the highway that separates the club's property from the road. Some of the sticks hit the vehicles. One or two hit a soldier. They littered the ground like little, nuclear pencils.

Sheriff Raymond's eyes grew wide as he saw dozens upon dozens of Slaughter Peninsula Posse members led by Gary Stonefence and Skinny Kenny stand up in the brush and come out from behind trees in the west-side forest. Every one of them was kitted up and ready to fight. The scene was compounded by the range's residents on the east side of the road.

"Fish in a barrel..." he slowly mumbled, realizing the Guard had the low ground.

For close to five hundred feet of the highway, they were caught between two forces above them on both sides. He looked at Phil and pulled the Constitution that the tired Marine had sent him out of his left breast pocket. "You are full of surprises, Mr. Walker," he said, thumping the tiny document against his other palm, thinking.

"Our duty is to be ready, Sheriff," Phil explained. He looked more closely at what the sheriff was holding. "It was the quote, wasn't it?"

The sheriff looked down toward the grill of the rig behind them, as if thinking thoughtfully. "No...no...not really." He handed the little pocket Constitution back to Phil. "Let's just say that your dedication to making sure I heard your message was a reminder of what's important. I may not be a strict Constitutionist like you, Phil, but you did remind me that government serves the people, even during disasters." Sheriff Ward Raymond smiled a bit. "What I saw unfolding out here today was the opposite of that. Call your folks down, Phil. You, too, Major." Phil stepped back a few paces and started calling people on the radio. Before he got too far away, the sheriff said to him. "We'll talk more about this posse thing in a day or two."

Charlie wandered over to Phil and waited until he was done speaking on the radio. "What quote?"

Phil looked down at the little book and then handed it to his best buddy. Charlie opened it and saw Phil's handwriting— "Men must be governed by God, or they will be ruled by tyrants." – William Penn.

TAHOMA'S HAMMER Plus 26 Days.

"GIT DOWN THERE, YOU SKANKY WHORE!" the one they called Jeremy said as he gave Natalie a shove.

Natalie twisted her knee when she hit the ground in the root cellar with a hard thud. She let out a fresh wail from the pain. It sounded raspy and weak, a result of a full week of crying, calling for help, and screaming in terror. Her nights were spent crying for her children. Only God knew what they were doing with Katherine. She lived in a fantasy in her mind where her boys found their way to her brother's cabin. *If he's even alive,* she bemoaned. Every time she found some nugget of hope in her mind, something else stepped on it. *For all you know, Bubby died on the first day.*

Hit another apple, Bubby! She'd drift back to her childhood in her mind, remembering a time when she and her brother would use a baseball bat to hit the last, mushy apples in the autumn that nobody wanted. She grew up calling him Bubby, because as a toddler she couldn't say brother. The name had been hers to use for him, and hers alone—until she had kids. His career in the Army and his falling out with their father had meant she'd spent much of her adulthood not getting to see him. They were close, though. Her memories of smashing rotten apples with Bubby were what she used to go to sleep. She did that, praying she wouldn't have another migraine when she awoke.

She had no idea how long she'd been down in the hole. They only brought her out to help with chores. There were seven of them —five men and two women, plus four kids. She was the only one that was a captive, as best as she could tell. She hadn't seen her precious daughter since *that day.* She groped in the dark until she found the old blankets covered in rat urine. She found herself trying to count the rats in the dark. Her fear of them had subsided until one of them bit her when she slept—which was still preferable to when one or more of the men got drunk.

Natalie felt that the worst injury was happening in the form of slow decay to her mind. She had severe diarrhea, hadn't been given much food, dirty water, beaten…and worse. She had severe rashes and infections, and now, a sprained knee. Roy had been murdered in cold blood, and her children were missing. There was no hope. In her mind, she was now just looking for an opportunity to end herself. She was high up in the snowy mountains. If she had escaped, she wouldn't last two hours in the elements—*if* they didn't find her and kill her. *God!* She begged in her mind for the millionth time, *please just kill me!*

REYNALDO ARRIVED several minutes after his advance team. It would be his third time that day he was visiting a captured "general." Each "meeting" was unique, crafted by the advance team with whatever tools were available. He had several more to attend that day. He got out of his armored SUV and stepped over a few bodies as he walked into the clubhouse from the rear parking area. The entire compound was surrounded by fifty of his best men.

Renaldo Hernandez walked into the room and surveyed his surroundings. He saw his special forces and smiled. "Brothers!" he called in English. "You've done perfectly. I knew I could count on you. Your families will never want for anything!" He gave them both a hug. "Go. Rest. You've earned it."

The handsome cartel leader proceeded to the business end of the structure, the old hotrod and chopper customization shop that was on the street side of the building. In the middle of the empty garage was Legion—naked and chained upside down with chain hoists mounted to the ceiling. Legion and his employees used to lift engines out of vehicles with them. Two separate hoists about ten feet apart were holding him in the air, one wrapped around each ankle. There were two more attached to the shop's large, metal parts shelves. They were attached low, near the ground. The four chain hoists were tense enough to have Legion splayed out like an upside-down, human "X."

Rey kind of chuckled when he walked in and saw it. *These sickos get more creative each and every time, don't they?* "Hello," he called out to Legion. There was a sack on his head, taped to his neck to keep it on.

"H-Hey! Hello! Are you the man in charge?" he yelled

nervously. He had never been on the receiving end before—it was a new experience.

"I am," Reynaldo acknowledged. In his own mind, he was quoting the Bible, though he doubted Legion would get it. "I understand that you were organizing a group to fight us…"

"H-Hey! Whoa! We can deal, alright? I got stuff, we got cooks, we got cash!" He was getting nothing from Reynaldo. "P-Please! Listen!"

Typical, Reynaldo thought. He gave a signal and the four warriors running the manual hoists began to retract the chain. The links wrapped themselves tighter into the ankles and wrists of the big biker, causing his begging to speed up and morph into screaming in agony. *I wonder which will pop off first…feet?…or hands?* He left the shop as Legion screamed for mercy. Rey didn't really enjoy the torture so much. In the end, they would just shoot him in the head. The torture served as a deterrent for other potential agitators. *I hope the Russians put up a better fight.*

30

New Beginnings.

Tahoma's Hammer Plus 27 Days.

Phil found Josh up at the growing graveyard in the north end of the field. "Thought I might find you up here," he said.

"I didn't know these guys and gals very well," Josh said, "but it doesn't mean their deaths mean any less to me." *And now I have to learn to deal with it without drinking.*

They were looking at seven, handcrafted wooden crosses. They weren't labeled yet, but somebody had made plans to make some nice markers.

"I can't believe Craig Wageman is gone," Phil said glumly. "Just a couple of weeks ago he helped me bury Hope Brazik in her own backyard. Now we've buried him." He went silent again.

Josh could tell that this was mounting on Phil too soon after Crane's death. "What about the others?"

"I didn't know Emily all that well," Phil said. "But old Tommy? He'd been a range member fifty-two years, if you can believe it. Joined when he was twenty!" The pair stared at the graves for a while longer, letting silence take over again.

Josh's curiosity finally got to him. "So, what's up? It feels like you want to say something."

"Well…We're a month into this thing. We've already been in a handful of scraps and firefights, and two funerals…" he trailed for a short moment. "And Payton's six plus months pregnant."

Ahhh…the doctor. "You wanna go press Stu?"

"I thought if we went together," Phil explained.

Josh looked back down at the graves and sighed. "Yeah, I'm done here for now. In fact, there's an idea I want to run past you." The two continued to chat as they strolled to the front end of the property and found Stu's office door near the rifle line closed. Hearing voices inside, they waited a few minutes. In short order, it opened as Fred's widow, Phyllis, left. She was coughing and sniffling from a chest condition. She kept her mouth covered with her sleeve and said hello as she passed Phil and Josh.

Stu caught sight of them and gave a small nod. "Can I get one of you to come pour?" he asked.

He'd set up a small table right next to the door. It had a small tub, soap, and a carafe of warm water that had been boiled earlier that morning. He started using the tub water and soap to wash his hands while Josh came over and helped him rinse. They had run completely out of napkins or paper towels, so he dried his hands on an old t-shirt rag.

"It's amazing how good something like a little warm water on the hands can feel when we've been without power for so long!" Stu said somewhat excitedly. "What's happening, fellas? You two look like the cat that ate the canary."

"Nothing gets past you, Stu," Phil quipped. "I imagine you already know why we're here."

"Ah," he said with a nod. "Time to poop or get off the pot, huh?" He led the two into the small room where they could at least get a little warmer. He and Josh parked on the bunk while Phil took the rolling stool.

"Something like that," Phil said. "We're not here to kick you out or anything. But it would be nice to know your intentions."

Stu took a slight breath and then sighed as he looked down at the floor between them all. "I do like being here, but…I have to go. I hope you guys understand."

"We do," Josh said, trying to get his two cents in. "I've thought a bit about this since our last talk." He looked at Phil, who gave him a small nod. "I want to go with you."

Stu was dumbfounded. "G-go with me? Why?" He realized that must have sounded rude. "Sorry. That came out wrong…but…why would you do that?"

"Don't get all emo, Doc," Josh said, chuckling. "It's purely self-serving! We'll get your folks and bring them back. That's all."

"Ohhh, you don't know my mother," Stu said, shaking his head skeptically. "She's not leaving. She might even stay out of spite just because I suggested she leave."

"I get that, Stu," Phil said. "But you might be surprised. If your parents are faring well, you might be surprised how much their perspective has changed. I mean—how much have you changed in a month?"

Stu was silent in contemplation. "You'd really go with me?" he finally asked.

"Yep. I might even drag my nephew along." He thought of Phil's recent escapade when he said, "There's strength in numbers."

"When do you think we could go?"

"The sooner the better," Josh said.

Phil concurred. "I'd like to run you through a little training first.

Make sure you can be useful in an ambush," he explained. "But in a couple of days, I'd think."

Stu thought about it, before standing up and sticking his hand out. "Thanks, Josh. I'd really appreciate it. I learned a couple of weeks back just how..." He froze up thinking about what had happened to Carmen. Josh and Phil looked at each other and then back at Stu. "Something happened to my travelling partner that... forever changed me."

Josh shook Stu's hand. "You don't have to explain, Doc. We're all changing." He looked at Phil. "And in some ways for the better."

PAYTON AND TONY'S BIG "COMMON" still had some minor details to finish before it would be one hundred percent complete. That wasn't stopping the celebration, though. The sheriff and several of his deputies had come out earlier in the evening. So had the leaders of several other groups on the peninsula, including the sheriff from nearby Mason County, Skinny Kenny, Gary Stonefence, and several others. It had been a productive day, which began with a service for the seven killed in the action—four range members and three Guard personnel. Gene Hackett had volunteered to lead the service. They also commemorated that it had been one month since the events had started. Plans were made for another get together for Thanksgiving in just a couple of weeks.

Eight had been wounded and had been transported to the temporary hospital at the Camp in Bartlett. It was the first example of how the agencies and civilians began to work together. "The summit" was not just discussing procedures and protocols for peacekeeping, but how to address crimes of need. People were going to starve in the coming months, there was no debating that. Better to solve that issue than arrest people. Josh instructed everyone in the methods that they had started mapping and scavenging. There were no more food banks and EBT cards—those with food were going to have to help those without. It was better for everyone to think it through together. There was a lot of work ahead of them.

After the guests had left that windy and wet evening, Josh and Payton sat near the one working fireplace in the new common. The roof was working well—it was dry and cozy despite the wind and rain. Their lawn chairs were touching. Payton reached out from under her blanket and over the armrest to Josh's chair, grabbing his hand. She pulled it back with her, under the blanket, placing it on the kicking bump in her belly.

"Whoa!" he said excitedly. "That was a big one!" The flames danced off the small tuffs of hair sticking out from under her beanie. Josh slowly pulled himself up and leaned over the armrests of the two chairs. He put his rough hand along the side of her jaw and neck softly, pulling himself over for a kiss.

After he relaxed and leaned back, Payton said, "It's about time, soldier. I was about to send out a search party for your sex drive!"

He laughed and smiled. "Ummm, sorry. I've just promised myself after two failed marriages and a bad bout of drinking that I would never make the same mistakes again."

"You think I'm a mistake?" Payton asked sharply.

"No. I think I am." She looked hurt. "I was the problem in both of my marriages...the common denominator."

"Don't flatter yourself, Bryant," Payton said. "I'm not looking for a husband. It's just lonely here at the end of the world."

Josh thought about his words carefully. "Look, I don't know all the answers. I don't even know the questions. But...I've had something going on lately in my heart...my mind. When I'm around you, I feel..." He shook his head. "Forget it. It sounds cliché and corny."

"You don't get off the hook that easily, mister!" she said. "Keep going!"

He thought some more. "I guess I feel...hope. I think that maybe, just maybe...I'm not meant to live the rest of my life alone." He looked into her eyes for a long silence, watching the fireplace in them.

"Maybe when you and the doctor get back, you can think about moving into the insulated cargo trailer with me and Savannah," she suggested. "Get to know each other a little better when she's at school!" she teased.

He laughed softly. "I have to be honest with you. This thing I'm feeling…it's bigger than me. Kind of…spiritual, in a '12-Steps' kind of way. With everything that's happened, I've come to realize that I'm looking for something I've never had."

"What's that?" she asked, grabbing his hand again.

He paused for a bit, finally admitting something he'd told nobody. "Happiness," he explained, looking into the fireplace. "It's almost like my life got a reset button when the quakes hit." He could see she was still missing the point. "I want to find God," he said openly and honestly. "I need to get my head wrapped around life, death, what comes next…" He could see she was hurt. "I still want this…thing we're doing. I just want it to mean something. To *know* that it will last the rest of our lives. For the first time in my life, I want to be in a relationship built on friendship, not sex and emotion."

"Sounds to me like you're looking for your soul mate," she joked.

Josh fell silent and looked into the stone fireplace once more.

You've found her, you jerk, she thought. *How long will it take you to realize that I'm in love with you?*

TAHOMA'S HAMMER Plus 29 Days.

"YOU BRING them back safe to us!" Payton joke-scolded Stu.

Stuart laughed. "I will." There was a small crowd bidding him, Josh, and Jeff a safe trip. The three of them plus Charlie and Phil were getting ready to get into the deputy's SUV.

It had taken Eli teaming with Josh to convince Alana to allow the seventeen-year-old to go on the mission. Jeff had proven very capable in Savannah's rescue and the attack on the meth-heads, but to Alana he was still a baby. Even Grandpa Don wasn't a fan of the idea. It ultimately took Eli's experience rescuing Phil to convince Alana. She was at the departing ceremony in the parking lot, giving Jeff the evil eye. "If anything happens to him, don't bother coming back," she said coldly.

Josh gave a little chuckle, "I know, sis, I—"

"Not joking, Joshua Bryant." She looked at Eli. "You'll wish you'd never met me, too," she said bluntly.

"Mom! I'll be fine," groaned the tall, blonde youth as he rolled his eyes. He leaned close to his mother for a hug and kiss to take the heat off his uncle and dad.

Charlie walked over to the group. "You guys all packed?" He glanced over at the open rear hatch on the rig where Stu was putting his bag inside.

"Think we got as much as we can reasonably carry," Josh said. He and Jeff started loading stuff into the back.

Phil walked over and mumbled into Josh's ear, "Let me help you with that, brother."

"Huh?" Josh almost laughed. "I got it. It's just a pack and a rifle." He had a "what's up with you" look on his face.

"I don't think you're receiving my transmission," Phil said, casting a purposeful glance across the parking lot at his daughter and granddaughter.

Josh followed Phil's gaze. "Awww…Roger. Wilco." He strolled over to the two ladies in his life.

Savannah grabbed him around the waist. "I wish you didn't have to go," she mumbled.

Josh tried to cheer her up with a smile. "I won't be long, sweetie. I just want to help the doctor and get him home safe and sound." He looked up at Payton.

"Be careful. Come home," she said, trying to not seem worried in front of her daughter.

Josh reached out and took her in his arms, giving her a sensitive kiss goodbye, not too long and not too short. "We'll be home in a few days, week at the top." He broke his grip and headed towards Charlie's rig. He looked back and smiled. *I could get used to all this attention!*

The three travelers piled into the middle bench, while Phil rode shotgun. He and Charlie were on a mission from the sheriff to begin recruiting for the north end posse. They would give the guys a ride to where a barter-for-ferry service had sprung up near the now un-drivable Hood Canal Bridge.

"You set, Doc?" Josh asked Stu as the short doctor was being squeezed into the middle like they were heading to Grandma's for Easter lunch.

"Ready as I'll ever be, I guess." Stu gave Josh a meaningful glance. "Thanks for doing this."

"No worries, Doc. Just promise me you can talk them into coming back, would ya? We'd kind of miss having you around here!"

"I'll try," Stu said as the five men departed the safety of the property. With the fanfare of a departing cruise ship, the green SUV started making the bumpy trip north on the Canal Vista Highway.

31

"We don't rise to the level of our expectations. We fall to the level of our training."
—Archilochus

Tahoma's Hammer Plus 30 Days.

"What is a posse?" Rey heard his boss, Javier Ortiz, on the other end of the HF radio ask in Spanish. Both he and Rey had taken the hand-held microphones over from their radio techs so they could talk directly.

"It's like when the American cowboys would follow their sheriff on a manhunt for a bank robber," Rey explained. "Citizens with guns." Javier actually keyed up his mic to laugh, Rey could hear.

"Careful, Reynaldo!" he warned jokingly. "They might run you back to Mexico on horseback!" He busted up laughing again. "Don't the idiots know that you obliterated their police?"

Oooo – need to reign that in a bit. "Only one portion of them, Jefe. Remember – that was just North Seattle."

"But that's the biggest city, Rey..." His boss's tone changed. "Don't tell me that you're having apprehensions, my friend," he warned.

"No, Jefe. I just want you to remember that there are police and Army units in many locations we still need to contend with."

"Then why are you focused on this posse, Reynaldo?"

All business. Good—he's listening. "Because that is the wild card, Javier. Once they figure out how to organize, they'll become an insurgency against us. Guerillas..." he explained. "We need to find the biggest one and set an example—just like with the local gangs."

"So why that one over on that peninsula?" His boss had clued in on Rey's concern. "Why does that one way over there make you worry, my friend?"

"Our sources tell us they are resourceful, well-trained, and..."

"And what." It wasn't a question.

"And they just struck a pact with the local police. They're joining forces. They've figured out how to bridge the divide with their elected officials. Soon they'll be providing the necessities for the people."

"Come on, Reynaldooooo," his boss said skeptically. "They don't have ships upon ships of food and medicine like you do! You're over thinking this. Stop worrying about little fish."

"No, Jefe. I agree that they'll have a rough time at the start. What worries me isn't what they do—it's what they believe...what they know. They won't just feed their own poor—they'll teach those poor to feed and protect themselves. They're going to remove the dependent mentality that's required for our business model to work. This, Jefe. This is why I want to start with them."

"So—what is your plan? You certainly can't take everyone over there. You need to hold the area you've gained, too."

"I have a plan to draw them out to me, Jefe. But first I need to gather some information from them."

"CAPTAIN, I don't need your excuses, I need your results," General Russel Driscoll told Navy Captain Marie Darnell via the secure video chat. "I want the Halsey certified for return to the fleet in three days! Clear?"

Three days! What are you smoking, General? "Crystal, sir. I'll need to talk to my chain about using some war-time waivers to make some of the tests and signatures disappear."

"Go ahead, Marie. I guarantee you they will approve."

"General, I understand need-to-know, but is there anything you can give me that will motivate my people? They've been burning the candle at both ends since the beginning, sir. I'm not sure if you remember that a lot of them lost their homes seven weeks ago." *Oops. Shouldn't have said that.*

The general in charge of all things military in the entire Pacific sighed and looked down briefly. "Captain, I know you regret saying that just now."

"Yes, sir."

"We're trying to get the task force re-loaded and turned around. And we know that your folks are heroes. We won't forget. Just let your team know that getting their jobs done now is *the most important* mission the shipyard has had since the last world war."

The 'last' world war. Marie caught what the general was throwing out there. "Roger that, sir. We'll have her ready for Captain Hawke to steam in three days."

"Good. Now. Have you figured out a plan for the El Paso?"

"She's too far gone, sir. She'll make a fine parts boat for the rest of the fleet, but the reactor was too badly damaged. We burnt through a lot of people's exposure limits getting her stabilized and buttoned up from the rain." Marie knew she had to tread carefully. "Sir—all due respect, I think I need to impress upon you that this shipyard is rapidly approaching a point of diminishing return if the Feds don't get some relief in here. My workforce is depleted, sir."

"Understood, Marie. I'll relay your concern to the Joint Chief Chairman tonight. Regarding the El Paso, I want you to get every usable part and classified piece of tech you can off her."

"Sir? That will be man-power intensive—"

"I know, Captain. I get it. I can't tell you why, but I can tell you that we have a watery grave in store for her. You should consider this your highest priority once the Halsey sets sail."

"MARTINEZ!" the Damage Control Locker Lead Petty Officer called out to Carmen. "Good job. Way to step up!"

"Aye, LPO. Thank you." Carmen never even looked up from rolling the hose back up into a donut. Just as every Marine is a rifleman, every Sailor is a firefighter. When the supercarrier U.S.S. Halsey was at General Quarters—battle stations—Carmen was assigned to one of the many damage control teams. Her primary job during those drills was to operate the valves that charged the fire hoses. Since returning to the ship, she had found a new passion for perfection.

Her shipmates were surprised she had come back, assuming she'd made it home on leave before Tahoma's Hammer fell. She was a different person—harder, meaner. She'd told none of them what she'd endured on the trip back. When they asked what coming all the way back had been like, she would just say, "Leave. Go find out if you wanna know so badly."

Carmen had thrown everything she had into being the best—at anything. It didn't matter what the task was—cleaning the deep-fat fryer, chopping onions, or rolling firehose. She was never going to be in a position to rely on anyone again. If her life was on the line, she wanted to be the person people asked what to do, not the person who had no idea what to do.

Most Sailors didn't value physical training as much as the Soldiers and Marines did. Carmen broke that mold. She was up at

0330 every morning except Sundays, working out. That way she would still be ready to start working in the galley by 0500. She was one of the breakfast and lunch cooks. After 1400, her day was usually over. She threw herself into the damage control manuals, learning every aspect of the job—firefighting, flooding, hull patches, and shoring. She was on a personal mission to cross over to the Damage Controlman rating—she was done with cooking.

There were many ways Carmen could have reacted to the atrocities that happened to her. She chose strength, knowledge, and perfection. Carmen was a warrior, and her leaders were starting to notice.

TAHOMA'S HAMMER Plus 32 Days.

THE PATROL BEING LED by Tyler Wilson was scouting a line of homes four miles north of the range. They were in a hilly area, horrible for radio communications. Some of the driveways were long, and so to make better use of time, Tyler had reluctantly agreed to split the team and work both sides of the road in two pairs. They had parked the truck near the main road and hiked in. The other pair were two of Lonnie's family—Kendell Kramer and Julia Everly. They had agreed to try to maintain radio chatter every fifteen minutes.

Tyler and Gene were working together, something that neither of them particularly wanted. Tyler could tell by the way that Gene talked that he'd finally figured out he was gay. Gene wasn't rude, but he was definitely not as sociable as he used to be. He spoke as if he was always talking to a cop or lawyer, carefully choosing his words. In his own mind, Tyler kept asking himself if he was guilty of the same judgmentalism that he felt Gene had.

They had just finished taking a small water break and eating a snack when Tyler realized they hadn't talked to the others for at least forty-five minutes. "Major League, this is Bull Durham, over." He tried again and shot Gene a look.

Gene took a turn. "Major League, comms and status report. Over," Gene said into his radio. "Might just be the batteries," he said to the team leader. "These things are dying faster every day."

"Could be," Tyler agreed. "Or our signals just aren't getting around in these hills." He did some thinking while he put away the remnants from the snack. He decided to stow the notes from the intel and scavenging, too. "Get the wagon ready, please. I think we should head back to the truck and look for them along the way. I'd rather get back too early than discover they needed help and we dropped the ball."

"I agree," Gene said.

The two started making their way back up the two miles of winding, hilly road. A while later, they rounded a curve and saw their two comrades sitting on the tailgate, rifles leaning against the truck about forty meters ahead. Tyler saw an older white van rise up out of a small dip in the road about two hundred meters beyond the other teammates. It slowed and pulled left at an angle. The sliding door on the right side opened, but all he could make out was the dark of the interior space and the motion of a body or two inside.

"*There* you guys are!" they heard Kendell call out gleefully. "Have any lu—"

"Move!" Tyler yelled at the other teammates just a bit too late as his brain caught up to his eyes. He raised his rifle, flipping off the safety as he levelled his sites.

ZZoooowooosh—Ka-Boooooommmmm! The swooshing noise and fiery tail of the RPG round were nothing compared to the explosion that sent the bodies—all thirty-seven pieces of their two teammates —flying in every direction. The fireball and shockwave from the exploding truck pushed out a concussion that knocked Gene unconscious and sent both men flying backwards several meters. Tyler was woozy, but he could tell there were now people running toward him.

He slowly pulled his shoulders off the ground, ears bleeding and ringing loudly. He was still dizzy and couldn't focus on the figures before him. The van drove up to within twenty meters of the burning wreckage. Six battle-hardened men jumped out and two of them held security, while the other four retrieved the fallen duo. They dragged them both back to the van, throwing them in and taking off without hesitation.

EPILOGUE

"If the country is good enough to live in, it's good enough to fight
for."
—Eugene Sledge

TAHOMA'S HAMMER PLUS 33 DAYS.

"MORNING, Sir. What can I do for you?" asked Sergeant Major
Greg Piercy.

"Thanks for coming right over, Sergeant Major. I know how
busy you are," Colonel Isiah Franklin stated. "I thought I'd bring
you up to speed on some new intelligence that just came in. It
shouldn't wait until tomorrow's daily threat report."

The senior NCO for the 5th Marine Regiment of the 1st Marine
Division scanned the room. *The XO and all three Battalion CO's. Must be
big.* The 5th was at Submarine Base Bogdon, shoring up the base's

smaller security detachment while "special toys" were removed from Washington State for National Security reasons. "Sir."

"Yesterday, sonic sensors on the south end of the base picked up a transient noise somewhere very close to the fenceline. The computers say it was an RPG."

"Sir?" *I'm being 'punked', aren't I?"* The Sergeant Major looked around and realized he was not being toyed with.

"Wish I was kidding, Sergeant. We phoned it in with a time stamp to Division and they were able to verify with satellite photos. They found what could only be described as the tail-smoke of a rocket blowing up a truck."

The sergeant looked past the colonel's shoulder as he was trying to recall anything in the prior intel briefings that would provide a clue "The cartel thing in Seattle?"

"That's our best guess, too," the colonel said, looking around at the three lieutenant colonels who were seated.

"This is certainly unexpected, sir," Greg said. "Orders?"

"For now, keep this contained to the Battalion Sergeant Major level. Pendleton is seeing what they can do to get us a permanent drone. We're also going to hold on to the Raiders and Delta operators a bit longer than originally thought."

"Understood, Sir." *And here I thought starving civilians were our biggest threat.*

"COULD THAT REALLY BE YOU, you little twerp?" Sticky asked his rifle scope. He had taken a lesson from his hunter, opting to lay in wait. Most of the homes on this road had been long abandoned. There was little activity at the ones that still had occupants. Shotgun's pirates had seen to that. As the off-loading vessels started to get boarded and robbed more frequently, the relief ships started travelling all the way around Vancouver Island and entering the Strait much farther east. As supplies dwindled, people began to huddle together in numbers. The Ford Expedition with blacked-out windows was the first sign of human activity he'd seen in two days.

The metallic gold vehicle was idling in front of the driveway to Stuart's parents' house. It sat there doing nothing for two minutes, driving Sticky mad in the process. *C'Mon! What's the hold up?* He could see a hooded figure in the near-side driver's seat, but there was no way of knowing if it was his target. *He's talking to someone. Probably in the back seat. C'mon. Step on out. Nothing to see here.* Sticky had set himself up on the covered deck of the house uphill from where he thought his target would appear. He figured it to be about a two-hundred-meter shot.

Suddenly, there was a loud bass thumping that caught Sticky's attention. He pulled his eye off the scope, looking to the right. At the crest of the road where it dropped back down the next slope, he could see a tricked out red Dodge Challenger stopped, almost as if it had been stalking the Expedition and found it accidentally. It obviously had a very customized sound system. He could hear rap music blaring loud enough to make the windows behind him vibrate a little. *What the actual hell! I should shoot you just for playin' that junk!* An uneasy feeling suddenly came over him.

He looked back in his scope and moved the rifle enough to reacquire the driver of the Expedition. It took a second as he steadied the eye-relief in the scope to realize that the passenger window rear of the driver was down. He made the micro adjustment and started to stare in, but since it was daylight hours, it was hard to see inside the vehicle through the scope. *Is that—? Is that a rifle?!* Sticky saw a flash of bright light as he pulled his own trigger.

— The End —

Continue the adventure with Cascadia Fallen: Spiritus Americae.

A NOTE FROM ME

Thanks for reading this book!

What would you do if you saw the Moon get destroyed? Grab a complimentary copy of my digital novella, The Splintered Moon by subscribing to my Reader Group at pkodell.com

Another great option is to go follow me on Amazon!

I also ask that you consider following me in the other usual hotspots: Facebook, Instagram, or BookBub. (Usually as P.K. O'Dell or @apocwriter6)

Thanks so much for reading this book! I couldn't do this without people like you! **Now, turn one more page to find my entire back-list of novels.**

ALSO BY AUSTIN CHAMBERS

<u>Cascadia Fallen Trilogy</u>

Book 1 Tahoma's Hammer

Book 2 Order Divested

Book 3 Spiritus Americae

Box Set The Complete Trilogy

<u>Blades of Grass Series</u>

Book 1 Venom Spear

Book 2 Dragon Unleashed

Book 3 Blood Red Sky

Book 4 Patriot Shield

Box Set 1 Books 1 - 3

Coming Early 2025!

Blades of Grass Book 5: Eye for an Eye

Blades of Grass Book 6: Fractured States

Seven Days 'til Mayhem: Echoes of the Just Book 1

Fourteen Days 'til Chaos: Echoes of the Just Book 2

Twenty-one Days 'til Anarchy: Echoes of the Just Book 3

ABOUT THE AUTHOR

"Austin" is actually Navy veteran and Dad-joke extraordinaire P.K. O'Dell. Originally from Austin, Texas, he worked most of a career in management at a naval shipyard. He and his wife tend to chickens and watch Combat Kitty slay squirrels near the Hood Canal in Kitsap County, Washington.

Made in United States
Troutdale, OR
10/29/2024